# PRAISE FOR
## *COYOTE DREAM*

"*Coyote Dream* brings together the songs of two cultures, twining family, food, love, and art into a narrative of love and life. A truly American story." —Jessica Barksdale Inclán

"A compelling love story matching an intellectual East Coast art dealer with a Native American artist. The cultures clash, sparks fly. . . . Think *The Horse Whisperer* and you'll have a sense of the magic of *Coyote Dream*. A bravura debut." —Elizabeth Forsythe Hailey

Written by today's freshest new talents and selected by New American Library, NAL Accent novels touch on subjects close to a woman's heart, from friendship to family to finding our place in the world. The Conversation Guides included in each book are intended to enrich the individual reading experience, as well as encourage us to explore these topics together—because books, and life, are meant for sharing.

Visit us online at www.penguin.com.

# COYOTE DREAM

## JESSICA DAVIS STEIN

FICTION FOR THE WAY WE LIVE

NAL Accent
Published by New American Library, a division of
Penguin Group (USA) Inc., 375 Hudson Street,
New York, New York 10014, U.S.A.
Penguin Group (Canada), 10 Alcorn Avenue, Toronto,
Ontario, Canada M4V 3B2 (a division of Pearson Penguin Canada Inc.)
Penguin Books Ltd, 80 Strand, London WC2R 0RL, England
Penguin Ireland, 25 St Stephen's Green, Dublin 2,
Ireland (a division of Penguin Books Ltd)
Penguin Group (Australia), 250 Camberwell Road, Camberwell, Victoria 3124,
Australia (a division of Pearson Australia Group Pty Ltd)
Penguin Books India Pvt Ltd, 11 Community Centre, Panchsheel Park,
New Delhi – 110 017, India
Penguin Books (NZ), Cnr Airborne and Rosedale Roads, Albany,
Auckland, New Zealand (a division of Pearson New Zealand Ltd)
Penguin Books (South Africa) (Pty) Ltd, 24 Sturdee Avenue,
Rosebank, Johannesburg 2196, South Africa

Penguin Books Ltd, Registered Offices:
80 Strand, London WC2R 0RL, England

First published by NAL Accent, an imprint of New American Library,
a division of Penguin Group (USA) Inc.

First Printing, September 2004
10  9  8  7  6  5  4  3  2  1

FICTION FOR THE WAY WE LIVE
REGISTERED TRADEMARK—MARCA REGISTRADA

LIBRARY OF CONGRESS CATALOGING-IN-PUBLICATION DATA:
Stein, Jessica Davis.
Coyote dream / Jessica Davis Stein.
p. cm.
ISBN 0-451-21315-7 (trade pbk.)
1. Women art dealers—Fiction. 2. Automobile travel—Fiction. 3. Navajo artists—
Fiction. 4. Coyote—Fiction. I. Title.
PS3619.T46C695 2004
813'.6—dc22               2004009240

Set in Bembo
Designed by Ginger Legato

Printed in the United States of America

PUBLISHER'S NOTE
This is a work of fiction. Names, characters, places, and incidents either are the product of the author's imagination or are used fictitiously, and any resemblance to actual persons, living or dead, business establishments, events, or locales is entirely coincidental.

*For my family:*
*My mother, Esther*
*My husband, Herb*
*Our children, Morgan and Kee*
*And in memory of my mother-in-law, Ruthie*

# ACKNOWLEDGMENTS

Sari Globerman—brilliant angel without whom this book would
  never have been published
Megan Rickman—for terrific notes and tons of moral support
Robert Guinsler—Agent Extraordinaire
My father-in-law, Charlie Stein, the blue-eyed fox who told the
  stories
Tom Rickman—wonderful writer and dear friend, whose
  professional notes and encouragement at the very beginning
  gave me the courage to continue
Eric Edson—for vigorous, challenging notes and generosity of
  spirit
The inspirational artwork of Allen Houser
Navajo Nation Historic Preservation
Judy Martin
Hopi Nation Historic Preservation
Rodina Huna, master potter who invited me into her home on
  Second Mesa many years ago
Terry Mogert
Corinne Cain, ASA, for a wealth of information
Marcy Posner
Murray Brown, who told me the truth
My dear friends and patient readers:
  Stacy Dalgleish
  Dianne Haak
  Steve Vinovitch

Bill Knoedelseder

Ariella Lehrer

Jo Dennis

Diana Reese Soltesz

Morgan Davis

Les Martinez

A Martinez

Caroline Mignini

Lissa Layng, for sending the manuscript to Elizabeth Forsythe Hailey

Ellen Edwards, soft-spoken editor, for minding the details

And Penny, who knew coyotes and grew old lying curled on the rug next to me as I wrote draft after draft

Quarry mine, blessed am I
In the luck of the chase.
Comes the deer to my singing.

NAVAJO HUNTING SONG

. . . there's a special providence in the fall of a sparrow.

*Hamlet,* ACT V. SCENE II

# PROLOGUE

She waited all night.

The full moon arched slowly across a clear sky. Boulders and brush gleamed silver and disappeared in shadow. The warm air carried a thousand scents: of earth and carrion, sage and sumac, but no hint of him. She sat taut, sifting through the desert sounds, listening for his footfall.

Every four hours she rose with a yawn and stretched the stiffness from her back. She pushed aside the brush at the entrance to the den and stepped through the yapping little bodies to the far end where it widened enough for her to lie down. The pups scrambled over each other to get back to her, frantic until each found its own teat. She cleaned them thoroughly, her warm tongue stimulating their bowels so that she could reconsume the digested milk. It was the only nourishment she took for twelve hours. By early morning she was ravenous.

She stood to shake, and the pups dropped off. She hid the den with brush, sniffed around the entrance, and yapped several times in quick succession, then turned to cross a stream and travel slowly down the hillside.

The moon was gone. In pallid, predawn light she descended the rocky foothills and moved across the desert, halting on a ridge behind the houses of Men bordering her territory. The scent of her mate was strong, mixed with carrion and human and lingering sulfur.

She approached low, hesitating every few feet to sniff the air and listen. Sightless eyes stared from his severed head sitting straight up on a rock. The rest of him lay nearby reeking of incipient decay. Soft whines and the insistent prodding of paws and snout would not rouse him. She nestled down, her chin on his torso.

The horizon brightened. She raised her head slowly, turning to spy a jackrabbit munching a tuber. Hunger rumbled in her belly. She rose silently and crept toward it. The rabbit paused on its haunches, ears twitching. She stopped. It took another bite. She inched forward. It stiffened. She pounced. The rabbit jumped out of reach, and her jaw snapped air. It bounded through the desert. She followed as it raced onto a gravel road, long, flat feet kicking pebbles in her face. She was inches behind when it dashed onto the asphalt—a roar more powerful than a mountain lion, a startled moment . . .

# PART I

# CHAPTER 1

**B**en Lonefeather's battered blue pickup leisurely wound down Henry's road on its way to the highway. Henry's wasn't the official name of the gravel road—it didn't have a name—but everybody called it Henry's because Henry Kanuho, Ben's grandfather, had built it. That was in 1932. He'd been thirty-four years old, the same age Ben was now, and the expense had been sizable. But he'd done it right, and it had remained unchanged since with no maintenance, except a few truckloads of gravel every now and then, snaking through the desert over eight miles, connecting the house to the highway.

It was around eight a.m. the third Saturday in May, and the Arizona high desert was full into spring. Red-brown earth stretched to purple foothills under an azure sky. Fiery blossoms engulfed ocotillos, the air so pungent with minty sage and poppies it tasted sweet. Seemed to Ben a shame, wasting such a fine day in town.

At the intersection with the highway, poised to make a right turn toward Lowman, he glanced across the expanse of blacktop and noticed three crows feeding on roadkill. He hung a left and pulled onto the shoulder to check it out.

For a moment the crows held their ground, claiming right of discovery. But as Ben advanced, the crunch of sand under his boots mingling with the drone of flies in the still air, they fluttered up cawing in protest and landed about ten feet away.

Ben squatted. Judging from the fresh smell, the coyote had been hit within a couple hours. He recognized her from the white markings on her feet and nose and the gold along her shoulders, one of the dozen or so that lived in the canyon behind his house.

He raised her muzzle with his thumb, revealing healthy pink gums and white teeth. Small and muscular with a bit of the pup left about her, little more than a year old. He brushed the flies away and squeezed one of the enlarged teats. Milk spurted up.

His eyes reflexively scanned the desert across the street toward the foothills. On an early morning hike three months back he'd come upon this female with a young male he'd never seen before. The two had been so wrapped up in each other that he'd been able to watch the courtship from behind a boulder. The eager male—big, mostly gray, black-tipped tail wagging, ears erect; the female—coy and teasing, nipping at his aggression. It was a couple minutes before they got a sense of him and took off.

From interest and observation through the years he'd learned something about most of the animals that shared the land. Coyotes mated for life, kept to a territory, lived in pairs or small families. Pups were born once a year in late April, early May. For the first month after she whelped the female stayed at the den, dependent on the male for food. Once the pups got their milk teeth and started eating regurgitated food, she'd leave them for short periods to hunt. The smooth, pink teats of this female, unmarred by punctures from sharp milk teeth, meant the pups still needed milk to survive.

He stood and gripped her rear legs to pull her off the side of the road into the desert, disturbing the crows again. She belonged to them now, and before the day was over, ants, flies, eagles, hawks, and buzzards would all get their share. Other coyotes might even feed off her. Soon her bones, picked clean and bleached dry, would crumble into desert dust.

He wiped his hands on his jeans as he headed back over the blacktop, bothered by the thought of the pups hidden in a den.

Be a challenge to find them, he thought. Better than spending the morning watching his clothes spin around in a washing machine. Laundromat was open twenty-four hours anyway. The market was open until six p.m. Only problem was the post office closed at noon, and if anything happened to his supplies he'd be in deep shit. Thirty pounds of uncut precious and semiprecious stones: red and pink coral, lapis, jade, opal, amethyst, garnet, dozens of seed pearls, a few small diamonds, and a pound of pure gold ingots. All the money he'd scrimped and saved for a year invested in one order. He'd gotten a notice in yesterday's mail it had arrived. Insurance required him to pick up the package himself and sign for it.

It was a risky move, putting everything he had into jewelry without a dealer in place. But if the Indian Market would let bygones be, by August next year he'd line one up and finally stop living hand to mouth.

He got back in his truck and made a U-turn.

He wasn't ready to begin work on the jewelry yet. The stones he had to cut on commission would keep him busy for another two, maybe three weeks. The package was as safe at the post office as anywhere. He could pick it up on Monday.

Grinning like a kid playing hooky, he headed back up the gravel road.

Within ten minutes, he'd passed the houses of his neighbors. Small wood-frame and cinderblock structures scattered along the three miles of road near the highway. A quarter mile beyond the last house he stopped and turned off the engine.

He reached under the seat for his daypack: bottle of water, two empty Mountain Dew cans, a snakebite kit, and a box of Hot Tamales candy. He left the cans on the floor, zipped the pack and slung it over a shoulder. Like a seal slipping off a buoy into the sea with barely a ripple of the surface, he passed between two boulders and slipped into the desert. Crossing the flatland swiftly, he picked up a deer trail into the hills, drawn by the secret depth of the desert's heart.

People commonly considered this part of the Navajo reservation a wasteland and spent a lot of time trying to find a way to tame it to a useful purpose. Divert enough water to make it suitable for grazing cattle. Fertilize the hell out of it for farming. Turn it green. In the end there was never enough water. Which was fine by him. He liked the desert the way it was, every hue and shade of brown from bone to lavender to red. Cutthroat, competitive, deadly for the weak or unprepared, it had its own way of keeping the riffraff out. Henry used to say the desert built character, and as a child Ben had learned to appreciate the lessons it taught about discipline and thrift and cutting down to the essential. He'd forgotten for a time, on the stormy road from adolescence to manhood, but he remembered now.

Henry had liked and admired the coyote—an unusual penchant in a sheep rancher, but Henry believed in balance and never took a narrow view.

"Truth is," he'd told Ben, "ranchers that watch their sheep don't lose many to coyotes. Lazy ranchers'll always complain, but coyotes kill vermin an eat garbage. Stop sickness from spreadin. World without coyotes be a pretty dirty place."

Most of the Southwest Indian tribes had stories about Coyote, the cunning trickster who always managed to get himself into trouble. Henry told them all.

"If a story's good, don't matter if it's Hopi or Navajo or Cheyenne. The Navajo's strength is in knowin a good thing no matter where it comes from."

Listening to him was like listening to music, and the tales told most often were the ones most loved. Ben's favorite was Hopi, the one about Coyote and the stars.

"At the very beginnin, when the world was just made and lookin like a new ball, Mother Earth give Coyote a jar to hold," Henry would begin, and Ben would settle in.

"That jar had all the stars, shiny and clean from a scrubbin. Mother Earth tol Coyote, 'I got things to do in town, but I'll be back soon as it's night. Hold the lid on tight. Don't open it for nothin.'

"Mother Earth had a plan for them stars. They was goin up in the sky to form pictures. Every star in its rightful place, neat an orderly. Coyote wanted to do what Mother Earth said, so he held on tight to the jar. Skunk asked to see what he was holdin, but Coyote wouldn't show him. Crow offered to trade him a ear a corn for jus a peek inside, but Coyote wouldn't do it.

"He held that jar all day long until late in the afternoon jus before the sun was about to set an he could see Mother Earth comin down the road from town. He knew once she come back he'd never get the chance to see all them stars bunched up together. Must be a sight to see, he thought. An before he knew it, he loosened the lid and lifted it up for a peek. Whoosh! All the stars come rushin out so fast they burned his nose. He put the lid back quick as he could, but he only saved a few a the pictures at the bottom.

"And that's the reason most of the stars are spread out all in a mess over the sky. And that's why, to this day, Coyote has a black nose."

It was hot by noon. Ben had about half his water left and was tracking among the rocks that bordered a small stream when a faint whine caught his attention. He stepped across the water, scaled a boulder and locked eyes with a red fox that looked up from the ground a few feet away. He jumped down; the fox vanished. At the base of the boulder, hidden by brush, he found the mouth of the den. He pushed the brush aside, thinking the nature of luck was all in the timing.

Three sturdy gray bodies with slanted yellow eyes and pointed ears backed up as he reached into the dank, feral den. Before placing the pups in the backpack, he noted two females and a male. The male growled and bit his finger with its gums.

"Save your fire, little man," he whispered, smiling.

# CHAPTER 2

**B**en drove through the open gate past the FRANK DAWSEN, DVM sign and followed the driveway around the back of the house. Dawsen came out of the barn wiping his hands on a rag and walked up to see why Ben was peering into the passenger side window of his own truck.

"Jesus." Dawsen laughed. "Coyotes."

"Their mother was killed out on the highway."

Dawsen grunted and opened the door. "Whew," he said, wrinkling his nose as he picked them up from the mess they'd made of Ben's laundry. Holding all three wriggling against his chest, he started toward the house. "Got a feeling you're gonna be even fonder a me than you thought," he called over his shoulder.

"Why's that?"

"Got the washin machine fixed."

• • •

Frank Dawsen had arrived on the Navajo reservation during the Vietnam War, a young veterinarian and conscientious objector, assigned by his draft board to spend two years bettering conditions for American Indian ranchers. He'd fallen in love with the place and with Anna Pierce, the daughter of one of the ranchers.

Many of the young men of the tribe had been drafted, and a number had been killed, Anna's boyfriend among them. After the war, the ones who returned had lost their youth and, in various respects, their chances. A privileged white man who'd sat out the conflict and used the opportunity to steal the heart of one of the prettiest of the Navajo girls was no longer welcome. Everyone expected Frank Dawsen to pack it up. But instead he dug in, creating committees, writing letters, making phone calls, attending hearings, in an effort to make sure the Navajo veterans got their fair share of government benefits in the way of psychological, medical, and financial assistance. Not everyone agreed with Dawsen's politics, but everybody came to like and respect the man.

Anna and Dawsen had no kids. Ben knew it was a source of sadness, but they compensated by making their house a home for whoever needed one. Ben had stayed with them when Henry died. He'd been eighteen and had spent the better part of a month in their spare bedroom, so drunk most of the time he couldn't stand up. Finally Dawsen had convinced him to join the army. He'd said it was against all his principles, but there was no sign of a war and it might be Ben's only chance at survival.

• • •

The two men walked into the house—Dawsen with the pups and Ben carrying his laundry. Ben stopped in the living room, noting the mess: dirty clothes strewn over the floor, a half-empty beer bottle lying on its side, liquor seeping into the carpet.

"Where's Anna?"

"Went to visit her sister in Albuquerque," Dawsen said airily.

"What'd you do?"

"Forgot the anniversary or some such."

"You gonna live like this til she comes back?"

"Maybe."

"She walks in and sees this mess, she's gonna turn around and walk right back out."

"You know where the washin machine's at," Dawsen said, nodding in the direction of the service porch as he continued through the living room.

Ben loaded the laundry and met him in the veterinary clinic, which claimed about half the downstairs of the house, glad to see it was as clean as usual. Dawsen handed him a pup and a warm, damp washcloth. They wiped the pups off; Dawsen examined them and put them in a cardboard box on the floor.

"Seem healthy. Whadda wanna do with em?"

"Figured you'd know."

"Nobody wants coyotes. Best thing is put em down easy."

"Then I'll take em."

"They're different from dogs. Never knew anyone to make a pet outa one."

Ben shrugged.

"You're gonna have your hands full." Dawsen chuckled. He gave each of the pups a shot, then washed up, leaning against the sink as he wiped his hands. "I got an idea. Hank Farrow brought his sheepdog bitch in this mornin to be spayed. I was gonna do it this afternoon. He's leavin her to board for a month cause he's goin to Seattle to visit Hank Junior. Thing is, she's just weaned a litter. Maybe she'd take on these pups for a couple weeks. I don't see what difference it'd make to Hank, cept he'd save boarding fees and it'd make your life a hell of a lot easier."

Ben didn't like asking favors, but he wasn't a fool.

Dawsen went out to the barn and returned with a black and white border collie. Ben squatted, and she came right to him, wagging her tail, her tongue warm on his fingers.

Dawsen picked up the box with the pups and carried it into his kitchen. He put the dog into a small area and cordoned it off with an expandable wooden gate.

"Thing is, some nursin dogs'll kill a strange litter of pups and some'll adopt em. You never know. Kinda like people. You never know til you find out." He picked up the little male and offered the box to Ben. "Let's see what happens."

Dawsen placed the pup into the area with the dog. Ben put the other two pups down next to their brother. The dog's ears pricked up. She whined with a worried look and tried to pick her paws up, either to avoid stepping on them or to keep them from touching her. The pups whimpered, stumbling around her feet. She curled her lip and growled.

"Come on, Lady," Dawsen said gently, stroking her head. She wagged her tail faintly. He picked up one of the pups and held it to her nose.

The dog smelled the pup and licked its head, once.

"Good girl," Dawsen said, nudging her chin with the pup's body.

She licked it again, several times. The pup wriggled, arching toward the dog. The dog sniffed its ears and eyes and licked them.

"Good girl," Dawsen encouraged, placing the pup back on the floor, where the other pups were squeaking and tumbling over the dog's prancing feet.

She looked between Dawsen and Ben in mute appeal. At

last, with a great sigh, she lay down, and in a flash the pups were scrambling through the unaccustomed hair to find the teats.

●  ●  ●

The two men walked out to the truck, Ben carrying the box with the pups huddled together asleep. Without a word said the dog followed, and when Ben opened the door she jumped into the cab. He put the box with the pups on the floor.

"How much I owe you?"

Dawsen scratched his head. "Twenty bucks? That's about what it cost me."

Ben reached into his jeans and pulled out a twenty-dollar bill.

"Bring her back soon's they're weaned. She's gotta be spayed. And those coyotes too. I want your word you're gonna neuter em at six months before the females come in season. I'm sick a getting calls to kill some half-starved animal nobody wants." Dawsen narrowed his eyes.

"It's okay, Man. One set of pups is all I can handle." Ben said, hustling around to the driver's side before Dawsen got wound up and went off on his neutering tirade.

Ben stopped at the grocery store in Lowman and bought mostly canned food for the week in order to compensate for the twenty dollars he'd spent at Dawsen's and the additional cost of dog food. By the time he drove back up the gravel road and parked in front of the long whitewashed wall at the base of the foothills, it was late afternoon.

His home consisted of a compound of three adobe build-ings built around a tiled central patio, the fourth side open to the desert foothills. Henry had started construction with a one-room house, suitable for bachelor days, and then expanded as the need arose.

Ben had built the third structure himself, keeping the style of the other buildings except adding half again the height. Inside was an unfinished rectangular room with a concrete floor. At the same time he'd wired everything, installed a generator and laid solar panels on the roof of the new building. He didn't have telephone service or own a TV. The property had its own deep, sweet well.

He set the box with the pups down in the center of the living room. They whined and yapped, clawing at the sides, while he unpacked his groceries and put the stuff away in the kitchen cupboards. Lady sat at attention next to the box, watching him.

He took his clean clothes out the back door into the next building. Almost as large as the main house, it incorporated two rooms. He used the larger as a studio. It had a wood-burning stove but no kitchen. The other, built originally as his parents' bedroom, had been his during childhood. He put the clothes neatly into the drawers of an oak bureau Henry had made for him.

When he'd first returned to the reservation, he'd tried using his grandparents' room in the main house because it had the bathroom, but after a few days he'd moved back into his old room and the pallet on the floor he'd had since he was a kid.

He filled bowls with food and water for Lady and was standing contentedly in the back doorway, watching the late afternoon sun turn the desert gold, when the approach of a pickup with thrashed shocks, chewing gravel, caught his ear. A few moments later his second cousin Alvin slouched into view through the front doorway. Almost as tall as Ben, he weighed about half as much and moved with disjointed clumsiness. He had an ugly patchwork of scar tissue down the left side of his face and neck.

Lady looked up from her food and barked.

Alvin froze. "W–what you doin with a dog?"

Alvin stammered, especially when he got nervous.

"Your lesson's tomorrow," Ben said. Alvin had taken to dropping by whenever he felt like it, and Ben wanted to put a stop to it.

"But you g-got a package," Alvin answered, eyes still on the dog. "Th-thought you might need it."

"You got it in the truck?"

Alvin nodded. "Had to s-sign for it."

Ben walked outside with Lady at his heels. Sure enough, the package with all his supplies was in the back of Alvin's truck. A wonder it hadn't been thrown out, given the speed Alvin drove.

"Don't do this again," Ben said tersely. "If I got somethin at the post office, I'll get it when I'm ready." He pulled the package from the back of the truck and shouldered it.

Alvin looked hurt. Maybe it would register.

Alvin lived with his grandmother Fanny at the bottom of the road, near the highway. Fanny was the widow of Henry's brother Dan. Since Ben drove past the house to and from anywhere, Alvin usually knew when he was home.

Ben barely remembered Fanny from his childhood. But he did remember Helen, her daughter, Alvin's mother. When she was about fifteen and he was ten, he and a few other boys had sneaked up and peeked in the window of a Chevy parked in front of her house to watch her suck off a marine in the back-seat. She'd run away with the guy, and rumor had it she'd turned to whoring and died in a brawl.

Out of the blue, Alvin had shown up at his grandma's a few years ago. Last year, forlorn and more like a kid than a twenty-two-year-old man, he'd come out to ask if Ben would take him on as an apprentice. Ben had no use for an apprentice, but he was mindful they were the last men of their clan on this part of the rez. He'd offered drawing lessons once a month.

"An you f-forgot to ch-check your mailbox," Alvin said, fishing in his pockets for a couple of envelopes.

"Jesus," Ben muttered, thrusting out his hand.

Alvin stepped forward and handed Ben the mail. Lady flattened her ears and growled. Alvin stumbled backward and hastened to his truck.

Ben rolled up the rugs from the floor, and the pups explored the living room while he heated a couple of cans of pork and beans and ate dinner. Their antics, toddling around on the slippery tiles, got him laughing out loud.

Late in the evening he sketched them with charcoal in the soft glow of lantern light. The dog lay on her side with her head resting on his foot, dozing coyotes, still attached, nursing intermittently in their sleep.

# CHAPTER 3

**I**t was August. The tin rattle of a lose filter in the vent above the doorway of the dining room indicated the air-conditioning was cranked up and flowing. Still, the Friedman home simmered. Outside, in lingering daylight, moist heat hung over the yard like fog. The hedges and rosebushes, the sycamore and birch trees, moved not a leaf, as if they'd been painted.

It was more than the heat that oppressed Sarah as she set the Sabbath table. She'd lived in this house in Woodbridge, Long Island, through all her childhood summers without the help of the air-conditioning, which had been installed eight years ago for her brother's wedding. And it was more than coming back to the familial home, per se. She had dinner with her parents at least once a month and sometimes the weight of disappointed expectations settled on her, but she assumed most people must occasionally feel disheartened coming home. After all, who really lives up to childhood hopes?

She imagined explaining her thirty-three-year-old self to the exuberant, outspoken ten-year-old in the picture on the wall in the hall. A stocky child with wild ginger ringlets in a bathing suit at the beach—could be entitled *Chubby Little Girl in Sand*. Well, kid, you do the best you can, but be careful what you put into the mistakes you make because you'll have to eat them.

Sarah's biggest mistake had been a four-year affair with a married man, her boss in an Upper East Side Manhattan art gallery. The job and his promise of a partnership in the business had evaporated when his wife happened to come home one day at lunchtime.

On to the next picture—*Voluptuous Adolescent With Acne in Prom Dress*. Don't worry, honey, this is a low point.

Thank God, at least she'd never have to go back to high school.

She had come into herself a bit late but eventually the chubbiness had proved to be baby fat, the pimples disappeared and she'd stopped growing at five feet six. Her hair had darkened to auburn, which along with fair skin, hazel eyes and a tendency to blush, were the primary legacies from her father's German-Jewish heritage. Ample breasts and an ironic perspective on them, as well as on the men whom they held fleetingly mesmerized—or who held them, fleetingly mesmerized—a gift from her Russian-Jewish foremothers.

No, it wasn't the unrealized promises of youth weighing on her tonight. The theme of roads taken or not had been played to death in therapy and she'd pretty much forgiven herself for screwing up her twenties. And after all, she was still young enough to have hope for the future.

*That* was the oppressive weight: the killing of hope on tonight's agenda.

She sighed and moved through the swinging door into the kitchen, where her mother stood at the counter ladling pan juices, along with carrots, potatoes and roasted garlic, onto a platter around a golden baked chicken.

"You make the dressing," Evelyn Friedman said.

Sarah mixed olive oil and vinegar with a pinch of salt and one of sugar, beat in about a teaspoon of Dijon and poured it over the salad. She turned off the burner under the asparagus and removed the sautéed spears to a small platter. She picked up the platter and the salad bowl and used her shoulder to push open the door between the kitchen and dining room, a hollow feeling of dread in her chest.

The sun shone low through the windows, burnishing the silver: candlesticks, challah platter, her maternal grandmother's cutlery. For a moment the table seemed aglow and timeless, or rather of another time, and quite beautiful. She thought of Germany and her other grandmother—her father's family when he was a child gathered around a Sabbath table like this one—and felt even more the apprehension of her approaching betrayal.

Evelyn, following through the door carrying the chicken, bumped into her.

"Are you all right? What are you doing stopping in the doorway?"

"Nothing. Where do you want the salad?"

Evelyn looked at her and whispered, "You have no business being angry at me. It's not my fault."

"But it's what you want."

"I want your father to have high blood pressure?" Evelyn hissed. "A heart problem?"

"You're glad he can't take the trip."

"That's different. I wanted him to *want* to stay home. I never wanted him to get sick." Evelyn looked at her daughter, sighed, and shook her head. "Move the challah platter next to Lisa and put the salad and vegetables in its place."

Sarah did as she was told and separated the candles so that Evelyn could put the chicken in the middle.

"Sam? Eli? Lisa? Dinner," Evelyn called.

The Friedmans gathered quickly. Sarah's father, Sam, sat at the head of the table; Evelyn at the foot; Sarah's brother, Eli, next to Evelyn; his oldest son, Aaron, next to him; his wife, Lisa, between Sam and Aaron. Sarah sat on the other side between her twin four-and-a-half-year-old nephews, Joseph and Jeremy. The little boys wiggled into their seats as Sarah poured their apple juice.

Evelyn covered her head with a lace shawl and lit the candles, chanting the Hebrew blessing. Sam stood and blessed the wine. Lisa helped Aaron pull off a piece of challah from the loaf.

"*Hamotsi leham min ha oritz,*" he piped, shyly beaming as he handed the bread across the table to Sarah. She repeated the blessing, grinning in surprise. He was seven.

"Really good," she whispered. She caught Lisa's eye and gave her a thumbs-up. Aaron smiled, showing both missing front teeth, and gleefully continued pulling pieces off the loaf, blessing them and handing them out.

Sarah glanced at Sam as he absentmindedly received his piece. She saw his quiet removal at family gatherings as an indication that part of him would always be with the others. He would forever remain caught between this family and the one he'd left behind.

Jeremy, on her right, reached across the table for his challah and knocked over his apple juice.

"Oh, Jesus," Eli groaned.

"Oops," Lisa said, going for the glass with mother reflexes, grasping it before the entire contents spilled.

Sarah stood to mop the tablecloth with her napkin and surveyed the platter of floating spears. "Umm, apple gravy on asparagus. We may have something here."

"That's a record. I don't think we were sitting more than five minutes," Eli said.

"Don't be silly," Evelyn retorted with a smile, rising. "You used to spill it before the candles were lit."

"I'll get it," Sarah said, motioning her mother to stay seated. She picked up the soppy platter and pushed open the door to the kitchen.

"I want more juice," Jeremy said, his mouth full of bread.

"Swallow the challah before you talk," Lisa answered as the door swung shut behind Sarah, muffling the voices.

She rinsed the asparagus, dried the platter, and added a little melted butter before returning to the dining room. Dishes were being passed and food served in the midst of overlapping conversations.

"Aaron had an adventure today," Eli told Sam. "Tell Grandpa where you went."

"How about trying some asparagus, Joseph?" Evelyn asked, picking up the serving tongs.

"The printers," Aaron piped.

"Yuck," Joseph said to Evelyn.

"What kind of printing do they do?" Eli prompted.

"Say 'No thanks, Grandma,' " Lisa corrected Joseph as she cut Jeremy's chicken breast into little pieces. She looked at Sarah, indicating Joseph's chicken. "Will you?"

"Offset," Aaron answered.

Sarah cut Joseph's little piece of chicken into five miniscule pieces.

"Right," Eli said, looking at Sam, who didn't respond. "Pop?"

"Hmm?"

"Sarah, give me your plate," Evelyn said, reaching.

"Offset printing, Daddy," Sarah said, handing the plate to her. "We were talking about it a few weeks ago, remember?

You said what a shame it was that the art of printing was dying."

"Oh." Sam nodded, looking at Eli.

"Yeah," Eli said. "Apparently Aaron's camp counselor agrees with you."

"Shelby," Aaron told him.

"Right. Shelby has a thing about printing."

"Her uncle's a printer, and it's really loud," Aaron said.

"Well, that's good," Sam said to Aaron.

"How is it?" Evelyn asked Lisa, referring to the chicken. "It's free range."

"Great," Lisa told her.

The twins' attention span for any activity involving adults ran out at about fifteen minutes. As soon as they'd eaten what they would—which was really just for show as an hour earlier in the kitchen Grandma had given all three boys heaping bowls of chicken soup with matzo balls—they were excused from the table to watch TV in the den. Aaron generally remained for a few minutes basking in the concentrated adult focus. No doubt, Sarah thought, reliving the halcyon days before the twin wrecking crew arrived to demolish his peaceful princedom.

He told them about his soccer team and the new uniform. "I got a practice game tomorrow."

"It's the first one," Coach Eli added. "So we'll see."

"I'll be there," Evelyn said. "Sarah, why don't you spend the night and go with me?"

"I can't," Sarah responded, pulling a sad face at Aaron. "But I'll try to come to the next one, okay?"

Eli glanced at Sam.

"Can I be excused?" Aaron asked his mom.

"I don't understand why you can't spend the weekend here," Evelyn continued to Sarah. "You're going to have to drive all the way back out for the wedding Sunday, anyway."

"Yes," Lisa answered Aaron.

"I have plans tomorrow," Sarah responded. "Eli? Will you e-mail me a game schedule?"

He nodded and glanced again at Sam.

"Eli? More chicken?" Evelyn asked.

"Yeah. Thanks."

Second helpings were served and a strained quietude settled on the table: subdued comments on the food, the heat, while knives and forks clinked against dinnerware.

"Pop?" Eli finally said.

"Hmm?"

"We need to talk about the Southwest trip."

Sam's eyes rested on Evelyn. She met his look without apology. "You won't listen to me or Dr. Kohn."

Every year for the last thirty, Sam had made a trip to the Southwest to buy art. And for as long as Sarah could remember, her mother had attempted to argue him out of it.

"I should make sure the boys aren't killing each other. Excuse me," Lisa said, picking up her plate and Aaron's. She disappeared through the swinging door.

Last year Sam had come home so exhausted he'd had to be hospitalized for a week. This year Evelyn had enlisted the help of Sam's internist.

"You're seventy-nine years old. How long do you think you can keep this up?" Evelyn asked rhetorically.

"I talked to Kohn a couple of days ago," Eli continued. "He says you need an angiogram, and you can't go driving across the country. You've got to take it easy."

"I talked to him too," Sarah said softly. "I'm sorry, Daddy, but Ma's right. What if something should happen? You'd be in the middle of nowhere, miles away from help. Can you imagine what that would do to us?"

"Can't do it anymore, Pop," Eli said. "It's too much."

Sam looked between them, and Sarah thought she saw a sliver of hope dying.

He sighed and shrugged in acquiescence.

Sarah watched Evelyn out of the corner of her eye. She expected a slight indication of satisfaction after thirty years of trying and then finally to have it accomplished so efficiently. But there was nothing she could read except relief.

• • •

Sam lay in bed rehashing the results of the evening's skirmish with Evelyn. He should have expected something of the sort. If he'd given it any thought, he'd have guessed from Sarah's particular solicitude and uncharacteristically quiet demeanor the past week at work that she was about to join the enemy. He sighed and rolled over to his side, pulling a pillow over his head to block Evelyn's soft snores.

He had no business being angry. Evelyn wasn't the enemy. She'd been a loyal wife and was entitled to fight to keep him safe, even from himself. At a time when there had seemed no alternative to death, she'd offered him a life, and like a sea crab stumbling upon an empty shell, he'd crawled in and lived there. He'd married, fathered children, prospered in business, forged relationships, all in an attempt to give form and create meaning for what he feared was simply a meaningless series of events. The man he had become was a stranger, his character molded long ago by circumstances beyond his control. Yet he'd chosen to live. Although he'd known there would be no intense pleasure, no untainted joy, he'd chosen life. And though he didn't love, he married and had a family. And so Evelyn was not the enemy, and a duty was owed.

As he lay in the dark, he pondered if the sum of his existence had been anything more than shadow play on a blank wall, or the desperate act of grabbing a twig in an endeavor to wrest himself from the quicksand of grief. That night it seemed that all he'd done for the past forty years was to fill a hollow shell.

• • •

Sarah spent most of the following day in her apartment anxiously consumed in a flurry of shopping, cleaning, cooking, wrapping presents. It was David Klein's birthday, and she'd invited him to her apartment for dinner.

She lived on the Upper West Side of Manhattan in a building of early-twentieth-century design; not terribly elegant, but properly described as having character. Her one-bedroom apartment on the eighth floor had a view into the central courtyard from the bedroom and the bath. She'd scoured the city for a year before she'd found it. In need of plaster, paint, and floor sanding, and with two old cats from the previous, deceased renter firmly in residence, she'd seen it for the tarnished treasure it was and snapped up the lease.

When the building had gone co-op a few years later, the occupants were offered first refusal at a price well below the market value. Evelyn had decided that owning her own apartment would be a good investment for Sarah, although Sarah suspected she meant it would increase Sarah's value in the marketplace of life. In any case, for her twenty-ninth birthday, her parents had surprised her with the down payment enabling its purchase.

Small but light-filled in the afternoon, with crown molding along the high ceilings and gleaming wood floors, filled with furniture she'd salvaged and repaired or scrimped and saved to purchase, it felt like home. Few lumps served up by the outside world couldn't be dissolved by a hot bath and an evening cocooned within its warm embrace.

It had been almost six months since her glance had connected with David's across the room at a gallery opening. He'd come up behind her at the refreshment table to pour a glass of wine and introduce himself. She'd already known who he was, but cleverly, for once, kept her mouth shut.

Second son of real estate magnate Herbert and socialite-philanthropist Paula, MBA from Harvard, sexy, smooth, rapidly moving up the ranks at Bloomfield and Sheeve, briefly married to someone in California, divorced a few years later, no kids. An undeniably great catch. The discovery, under her circuitous guidance, that they had mutual friends and had even attended the same high school in Woodbridge, seemed to surprise and please him.

"I don't remember you," he'd said. He'd been three years ahead, dreamy and unattainable.

"Well, I remember you," she'd answered brightly. "You had the lead in *Cabaret*."

"No." He'd laughed. "That was *Barry* Klein."

Which, of course, she'd known.

He'd called three days later to ask her to dinner.

She hadn't tumbled into his bed, which surprised him. Women did. He expected that they would. He was very nice-looking. Not tall but trim, with a strong jaw, straight nose, golden-brown eyes, and adorably long eyelashes. Determined to play it smart, she'd held back. Surprisingly, he'd been willing to invest almost two months taking her to dinner and a movie once or twice a week, without much more than few good night kisses. When she had sensed that his interest in dinner conversation had peaked, she'd gone home with him and kicked up the heat, doing her best to make it worth the wait. The next morning, he'd ordered breakfast delivered and they'd eaten in bed. She left and then agonized for three days until he called her. It stung, but he apologized, citing work. She pretended not to notice, to be horrifically busy at work herself, and said she couldn't see him until the weekend.

An exhausting game, but it appeared to have paid off. He called every couple days. They saw each other for lunch a few times a week and spent either Friday or Saturday evening together, generally ending up at one of their apartments for the night. Twice he'd surprised her at work with a flower delivery and card saying he was thinking of her.

She felt on the verge of falling in love. Why not? He was Jewish, successful, attractive, charming, and principled—he'd begun the process of leaving Bloomfield to start his own business management firm, and she judged his considered, above-board approach ethical as well as smart.

She wanted to stop playing. She was warm and nurturing and affectionate; it seemed absurd to keep pretending otherwise. Her friends advised her to hold back, but what was the point? Either he had feelings for her or he didn't.

# CHAPTER 4

That Sunday evening, bridesmaid for the fourth time in as many years, Sarah turned on the tap and sighed at her pasty reflection in the gilt-edged mirror above the sink. Why couldn't decorators give more thought to the lighting in ladies' rooms? Or didn't harsh overhead lights make everybody's skin sallow and highlight blue circles under their eyes? The full-skirted pink dress and matching wide-brimmed hat Lauren had chosen did nothing to help. Actually, she should be happy David hadn't come.

At least this would be her swan song as a bridesmaid. Lauren was her last close friend to settle. Down, she mentally amended. She pulled a compact out of her purse as her mother opened the door.

"Oh." Evelyn's tone arched in surprise, as if she hadn't just followed Sarah into the restroom.

"Hi, Ma. Having fun?" Sarah chirped, forcing a bright smile. She replaced the powder and pulled out a lipstick.

Evelyn gave an equivocal grunt and joined her at the sink. "He seems like a sweet man."

The groom, Louis Feldmar, full partner in a successful business law firm—Sarah had dated him a few times. "And a mensch," Evelyn continued, running a comb through the front of her hair. "Ruthie says he paid for his brother's education."

"Yes. He's a nice person," Sarah replied, inching toward the door.

"He's reasonably attractive."

"I suppose." He was short and balding.

"I hear they're looking in Miramar." Miramar: beautiful older houses, expansive lawns, every girl's dream. Sarah grasped the door handle.

"Sarah?"

"What?"

"Did you at least give him a chance?"

"Ma, he wasn't right for me, but I thought he might be right for Lauren. And you know what? He is. Let's be happy for her, okay?"

"I'm happy for her." Evelyn paused for emphasis. "You know, when you were a little girl, I always knew which present you'd open first."

"So?"

"A pretty package doesn't mean what's inside is gold."

"Gee. I never thought of that. Thanks for telling me."

"Don't be sarcastic. I just hate to see you wasting your time on no-goodniks. You deserve better."

"Call me an idiot, but I'd like to be in love with someone before I decide to marry him."

"Sometimes it's more important for someone to be in love with you."

Sarah's grip on the door handle tightened. Trust her mother to find the soft underbelly and thrust. Since her first crush on Jonas Burnside in second grade, Sarah had always been the one who cared more, sometimes the only one who cared at all. But then, she reflected, hadn't she learned all she knew about love from the woman standing at the sink? She'd spent her childhood watching her mother scurry after her father.

"Where is David Klein tonight?" Evelyn asked pointedly. "I'd like to meet him."

"I told you he's just a friend."

"His parents had an anniversary party last week. Molly said there were at least seventy people. Did you know?"

Sarah hadn't, and the information struck another blow to her battered ego.

"When a man is serious about you, he takes you to meet his family."

Tell me something I don't know, Sarah thought, pulling the door open and walking out.

Back in the old neighborhood—literally—the Crystal Room of the Belmont Hotel. Not much had changed since her Bat Mitzvah. Same overdone cut-glass chandeliers, same gold-flecked mirrors. They'd repainted the gilt and hung trendy brocade wallpaper, but it was still just a large cavernous space, used for professional meetings and conventions, attempting to pass itself off as a ballroom. And here she was too, in many ways the same insecure, conflicted little girl she'd been, attempting to pass herself off as a self-determined woman.

She moved around the dance floor with Arty, Lauren's fourteen-year-old nephew, sharing pointers on how to dance

slow without crippling his partner, acutely aware of her
mother and her mother's closest friends, Molly Lieberman and
Ruthie Slotkin, sitting at a table with their husbands, observ-
ing her. She found it impossible to keep from evaluating her
life as they saw it: lonely apartment in Manhattan, working in
her father's store.

"I had my Bat Mitzvah party in this very room twenty
years ago," she told Arty, inadvertently interrupting his concentration. He lost count and stumbled over her foot.

"Uh, sorry," he said, coming to a standstill. Conversing
while dancing was beyond his experience, or skill level.

She smiled. "Never mind, go back to counting."

The party that night had been a pivotal moment in girlhood—
her first strapless dress, her first glass of wine, her first kiss—
like a movie teaser promising a whammy of a film. A marquee
had materialized in her imagination: *The Future,* starring
Sarah Friedman. The road of infinite possibilities stretched before her.

Where had the time gone? Squandered on unfortunate
choices and her inability to lead with her head and keep her
eye on the ball. The affair with her boss had been by far the
worst waste, not to mention lapse in common sense and
morality. She'd landed on her ass in the street at twenty-eight
with nothing to recommend her but a bachelor's degree in art
history and four years of missed lunch.

Museum jobs were nonexistent, even gallery work was in
tight supply, and after two months of looking for something
with a possible future, she'd gone to work for Sam, selling furniture and folk art at Shoen's, the store he'd inherited from
Evelyn's father. Not what she'd imagined after years of rushing
to every contemporary exhibition in the city. Her social life
hadn't exactly taken off either. A series of intermittent, disappointing dates occupied the following years, punctuated by

several even more disappointing relationships, the most positive aspect of which had been their brevity.

So here she was, back in the Crystal Room, the road of infinite possibilities having apparently led in a circle.

Shortly after her thirty-second birthday she'd had a dream that she was swimming across a vast lake. She couldn't see the shore and knew she was too tired to make it. She panicked, flailing about, and woke up with an anxious knot in her guts.

Seemed a fairly straightforward message from her unconscious. So when David came into her life, she'd thought he was the lifeboat. And up to last night he'd given every indication of being a man enamored.

He'd been a half hour late and had come in with a rather cursory apology, his glance taking in the lovely, romantic table she'd set: candlelight, brocade silk swatch for a tablecloth, red roses in a low crystal vase at the center, two antique gold-rimmed china plates, painted crystal glasses, borrowed silver cutlery, a tossed salad on the sideboard next to a chocolate walnut torte resplendent on a Victorian cake plate. He'd made a show of breathing in the cooking smells: chicken picatta, gnocchi in brown butter, grilled eggplant.

"Wow. Looks great, smells wonderful. You must have worked all day."

And suddenly she knew she'd done too much.

She couldn't very well hide the gifts next to his place at the table: an expensive woven scarf for his favorite jacket, the CD from *The Big Chill* because they'd rented the video together, a bottle of the favorite cologne he'd run out of. The only gift she could have held back was the new black silk teddy under her dress—but she hadn't.

Instead she'd redoubled her efforts to make it great. As if trying harder ever—ever—worked with a man.

He'd waited until after the sex.

"Sarah . . . I like you, a lot," he'd said, lying on his side in bed facing her, his expression a model of apology. "But I'm afraid you want more than I'm prepared to give at this point. I'm starting a new business. I can't afford to split my focus."

She'd nodded numbly, feeling a fool, wishing he'd go before he said anything else. "I understand."

"Look, you might be the one . . . I don't know. I do know I need to take some time and space to think about it."

She'd gotten up and pulled on her robe. "It's late. I think you should go home to do your thinking."

She'd gone into the kitchen to start on the dishes. He'd come up behind her a few minutes later, re-dressed in his suit. Hands on her shoulders, a kiss on her cheek. "I'll call in a few days," he'd whispered.

And she'd probably be there, waiting next to the phone. But she wouldn't pick up, and she'd wait for him to call again before returning the call. Then she'd feign a hectic schedule— her voice cheery and cool. Maybe, if he hadn't already met someone else, she could retrieve the situation.

● ● ●

After the dance, on the way back to her seat, Sarah dutifully stopped at the table where her parents were ensconced to pay respects to the Slotkins and Liebermans.

"Your mother says you're seeing David Klein," Molly Lieberman said.

"He's just a friend." Sarah visualized climbing over the chicken Kiev to strangle Evelyn.

"It's such a small world," Molly continued.

Too small in Sarah's opinion.

"Paula Klein and I play bridge. She has three sons. David is the middle one, isn't he, Sarah?"

"Yes."

"The doctor?" Ruth Slotkin piped up. "David Klein the cardiologist?"

"Business manager," Sarah mumbled. She pictured the conversation between Molly Lieberman and David's mother about "poor Sarah Friedman" at the next bridge game. Her stomach turned over.

"They had a lovely party last Sunday," Molly said. "Victor Belinni catered. He did something wonderful with salmon baked in pecans. You should ask David about it."

The band struck up again. Evelyn used the opportunity to pull Sarah toward her. "You're wasting your time on that one," she whispered.

"Mind your own business," Sarah hissed back through clenched teeth. She straightened up and caught her father's eye.

Sam sat in morose reserve, like a swan among geese. Sarah wasn't the only one feeling desperate.

"Daddy? Dance?" she asked.

He stood immediately, looking quite elegant in his tux. Sarah took his arm with a squeeze. "Thanks," she whispered.

On the dance floor he took her into his arms with a sad smile.

"Have you forgiven me?" she asked.

"There's nothing to forgive."

"I'm so sorry, Daddy."

She felt doubly guilty because she didn't really care about the American Indian ceramics and wood sculpture Sam drove across the country to buy. It was a tiny portion of their business, really more of a hobby for him. The clientele consisted almost entirely of older collectors, not the young upscale urbanites she cultivated with vintage furniture and high-quality pieces of folk art and craft.

But Sam loved "art from the heart of America." The three artists he visited every year were dear friends. They lived scattered through the Southwest in remote places. She'd tried to talk him into having their work shipped, but he insisted it must be picked up. No amount of insurance could cover the loss if even one piece was damaged, because each was irreplaceable.

That was the reason he gave. However, she knew, as much as anything, it was the trip itself he loved—attending the Indian Market in Santa Fe, purchasing pieces from new craftsmen that caught his attention, getting away on his own for three weeks.

"We could use this as an opportunity," she said gently. "There are wonderful artists in New York looking for representation. Why don't we find one or two we believe in and take them on? There's nothing I'd like better than to ease out of the craft and furniture business and deal in fine art. Who better to teach me than you?"

It wasn't a new idea, but it had been a while since she'd brought it up.

"We'll see," Sam sighed.

His sadness broke her heart. The Indian Market would open in less than a week, and for the first time in thirty years he would miss it.

"What if I went?"

"Where?"

"The Southwest. I know it's not the same as going yourself, but I have an idea of what you like, and I could finally meet Alan Trublo and Camilla Huna and Jon Wilbur," she said, the idea taking hold. At least she wouldn't be sitting in her apartment waiting for David's call.

"I've already written to Jon. I was going to call Camilla and Alan."

"Well, you still can. Tell them your daughter's coming. I'll meet people you care about, see the places you love, and come back with beautiful things to tell you about it. Doesn't that sound better than nothing?"

"I suppose so," he said.

# CHAPTER 5

**S**arah drove slowly along the highway between Lowman and Many Hills, searching the side of the road for mailboxes and ignoring the blaring horn from the eighteen-wheeler riding her tail. She spotted the grouping of five or six dilapidated containers, flicked her turn indicator, and slowed even more for the turn. The truck roared past, horn still blasting. The driver flipped her the bird through his open window.

"Oh, screw you too." She laughed as the car slipped smoothly onto gravel.

It was a Friday, one thirty in the afternoon. Under the cloudless sky a light breeze stirred the desert brush. So far the weather in New Mexico and northern Arizona had been mild and dry, rather than the sweltering heat she'd pictured.

She was feeling cheery, buoyed by the glorious day and a brief phone conversation with David that morning.

In spite of his promise to call in a few days, it had taken him more than a week. Then he'd left a message on her machine during the daytime, when she was presumably at work, apologizing and explaining he'd been so busy he'd "lost track of the days." She'd listened to it from her hotel room in St. Louis.

The second message three days later, in the evening, had been more forthcoming. Why hadn't he heard from her? He supposed she was angry and suggested they meet for a quick bite downtown to talk things over. She'd heard that one in Santa Fe.

The third message two days later—left on her machine at seven a.m.—tersely asked her to call him. She'd heard that one last night and returned the call early this morning, from a motel in Gallup.

"Hope I didn't wake you," she'd said cheerily.

She hadn't—he'd just showered.

Keeping her tone light and friendly, she told him where she was and apologized for not calling sooner. "This trip was completely spur of the moment. I've been so busy and involved I didn't even think to check my machine at home until last night, and then it was too late to call. Truly, I'm not angry. In fact, I'm convinced you were right to step back."

He'd been disarmed and had relaxed and warmed up. Relieved, he said, to know she was still speaking to him. He'd seemed genuinely concerned about her safety, said he missed her, and asked when she'd be home, eliciting her promise to call.

She'd calculated it would be six days, told him five, and planned to call in eight. She wanted to give him time to call first, but not too much. His interest was slightly piqued. It wouldn't do to count it as anything more than it was, or string it out too long.

Just one little detour, perhaps two hours, and she'd be back on the highway to the Hopi reservation to visit with Camilla

Huna. She'd spend the night near there, and if she started early
the next day, make it to Alan Trublo's back in New Mexico by
late tomorrow afternoon, already headed toward home.

The gravel road wound around, twisting into the desert.
Apparently it had been built to circumnavigate the vegeta-
tion and large boulders alongside it. Judging it impossible to
maintain traction at more than twenty miles an hour, she
settled into the slow pace, turned up her CD of *La Bohème*
and looked out the window. For the first time in ages she wanted
to paint the picture she saw—red earth, sparsely vegetated
and strewn with massive boulders against a deep, vast sky—
wild and harsh yet compelling. No mystery why Georgia
O'Keeffe had fallen in love with the desert and spent her life
capturing it on canvas.

Sarah had been an art major for two years of college until
she'd switched to art history. She'd already begun to suspect
she didn't have real talent, but it was the succinct critique of
one professor—Dr. Delman Hines—that convinced her to
drop her brush immediately. He'd posted his evaluations next
to the sophomore final projects exhibited in the main hall of
the department.

She still went clammy at the memory: standing in the large
room filled with students, parents, friends, reading the neatly
printed bold red ink note next to hers: C-. Insipid saccharine
work. Lacks matter, passion, and edge.

Not much left to lack as an artist except the guts for public humiliation. She could happily live the rest of her life without ever facing that kind of mortification again. And although
it seemed cruel at the time, he'd probably done her a service.
She wasn't cut out for the artistic life, being by birth and inclination middle class, sociable, and conforming. She had no
desire to set herself apart from society or bear the censure of
the world. Her taste in lifestyle centered on a nice home in a

good neighborhood, not a warehouse in Queens. And it turned out she loved art history.

Nevertheless, even with all the rationalization, it had hurt to let go of the dream. Primarily she supposed because she'd wanted to do it for Sam. Throughout her childhood he'd told her that art was humanity's answer to barbarism. "Artists are the best of us. A beautiful piece of music, a great sculpture or painting, can make you a little proud to be a human being."

She remembered, as a child, begging him to take her along on Eli's first trip to the Metropolitan Museum where, unlike her brother, she'd been willing to behave in the manner required, no whining or asking to leave. After Eli had been relegated to the lobby with a comic book, she'd stayed next to Sam for hours, basking in his approval and the conviction, shared by Eli, that she was his favorite. Precious time alone with her father—his hand occasionally on her shoulder, guiding her, positioning her for the best view, or absentmindedly patting her head—had been worth the stress of maintaining decorum. Although he had little patience for childish comments or questions, he'd shown her a way to stop and really look and think about what she saw.

"Is that woman happy or is she sad?" he'd ask, staring into a painting. "What is she thinking? Why did the artist choose a red scarf and not brown or green?"

Despite his emotional reserve, Sam had done his best as a father, and she was glad she'd made this trip for another reason besides the wake-up call to David. Although Sam hadn't seemed particularly enthusiastic about it, being here brought her closer to him. She could almost hear his voice expressing thoughts about the immensity and grandeur of the country, the vast horizons and deserted roads that slowed time and gave perspective.

She'd driven all day in order to arrive in Santa Fe the third night, in time for the last day of the Indian Market. Many of the artists were gone, but she'd picked up a number of pots at special last-day prices and enjoyed the colorful tribal celebrations. She'd spent the next day shopping for gifts to take back to her family. The following morning she'd driven to the Taos Pueblo to meet Jon Wilbur, a small American Indian in his mid-sixties with a melodious voice, who'd taken delight in showing her around the Pueblo and introducing her to everyone they met as "Sam's daughter." The people were very friendly, although she got the feeling not everyone knew who "Sam" was.

Jon, a nontraditional folk artist, worked primarily on commissions Sam arranged, and every year he made several special pieces for Shoen's. This year he'd carved two three-foot wood totems with brightly painted faces and sculpted a large black ceramic pot encircled by the long, winding body of a magnificent snake, its head resting on the lip.

They'd wrapped the totems in bubble wrap and boxed the pot. After carefully setting them in the back of the Volvo among the other boxed pottery, Jon had produced several thick pieces of foam to lodge between them, for which Sarah was extremely grateful at the moment, given the curves on the gravel road.

Within about fifteen minutes she'd driven three miles and passed five small and randomly scattered houses. The man at the post office had told her it would be at least eight miles up and there would be nothing after the first three miles. She was operating on instinct and faith. Instinct, when she'd spotted the gold necklace in the window of a gallery in Santa Fe, and faith that the old man had given accurate directions to the artist's house, in spite of his strange smile.

Shoen's didn't carry jewelry, at least they never had. But in Santa Fe her attention had been captured by unique pieces at several galleries. Extraordinary hand-cut stones and beads in liquid settings or inlaid in beautiful patterns, precious and semiprecious gems, and everything, even the clasps, fabricated by the artists. Hip and delicate, with an Indian feel but far from clunky silver and turquoise, it was nothing like anything she'd seen in New York and she was certain it would sell. That is, if she could get it at an affordable price.

Most of the pieces she'd liked had been the work of a few highly regarded artists who had taken major prizes at the Indian Market and had exclusive deals with local gallery owners. Then she'd spied an exquisite necklace in a small shop off the main square.

A chain of gold, hammered and twisted into a delicate lacy vine and scattered with red coral beads. It was serious jewelry, but light and airy enough to wear with jeans. She'd asked about the artist.

"I don't know," the saleswoman answered. "The owner bought it yesterday from a wholesaler. I can tell you it isn't collectible as art because it's definitely not by one of the top names. It's just a beautiful necklace."

A wholesaler? If the artist was selling through a wholesaler, he or she didn't have a dealer.

"What does this mean?" Sarah pointed to a tiny engraving on the back of the clasp.

"Oh, that's probably the artist's signature," the saleswoman answered.

"Really? It looks like a feather. Is there any way you can find out?"

"I could call the owner at home, I guess."

"Would you?"

The owner said the wholesaler had told her the artist was a Navajo named Lonefeather who lived near Lowman, Arizona.

She'd looked up Lowman on the map and realized she'd be passing within a few miles of it on her way to the Hopi reservation. Information didn't have a telephone listing, but she'd driven to the town anyway. It had been surprisingly simple. She'd asked an old man sitting on a bench in front of the Lowman post office if he knew where she could find a jeweler named Lonefeather.

"Ben Lonefeather," he'd said, chuckling at a private joke.

She'd been listening to the same CD for hours. A third go around of Musetta's aria was one too many, so she pressed eject and the search button for the radio. The odometer indicated at least two miles to go, and she could get nothing on the radio but static, so she riffled through the CDs scattered on the passenger seat for something interesting. She glanced back up and shrieked, hitting the brakes and swerving to avoid a brown rabbit poised in the center of the road a few feet ahead of her.

The tires lost traction. She lifted her foot off the brake and tried to turn into the skid, but the car slipped off the road between two boulders and bounced into the desert. She pumped the brake but the car kept bumping along, knocking against several rocks, heading straight for a huge boulder. All she could do was grip the wheel, attempting to turn. It felt locked, as if the car were in tracks. She screamed again, pulling as hard as she could against the soft ground. The car skidded sideways, skimmed the boulder, and smashed through some brush, rising up over a large rock before coming to an abrupt halt.

Dizzy and shaken, she opened her eyes and turned off the ignition, gulping air, weak with relief.

She pushed the door open and climbed out. Her momentary euphoria evaporated as she stepped into sand over the top of her new cowboy boots—light brown calfskin, purchased in Gallup that morning. The car, impaled on the rock, listed to the right, hissing dreadfully as water and antifreeze dripped out

into the red earth. She stood sinking—literally and figuratively—
for several moments before she thought to check the boxes in
the back.

At least the pottery seemed okay. She shut the hatchback
and leaned against it, hoping to catch some sound of humanity—a car, a radio, anything—but she heard absolutely nothing.
At least there was no dead bunny on the road. It was obvious
the car would need to be towed. She had her AAA card with
an 800 number in her wallet.

Her cell phone couldn't pick up a signal. She tried punch-
ing in the number anyway, walking around the car and turning in different directions, but all she got was a No Service
message on the screen. The important thing was not to panic.
There were hours of daylight left, plenty of time to get help.
She simply had to remain calm, continue checking the phone,
and make a choice—three miles back to the little houses or
two miles on to the jeweler.

She took her purse and cell phone, locked the car, and
plodded through the sand to continue on in the hope that Ben
Lonefeather was a kind man who'd give her a hand.

Her feet began to bother her within a few minutes. She assumed it was just the unfamiliarity and heaviness of cowboy
boots. It would pass as she got used to them. After all, they
were made for walking, right? But the walk was interminable,
and by the time she realized the extent of her folly, she had
painful blisters and the Volvo was far behind her. The phone
still couldn't get a signal.

She stopped and sat on a boulder looking around, straining
to see or hear any indication of an approaching car. The silence
was a bit unnerving, and sitting gave her throbbing feet little
respite as they'd swollen into every inch of boot. She considered trying to pull the boots off. But her stockings were no
doubt shredded—it felt like her skin would come off in shreds

as well—besides the fact that walking barefoot on the gravel would be impossible. She glanced down into the desert next to the road just as some sort of awful-looking thing, a scorpion or tarantula, crawled out from under her boulder. With a squeal, she grabbed her purse and jumped away to resume hobbling up the road, still shivering from the encounter.

At four o'clock she'd been walking for almost an hour. Surely she must have walked more than two miles. How much farther could it be? What if the old man had been wrong or she'd misunderstood and was on some strange, endless road? Or it ended in an abandoned house inhabited by lizards and snakes? What kind of person would choose to live in the middle of the desert?

At four twenty she realized her cell phone was missing, likely a casualty of her narrow escape from the murderous insect. At four forty-five she rounded a bend, swallowing tears. And there! Maybe a hundred feet ahead was a blue pickup parked near a long whitewashed wall. The road widened along the front of the wall for turning around and parking.

"Thank you, God," she whispered.

No knocker or bell, and the front door was too solid to register her knock. Even banging with the flat of her hand netted only soft, dull thumps.

"Hello? Mr. Lonefeather?" she called.

No response.

"Hello? Anybody?" she yelled, grabbing and juggling the door handle, which surprisingly gave readily.

She pushed it open: a lovely light-filled room, terra-cotta floors with beautiful woven rugs, wood furniture that appeared handmade, a couch and two large chairs facing a round adobe fireplace, a bookcase along the wall. Definitely more craftsperson than serial killer—possibly, from the taste and immaculate condition of the place, Mr. and Mrs. Craftsperson.

Through the open back door, she could see a patio and hear the muted drone of a power tool.

"Hello," she called breezily. A medium-size gray dog with a red bandanna around its neck appeared in the doorway and stared at her. Like a wolf, she thought, but smaller. The animal walked quietly through the room toward her, its ears erect.

"Hi, doggy," she said.

It didn't wag its bushy tail. She held the front door, ready to bolt if it showed any sign of attacking. But after making a thorough study of her boots, it turned, apparently satisfied, and walked back the way it had come. She followed slowly past a small dining table and four chairs and the kitchen area, out onto a lovely tiled patio, enclosed by two additional adobe buildings. Only the fourth side remained open to the empty desert and foothills. The hammering noise came from the tallest of the buildings.

She limped up to the open doorway and peered inside.

Sunlight streamed through high windows from both sides of the cavernous space, illuminating a cloud of white dust floating in the air and covering everything, settling like snow over great, tarp-covered mounds along the walls. Near the doorway a man worked a large block of marble with a small handheld jackhammer, his back to her. He seemed extremely tall, shirtless, wearing jeans. His head was covered by a paper surgeon's cap, strings from a surgeon's mask knotted at the back of his head. Sweat revealed dark skin and a muscular back under the white powder. The mask and the hammer muffled his voice, but it sounded like he was talking to himself, or singing.

Several sharp yaps, between a bark and a whine, pulled her glance to the right. Three wolf-dogs stood in a line about four feet away, staring at her. Their curled lips revealed shiny, sharp, white teeth.

The man suddenly whirled around, a ghostly apparition like some mad doctor: goggles hid his eyes, the mask covered his nose and mouth, the jackhammer, abruptly silenced to a hum, hammered the air.

Sarah gasped and tried to step back, but one of her bootheels caught and she couldn't move it. The dogs, ears flattened, fangs bared toward her throat, crept forward.

"No!" she cried, terrified, shaking her good leg at them. "No! Stay away!"

The man turned off the jackhammer and pulled down the mask.

"Back," he said casually. They immediately relaxed and retreated, wagging their tails.

"Mr. Lonefeather?" Pain shot through her foot as she succeeded in wrenching the boot out of the patio tile. "My name is Sarah Friedman. I'm sorry to barge in on you, but my car went off the road a few miles back. I'm sure it needs to be towed." She paused, but he didn't respond. "I guess I startled you."

He left the jackhammer on the table and came out of the building pulling the goggles off his head. The cap fluttered to the ground, releasing long, dark brown hair over his shoulders. Even taller than he'd appeared at first, he regarded her without the least hint of a smile.

"Would it be all right if I used your phone?"

"Don't have one."

"You're kidding."

"What were you doin on my road?"

"I was hoping to buy jewelry. You make jewelry, don't you?"

"You a wholesaler?"

She shook her head. "I work for a gallery in New York. I'm here on a buying trip. I saw one of your necklaces in Santa Fe.

The salesgirl told me they'd purchased it from a wholesaler. I thought perhaps you didn't have a dealer and might be interested in what we could offer. So I tracked you down." His stare was disconcerting so she rattled on. "I don't know what the trader paid, but I think we could do better, considering the price at the gallery."

He gave a short, humorless snort. "Sold everythin two weeks ago."

"Surely you must have things you kept or something you're working on?"

He didn't answer, nor did his expression afford a glimmer of interest.

Sarah swallowed. "Well, I'm sorry for bothering you." She took a step back and her toes screamed. "Um, do you mind if I sit down for a minute? My feet are killing me."

"Suit yourself." He kicked the door shut and leaned against it, his arms crossed.

She sat on the bench. One of the dogs came over to rest its chin in her lap, looking up in apologetic appeal. She patted its head. "It was clearly foolish of me"—she met the man's gaze and smiled with all the charm at her disposal—"but I loved your necklace, and it was such a pretty day. You have no idea how nice it is to see the whole sky. I mean without buildings. Well, I suppose my attention wandered. All of a sudden there was a bunny in the road. I swerved and . . . Look, I've obviously interrupted your work. I really am sorry. I'll happily pay for your time and trouble. I just need a ride into town."

He swore under his breath, turned and went back inside the building, reappearing a minute later and walking past her without a glance. She followed painfully through the house to the truck parked in front, where he waited in the driver's seat. He started the engine.

"Thank you very much," she said, forcing a smile as she

climbed in. As any further attempt at conversation seemed a waste of energy, she contented herself with staring out the window. She kept her eyes open for the cell phone, but chose not to say anything about it unless she actually saw and could identify the boulder, which turned out to be impossible.

They stopped at the Volvo, marooned in a red desert sea against the backdrop of deepening afternoon sky. The car looked like it had been stabbed through the heart and, if left alone, would remain forever a heap of rotting metal.

He got out, strode to the car and walked around it, bending over to examine underneath the front where it rested on the rock. She hobbled after him and unlocked a side door. Grabbing her suitcase and pulling it out onto the ground, she rummaged to the bottom for tennis shoes and socks, the most precious of all her worldly possessions at the moment.

She spoke without looking at him, hating to ask yet another favor. "I've got a lot of art in the back of the car, mostly pottery and quite valuable. It shouldn't be in the car when it's towed. Would you mind helping me load it into your truck so I can keep it with me?"

He grunted in what seemed assent.

"Great," she said, limping over to the passenger side to sit down and pull off the accursed boots. "Just give me a minute," she called, pushing against the ground for leverage, gritting against the pain. The boot locked her foot in a vice, absolutely immovable.

He opened the back hatch, removing and carrying the wrapped pieces and the boxes to his truck while she struggled unsuccessfully with one boot and then the other, fighting tears of frustration and pain.

He came around to the side of the car. "Here," he said, bending over and taking hold of the boot with which she was currently engaged, the left as it happened. "Hold on and relax."

She gripped the doorframe and extended her leg as he pulled steadily, applying pressure to the toe and heel. The boot slipped off. Her stockings were tattered and bloody, her heel and the tops of her toes almost as red as the polish on her toenails.

"Jesus," he murmured, staring at the foot for a moment before taking up the other boot.

• • •

Sarah watched through the rear window as the truck bounced. He'd set as much of the pottery as possible in the cab, on the floor and in her lap. He'd used some canvas and rope he had in the back of his truck to secure the larger boxes he'd placed there. The boxes appeared stable.

"What gallery?"

"I beg your pardon?"

"The necklace. You remember the name of the gallery?"

"Um. Blue Bird? Blue Parrot? Something like that."

"How much they want?"

"Fifteen hundred dollars."

"How long they had it?"

"The saleslady said a day."

"What'd you get at the Market?"

"Pottery, some beautiful pieces. You can see them if you'd like."

"Where else you been?"

"Uh, Taos, Gallup, Albuquerque. I'm on my way to the Hopi Mesas and then I start back. I have another stop near Four Corners."

"What's the name a your gallery?"

"Shoen's Furniture and Gallery."

"Furniture, huh? Where's it at?"

"Upper West Side. Do you know New York?"

"I been there," he answered.

He seemed to have exhausted his interest, and for the next twenty minutes they rode in silence.

• • •

"No way you gonna get a tow til Monday," the gas station attendant, a young man with a crossed eye, shaved forehead, and a long queuelike braid down his back, intoned lazily.

"Monday?" Sarah screeched. "Oh, no, you don't understand. I've got to get back to New York."

"Big Jack's in Flagstaff. His sister's weddin. He's got the Triple A contract. Owns the only tow truck for forty mile. But once he gets to it, he can prob'ly fix whatever's wrong. If he can get the parts. You know a Volvo dealer?"

"Don't you?"

The attendant shrugged. "Big Jack prob'ly will. Never seed a car he can't fix."

She wanted to scream in frustration at the two men regarding her with indifference, at herself for her folly, at an uncaring universe. She took a deep breath and unclenched her fists. It certainly wasn't their fault. It was a situation. Temper wouldn't help.

She dialed information from the phone booth. No dealer in Gallup or Flagstaff. The operator suggested Albuquerque. Bingo.

The salesman who answered told her that the service department was closed for the weekend.

She called AAA. The operator confirmed what the attendant had said. Big Jack's Towing was it.

She hung up the phone, frustration giving way to the reluctant realization that she'd be spending the next few nights where she was. A glance down the main street of downtown Lowman netted a coffee shop, a hardware store, and the Lowman Laundromat. No other tourists in sight. She might be the only white person around.

Lonefeather came over to the phone booth.

"You want a ride to the motel?"

"Yes," she said, smiling in spite of herself. "I do. Thanks."

Only two pickups occupied the parking lot, but the Lowman Motel had a No Vacancy sign propped up in the office window.

"I can't believe they're full," she said. "Is this the only motel?"

"Could be they forgot the sign."

"Right. Would you mind waiting?"

He shrugged.

She hit the little bell on the wood-grained Formica counter. It took several seconds for a middle-aged Indian man in a red apron to open an inner door, infusing the air with a sizzling strong scent.

"Somethin I can do for you?"

"Hello," she trilled with her friendliest smile. "I'm sorry to bother you, but my car broke down and I need a room for a few nights."

"We're full." He turned to go back to his cooking.

"How can you possibly be full?" she implored. "There are no cars in your parking lot. The town is empty. Who could be here to fill this place?"

He stood wavering for a moment before leaning into the inner apartment.

"Deloras?" he called. "Get the liver fore it burns, okay?"

"Why, where you goin?" a woman's voice responded.

"Nowhere. I'll be right there." He closed the door and motioned conspiratorially for Sarah to come closer.

"We ain't full," he whispered. "My wife jus likes to say that cause she thinks it sounds better. The plumbin's broke.

Cesspool's backed up, and we ain't got running water. Gotta lay all new pipes. Gonna take three, four days."

She imagined this might be what it felt like to be stuck, sinking in tar. "Can you recommend another motel?" she asked.

He wrinkled his brow. "Closest is thirty miles out on the highway. Don't know as I'd recommend it though."

"Where can I rent a car?" she asked.

He told her an hour and a half away, in Gallup or Flagstaff, take her pick.

She plastered a meek smile on her face and limped back out to the truck to throw herself on the mercy of Mr. Lonefeather.

"I've got to get a car so I can stay out on the highway while they fix the Volvo. Do you know where I can rent one for a few days?"

"Nope," he said.

"Is there a bus to Gallup or Flagstaff?"

"Not tonight." His eyes were unreadable, so dark the pupils disappeared.

"Oh," she sighed, beginning to dislike this man. "Then, do you think there's any way you could possibly give me a ride? Of course I'll pay whatever you think is fair. And if you don't want to drive back tonight, I'll cover a hotel room for you."

He leaned over and opened the passenger door.

"Get in."

As he drove he turned the volume on the radio up. Pushing button after button until apparently satisfied, he settled back, humming along to the worst, most twangy, brokenhearted country western lament she'd ever heard.

# CHAPTER 6

Instead of proceeding to the highway, he drove out of Lowman on a back road and turned into a long driveway, past a sign: FRANK DAWSEN, DVM. He followed the driveway along the side of a white, two-storied clapboard house and stopped between the rear of the house and a red barn.

"Doctor's a friend of mine. He'll take a look at your feet."

A veterinarian? Was he kidding?

"There's no need, Mr. Lonefeather," she said. "Really, all I need is a ride into Gallup. Or Flagstaff."

"Wait here."

Sarah watched him go into the barn. A few minutes later he came out with a gray-haired white man who walked to her side of the truck. She rolled down the window, and he reached in to shake hands.

"How you doin? Frank Dawsen. But nobody uses Frank cept my wife. You better call me Dawsen or I might get you

confused with her, an then who knows what would happen?"
Impish blue eyes, fair-skinned rosy face, upturned sunburned
nose. About sixty, Sarah guessed.

"Nice to meet you, Dawsen. I'm Sarah."

"Nice to meet you too, Sarah. I hear you got blisters."

"I do, but nothing that requires medical attention. A few
Band-Aids would do the trick."

"Come on into the house and we'll get you fixed up.
Annie's making tacos so you're gonna get wrangled into staying for supper." He opened the truck door and held out his
hand to help her down. She winced. He took her elbow.

"Last time Ben showed up here with a medical emergency
was bout a year an a half ago an it was motherless coyote pups,"
he said, walking slowly with Sarah. He shot a glance at the
other man with a quick grin. "I'd say your luck's improvin."

Ben Lonefeather ignored him, striding ahead.

Coyotes, Sarah thought. No wonder they'd looked so
strange.

"The Gorman boys are here," Dawsen called. "Millie an
Tom'll be coming for supper after work."

Lonefeather turned back, his hand on the screen. He did
not look pleased.

"Guess we'll be havin a dinner party," Dawsen continued,
smiling as they passed him at the door.

"Damn," Lonefeather muttered.

Dawsen winked at Sarah. "He's not much for parties."

They entered a large living room, permeated with the kind
of well-used ambiance people give a house when they care for
comfort but have no eye for decorating: faded overstuffed sofa
and chairs with worn spots; pine tables and mismatched lamps,
shades askew; books and belongings scattered on the floor and
coffee table.

The scent of something wonderful cooking—possibly a

stew seasoned with cumin and sage, Sarah thought—drew them past a group of children sprawled on the rug in the center of the room and through a doorway into an old-fashioned kitchen. Yellow tiles on the counter, a Formica breakfast table with wooden chairs, a freestanding stove where a heavyset, middle-aged Indian woman watched over several bubbling pots.

Lonefeather preceded them through the door.

"Ben! You devil," the woman cried, rising up on her toes and kissing his cheek. "Where you been? I was startin to worry. Thought you mus be sick or starvin."

"I got caught up in jewelry and stuff," Lonefeather said. He used a potholder to lift the lid off a cast iron pot on the stove, intensifying the rich aroma of the room. "Smells good."

Dawsen made the introductions.

"Nice to meet ya," Anna said, taking Sarah in with a nod. "Frank, get Sarah some lemonade and set two more places."

"Ginny?" Dawsen called into the living room. "Can you come in here?"

He turned to his wife. "Sarah's in need of some bandaging."

An Indian girl of about ten came in, followed by a younger boy. Dawsen patted the girl's head. "Ginny, set two more places at the grown-ups' table."

"I'll get the glasses," the boy volunteered.

"No, Frankie," Anna said quickly. "You get the silverware."

"Come with me," Dawsen said to Sarah.

Much of the downstairs area of the house had been converted into an animal hospital. She sat on a chair in the examination room to remove her shoes and socks. Dawsen whistled one low note when he got a look at her feet.

"You got some blisters goin there, little lady. Must hurt like hell."

"They do."

He sat in front of her on a small stool with wheels, pushing her jeans up gently.

"How far up?"

She pulled the jeans up to show him the raw patches on her shins.

"Nice ankles, and I like your toenails. What's the color?"

"I think it's called Red Passion. Or Passionate Red."

"Passion, huh?" He chuckled, dabbing the raw skin with a cool ointment. "Does it work?"

"You're the first man to notice. You tell me."

"I'm too old to remember. Better show em to somebody younger." He held up her foot, looking over at Lonefeather, who was standing in the doorway.

Lonefeather ignored him.

"Too bad." Dawsen winked at Sarah. "I guess it's been so long he's forgotten too."

Sarah felt herself color. "Well, I'll just have to wait until I get back to New York to test it."

"I don't know. Maybe if you stick around here long enough, one of us'll get his memory back. You got any go-aheads?"

"I beg you pardon?"

"Go-aheads? Thongs? Any kinda shoe that won't rub?"

"I've got a pair of sandals in my suitcase."

Ben Lonefeather left the doorway. Dawsen placed cotton between her toes and covered the blisters with gauze.

"Leave the dressing on overnight. Keep from gettin stains on your bed linen. After that let the air get to em. Don't put Band-Aids on, or they'll be botherin you into next week."

Lonefeather returned with the sandals, handing them to her without a word.

"I can't tell you how much better that feels," she told Dawsen.

"Glad to help."

She used the bathroom between the clinic and the kitchen and then realized she'd left her tennis shoes in the clinic. The door was shut, but she could hear the men in conversation. She raised her hand to knock, then stopped.

"Bullshit," Dawsen said. "I ain't sleepin in the barn when you got a room goin to waste. Do you good to have company."

"I got work to do."

"Pretty little thing . . ."

"Keep her here, then."

"What's the matter? You dead?"

"She's nothin but a pushy white broad thinks she can buy her way to whatever she wants. Jus keeps shovin money at me."

"Aw, hurt your pride, huh? Didn't see you was—"

"Didn't hurt nothin. She'll be more comfortable here."

Sarah's face burned as she walked into the kitchen and offered to help Anna, who handed her a glass of lemonade and waved her toward the living room to rest her feet.

Ginny sat in a corner of the sofa looking at a magazine. Frankie and two other boys were engrossed in a board game.

Sarah, mulling over whether she'd been culturally insensitive, took a spot at the other end of the sofa.

"You can't move that piece, fish face," Ginny said to Frankie.

"Mind your own business. I can, can't I, Billy?"

"It's going the wrong way," Billy, an older boy of eleven or twelve, answered.

"That's because Chippy put it down wrong."

"Did not," a little boy piped.

"Labyrinth," Sarah said, looking at the board. "My nephews play that game."

For the next half hour she served as final arbiter. Glad to get her mind off Lonefeather, she discovered that Ginny was ten years old and Frankie was eight. They were not the Dawsens' children or grandchildren but their great-niece and -nephew sent to the reservation for the summer, according to Ginny, to learn to appreciate their culture. Frankie thought it was because Phoenix was too hot in the summer and the trailer didn't have anything but a swamp cooler. Billy and Vernon, who was called Chippy because he resembled a chipmunk, brothers of eleven and seven, lived a few blocks away from the Dawsens with their parents. Billy and Frankie shared an interest in sports, especially baseball. Chippy was a good reader, and Ginny missed the ice rink in Phoenix where she skated every day after school.

"Where are you from?" Billy asked. He was a cute boy with dusky skin, mischievous eyes, and dimples.

"New York City. Do you know where that is?"

"Yeah," he said sagely.

"Hey, guys." An Indian man, mid-thirties, in slacks and a white polo shirt, opened the screen door, holding it for an attractive Indian woman in a pantsuit with short hair and a bright smile, carrying a large glass pie plate.

"Mommy!" Chippy exclaimed, jumping up and running to grab the woman around the legs.

"Chippy, you're gonna knock me over. Here." She bent, handing him the pie. "Take this to Anna."

"Hey, Dad," Billy said, standing up. "Did you get it?"

The man, showing the same dimples, tossed a baseball glove he'd been hiding behind his back.

Billy caught the glove, slipping it on and pounding his other fist into it. "That's so cool. It's from the Diamondbacks' equipment room," he told Frankie. "My dad's building a vacation house for the owner."

The couple introduced themselves to Sarah as Tom and Millie Gorman.

"You a friend of Anna's?" Tom asked.

"I'm just a wayward traveler."

Anna peeked through the kitchen door. "Millie. Tom. Good timing. The bread's just ready. Ginny, go get Carl."

Millie went into the kitchen, and Ginny ran through the hall and up the stairs.

"Okay, guys, put the game away and wash your hands," Tom said.

"Dinner! Frank? Ben?" Anna's voice called.

Tom Gorman abruptly glanced sideways at Sarah, cool and appraising.

The dining area extended off the living room in an L, with access to the kitchen at the end. The Dawsens served dinner on a weathered pine table covered with a crocheted lace tablecloth, set for seven. The seventh place was taken by an old Indian man who, having apparently worked his painstaking way downstairs, materialized from the hall and took a seat just as Anna came in carrying a platter heaped with golden rounds of bread and a large bowl of beans.

"Here's your fry bread, Carl," Anna said, placing the platter in front of his place. "No point in introducin you," she explained to Sarah. "He's deaf as a post. Don't know us half the time. Never mind what he says—we jus smile and nod."

Dawsen came in carrying a large bowl of salad and small bowls of grated cheese and onions, followed by Ben Lonefeather with a platter of stewed meat. Lonefeather paused midstep, eyeing Tom Gorman, who stonily stared back. Anna looked between them and then at Dawsen, who shrugged.

"Tom," Lonefeather finally said with an icy nod.

"Ben," Tom answered in the same chilly tone.

The children carried plates that had been assembled in the

kitchen to the coffee table, and Millie joined the adults with a glance at Tom.

"What do they think?" Anna asked Millie quietly.

Millie turned to her, speaking under her breath. "They think it was a transient."

Anna nodded. "As awful as it is, it'd be worse if it was someone here."

"A child was killed a month ago, Sarah," Dawsen said softly. "A little girl from Many Farms. Millie's the Lowman chapter community involve coordinator. She's been assistin the federal investigators."

"They were all over the area looking for clues but didn't come up with nothing except what the tribal police already knew," Millie continued in an undertone. "She was playin near her house one minute and the next she'd disappeared. Now they're contacin companies that use trucks to ship across country, checkin speeding tickets, credit cards at truck stops, that kinda thing."

"What are you whispering about?" Ginny asked, looking over from the coffee table.

"Nothin," Anna answered. "Tom, pork?"

"Sure, thanks."

"They think there's a connection with the animals?" Dawsen asked.

"Not at this point."

"What animals are you talking about?" Ginny interrupted.

"The animals I gotta see to tomorrow," Dawsen replied loudly. "Annie, Sarah needs a place to stay for a few nights. Her car ran off Henry's road into the desert."

Anna looked at Ben Lonefeather, who seemed to be in his own world, oblivious to everything but heaping beans onto the disk of bread on his plate. She smiled reassuringly at Sarah. "Well, you can stay with us. Frankie's been hankerin to sleep out in the barn all summer. And I'd enjoy another woman in the house."

"No, I ain't," Frankie piped up from the coffee table before Ginny jabbed him with her elbow. "Oww, why'd you do that?"

"Little pitchers have big ears." Anna chuckled.

"Sarah, you ever had Navajo tacos?" Dawsen asked.

"No. They look wonderful . . ."

"I don't want to sleep in the barn alone," Frankie wailed.

"It's okay, honey. Uncle Dawsen'll sleep out there with you," Anna called to him.

"She's welcome to stay with us." Millie turned to Sarah. "All we got is a couch in the living room, but we can close it off so it's private."

"That's very kind. It seems like I'm putting everybody out. What I really need is a car. You wouldn't know where I could rent one for a few days, would you?"

Millie looked at Tom. "I don't. Do you?"

He shook his head. "Sorry."

"We'll figure somethin out," Anna said to Sarah.

Sitting between Millie and Dawsen, Sarah felt like a person in regular speed trapped in a slow-motion movie. She longed to jump up and resolve her situation. Surely there must be one person on this reservation who wouldn't be insulted by the offer of payment for a ride to Gallup or Flagstaff?

"Start with the bread on the bottom," Dawsen said, handing Sarah the bread plate. "Then add the beans an the cheese."

"Frank's a vegetarian," Anna said, extending the platter of pork. "I keep the meat separate."

"Oh, none for me, thank you," Sarah said.

"Then just add onions and the salad on top."

The airy bread reminded Sarah of pouri from India. "Mmm. The beans are delicious," she said. "What's in them? Chipotle peppers?"

"Yeah," Anna answered. "I smoke em myself."

"I'd love the recipe."

Anna Dawsen looked pleased.

"He snores," Frankie's voice carried from the other table.

The other boys laughed.

"Shut up," Ginny hissed.

"Do you like to cook?" Millie asked.

"I love to cook, but I don't make beans often."

"What do you make?" Dawsen asked.

"All kinds of things. Italian mostly and Chinese . . ."

"My mom makes spaghetti. That's Italian," Chippy told Ginny.

"No, it's not," Billy scoffed. "It's American. Pasta is Italian."

"It's the same thing."

"Is not."

"Is."

"You know how to make chicken parmesan?" Ben Lonefeather didn't look over or miss a beat ladling beans onto his second piece of bread.

Tom and Millie Gorman exchanged a look across the table.

Sarah flushed. "Um, I used to. I haven't made it in a while. I think it's pretty simple. You just bread and sauté chicken breasts and then bake them with sauce and cheese."

"Sounds good," Dawsen said.

"Would you write it out for me?" Anna asked.

"Of course."

Immediately after the pie, Tom and Millie excused themselves as the boys had to be up early for a ball game. Millie prompted Billy and Chippy to thank Sarah for playing Labyrinth with them. Sarah noticed none of them said anything to Ben Lonefeather, who had retired to the kitchen with his dishes. Dawsen went to the barn to see to a sick dog he was boarding. Anna took Frankie upstairs to have a talk.

Sarah and Ginny continued clearing the table, carrying everything into the kitchen where Lonefeather was up to his elbows in soapy dishwater. Sarah found a dish towel to help Ginny dry.

"Ben," Anna spoke sternly from the doorway. "I wanna talk to you. Ginny can take over washing."

• • •

After tidying the kitchen, Sarah wrote what she hoped was a reasonable recipe for chicken parmesan on a piece of notebook paper Ginny gave her. Then she sat on the sofa watching Carl cut one long spiraling piece of peel from an orange with a small knife.

"In the wrist," he mumbled to himself, "in the wrist."

Lonefeather came downstairs and stopped a few feet away. "It's too crowded here. You better come with me. I got a room."

She said good-bye and thank you and remembered to go back to the clinic for her tennis shoes.

He was waiting in the truck with the passenger door open, a country station blaring on the radio. She shut her door, and he took off.

She reached over and lowered the volume on the radio.

"If it's not too much trouble, could you take me to the motel on the highway? I'm sure I can handle the situation from there in the morning."

"You'd be better off at my place."

"Look, I overheard some of your conversation with Dawsen in the clinic. It wasn't intentional. I don't usually go around eavesdropping, but actually I'm glad it happened because otherwise I wouldn't have known that I offended you. I'm very sorry. I appreciate how you've gone out of your way for me. The motel will be just fine. Really. And if you can think of any way I can repay you for your trouble, that you wouldn't find insulting, just let me know."

"It's a fleabag next to a gas station," he said wearily. "Anna says it ain't safe for a woman alone. An how you gonna get back to take care a your car?"

"Isn't there a bus or something?"

"There's no bus stop out there."

"Is there a taxi?"

"No." He sighed. "Okay, if I been rude, I apologize."

Apparently, Anna Dawsen had taken him to task. Sarah turned to stare out the window, considering what to do. He made the turn onto the gravel road and stopped. Except for the truck's brights eerily highlighting the boulders along the edge, everything was black.

"I got no problem taking you out there," he said. "Up to you."

"You think I'm a spoiled white woman who has no business being here."

"Didn't say that."

"No, you said I was 'a pushy white broad who thinks she can buy her way to whatever she wants.' "

He shrugged.

"But doesn't everyone have to pay for what they want?"

"Not always with money."

"Oh, I see. So you're saying that if I'd simply asked politely for a favor, a very big favor as it turns out, you'd have been pleased to help me?"

He thought about it. "Prob'ly not."

"Then what did you expect me to do?"

He was silent.

"Apart from the term 'broad,' which, by the way, is so old-fashioned it isn't even that insulting, there's another thing that bothers me—the use of the word 'white.' It strikes me as racist."

He gave a short laugh.

"What's funny?"

"Your defense. Like in the best defense is a good offense?"

"I'm not being defensive. It's a legitimate point."

"Describe me."

"Well, you're tall, you have long hair for a man, brown eyes . . ."

"Bull . . ."

"What?"

"If you was to describe me to one of your friends, the first word out of your mouth would be 'Indian.' "

"No, the first word out of my mouth would be 'He's.' " She paused, permitting his point. "The second would be 'Indian.' "

He smiled faintly. "Okay. I apologize for callin you a broad."

He started the truck and looked at her. She considered her alternatives and decided humble pie was better than a fleabag.

"If it's truly all right with you, I'll stay at your place tonight."

He put the truck in gear. She noted he drove the gravel road slowly, both hands on the wheel. He'd probably driven it a million times, but he didn't take it for granted. When a rabbit jumped out in front of him, he'd be prepared to stop in time.

"How much you figure you'd a paid for the necklace?"

"What did the wholesaler pay?"

"You figure what, half? Seven-fifty?"

"Probably."

"Shit," he said.

"What did they pay you?"

"It was a lump sum for a year's work. Broken down, that piece, bout four hundred."

She considered asking how much the gold and coral had cost but decided it would be like rubbing salt in a wound. Certainly a huge proportion of his gross had gone for supplies, not to mention the hours and hours of labor. What a shame. She'd have happily paid him seven-fifty.

When they got to the end of the road he turned the headlights off, and the wall, bright a moment before, almost disappeared in the night.

"No moon," he said. "Leave your door open." He carried her suitcase, and she followed him through the large room she'd seen before—shadowy now, lit only by the interior light coming from the truck—into another room and darkness. She stood still, listening to him move things around. He opened and shut a drawer abruptly, and her heart lurched, panicked by the isolation.

He struck a match to light a lantern, illuminating a double-size wooden four-poster bed between matching nightstands. A Navajo blanket, intricately woven in muted blues and browns, covered the bed. The stands each held a lantern and several pieces of Hopi pottery. At the foot of the bed a large wooden trunk rested on a stunning rug, woven in the same muted shades in patterned rows, with a slender zigzag of red added throughout. A six-drawer dresser stood against the wall facing the bed, above which hung a mirror in a wooden frame.

"It's lovely, like a room in *Country Home* . . . a magazine. Who made it all?"

"Grandparents." He moved her suitcase against the wall and opened the trunk.

Everything was fine. The Dawsens, clearly decent people, knew where she was, and it didn't seem that Ben Lonefeather had any intention of doing her harm.

He removed a set of embroidered linen sheets from the trunk. "You can put these on the bed."

"Oh, my God," she said, running her finger along the delicate pink and yellow flowers embellishing scalloped edges. "They're incredible. I can't sleep on these. Don't you have any plain ones?"

"Bathroom's in there. Only got the one. Clean towels in the cupboard. You need anything else, I'll be up for a while."

"Thank you."

He nodded and left, shutting the door behind him.

She made the bed. The homespun linen—infused with the scent of cedar from the trunk, heavier and denser than cotton but very soft—seemed to contain something of the woman who'd sewed them, probably as a young girl, to pack in her hope chest. The femininity of it moved her. Such an intimate, romantic gesture, to make bed covers to share with your future, unknown husband.

The day caught up with her. Leaving her clothes in a heap, she slipped into an oversize T-shirt, dizzily washing her face and brushing her teeth, before blowing out the lantern. She remembered the bed linen and got up, rummaging in her suitcase for a pair of socks to pull over her shins and cover the gauze Dawsen had wrapped on her wounds.

Gazing out the open window at the stars, she caught fragments of Lonefeather's low voice on the patio, talking to the coyotes. What kind of person kept coyotes as pets? A few moments later, to the strains of a guitar, they started howling—or yapping—short, high-pitched notes, almost like dogs crying, but not. Really like nothing she'd ever heard. It lasted perhaps five minutes. Then there was just the guitar.

Half awake. Sounds of water. Sarah opened her eyes. A moment later he emerged, a towel around his waist. She stayed still, heart thumping. He *had* said there was only the one bathroom. He walked past the foot of the bed, his body silhouetted in the hazy light from the lantern in the other room, loose hair flowing over his muscular back and shoulders. Like an ancient god. In the doorway he turned in her direction, eyes in shadow.

"Night."

"Good night," she whispered.

# CHAPTER 7

**S**arah awakened in full sunlight to clamorous birdcalls. Her watch read ten to seven, ten to nine in New York. Saturday. David would be at the gym.

The bathroom, remarkably clean, contained an old freestanding tub with a circular shower curtain suspended from above, a toilet with overhead water container and chain, and a large white pedestal sink, no counter for toiletries. She set her razor, shampoo, conditioner, and foaming face cream on the floor next to the tub and her toothbrush and paste on the rim of the sink. The shelves in the medicine cabinet held generic shampoo, toothbrush and paste, deodorant, a bottle of aspirin. A small built-in cupboard had towels, rolls of toilet paper, and cleaning products.

She sat on the toilet to remove the gauze and evaluate the red sores on her toes, the tops of her feet, her shins and heels. She ran the water, which was plenty hot—too hot, in fact, for her screaming shins. She managed to endure a tepid shower. Afterward, she towel-dried her hair, dressed in shorts and a T-shirt, and slipped the sandals gingerly over her toes.

No sign of life in the main room, but there was ground coffee in the refrigerator and a dented aluminum coffeepot sitting on the kitchen counter. The stove used propane. She followed the instructions, which were engraved on a plaque in the center of the burners, and brewed a strong, full pot. No milk or creamer, so she carried it, black, through the open door, and outside to the redwood table on the patio.

The building where he'd been working the day before was locked with a padlock. However, the door to the smaller building was open, and as soon as she sat down, one of the coyotes walked out toward her. It stopped a few feet away, staring directly at her, in much the same way as a cat. A moment later the other two appeared in the doorway.

"Come on. It's okay," she called, extending her hand. They came forward quietly, with more dignity than dogs, to sniff her hands and feet. One of them gently licked her sore toes and shins. They permitted her to pet their soft heads. Then, as if on some signal, they turned and walked back through the door they'd come out. She picked up her coffee to follow.

The room, similar in shape to the main room of the other house, had the same terra-cotta floors, whitewashed walls, and huge, hinged windows. At the back there was an arched doorway through which she could see a neatly made futon mattress on the floor and a wooden dresser. He apparently used this house for sleeping and as a studio. He had easels stacked against the wall, a long table with a couple of high-powered lamps and a stool, a large double sink recessed in a long counter stacked with labeled plastic containers and tools. More tools hung from the walls, and there was a drafting table, where he stood drawing.

Dressed in a T-shirt and jeans, his hair tied in a ponytail with a cord, he sang softly to himself, ignoring the coyotes winding around his legs. She couldn't tell what he was drawing, but she hesitated to interrupt him and soon stepped away from the door to wander across the patio and into the desert, where she found the wild remnants of an herb garden: rosemary, sage, thyme, mint.

She picked sprigs of the sage and thyme and scurried back into the kitchen to scavenge the contents of the almost barren refrigerator. A mushy tomato, a few stalks of celery, a moldy container of cream cheese, one beautiful onion, half a banana squash, a carton of eggs, and a cube of butter. He had a decent knife and a frying pan.

She separated the herbs from the stalks and ripped the leaves with her fingers, chopped the vegetables, sautéing them separately, beginning with the onion, to flavor the pan, then the celery and the squash. She diced the tomato and beat six eggs with a fork. There was a bit of cream cheese left under the mold, and it tasted okay.

She washed the pan, swirled a chunk of butter to sizzle, then poured in the eggs and seasoned them with the herbs and a little salt. As soon as they set, she dropped the cream cheese in dollops, giving it a chance to melt for a moment before spreading it with the back of a spoon over half the eggs. She added the vegetables and, using the knife, carefully folded one side over, waited a minute, and flipped it.

The scent of herbs infused the little house. She'd set the places and was putting some extra stalks of sage in a small double-spouted Hopi wedding vase at the center of the table when he walked in.

He had a killer smile.

He closed his eyes and gave a little moan with the first bite. Sarah couldn't help but feel smug, even if it was only an omelet.

"This is gourmet. How'd you do it?"

"Just used what I found. Who planted the herb garden?"

"My grandma."

"Is she the one who made the sheets?"

"I guess. Moved your boxes to the storeroom after you went to sleep. Figured you'd rather they was locked up."

"It's a storeroom? You were sculpting there yesterday, so I assumed. . . . What do you store?"

"Your art."

"Ah." She smiled. "I suppose if I asked what the sculpture was going to be, you wouldn't tell me."

In the process of taking in a mouthful, he responded by a slight inclination of his head, indicating she was correct.

"Okay. I've got another question—why weren't there any lights last night?"

"Turned the generator off before we left yesterday."

"You mean the only electricity you have is from a generator?"

He chewed thoughtfully. "You done any thinking bout where you're gonna stay til your car's fixed?"

"Well, I thought . . . hoped you'd be willing to store the art for a few days and you'd be good enough to take me some-where to catch a bus to either Gallup or Flagstaff. I know I'm really putting you out . . ."

"Then what?"

"I'll rent a car, check into a hotel, and come back on Mon-day to deal with the Volvo."

He shoveled another forkful. "Lotta driving. An you still gotta return the rental an take the bus back to get your car." He glanced up.

"I don't see an alternative."

He nodded and took another bite, using his finger to push the last bit of omelet onto his fork. He picked up his plate and carried it to the sink. "Got somethin to show you."

She followed him to the studio, where he'd laid out several pieces of jewelry on the table: two hammered and linked gold chains with beautiful pendants—a lizard and a bear—inlaid with pieces of turquoise and red and pink coral, and a lovely multistrand seed pearl necklace with an inlaid turquoise and lapis clasp.

"You said you didn't have anything left."

"Made the chains an set the turquoise this morning."

"What are these?" she asked, indicating the drawings on the drafting table.

"Ideas for supplies I got on hand. Could do em in a couple days."

Two necklaces: diamond shapes of gold inlaid with slivers of lapis, pink coral, and garnet linked by gold chain.

"I take it you don't have a dealer?"

"Right."

"What were you thinking?"

"Half what you'll get. Not consignment, up front."

"We've never carried jewelry. I don't know what to expect. Thirty-five hundred?"

"Five thousand."

"I can't go that high. It's a new market. I'm not sure I'll even be able to generate any interest."

He shrugged.

"How about four thousand?" she offered.

"The materials alone cost over two."

"Forty-two hundred. That's as far as I can go."

"Forty-five an you can stay here until your car's fixed."

"Forty-four, and I'll cook."

"Deal."

# CHAPTER 8

They bumped along the road under a deep blue sky spotted with cotton-ball clouds, passing the forlorn Volvo.

"Were you at the Indian Market?" she asked.

"No."

"I thought that was the best place to sell jewelry, especially if you don't have a dealer."

"Didn't get in."

"Why not? You're certainly good enough."

"Had trouble there a few years back."

"What kind of trouble?"

"Got in a fight, knocked over some pottery stalls." He turned on the radio to country western twang.

"I bet you think I'm really nosy."

He gave a short laugh.

A few minutes later he turned the radio off. "Quit drinkin six years ago. But I got a residue from stuff I did."

"You don't drink at all anymore?"

"One day at a time."

"Well, I'm glad you told me so I won't use wine in the food. Is there anything else you can't eat or don't like?"

"Nope."

He took her to a standard supermarket stocked with regional items, such as numerous varieties of dried beans and peppers and rows of pork parts, including feet, in the meat section. She searched the aisles quickly, locating things she could use: chicken, a leg of lamb, flour, a can of tuna, packaged mozzarella, parmesan from a container would have to suffice, cottage cheese, eggs, brown sugar, butter, vinegar.

"Ah, there we are," she cried, delighted to spy a bottle on the top shelf among the oils.

"What?"

"Olive oil. I was afraid they wouldn't have it."

He reached up for the bottle. "Extra virgin? Woulda thought one was enough." He grinned, handing it to her.

As they continued through the aisles, gathering items, she discovered a few surprises, like a dusty bottle of capers.

"Whadda you gonna do with that?"

"You'll see," she said.

"What kind of vegetables do you like?" she asked, dubiously looking over a limp and meager choice.

"The kind they sell at the farmers' market on the other side of town."

She pulled out her wallet at the check stand as he reached in his pocket for a wad of money.

"I don't want to insult you, but my paying for the food seems part of the deal we made."

"The deal was for labor. The cost of the food should be split. An I should pay more cause I'll eat more."

"I see. Well, if it's just labor, then I should fill your gas tank and pay for the utilities I'm using in your house. We'll prorate whatever you spend, including wear and tear on your generator, so we can split the cost."

He put the money back and raised his hands in the air. "Okay, you get the food. I'll cover the produce."

They bought garlic, onions, lettuce, potatoes, tomatoes, summer squash, zucchini, corn, green beans, peaches, apples, and pears at the farmer's market.

Before they left Lowman, they stopped at the gas station so Sarah could use the phone. She called her parents and left a message on their machine. She'd had a little "car trouble," she said, nothing serious, but it would take a while to get it fixed. She told them she'd lost her cell phone and didn't know where she'd be staying so she couldn't leave a number. She'd call back on Monday when she knew what the problem was with the car.

She checked her answering machine at home. Two messages: one from Bloomingdale's about a skirt she'd ordered and one from a cable company offering her free service for the month.

They arrived back at his place just before noon. After carrying the groceries into the house, he went out to the studio, leaving her to unpack and organize.

At seven that evening she put the finishing touches on the table with a flowered cotton tablecloth from the 1950s discovered in the trunk at the foot of her bed, a votive candle, and a bougainvillea clipping in the vase at the center. She'd freshened up for dinner and changed into a summer skirt.

"Whoa," he said, stopping at the back door, a smile transforming his face. He disappeared and returned with clothes over his arm, emerging from the bedroom a few minutes later in a blue cotton shirt and clean jeans, his hair slicked back.

"Need help?"

"No. Just light the candle and sit down. I'll bring your plate."

He struck a match and watched her set the food on the counter in the pans she'd used for cooking. Chicken parmesan with fresh marinara and mozzarella, gnocchi in brown butter garnished with thyme, sautéed yellow squash and zucchini with onion, soda rolls, a platter of fruit and cheese for dessert.

His eyes shone as she placed the plate in front of him.

"I'm real proud a the deal I got."

"You'd better taste it before it gets cold, or you might not think so."

She placed a large bottle of club soda on the table with two glasses. He poured some into each glass and leaned forward to smell the food. But he didn't start.

"What?" she asked from the counter.

"I'm waitin."

She came to the table with a sparse plate. "Okay, dig in."

He raised his glass. She picked hers up.

"To good deals," he said, touching glasses.

"Good deals."

He picked up his knife and fork and sliced into the chicken, spearing the piece with several gnocchi and a bit of squash, savoring the mouthful with his eyes closed. She tried hers, concerned the chicken might be dry, but it was quite moist and surprisingly good.

He swallowed and took a sip of water. "Lady, you are some cook."

"Lady?"

"What's wrong with 'lady'?"

"It's one of those generic names men call women, like honey or babe. But maybe I shouldn't complain. It's better than broad."

He shook his head with a laugh and then proceeded to eat

with a gusto she'd rarely seen. Not that he rushed. He chewed slowly, tasting every bite, making appreciative noises, sometimes closing his eyes. Certainly a change from the taciturn man she'd met yesterday.

"How come you're not married?"

"Oh, my God," she said, setting her fork down. "I can't believe it."

"What now?"

"Do you know that's the first personal question you've asked me?"

"So?"

"So here I am, in the middle of the desert, having dinner with a complete stranger, and the first thing you want to know about me is the same thing my mother's driving me crazy asking. Why? Is there a big S on my forehead?"

He chewed thoughtfully, regarding her.

"Or is it because I enjoy cooking and do it well? It's odd, isn't it? If a man cooks, he's a chef. If a woman cooks, she must be desperate for a husband."

"I'm gonna get some more," he said, picking up his plate and heading for the counter.

"Okay, maybe I'm a little sensitive on the subject. It's just that the last time I cooked dinner for a man, he decided it meant my feelings for him must be 'too intense.' I'm trying to understand the connection."

David's condescending expression, when he told her he needed space, flashed into her mind, and she had the urge to slap it off. On edge, she picked up her fork.

Ben Lonefeather didn't seem to notice her annoyance, being fully occupied scooping chicken and gnocchi onto his plate. A task complicated by the lack of proper utensils.

"But you know," she continued, "it is funny, because there are all kinds of things I want to know about you. I have a million questions. And why you're not married is *not* the first that comes to mind."

He sat back down with a satisfied smile.

"Food's gettin cold," he said.

He finished his meal, ending with a final, perfectly orchestrated bite. "You done?"

She nodded, and he carried the plates to the sink, returning with the platter of cheese and fruit.

He picked out an apple, sliced a piece, and popped it into his mouth. "Okay, go head."

"With what?"

"You said you had a million questions."

It took a moment to decide where to start. "Did you grow up in this house with your grandparents?"

"Yep."

"What happened to your parents?"

"Killed in a car crash when I was two."

"How sad."

"I guess." He shrugged. "Don't remember em much cept I get a hazy image a my mom now an then. Long hair, smilin face. Name was Amelia."

"What about your dad?"

"Named John. They was real young—she was nineteen, he was twenty." He sliced another piece of apple, chewing with a furrowed brow.

"What?"

"Must a been tough for my grandparents. He was their only kid. Don't know as it made much of a difference to me though."

"What were your grandparents like?"

"She was Hopi. Lots a family an friends. Loved company

and goin visitin. Henry was Navajo, liked it quiet. Most content when it was jus the three a us at home. Hated when she
was gone. "Runnin round,' he called it. When she died he fell
apart. Never got over it."

"How old were you?"

"Fifteen. Day they buried her was the first time I had a
drink."

He stood and began clearing the table. Sarah joined him,
and for the next few minutes they worked in companionable
silence. He ran hot soapy water in one side of the sink and
clear water in the other. She picked up a dishcloth, and they
stood next to each other, washing and drying in quiet rhythm,
the last rays of sun streaming through the windows.

"You know anythin about Indians an liquor?" he asked.

"Just the stereotype, I suppose."

"Some kinda metabolic thing. From that first drink, I was
gone. No possibil'ty a moderation, jus sober or drunk. For the
next thirteen years it was mostly drunk."

"It takes a strong person to beat something like that."

He rinsed the last dish and pulled the plug. "Why don't you
make some coffee?"

They took it out onto the patio. The sun had set. Orange
and pink feathers of cloud laced the twilight. He sat across
from her at the redwood table. Her earlier emotional turmoil
had dissolved. Absorbed, she thought, by the quietude, so different from the city. Too much of it would drive her crazy. She
craved the fast-paced pulse of Manhattan, the rush of being at
the center of the world. But a little leisurely peace seemed a
nice change.

"You grow up in New York?"

"Long Island, in a Jewish neighborhood. Jews can be quite
insular. I mean," she explained, "we stick to ourselves. Have
you ever met anyone who was Jewish before?"

He shrugged. "Don't know."

"Of course." She smiled with mild sarcasm. "And why would you care?"

"You ever met a Cree or a Sioux?"

"No, but I just met a number of people from the Pueblos when I was in New Mexico," she said smugly.

"Notice any difference between them an the people you seen around here?"

She tried to think but couldn't come up with anything. "Touché," she said sheepishly, wondering if he understood what touché meant.

"You were sayin Jews stick to themselves. Why's that?"

"For a lot of reasons, I suppose. Partly because we're afraid we won't fit in, and, on the other hand, we're afraid maybe we will and then we'll forget who we are. My father lost his family in the Holocaust, so for us it's about continuing our Jewish identity."

"Holocaust? You mean in Germany?"

"Don't tell me you don't know what the Holocaust was," she said rather sharply.

"Yeah, I do. Jews killed during World War Two. I jus never met anyone lost someone in it. Your dad lost his family, huh?"

"Yes, his parents and two sisters."

"How come they didn't get him? He hide or somethin?"

"They sent him to his father's cousin in New York. His parents were working on visas for all of them. My father was the youngest, but for some reason his came first. So he left Germany when he was fourteen, expecting the rest of them to follow in a few weeks. He never saw any of them again."

"Why couldn't they get out?"

"My grandfather waited too long. He owned a large department store in Cologne. He and my grandmother had built it from a small tailoring shop, and he couldn't stand the thought of losing everything they'd worked for. So he turned a blind eye to Hitler and decided the Nazis were a passing fad. My grandmother—her name was Sarah and she was wonderful, very smart and stylish; my father adored her—well, she could see they were in trouble, and she begged him to leave, but he kept saying the Germans would wake up and see what a mistake they were making and the whole thing would blow over. Also, some of his customers were Nazis, so he was convinced they would leave him alone. Then in 1938, on one night—we call it Kristallnacht, the night of broken glass—the Nazis destroyed all the Jewish shops and stores in Germany, including my grandfather's. He finally realized they had to get out and started trying to get the visas, but by then it was too late. My father got to New York a month before Hitler invaded Poland."

"Musta been tough, a kid alone in a foreign city."

"I don't know. He talks about his family and Germany when he was a child, but not much about what happened after he came to the U.S. He says Kaddish every year for the Reeses, the people who took him in. It's a special prayer for the dead. They didn't have children of their own, and I'm sure they were kind to him. All I really know is that he went to high school in Manhattan and as soon as he graduated joined the army. After the war he went back to Germany and found out what happened to his family. It took months, but he traced them to Auschwitz, a concentration camp. His mother died first, from typhus, then Elizabeth, his oldest sister. A year later Gerta, the younger one, was shot for trying to escape. His father was the last. His name was Joseph, and he survived until 1943 and died in the gas chamber. I think it almost killed my father to find out. His sisters were only twenty and twenty-two when they died. Elizabeth was gentle and brilliant. She was going to be a doctor until the Nazis barred Jews from the university. Gerta was a rebellious redhead."

Ben got up to get a lantern from the house. Sarah breathed in the warm scent of desert turning into night, surprised by the turn the conversation had taken. It had been years since she'd told anyone her father's story.

But he was an extraordinary listener—very still, without interjecting or even nodding, simply using an occasional question to draw her out. Was that part of his culture? Or was the thought that it was cultural in itself stereotyping?

He returned and set the lantern on the table. Before she could even begin to offer a change of subject, he was sitting as before, his eyes intent on her face.

"What did your dad do, when he found out?"

"He went back to New York and stayed at the Reeses'. He wouldn't leave their apartment. He didn't eat much or sleep. I think he wanted to die too, but he couldn't because that would mean Hitler had won. Then, one Friday night, Milton Reese came into his room and insisted he shower and get dressed and go to temple with them."

She looked out into the darkening sky as the first stars appeared. "The building was packed. On a normal Friday night the temple was never even half full. That night there must have been a thousand people. Somehow people moved closer together and made room for them. More people came in, and people made room for them too, until there was no more room. Then people stood in the back. The Reeses told him it had been the same for weeks, all over the city. Jews filling the temples as a way to prove to the world and to each other that, in spite of the horror and the impossible number of deaths, Hitler's 'final solution' had failed. At the end of the service, everyone stood and put their arms around each other, and the rabbi began to read the names, all the family and friends lost to members of the temple. My father heard his family's names among all the others. Then a thousand voices said Kaddish."

The lantern flame danced behind the glass, casting a shimmering circle around them.

"He says that's what saved him. His people and his religion."

"He named you Sarah. For her, his mother."

"Yes." She smiled faintly. "It's a lot to live up to."

"How come?"

"It's an obligation, to my father, to all of them. Or at least that's what I feel. As if somehow I've got to make up for what happened. I know what's expected. The kind of marriage I'm supposed to make, the way I should raise my children. When I was growing up I couldn't bear to think I'd upset him or made his life more difficult by getting bad grades or wasting time with inappropriate friends. Which, of course, my mother used to full advantage. But then, that could just be an excuse."

"For what?"

"For going along, seeking approval. I'm a very conventional person. I suppose all I've ever really wanted was to make my parents proud of me. Unfortunately I'm not a brain or an athlete, so the best I can be is a good daughter. You're tricky," she said with a laugh. "I was supposed to be asking you questions."

He inclined his head, waiting.

"Do you consider yourself Navajo or Hopi, or both? Or is that a stupid question?"

He took time answering. Nothing about him seemed rushed or slapdash. She'd felt a difference in the pace of people here, last night at the Dawsens'. But then it had been frustrating.

"It's a good question. I'm a quarter Hopi. That's all you need to be part a the tribe, but it's got to come through your mother. When I was twelve, my grandma felt bad cause I couldn't be initiated. I tol her it didn't make any difference to me. I'm Navajo, like Henry."

"Is it common for Hopi and Navajo to marry?"

He shook his head. "Specially not then. Met one day in Tuba City. Her dress got caught in a doorway, on a hinge. Henry unhooked it an they looked at each other. He found out who she was an went courtin. Wouldn't take no from anyone but her. An she wouldn't say it. They finally had to run off. She didn't make up with her folks til after my mom an dad died. Tol me she'd learned her lesson. 'Life's too precious to hold a grudge against someone you love.' "

"Was your mother Navajo?"

"Cree, from Montana."

"How did your parents meet?"

"At a boardin school. Not the fancy New York kind. Those days, the BIA had it set up so all Indian kids had to go. The idea was to get em away from their tribes an mix em together. Get rid a the different traditions an languages. Suppose to help em adapt to white society." He smiled ironically. "But that's where they met. She came from a bad place. Was up there once. People lot worse off than here."

"Did you go to a boarding school?"

He shook his head. "They changed the law by that time. I went to high school in Many Hills. Played baseball. Raised hell. After my grandma died, Henry kinda disappeared into himself, and I was left on my own a lot. Did some bad stuff. Hated everything bout livin here. Tried my best to get away. Joined the army, bummed around. Woulda skinned myself, if I could. Only come back cause I was broke an had nowhere else to go."

"And now you love it."

"It's home."

Her watch read a few minutes after midnight, but Sarah wasn't tired.

"Shall I make some tea? Or do you want to go to bed?"

He looked at her with a quick grin. "Sure. Tea would be good."

They made it together and carried the cups back outside.

"Do you have a girlfriend?"

"Nope."

"You say that as if you're happy about it."

"I ain't sad about it. It's not somethin I'm missin."

"Don't you get lonely?"

"Not usually."

"But sometimes?"

He shrugged, looking out over the dark desert, stroking the head of one of the coyotes that rested in his lap. The other two were lying near his feet, curled together.

"Which one is that?"

"This here's Sage."

"She's the sweetest, isn't she?"

"Yeah."

"And the largest is Littleman? I think he's the first one I saw."

"Prob'ly. He's usually out ahead, the bravest or the dumbest. I ain't made up my mind. Eagle's the smartest. No question." At the sound of her name, the coyote stood up and shook, nudging Sage out of the way to get close to Ben. "We play hide an seek. She can find anythin, a crust of bread, a dirty shirt, no matter where it's at."

The displaced coyote moved over to Sarah and put its chin on her knee. "If you're Sage, why do you smell like rosemary?" she asked, bending forward to nuzzle the velvety head.

She looked up and met Ben's eyes. "Now will you tell me what's in the storeroom?"

He expelled a short breath and chuckled to himself. "You know what they say bout curiosity?"

"I'll take my chances."

"Jus art, sculpture mostly, some paintins. Everythin I done besides jewelry for the past ten years."

"Why keep it locked up?"

"Prob'ly so a pretty woman from the big city would think I was a man a mystery an sit out on my patio all night talkin to me."

"Stop." She laughed.

"There's no big secret. I'm jus not inclined to show it to anyone."

"Would you let me see?"

"Why? So you could tell if I'm any good?"

"I'm not a critic. I'd just like to see it."

"What do I get out of it?"

"I don't know," she said, surprised. "Why would you make art if you didn't intend to show it?"

For a moment, from the intensity of his look, she thought he might be annoyed, but then he stood with a laugh, shaking his head. "I'm goin to bed. Mind if I use the bathroom first?"

•  •  •

She sat on the sofa waiting. Sage jumped up and curled next to her. The other two coyotes sat on the rug in the middle of the floor.

He opened the door from the bedroom, wrapped in a towel, moist heat emanating from his hair and skin.

"That was quick," she said, conscious of sheer masculine power and the smell of soap as they passed each other.

"Night," he said, his dark eyes unreadable.

"Good night," she said, closing the door behind him.

•  •  •

Sarah lay in the shadowy room, wrestling with jumbled thoughts and images. David backing away from her—had she really seen, or just imagined, the victorious look in his eyes? Her father's slumped shoulders. The awful feeling of betrayal she'd felt siding with her mother. Was it right or simply selfish to rob him of what he loved so much? Evelyn's infuriating concern. Suppose she was right, had Sarah blown all her chances?

She tried breathing deep and listening to the stillness— loosening her grip on everything but the peace of the moment. It took a while but she finally drifted to sleep.

• • •

Ben tossed on his pallet, feeling as if a blocked confluence between his mind and body had opened and, like blood to an arm that's fallen asleep, flooded him with a tingling ache.

When was the last time he'd been with a woman? Sally, middle-aged waitress at Stuckey's out on the highway. He saw her every once in while when he needed a warm body in the dark. He couldn't remember how long it had been.

Couldn't remember the last time he'd had a conversation with a woman besides Anna. Couldn't remember the last time he'd been so talkative, or listened to a story and been touched.

Not since he stopped drinking.

He got up and stood in the doorway, looking out over the patio, juiced up and wide awake. Dawsen was right; he'd been living like he was half dead. He'd gotten as far to the outlying edge of humanity as he could without falling off.

For the first time in a long time, he felt like taking a step back in.

# CHAPTER 9

**S**unday morning Sarah awakened in a pool of sunlight and listened to the birds for a few minutes before hopping out of bed to take a shower.

Ben wasn't in the house, but there was a fresh pot of coffee on the stove. She took a cup out to the patio. Clouds moved rapidly across the sky, hiding and revealing the sun, transforming the world from gloomy to dazzling in a moment. Warm air dense with moisture enveloped her. Electricity ruffled the hair on her arms.

The storeroom door stood open.

She walked to the studio and peeked in. He was sitting on a stool bent over the long worktable, a lamp shining on his hands as he used a small pump drill to make holes in tiny beads of red coral. The coyotes, lying on the floor at his feet, raised their heads to look at her but didn't get up.

"Had cereal for breakfast," he said, without turning around. "Won't want nothin til lunch."

She cleared her throat. "I noticed the storeroom's open. Do you mind if I have a look around?"

"Suit yourself."

•  •  •

The room had been swept clean of white dust. The block of marble still rested on a low platform near the door, but the canvas covering had been removed from everything else. She started with the paintings stacked against the wall to her right.

The first were oil scenes of old Indian life: braves hunting buffalo on horseback, war parties, villages with tepees and campfires. Perhaps two dozen of them, rendered almost as cartoons. Figures outlined in black, filled in with ripe, rich colors, loaded with action.

Next came darker, more realistic pictures, lush and emotional details of modern reservation life. A line of disaffected, lost souls waiting for welfare checks in front of the post office. A grouping of young men drinking beer, posing as if for a photograph, around the body of a deer in the back of a pickup. A woman sitting by a window in a small, bare house, staring out at the looming sky. Studies of shadow and light, technically masterful.

She moved next to a series of six woodblocks against the back wall. Rectangular panels, probably eight feet high by four feet wide, fashioned of dark wood, beautifully carved with symbols and figures reminiscent of those found in sand painting, colored in earth tones. Along the boarder, about eight inches wide, he'd painted bathroom-type graffiti pictures and bumper sticker phrases—like Fight Poverty, Kill a Beggar; Shut Up and Open Your Mouth; Keep America White; If You Don't Like It Go Home—in red, white, and blue.

In the far corner of the room, he'd created a life-size camp scene made of wood, metal, papier-mâché, fabric, dirt, found items. A tepee with three women inside on a blanket, nursing babies, two children playing in the dirt just outside the opening. Three men sitting around a campfire with two horses grazing nearby, dogs and sheep surrounding them. The figures were clothed in traditional dress.

An idyllic scene, except that all of them, animals included, had been decapitated. Their heads lay next to them, eyes open, faces expressive of whatever they would have been doing had they been left intact—talking, smiling, laughing—as if they'd been caught at one instant in time and their lives severed. Every element—the rattle gripped by the baby as it sucked, a dog rolling on its back for a scratch, the gentle fellowship of one man's hand resting upon another's as they shared a laugh—heart-stopping.

Filled with rage, pain at their core, superbly done, the images sent shivers up Sarah's back as she walked around the circumference. No wonder she'd felt comfortable talking to him last night. He was on intimate terms with the holocaust of his own people. He'd found a way to transform it into art.

The three remaining pieces were marble sculptures set near the center of the room.

The first, three-quarter size: a man kneeling, holding the body of a deer in his lap—a reflection on Michaelangelo's *Pieta*? The back of the stone left simply rounded and polished.

The next, on a pedestal: the life-size head of a horse—smooth, silky curves of mane, flared nostrils, wild eyes, an arch to the neck. Mortality captured in timeless stone.

And last: the life-size figure of an Indian man—shirtless, barefoot, dressed in jeans—standing, face upturned as if to the wind, long hair blowing back. His arms would have been raised in the gesture of a supplicant, except they had been severed, the marble left rough at his shoulders. The two arms rested at his feet, on the elbows with palms up, persisting in their mute plea to an unheeding god.

•   •   •

She made her favorite salad by rote. The same salad she made at least once a month in Manhattan. Usually on a Sunday so she could eat in front of the TV watching *60 Minutes*.

In the city she kept her windows closed against the clamor: cars and buses, horns, sirens, jackhammers and shouts that permeated glass and walls, a constant drone of which she was no longer conscious. Here there was no escape from the quiet, but her thoughts bellowed as loudly as a full orchestra in the living room. In New York, her closed apartment offered a haven from the tumultuous city. Here the doors and windows opened to the natural world, and it was the turbulence of her own mind that closed her in.

She boiled the green beans to bright crispness, adding them to the lettuce, tomatoes, tuna, capers, and boiled potatoes cut in thin slices, and tossed it all with vinaigrette. She buttered the slices of bread, pressed the garlic, placed it under the broiler, her thoughts whirling.

She had no idea what to say. Was he kidding her, or had he really not shown his work? Had she sounded like a condescending ass when she felt compelled to define the word "insular"? Thank God she hadn't gone on to explain "touché."

He went directly into the bathroom and came out with washed hands, his hair combed, to sit down quietly at the table. She'd found green cloth place mats in one of the kitchen drawers and put sprigs of sage in the wedding vase.

She carried the salad over in a bowl with two spoons for serving and practically dropped it in front of him to rush back for the forgotten bread.

"I burned it a bit," she said, showing him the cookie tray with the slices of toast, black around the edges. "Should I make some more?"

"It's okay." He served himself a heaping portion of salad and took four pieces of toast.

She served herself a little, took a deep breath, and cleared her throat.

"I don't know what to say to you. I feel off balance and pretty foolish. Your work is brilliant. But, of course, you must know that."

His eyes narrowed, and he looked at her quizzically. Then slowly the tension in his face relaxed. He grinned and finally laughed, leaning back, lifting the front legs of his chair off the floor.

"Whoa. Man, that feels good. You're wrong. I didn't know what you'd think. I tol myself it didn't matter, but I lied."

"You honestly haven't shown your work to anyone?"

He shook his head.

"You could line up a dealer and have a one-man show in New York by the end of the year."

"Won't be ready by the end a the year. But I appreciate the vote of confidence."

"Why are you wasting time with jewelry? I mean, it seems to me you should be sculpting full-time."

He shrugged and let his chair fall back. "Gotta make a livin. The jewelry's fast. Took me a while to get the hang a it, but I can churn it out now. Figure, if things work out with our deal, I can make enough in three months to live on all year. Maybe buy two pieces a marble."

"But how can you make any money if you use more than half of your gross for supplies?"

A sly grin crossed his face as he looked down for his fork and stabbed some salad.

"You said the materials cost you over two thousand dollars."

"We was negotiatin," he said, stabbing salad.

"How much did they really cost?"

"Can't say exactly. It was leftover stuff." He looked up. His loaded fork paused on the way to his mouth. "Maybe eight hundred."

She stared at him, completely thrown. He gazed back unabashed and took the forkful. She turned her attention to the salad, perplexed by his savvy and her own gullibility.

As he dug in, expressing his eating enjoyment in moans, much as he had last night, a humorous observation by one of her friends popped into Sarah's mind: If you want to know how a man makes love, watch him eat.

"Oh, man, that's good," he groaned with his eyes closed.

She stifled a giggle.

"What's so funny?" he asked, opening them.

She shook her head, feeling giddy. "Nothing."

But when he took another mouthful and moaned, she couldn't help bursting into peals of laughter.

"Sorry," she snorted.

He waited.

She took a deep breath. "I apologize. I just remembered something a friend of mine once said—it's not important."

"If you're gonna laugh at my eatin, I wanna know why."

"I'm not laughing at your eating, exactly. It was just a stupid comment."

"About what?"

"About a connection between the way a man approaches food and the way he approaches . . . oh, forget it—it was silly."

"An the way he approaches what? Women?"

"Well, sex."

He nodded seriously. "You think it's true?"

"I don't know. I just think it's funny."

"Seems to me, if it works on men, it prob'ly works jus as well the other way round. Look at you. You're real careful how much you take. An then you pick at it an don't finish. Sound right?"

"And I was worried about insulting you."

"You didn't insult me. I enjoy eatin." He took several large bites of toast, smiled at her, and licked his fingers. "Yep, I enjoy eatin a whole lot," he said.

Sarah felt herself color. "Hmm. So I've noticed."

"You want any more?" he asked, indicating the remains of the salad.

"No. Thanks."

He smiled and finished it off. "Man, that was a good salad. I never tasted anything like it. What are them little salty things?"

"Capers."

"Real good."

He went off cheerfully to the studio to work on the jewelry.

Sarah washed the dishes, still emotionally off balance. As if she'd been walking along a familiar path daydreaming and then suddenly looked up to find she had no idea where she was. She brought in handfuls of rosemary, thyme, and sage from the garden to add to a marinade of minced garlic cloves, olive oil, mustard, vinegar, salt, and pepper, and rubbed the pungent mixture into the slice she'd made in the deep lean muscle tissue of the leg of lamb. She felt uneasy, anxious.

Suddenly Littleman raced into the house, yapping, a ridge of bristling fur down his back, his teeth bared. She spun around to see a young man hunched in the front doorway, his eyes as wide in surprise as hers.

"Uh . . ."

"Yes?"

"Hey, Alvin," Ben said from the back door. "Forgot you was comin. Sarah, my cousin, Alvin."

He signaled Littleman, and the coyote followed him out the back. The young man stepped inside.

Tall and very thin, he reminded Sarah of a puppet on strings. Cowlicks shot his short brown hair out at odd angles, and his skin was quite fair except for a prominent red scar down the side of his face. He wore a long-sleeved shirt and carried a backpack.

Sarah wiped the marinade off her hand and extended it.

"How do you do, Alvin."

She caught him in the middle of removing the pack. He fumbled it, switching hands, and knocked over the Hopi wedding vase on the table.

"No harm done," Sarah said, righting the vase.

Alvin looked toward the back door where Ben had disappeared, then ducked his head and riffled through the backpack.

Ben returned without the coyotes. He caught Sarah's eyes. "Alvin's here for a drawin lesson, an I got an idea if you're willin. He's ready for some figure work."

• • •

Ben placed Sarah behind a bowl of pears outside at the redwood table, her head on her hand. Reflecting.

The men stood at easels, drawing with pencils.

"It's all in the way you see it," Ben said after a few minutes. "Seems to me she's confused. Like maybe she wants somethin but she's hesitatin bout takin it. Could be a pear, could be something else."

"Alvin?" Sarah interjected. "Did you grow up on the reservation?"

Alvin shook his head, his attention riveted on his drawing.

"He grew up in California, only came here a few years ago," Ben told her.

Sarah got up to remove the lamb from the refrigerator so that it would be at room temperature when she roasted it, using the opportunity to look at their sketches before taking her seat again. Alvin's focus was the bowl of pears, and he didn't appear to have much talent, but Ben had detailed a very pretty, somewhat pensive woman—the light in her eyes, the fragility of her neck, the full mouth, an interplay of elegance and sensuality.

"May I have it when you're finished?" she asked.

"Sure. If you pose for another one I can keep."

"Not now, though, I have to get to my dinner."

Twenty minutes later, drawings completed, Ben took the easels back to the studio. Sarah returned to the kitchen; Alvin wandered into the house and sat on the sofa.

"You better go," Ben said when he saw him. He picked Alvin's backpack up from the table and walked to the door.

"There's plenty," Sarah said.

•  •  •

"How c-come I can't s-stay?"

They were standing next to Alvin's truck, Ben still holding the backpack.

"I gotta work."

"Sh-she s-said there was plenty."

"She was just bein polite."

"I ain't had a c-cooked meal s-since Grandma died."

"Go on over to Dawsen's."

"I d-don wanna drive all the way over there. Maybe they already got c-company. Why c-can't I eat d-dinner w-with you?"

Ben sighed and wondered why he always got sucked in.

When Alvin had first come out looking for work and Ben told him he didn't need anyone, Alvin walked away like a whipped dog. That's when he'd called him back and offered the lessons. Maybe he'd seen some of his lost teenage self in his second cousin, or maybe he'd thought he could impart a sense that art was more than gluing turquoise into junk for tourists. After two years he couldn't remember, and he'd come to believe any similarity between them was imaginary or hidden so deep it might as well be.

"Okay," he said. "But I'm takin the coyotes up to the water-fall. I'm movin fast an I ain't talkin. Think you can handle that?"

"Th-thought you s-said you had to work."

"I can't work with you hangin around."

"What about her?"

"What *about* her?"

"Sh-she's hangin around."

"You're pushin it, Alvin," he said, starting back to the house. "You stayin or goin?"

"S-stayin."

Ben walked in and leaned against the counter close to Sarah, watching the pulse at the base of her throat as she struck eggs against the bowl and separated the shells with her slender fingers.

"Alvin's stayin for dinner, if it's okay."

"Of course it's fine," Sarah said, beating the eggs with a fork and pretending to ignore his proximity. She turned to smile at Alvin. "I'm glad."

"We're gonna take the coyotes for a hike," Ben said. "When you figure we'll eat?"

"Two or three hours. But don't you think it's going to rain?"

"Maybe tonight. You okay?"

"Absolutely fine."

• • •

Ben moved swiftly, but Alvin kept up.

"Th-thought you didn't want a g-girlfriend," he said after a few minutes silence. "Th-thought you s-said gettin laid was more t-trouble than it's worth an havin a woman around would d-drive you nuts."

Ben pushed on, climbing faster, either to outdistance Alvin's comments or to wind him so he'd stop talking.

• • •

Sarah kneaded the dough, warm and elastic with life, into a smooth ball, then rolled it as thin as possible and cut one-quarter-inch-wide strips. The strands, like creamy ropes of mermaid's hair, clung together and had to be cajoled gently apart and straightened on the floured counter and tabletop to dry. Midway through the process she realized there wasn't enough surface.

She held a clump of drooping locks and looked around, spying the bookcase. *Tom Sawyer, Robinson Crusoe, Twenty Thousand Leagues Under the Sea* shared the shelves with *Sculpture Inside and Out, The Complete Henry Moore, Tao Te Ching, The Way of Zen*. Issues of *National Geographic*, in order by date, completely filled the two bottom shelves. But the top housed only a few pieces of Hopi pottery.

Ben's tidiness amused her. She suspected he thought her messy, as he'd arranged her cosmetics in a line on a shelf in the medicine cabinet. She wondered how he'd deal with flour and pasta on his bookcase. She moved the pottery to the end table, wiped the surface of the bookcase, already remarkably clean, and dusted it with flour before spreading the last of the pasta across it.

She put the lamb in to roast, sautéed vegetables for primavera, mixed and baked two dozen sugar cookies. She'd just placed the warm cookies in an old lidded tin she'd discovered in the cupboard when the coyotes returned.

They raced in, a pack on a hunt. Littleman and Sage bumped against her legs, searching for scraps on the floor. Eagle quickly discovered the unguarded treasure on the bookcase and pulled up on rear legs, tongue slurping up half the strands. Without thinking, Sarah screamed, "No!" and rushed over to grab them. The coyote actually stopped long enough for her to scoop what was left of the linguini.

"Stop," she yelled as she turned to see Littleman, his head on the table, poised to gobble the pasta in front of him. He paused, looking at her as she ran over to gather the strands. Cushing them together in her hands and holding her arms up, she moved toward the counter with both Littleman and Sage jumping around her attempting to bite the ends of the strips she'd managed to save. She had no idea where she got the guts, but she was damned if they were going to eat her pasta.

Eagle's paws were on the counter, her tongue stretching toward the mound of pasta at the rear. "No! Stay away," Sarah yelled. She bumped the coyote with her hip, dropped the remaining pasta on the counter, and leaned over to protect it with her back, fairly terrified of being attacked.

Ben laughed from the patio door.

"Leave it," he said. The coyotes immediately retreated, innocently nosing around the floor for scraps.

Sarah straightened up. "How long were you standing there?"

He shrugged, grinning.

"You wouldn't think it was so funny if they'd eaten it all," she snapped. "Why didn't you help?"

"Looked to me you could handle it." He bent to pick up a comb that had dropped from her hair. "You're fierce," he said, his body damp, his hair wet. He was very close. "You got flour on your nose," he said, running his fingers through the side of her hair to replace the comb.

Alvin appeared in the doorway. Sarah took the comb, moved away from Ben, wiping her nose with the back of her hand.

"Where did you go?" she asked.

"Swimming," Ben answered. "Got a waterfall a couple miles up the canyon. Maybe if you stay long enough for your feet to heal I'll take you."

"It's a hard c-climb," Alvin said doubtfully.

Sure enough, Ben wiped off the bookcase and replaced the pottery before he went back to the studio to work. Alvin sat at the table with a sullen expression while Sarah boiled and strained the pasta and set the table.

"Do you have a job, Alvin?" she asked.

"I g-garden an b-babysit."

"So you have two jobs?"

He stood up and walked outside.

• • •

They dined by the light of the setting sun, an uneasy meal.

Alvin took little, ate less, and said nothing. Ben ate three plates full, his conversation limited primarily to positive comments about the food. Sarah finished her plate. Then both of them sat at the table watching Alvin push his food around. When Ben asked him if he was done, he shook his head and took a small bite of the now cold meat.

"Shall I make coffee to go with the cookies?" Sarah asked.

"What kinda cookies?" Ben said with exactly the inflection her nephews used when Evelyn baked cookies.

"Just sugar."

"Nobody's made me cookies since I was a kid." His shining eyes sought hers.

"I d-don't d-drink c-coffee. You g-got c-cocoa?"

"No," Ben said. He stood up to clear the table. "You done?"

"I g-guess," Alvin said, watching his plate disappear.

Sarah brought the cookie tin.

"Okay," Ben said to Alvin with finality. "Take a few for the ride. Say thank you an good night to Sarah."

"Night," Alvin mumbled, avoiding her eyes. He reached for several cookies, picked up his backpack, and slumped out.

"You wanna make coffee now?" Ben suggested as he carried the last of the dishes from the table. "We can wash up while it's brewin." He reached under the counter for the detergent and the drainer.

"Has anyone ever mentioned that you're a bit anal?"

"Huh?"

"Honestly. You're the neatest man I've ever met. There isn't a speck of dust anywhere."

"So?"

"So nothing," she said, filling the coffeepot under the faucet. "Except I understand why you don't like visitors. It must drive you crazy to have to keep replacing the cap on the toothpaste and continually reorder your kitchen utensils." She searched the cupboard, trying to remember where she'd put the coffee.

"Maybe it's you that's too sloppy," he said, running hot water into the sink. "You lose things, ever notice? Check the refrigerator."

She rolled her eyes and opened it to pull out the can.

"An I might as well say," he continued, "it'd be a kindness to make the bed. Every time I use the bathroom I gotta pass it all rumpled from you lyin in it. Givin me all kind a thoughts."

As she could think of no appropriate rejoinder, she made a mental note to make the bed, picked up a dishcloth, and changed the topic. "Well, I don't think the dinner was a success."

"What you talkin about? That meat was great."

"It was good, but the pasta primavera was disappointing, not at all worth the effort. I should just call it noodles primavera."

"Tasted fine to me."

She laughed. "Everything tastes fine to you."

"Some things taste better an others. I like noodles. You criticizin my eatin again?"

"I'm simply pointing out that you're not particularly discriminating. You eat whatever's in front of you."

"We still talkin about food, or we back onto sex?" He faced her. "Cause I'll eat a can a pork an beans, if that's the best I got. But I know the difference between pork an beans an that lamb you fixed tonight. An I like the lamb a whole lot better. Truth is I bet I'd rather eat the food you cook than anythin I ever ate."

"Hmm," she said, choosing not to pursue the analogy further.

"Hmm," he said, unplugging the sink. He poured two cups of coffee and took them to the table. "Let's see about these cookies," he said. He took a bite and grinned. "Oh, man, these are good."

"I don't think Alvin enjoyed the dinner. He seems a little strange. Or maybe he just didn't like me."

"It ain't you. His grandma died six months ago. He's havin a tough time."

"How old is he?"

Ben shrugged, picking out another cookie. "Twenty-two, twenty-three."

"How did he get the scar?"

"Some kinda accident with boilin water when he was a kid."

"What a shame."

He reached for another cookie. "Everybody's got scars."

"Maybe that's true, but most of them are hidden."

He regarded her seriously. "Yeah, you're right. He's got a rough road."

"Is that why you give him drawing lessons?"

"His grandpa had a lot a mental problems. Henry took care a him, an when he died Henry took care of Fanny. Figure he'd want me to look after Alvin. I don't do much." He took another cookie.

"His skin is light. Is he part white?"

"Must be. His ma run off with a white guy when she was a kid." He picked up another cookie.

"So Alvin lives by himself, since his grandmother died?"

"Yeah."

"He seems lost and lonely."

"Aw he jus needs to get laid. I mean, he needs a girl-friend."

"Maybe he doesn't want a girlfriend. He could be gay."

"A queer?" Ben snorted.

"A homosexual. It's possible."

"He's young an scared is all. I'm gonna save the rest," he said, replacing the lid and taking the tin to the counter. "I got a little work left on the jewelry. Then I was hopin you'd keep your promise an pose for me."

• • •

He brought the jewelry in about an hour later—five exquisite necklaces. Sarah wrote a check from Shoen's, grinning when she handed it to him. "I'm real happy with the deal I made."

"Good. You ready to model? I wanna catch you by lantern light, on the couch. Nude, if that's okay."

Her smile faded. "We didn't say anything about nude."

He regarded her seriously. "I ain't makin a move, if that's what you're thinkin. I'm askin a favor. It's been too long since I had the chance to draw a woman from life."

"Well, I suggest you hire someone."

His brow furrowed. "There's no one round here under-stands what I do. I can't 'hire someone' unless I go into Tuba City for a hooker. Thought you understood about my work."

"You're a brilliant artist, but I'm not a professional model. I don't feel comfortable taking my clothes off in front of you."

In college she'd drawn her share of nudes, both female and male. She knew the importance of life drawing to an artist. She felt somewhat adolescent and prudish, especially in the light of what he'd shared with her that morning. He'd certainly bared himself. Still, it was out of the question.

"Aw, never mind. You got a robe or somethin soft you could put on?"

Incredible relief. "A robe."

It was short green silk, watery and thin. The outline of her bra showed, and she looked ridiculously prim. She took off the bra. Her nipples announced themselves and the robe clung, like an advertisement for breasts. She searched the depths of her suitcase and came up with a compromise in the form of a camisole. Her nipples still pointed, but the double fabric fell away from the outline of her body.

She sat down nervously on the sofa while he set up his easel. He looked up and took her in. Their eyes met.

"Uh, you look kinda stiff. Could you move into the cor-ner an put your legs up?"

She did as he asked, pulling the robe over the top of her thighs.

"An would you mind taking the combs out?"

She removed the combs and ran her fingers through her hair as it spilled over her shoulders. She felt dangerously sensual, and had the impulse to stretch like a cat and let the robe fall open in the lantern light. She shifted self-consciously and glanced at him. He eyed her dispassionately, with about as much agitation as if she were a bowl of fruit.

"Can you turn a little, into the light? An would you mind resting your arm on the back of the couch? Yeah, like that. Tilt your head."

He asked twice if she was tired, otherwise he didn't speak. After a while he began to sing to himself, an unrecognizable, almost tuneless song.

An hour later he put down his pencil.

He left the drawing on the easel and went to the back door, staring out into the night while she looked at it. A beautiful woman, her body in shadow, reclined on a sofa—soft and sensuous, bright eyes, a secret smile, hair tumbling over her shoulders.

"It's lovely," she said. "Really wonderful."

"Come here."

She walked to the door. He gave way, and she moved a little in front of him to stare out as a bolt of lightning, the length of half the sky, lit the world with a ghostly pale light. Several seconds later came the sound—a crack and rolling—like the cosmos was splitting.

She jumped back, touching his chest. He wrapped his arms around her from behind. Her pulse raced, making her dizzy, and she leaned against him, gripping his arms. He tightened his hold.

Another bolt zigzagged across the sky, huge and distinct, a miracle of pure light etched in the dark.

"You feel so good," he whispered.

She stood immobile, shocked by the extraordinary power in his body, like a wall behind her. The ground shook from echoing thunder. His warm breath on top of her head sent

shivers down her back. She felt out of control and frightened. By the power of the electrical storm, the vastness and
isolation. By the force of the man who held her, a man she
hardly knew.

She clutched his arms. Warm skin covered muscles of steel.
What if he refused to release her? Was that what she wanted?
What kind of silly game was she playing at the edge of
nowhere with a man so strong that any man she'd ever met was
a joke beside him?

• • •

He felt her delicate ribs, the rapid heartbeat, the soft, full
swelling of her breast resting on his arm. He bent to her, in-
toxicated by her scent. She trembled. Instantly the tremor
pulsed through him, transformed into white-hot throbbing in
his guts and loins—the reckless, painful need to claim, to pos-
sess. It took all the strength of will he could summon to keep
from pulling her back against him and shoving his hands inside
the silken fabric to take her. He released his grip and stepped
back. She stumbled a little but regained her balance without
his help.

"Ah, guess I'm more tired than I thought," he said. "Night."
He turned quickly and left her on the patio.

• • •

Two of the coyotes followed him, but Sage stayed behind.
Sarah sank onto the redwood bench. The coyote rested her
head in Sarah's lap as she tried to make sense of what had happened. The thunder had startled her, and somehow she'd
ended up in his arms. She'd been so disconcerted by his physical presence that instead of making light of it and moving,
she'd gripped on to him and stayed. He'd become aroused, and
she'd gone rigid and cold, afraid he'd take advantage. He'd

backed off immediately, but she didn't blame him for being annoyed. Talk about mixed messages.

She got up to go into the house, and Sage followed her into
the bedroom. The coyote seemed content even with the door
closed, and when Sarah came out of the bathroom Sage was
curled on the bed, asleep.

# CHAPTER 10

**A** knock on the bedroom door woke her.

"Hmm?" she murmured.

The door opened a crack. Sarah sat up, instantly awake. Sage jumped off the bed with a yap, wagging her tail.

"If you want a shower, you better get up," Ben said, letting Sage out before he shut the door.

They were at the gas station in Lowman by eight o'clock when Big Jack Farland, a small, skinny Indian, arrived. He greeted Ben impassively and listened without comment as Sarah related her story. When she'd finished he held out his hand.

"Need the key," he said.

She fished around in her purse and came up with her keys, then both men watched as she manipulated the Volvo key off the circle.

"Check back after two," Big Jack said, walking toward the office.

"Don't you want me to show you where it is?"

"I'll find it."

"I can stay here and wait," she said to Ben. "There's no reason for you to lose an entire day of sculpting."

They were being careful with each other.

"Too late for today," he said. "You wanna see Canyon de Chelly?"

After last night, she didn't blame him for being cool.

"I'd love to, if you really don't mind playing tour guide."

•   •   •

A deep, slender gash carved into the red land by patient water over a million years, Canyon de Chelly might be less imposing than the Grand Canyon, Sarah thought, but it was more magical, with its steep sides falling below them for a thousand feet. A spire of red earth, rooted in the canyon floor, rose almost to the edge and split like two fingers pointing the way to the sky.

"Spider Rock," Ben said.

Perhaps a stone had been in the river's path initially, when it began its slow creation of the canyon, causing it to circle and, like a sculptor, remove the excess.

"This here's the heart of the Dine'," Ben told her. "That's what we call ourselves, means 'the People.' Guess all people think they're *the* people."

"Well, I am one of 'the Chosen.' "

"Chosen for what?"

"Good question and one we repeatedly ask. There are a lot of jokes on the subject, mostly ending with some kind of 'couldn't you have chosen someone else' punch line. Supposedly chosen to receive the Word of God, in the form of Torah, the first five books of the Bible."

As they walked along the edge with an airplane view, Sarah could see a thin ribbon of water winding its way through the center of the canyon floor among trees and through patchwork fields of farmland dotted with tiny houses. It looked like a fairyland.

"Can we go down?"

"How're your feet?"

She'd put her tennis shoes and socks on that morning. "I'm game."

They descended by a switchback trail. Ben pointed out the cliff dwellings, built from sandstone and earthen bricks along the canyon walls by the mysterious Anazazi. The ruins were extraordinarily beautiful—sand-colored, crumbling, ancient apartments. They'd been found, as had other cliff dwelling communities in the Southwest, filled with clay cookware, tools, farming equipment, weapons, and other articles of everyday life, as if the inhabitants had left in a hurry and intended to return momentarily. Instead they'd vanished without a trace, leaving the mystery.

"Speculation bout why they left runs along three lines," Ben told her. "Prob'ly all connectin right at the time. A fourteen-year drought, marauding war parties, an their abuse of the environment."

"Where did they go?"

"Nobody knows for sure, but I think to the Mesas. Hopis showed up there bout that time. They live in pueblos. Course not pretty ones. But if it was them, they learned a good lesson. They picked a place no one else wanted an always give back somethin for whatever they take. Been farmin the same soil for a thousand years an still manage to get a livin off it."

The canyon was quite cool at the bottom, sheltered by the steep walls. He showed her some caves he'd played in as a child and led her through a peach orchard to the narrow river where they sat on the bank watching silver trout dart in sunlight and disappear in shadow.

In answer to her questions he told her more about his life. How when he was eighteen and Henry died, Dawsen had persuaded him to join the army.

"Did basic trainin in Oklahoma an then was stationed in Frankfurt."

"You've been to Germany?" she asked, surprised.

"Didn't see much of it outside the base. Mostly I jus remember the beer," he said, glancing at her with an abashed smile, suddenly close and warm.

"Did get to Paris though," he continued, "on a four-day leave. Blew me away. Never thought people could build a city like that. Four days I jus wandered around gawkin. Watched the light change the stones at Notre Dame Cathedral. Climbed up where you could see over the river an the city. Went to the Louvre, an the Jeu de Paume, an a couple other museums. When I was a kid I always drew stuff. Henry tol me I was gonna be an artist, but I forgot about it til I got to Paris."

She wanted to reach out and give his arm a squeeze—a natural gesture with people she liked. But she restrained herself. No more mixed messages.

"We're going to be friends, Ben," she said, smiling at him instead. "You send me all your jewelry, and I'll sell it for big bucks. And then, when you're ready, we'll find someone to represent your art."

He cocked his head. "Thought you wanted to do it."

"I don't have the experience or connections you'll need. You should have a great gallery behind you."

"Then what do you get out of it?"

"Aside from the incredible profit off your jewelry and the pleasure of helping to discover a wonderful artist? Maybe someday, when you're famous, you'll give me a deal on one of your pieces."

She smiled. He didn't. His eyes held hers. She felt herself flush and turned away toward the stream.

A misty rain started as they walked back up the trail on their way out. Sarah was able to keep up, although her feet were bothering her. Even if the blisters reopened, it would have been worth it.

"What happened after you got out of the army?"

"Took advantage of Uncle Sam's offer. Went to the University of Arizona. Was a guy there, Alan Trublo. I wanted to study with him."

"I know who Alan Trublo is," she said, stopping to rest. "I'm going to see him before I go back to New York."

"How come? He's not sculptin anymore." His brow furrowed.

"He's a friend of my father's. Is something wrong?"

"Climb on that rock. I'll give you a ride."

"Don't be silly. I can walk. I just have to go slowly."

"Yeah, but I wanna get out a here before midnight."

He lifted her effortlessly, his hands running along her thighs to connect under her butt. "Don't get all excited," he said easily, walking at twice their previous pace. "I'm only doin this so I can move faster."

She bounced and wrapped her arms around his neck, legs around the warmth and breadth of his back. He felt so solid under her and smelled so good, of soap and earth. Just for a few minutes, she thought dreamily, what's the harm in relaxing against him and enjoying the heat and power of his body? They passed through the mist, and the sun came out, warm on her back.

At the end of the trail she slid off. He turned. Their eyes locked, sending an electric current down the center of her body. Her mouth went dry; she couldn't swallow.

He took a step and lifted her chin with his finger. His lips brushed hers. The rhythm of her blood hammered in her ears. She stood riveted. He bent to her again, gently parting her lips with his, the tip of his tongue grazing the inside of her upper lip. He drew back, and with a slow smile he ran his hand along her cheek to the nape of her neck. His eyes held hers as he applied a gentle pressure, guiding her forward until their bodies touched. He bent and lightly opened her lips again, flicking her tongue with his.

As he pulled back a moan escaped her, and she ran her hands up his arms to his shoulders, rising up on her toes to press against him. His smile dissolved. His hands came down her back, cupping her butt, lifting her. His lips seared hers. His tongue, harder now, explored the length of her tongue and the recesses of her mouth. She bit down and sucked. He groaned. His arms shook, gripping her. His erection seared through his jeans and her shorts. She opened her legs to feel it closer, her arms and legs like jelly.

He withdrew his tongue and lightly kissed her again before setting her down. He kept his hands on her shoulders until she regained her balance.

"Jesus," he said with a chuckle, his eyes dancing. "Look," he said, indicating behind her.

She turned for a final view. A perfect rainbow arched across the magnificent red canyon. He moved beside her, laid his arm across her shoulders and kissed the top of her head. She slipped her arm around his waist and knew she would remember that moment for the rest of her life.

# CHAPTER 11

**B**ig Jack had diagnosed the problems and contacted the dealer in Albuquerque. They could ship the necessary parts by truck. They were waiting on Sarah's okay. "Radiator's got a hole in it, the crossmember's bent, an the engine mount's broke," Jack said. "An the two flats. They get me the parts tomorrow afternoon, you can have it by late Wednesday, Thursday at the outside."

It was an expensive little accident. She told him to go ahead and called her parents' home from the pay phone to let them know she'd be in Lowman until Thursday.

Evelyn answered the phone, and Sarah realized it was only five p.m. in New York. Her father was still in transit from the city. She'd have to deal with her mother.

"So where are you staying?"

Sarah licked her lips and took a deep breath.

"I've met some nice people," she said lightly. "A couple

with children. There was no room at the motel, some problem
with the plumbing. Anyway, these people have been very kind.
But they don't have a phone, so you can't . . ."

"How could they not have a phone?"

"It's out of order. There was an electrical storm and repairs
here take forever. Tell Daddy I've picked up some terrific
pieces I can't wait to show him. It's gorgeous here. I know why
he loves it."

"I hate not to be able to reach you. What if something
should happen?"

"Is Daddy all right?"

"He's fine. I mean just in case."

"I'll call when I can. Make sure he knows I've been delayed
by almost a week. He might want to alert the people waiting
for me."

Sarah hung up and opened the glass door.

". . . the fuck didn't you say somethin this mornin when I
was here?" Ben roared. Big Jack stepped back cautiously, moving toward his office, waving a conciliatory hand as if to stop
Ben's anger with it.

"Chill, man. Thought you knew and wasn't interested."

"Shit." Ben caught a glimpse of Sarah out of the corner of
his eye. "Come on," he said, indicating the truck.

She climbed in, and he stepped on the gas.

"What's the matter?"

"A kid's missin. The Gorman kid. You met him at
Dawsen's. Disappeared yesterday afternoon. Apache County
Sherrif's Department's here an search parties been goin out
since dawn."

"Which one?"

He looked puzzled.

"Billy or Chippy?"

"The older one."

He pulled into a city park several blocks up the street.
The lot was three quarters full with dozens of pickup
trucks. They walked through the park into an indoor gym,
passing a half dozen men milling around a deputy near the
entrance. The men stopped talking as they walked by, but no
one said anything, nor did Ben greet anyone. One of them
gave a curt nod in his direction. The others watched them
in silence.

A long table had been set up in the middle of the room,
covered with a topographical map marked with red and green
plastic tacks. A paunchy white deputy with sergeant's stripes on
his shoulder and Warren on his ID pin stood in front of it,
peering down. Ben asked what he could do. The deputy's watery eyes barely acknowledged him and skimmed over Sarah
before turning back to the map.

"The green's where we been. The yellow's what we're cov-
erin. The red's where we ain't got to yet. We found his bait an
tackle here." His stubby finger, nail bitten to the quick, pointed
to a small blue spot. "You know it?"

"The reservoir," Ben said. "Swam there as a kid."

"You can join Jim's group." He indicated the men they'd
passed near the door. "They're fixin to go out again in few
minutes."

"I track alone."

The deputy looked up sharply.

Sarah spotted Anna Dawsen coming through a swinging
door, balancing several foil-covered cookie sheets and a coffeepot, heading for a table at the far wall. She moved across the
room to help clear some space on the overloaded table.

Anna thanked her and set the cookies down among half-
eaten cakes and brownies and cupcake tins. Sarah took the coffee over to a smaller table set for coffee service and poured the
contents into a large electric percolator. She restacked the sty-

rofoam cups and used a napkin to wipe up spilled powdered creamer and half-used packages of sugar.

Ben touched her arm. "I'm gonna get the coyotes. I'll take you home."

Anna glanced over. "Glad you're here, Ben. Frank was lookin for you. He's out with a group, left a few minutes ago." She stacked her empty cookie sheets together and headed back through the swinging door.

"I'd like to stay and help," Sarah said.

"Don't know when I'll be able to come back an get you."

"Whenever. I'll be fine."

• • •

The chatter of a half dozen heavy brown-skinned women dropped off abruptly as Sarah followed Anna into the kitchen. Their averted eyes, mismatched clothing, and deferential nods when Anna introduced her reminded Sarah of the Hispanic women who served as cleaning ladies in New York.

But these women weren't immigrants. They'd been born in the U.S., as had multitudes of generations stretching back to a time before the *Mayflower*, before the *Niña, Pinta,* and *Santa Maria*, before Leif Eriksson. Still, that didn't alter the fact that they looked like they lived in the third world. Whose fault was that? Sarah thought. And who defined the numerology of worlds in the first place?

Anna left, and the women resumed brewing coffee, washing and drying the used cake and brownie pans, speaking a language Sarah assumed was Navajo. In spite of her attempt at friendliness, they treated her with the same reserved deference she'd received when she'd gone into the kitchen at Lauren's shower to prepare a soufflé in the midst of the housekeeper and her assistants—a clearing of space around her and the tacit communication that she was encroaching.

"Is there an extra sponge?" she asked. After a rather bela-
bored search, one was located. She took it into the gym to
wipe the tables. The name Lonefeather and muffled laughter
reached her from behind the closed door.

Over the next several hours, two search parties came and
left again, and a collection of women delivered sweets they'd
baked at home. Sarah took on the task of keeping the tables
neat and clean, consolidating the desserts, carrying used cake
tins and pans into the kitchen for washing. No one spoke to
her except one of the deputies, a fair-haired young man named
Roy with a gold tooth at the rear of his smile.

Alvin came in with a group, and she walked over, happy to
see someone she knew.

"How's it going, Alvin?" she said.

"Okay," he mumbled, avoiding her eyes.

"I think there might be some cocoa in the kitchen. Want
me to find out?"

He shook his head and walked away. He didn't join the
crush for coffee and sweets. She glanced up once and saw him
standing alone by the doorway. When she looked for him a
few minutes later, he'd left the gym.

Maybe he disliked white women, or women in general; or
maybe he resented an outsider spending so much time with
Ben, whom he obviously adored. Whatever. There didn't seem
to be anything she could do about it.

By six p.m., only two old women remained in the
kitchen. Sarah was sitting in the gym on a folding chair, listening to Sergeant Warren talk to the search parties on a
radio, when Anna Dawsen returned with a cake. She unwrapped the tin foil exposing a lopsided chocolate confec-
tion. "Ginny made it."

"Gorgeous. But I don't know who in the world could still
be interested in dessert. There have been more cakes and cook-

ies through that kitchen in the past three hours than I've seen in my life."

"Everyone wants to do something. They'll stop now. Have to make dinner for their own families. The men will come in from searchin in a couple of hours, when it gets dark. They'll probably finish what's left here. Then their wives'll be mad at them for spoilin dinner. Unless they find Billy. Then no one will be mad about anything. What are you gonna do now?"

"Wait here for Ben."

"I wonder if you'd mind watchin some kids? I got a house full: my niece's two, Chippy Gorman, and a bunch from the neighborhood whose moms work an dads are out searching. I'm gonna stop by Millie's. She's waitin at home in case Billy shows up. Can't even make a phone call. If she wants company, I'd like to stay. My brother's son, Edgar, is watchin the kids at my house now, but he's only fifteen. I can't leave him in charge for too long."

• • •

Millie Gorman was sitting on the top step of the front porch holding a telephone when they pulled into her driveway. The cord stretched into the house. She looked over with haunted eyes as Anna got out of the car with a casserole dish. Sarah waited in the passenger seat.

Anna put her arm around Millie, and Millie leaned against her for a few minutes. Then she sat up and shook her head. Anna rose and came back to the car.

Millie, holding the casserole and the phone in her lap, vacantly watched the car back out of the driveway.

Anna sighed. "She says she's better off alone. She's half out of her mind, blamin herself and Tom."

While they drove to her house Anna related the series of events.

Yesterday morning, Millie wouldn't let Billy play at a friend's house because his room hadn't been cleaned up. He sassed her about it. She grounded him, and he called her a bitch.

"He's gettin full of hisself lately, adolescence rearin its ugly head. Tom heard it an tol him to apologize. But Billy's too stubborn an proud. He takes after Tom in that. Tom gave him a strapping, but he still didn't apologize, so Tom sent him to his room to think it over.

"Sometime durin the afternoon he packed his backpack and sneaked out. They didn't know he was gone til around four in the afternoon. They was sure he'd come home when it got dark and he got hungry. Around nine p.m. they called the tribal police. The Apache County Sheriff was notified at six this morning.

"She's bein hard on herself because they waited so long to call the tribal police. Billy's the kinda kid you expect to run away for a few hours. Always into somethin. They been to our house more times in the middle of the night with him than any other child in Lowman since Tom was a kid."

"Didn't the tribal police wait a long time too? Before calling the sheriff's department?"

Anna sighed. "Maybe. Nobody likes askin for outside help. They prob'ly woulda waited another day if it wasn't for the little girl from Many Hills. She was about Billy's age. Disappeared walkin home from a neighbor's house. That's really what's got Millie so worried."

"But the other night she said they thought the person was a transient."

"Everyone wants to believe that. But for the last year or more, animals been found in the desert around the reservation, rabbits an sheep, coyotes an foxes, even a dog once, with the heads cut off an set up on rocks near em. The child's head wasn't cut off, but she was strangled and left shoved against a boulder so it looked like her head was settin on top."

They pulled past the gate and parked. Loud voices of TV mixed with children's laughter wafted out through open windows.

Edgar greeted them at the door and assured Anna that everything was all right. She checked the den anyway, counting heads, then gave Edgar five dollars and told him he could go.

"You want a cup of coffee?" she asked Sarah.

"I think I've had all the coffee I can drink for one day."

"Well, you can keep me company."

Sarah followed her into the kitchen. "I hope you don't think you have to entertain me."

"I don't. Jus need to put my feet up an relax for a little while. You can help me feed the kids if you want. Frank won't be back for a couple hours."

They sat at a small table in the corner of the kitchen.

"Why do people wake you in the middle of the night?"

"Habit. Their parents brought them, so they bring their kids. Nearest hospital's forty miles, in Willard. Mostly they come cause a accidents—broken bones, concussions, falls from ladders, burns from chemistry kits. Frank's a good doctor, even if he is a vet."

"You don't need to convince me." Sarah smiled. "Whatever he put on my blisters helped them heal extremely fast."

"How're you getting on at Ben's? If you don't mind my askin."

The kiss at Canyon de Chelly zipped through Sarah's mind. "We have a deal," she answered lightly. "I do the cooking in exchange for lodging while my car is being repaired. So far it's working very well. I'm going to take some of his jewelry back to New York with me."

Anna nodded and sipped her coffee.

"I get the feeling he's not very popular around here. Millie and Tom certainly don't seem to care for him."

"You're right to say he's not too popular."

"Would it be prying to ask why he's disliked?"

Anna shrugged. "Everybody else knows about it. Ben used to be a heavy drinker, caused a lot of heartache."

"He told me he has a residue of regrets. But he stopped drinking years ago. Surely he didn't do anything so terrible people can't get over it by now?"

"People take their own time gettin over things. An Ben won't go out of his way to make it easier for em. More an anythin that's what makes the trouble. He won't reach out." She paused, looking at Sarah. "I was glad to see him today."

"How long have you known him?"

"Since he was a baby. Henry's father an my grandmother was the same clan. Henry and Alma was friends a my folks an Henry was the one talked my dad into letting me marry Frank, and talked Frank into stayin when things got rough after the war. He was best man at our weddin. I guess we stuck with Ben through the worst of it cause a him."

"What happened with Tom and Millie?"

Anna got up from the table. "Let's get dinner for the kids."

They boiled hot dogs and diced potatoes for salad, mixing them with hard-boiled eggs, celery, mayonnaise, salt, and pepper. They toasted the buns, peeled and cut up carrots, set out condiments, and poured soda into plastic cups. While they worked, Anna told the story.

Millie Bulton, Tom Gorman, and Ben Lonefeather had gone through school together. Tom was big and tough with a mischievous streak that always seemed to land him in trouble. The other boys respected him, and early on he became a leader. Ben was a slight, quiet child who drew pictures and liked to play with girls. He endured a lot of abuse from Tom's group, but it didn't seem to faze him.

By the time they were in sixth grade Tom's dominance had gone unchecked for so long he'd grown into a bully, frightening the other kids with threats of violence if they didn't give over any possession he coveted. One day he took Ben's prized drawing pencil. Ben, who was pretty much a loner by then, challenged him to a fight after school.

All the kids thought Ben was crazy, that Tom would kill him. And, at first, it appeared they were right. Tom knocked Ben down and climbed on his back. But Ben refused to yield, so Tom picked up a rock and threatened to bash his head in. Ben told him to go ahead. Finally Tom twisted Ben's arm behind him. But he wouldn't give. It got quiet. The kids stood around waiting for Ben's arm to dislocate. Suddenly Tom let go and climbed off. Ben got up. He said his arm hurt but it was okay. He stuck out his hand to shake. From then on they were best friends.

As they got older, both boys changed radically. Their roles reversed. By high school, Ben had filled out and grown taller than Tom. Handsome as the devil, he got to be wild, drinking and carrying on with a different girl each week.

Tom went a different route and became a serious student, his sights set on college and on Millie. By senior year, he and Millie were engaged.

One afternoon, a few days before graduation, Millie was home alone when Ben showed up half drunk with a confession to make. He couldn't stop thinking about her. That's why he didn't stay with any girl for more than a couple of nights. Millie decided she was in love with him. The next day her mother discovered a bloodstain on Millie's sheet, and Millie was too naive to deny she'd lost her virginity. Everybody simply thought Tom had finally prevailed until Tom and Ben had a terrible fight, the upshot of which was that Tom landed in the emergency room at the hospital in Willard with a broken nose and three broken ribs. Millie waited for Ben to come to her. He never did.

"Tom went away to college in Colorado. It took Millie a year to come to her senses and follow him, patch things up. I don't think either of em will ever forgive Ben."

"Have you considered that maybe Ben meant what he said to her?"

Anna smiled. "Yeah, her and a dozen others. I love him like he was my own son, but even I got to admit he's a sweet-tongued devil, say any damn thing in the world to a woman to get what he wants."

Oh, God, Sarah thought, a player? In the middle of the desert? On an Indian reservation? Trust her to find him. She should have known; nobody kissed like that without a wealth of experience.

The children ate and their parents came one by one to pick them up. No one had any good news. Ginny and Frankie went upstairs to get ready for bed. Anna and Sarah were sitting on the sofa in the living room when Dawsen opened the front door, dark night behind him.

His eyes met Anna's, and he shook his head. He noted Sarah with mild surprise.

"Where's Ben?" Dawsen asked.

"He went searching," Sarah responded. "I don't know where he is now."

"Well, he wasn't with any of the search parties. They all checked in before we left."

"He wanted to track alone with the coyotes."

"You're kidding."

"He was supposed to come back to the gym for me."

"Nobody's at the gym but the deputies, camping out. He

probably went home first. People round here don't cotton much to coyotes. He keeps a low profile. We should call Sergeant Warren an leave a message you're here."

Sarah already had.

The three of them ate potato salad and grilled cheese sandwiches. Sarah expected Ben any minute, but he hadn't arrived by the time they finished.

"I can take you out to his place if you want," Dawsen said. "Maybe he had a problem with his truck or somethin. Might run into him on the way."

"Would you mind?"

"No problem. I'd take you to the ends of the earth, long as it's okay with Annie."

# CHAPTER 12

**B**en left Sarah at the gym with two thoughts on his mind. The first—concern for Billy Gorman and for the whole reservation if something bad happened to him. The second was Eagle. He stopped by the Gorman house. Millie answered the door, guarded and scared, as if she expected bad news.

"Heard about your son. I got a dog. She's a good tracker, but I need somethin to give a scent. Could you let me have a piece of clothin, maybe somethin he wears to sleep?"

He waited on the porch for her to come back, staring at his boots, feeling like he always did around her, like a lying sack of shit.

"This is what he slept in the night before last." She handed him a T-shirt.

He turned and started away.

"Ben?"

"Yeah?"

"Thank you," she said stiffly before closing the door.

•  •  •

Coyotes scavenge in the wild. He knew they'd discover a
dead body without the help of a shirt, but he was hoping
they'd use their exceptional sensory ability to find the boy
alive. The trouble was how to get them to know what they
were looking for.

Since they were pups he'd played a hunting game with
them. He'd hide a piece of bread and they'd find it. From early
on it was clear Eagle had more skill and interest than the other
two combined. One day he caught her chewing on an old
shoe of his, and he'd decided to see if she'd be interested in trying to find something besides food. He took the shoe, told her
to stay, and hid it in the bathtub. He released her from the stay
and sat down at the table. She dashed into the house and came
out with it in under a minute. The funny thing was she didn't
go back to chewing it. She dropped it at his feet and looked
up at him, like she wanted him to do it again. Like it was
something she'd been thinking of all along and she'd just been
waiting for him to get it.

They'd moved on from shoes to all kinds of things. The
game formalized with the word "find," and he'd started doing
it outside in the desert. Sometimes the other two played along.
They lost interest when he hid things they didn't care about
finding. But it didn't matter to Eagle; she'd look for anything.

The problem was he'd always shown her what she was supposed to find. After he let her smell Billy's T-shirt she jumped
all over him trying to get into his backpack, where he'd put the
shirt away. He pulled it out and carried it in his hand so she'd
know that wasn't what he wanted, but he couldn't figure a way

to get her to understand it was the scent that mattered. After sticking by him for a while, all three took off. As far as he knew, they were running all over the foothills hunting for a dirty T-shirt.

The area he'd been given was not one the deputy, Warren, considered important. He searched for more than an hour anyway, climbing rocks, looking for a trail. About halfway through his search he remembered an elusive cave he'd discovered once, when he was twelve, in the hills above the reservoir. It was high up and hard to find. If the kid was running away, that cave would be a pretty good place to hide out.

The instructions were to check back in at the gym as soon as he was sure his area was clean. But he didn't want to waste the time. Instead, he called the coyotes and drove to the reservoir. He parked his truck among the others on the shoulder of the road at the trailhead.

A dirt path ascended rather steeply for about a mile before leveling off and reaching the reservoir itself. He kept the coyotes on a rope, concerned about running into other searchers. When he neared the water he moved off the trail. Three deputies were sitting on the rocks around the pool. He backtracked before they saw him, then continued on up, out of sight behind them. After a short climb he picked up a deer path and moved swiftly into the hills.

The deer path ended after about a quarter mile. He untied the coyotes and let them smell Billy's shirt again while he looked around. All he remembered was a tough climb up through boulders and stumbling onto an old trail that led to the cave.

He searched until sunset, high up and far back in the foothills, well off any trail, climbing with his hands and feet and the rope. There was no sign of the kid. No candy wrappers, gum, footprints, broken brush, nothing. The coyotes had disappeared. For the first hour, he kept calling them back to smell the shirt, but they didn't get it and lost interest. The last he saw them, Littleman was bounding down the canyon after a jackrabbit, the females at his heels.

He hated to give up without finding the cave, but it was useless and dangerous to continue searching after dark. As it was, he barely had enough daylight left to make it back to the truck. He'd try again tomorrow, start from the reservoir, maybe leave the coyotes at home. He whistled for them and began the descent.

They didn't respond. He whistled again. He climbed a boulder and stood up, the dusky canyon spreading out below him. He heard a faint yapping and saw Eagle far below heading toward him. She stopped about fifty feet away, yapping and turning in circles. When he took a step toward her, she began to descend the way she'd come.

She stayed in sight as he climbed down. After about fifteen minutes he found the trail he'd missed on his way up. Narrow and steep-sided but the going was easier. He walked on for another ten minutes, the sky darkening. Then Eagle disappeared.

He whistled. They answered from directly beneath him. He peered over the perpendicular drop. Eagle and Littleman looked up from a ledge about twenty-five feet below. He searched for a path, but in the gathering gloom he was rapidly losing the ability to see much. He called them, hoping they'd come up and show him the way, but they just kept yapping. It was impossible for him to jump, and a long, slick boulder beneath him made it too steep to climb.

"Billy? Billy?" he called hopefully. There was nothing on the ledge but the two coyotes, no sign of Sage. He secured the rope around the top of the boulder and began to descend.

As he inched his way down, his legs slipped off, leaving him hanging in midair, above the canyon. He lost sight of the coyotes in the struggle to regain his footing. When he saw the ledge again, only Eagle was there, sitting on her haunches, waiting for him. His rope ran out, and he had to let go and drop about two feet. The ledge extended into the side of the canyon and became the floor of the cave he'd been looking for.

As his eyes adjusted to the dim light he made out a figure against the back wall, Sage curled next to it. He pulled out a penlight from his pocket.

Sage looked up and whined but remained where she was, unwilling to disturb the sleeping boy, whose arm was wrapped around her. The tiny flashlight revealed one of the kid's legs twisted strangely and dried blood along a rip in his jeans.

He moved to the child and touched his shoulder.

"Billy? Billy? Wake up."

His eyes opened, frightened.

"It's Ben Lonefeather. Remember?" He shined the light on his own face. "We met at Dawsen's?"

Billy blinked a couple times.

"How you doin?"

"Okay, I was scared til the dogs came. I been here all night an day. Think my leg's broke."

Ben shook his pack off and pulled out a bottle of water. He held the kid's back to give him a long drink. Billy's open pack lay in the dirt next to him with nothing but an empty box of crackers and some matches.

"I'm gonna take a look at your leg."

He used his knife to cut the jeans from the rip down to the end and struck a match. It was black and blue, swollen twice its normal size; the bone protruded from a long, oozing gash in the skin. No way in hell they were going to climb up the trail and out of there.

Billy looked at the leg, then up at Ben before the match went out. "It don't hurt much, cept if I try to move," he said.

Ben walked outside and stood gazing into the gray canyon.

Delay might be serious with a leg that bad. He could leave the coyotes and try to make it out himself, but it was a treacherous climb. If something happened to him, they'd never find the kid. Or they'd find him too late.

He walked back inside.

"We gotta stay here til it gets light."

He shined the little light around the cave, kicking himself for not replenishing his pack. All he had was another water bottle and a box of Hot Tamales. He took the light and went back outside to search for anything he could use to make a fire. The ledge was as bare as the cave.

He emptied his pack and rolled it together with Billy's to make a pillow. He lifted the kid to get it under his head and gave him the light to hold and the candy.

"In the mornin I'm gonna climb out and get help. You gotta wait here alone for a while, don't know how bad your leg's hurt. We're gonna let the rescuers come and get you."

"Can the dog stay?"

"She's a coyote. Name's Sage. From the look a things, she's gonna be next to you long as you want."

Ben sat at the kid's feet and leaned against the wall.

"My dad's gonna kill me."

"I don't think you need to worry bout that. He'll be too glad to see you."

"You don't know my dad."

"He ever tell you bout the time, when he was twelve, he stole his daddy's truck and ended up in a ditch?"

"My dad?"

"Or bout when he got crayons stuck up his nose and had to go to Dawsen to get em pulled out?"

Suddenly Littleman and Eagle rushed into the cave. Eagle regurgitated a dead rat onto the cave floor, its tail still intact. Littleman dropped a half-eaten jackrabbit in front of Ben.

"What are they doin?" Billy asked, shining the little light over the smelly remains.

"Tryin to bring us dinner."

Ben used the empty cracker box to carry the carnage outside.

"Tell me more of that stuff bout my dad," Billy said when Ben returned to his place.

There were lots of stories. About Tom's mishaps, about the winning baseball season when Tom was pitcher and Ben was catcher. Good times with a boyhood friend he'd forgotten. He talked for quite a while until the kid fell asleep.

When he woke a few hours later, feverish, Ben gave him some water and carefully stripped off his shirt and jeans to keep him cooler, using them to cushion the ground underneath him. After a few minutes his breathing got slow and regular again.

Ben couldn't sleep himself. He wondered where Sarah was, if she'd gotten a ride out to his place. He pictured her on his couch in that robe, shy and bold at the same time. He'd almost blown it, pressing too fast. She needed to be teased into it slowly, until she turned on. Then she was like a ball of fire.

Billy woke, groaning in pain, calling for his mama. Ben got him to take some water and used a little to wipe him off, trying to get the fever down. He slept again, but fitfully. Ben sat down near his head.

The kid was the spitting image of Tom, inside and out. Bluster covering a soft heart. He'd taken Tom's measure early on and had known by the sixth grade, when he challenged him, that for all Tom's big talk he lacked the instincts to go for the kill.

Tom Gorman was a strong man with a loving nature that made him vulnerable. It would destroy him if anything bad happened to Millie or one of the boys. Ben had never been able to understand what it was that made a man get himself into a situation like that. Tom had been little more than a kid when he'd jumped into it with Millie, and Ben had just figured it was Tom's weakness. But sitting in that cave next to Tom's son, for the first time since they'd known each other, he considered the possibility that Tom Gorman was braver than he was.

At the first sign of light he located the fissure in a boulder on the far side of the cave that created a natural series of small steps up to the trail. He checked the cave; the boy was still asleep. Sage looked at him but didn't raise her head from the kid's chest. He motioned her to stay; the others followed him. By sunrise he'd made his way back to the reservoir and was climbing into his truck as a couple of deputies pulled up. He told them about the boy and they radioed for help. He locked the two coyotes in his truck, and a deputy poured him a cup of coffee from a thermos, while he waited to lead the medical rescuers back up to the cave.

● ● ●

The coyote's lip curled at the paramedics, and she emitted a low warning growl. Billy's eyes opened, feverish, unfocused.

"You're gonna be okay now," Ben told him. "These people are gonna take care a you. But we got to get Sage outta here so they can do their work."

He called the coyote softly, moving back. She stood and shook, then came to him. The rescuers gave them a wide berth as Ben started back down the trail.

"Good job." Sergeant Warren, waiting at the reservoir, extended his pudgy hand and granted Ben a moment of red-eyed respect. "I never woulda believed coyotes would do somethin like that."

"Appreciate if you could keep it quiet. No need to call attention to them, or me," Ben said.

By the time he got back to his truck, word of the rescue had spread and people were arriving. Light-headed from hunger and lack of sleep, he didn't want to stick around. All he wanted was to find Sarah and head home. He was on his way into town when he spotted Dawsen's truck heading toward him. They rolled down their windows as they passed each other, and Dawsen told him she was waiting at his place.

# CHAPTER 13

When he got home Sarah was up and dressed. She'd been washing clothes in the sink, and he could make out a lacy bra through some wet spots on her little cotton T-shirt as she walked in from the patio, smiling at him. The house smelled of coffee and her shampoo.

"Are you all right?"

"Yeah," he said, bending under the sink to fill the coyotes' dishes with dog food. "Glad you're here."

"Where were you all night? You look exhausted."

"Got stuck in a cave. Too dark to climb out."

"Did they find the boy?"

"Yeah." He placed the bowls on the patio. Among her T-shirts drying on the line outside she'd hung panties, tiny white, black, and red bits catching the morning sun, sparking his imagination.

"Is he all right?"

"Think so. They're takin him to the hospital in Willard."

"That's wonderful news."

"I'm gonna take a shower. Think you could make me some eggs or somethin?"

"Absolutely."

He ate three eggs and five pieces of toast and leaned back with a cup of coffee, revived by the food and by the pert nipples pointing at him in spite of the bra and the T-shirt.

"That's better," he said.

"Instead of drinking coffee, why don't you go to sleep?"

"Hmm. Bet your bed's still warm."

"Sleep. According to rumor, you don't need another notch in your belt." There was something new behind her eyes—a slight removal.

"Huh?"

"I had an interesting talk with Anna yesterday. You've got quite a reputation."

"Oh, yeah?" He tried to toss it off. "What'd she say?"

"That you were a sweet-tongued devil. I took it as a warning."

He saw it then, although she smiled. The door he'd sensed opening under his persistent press shut firmly in his face. The invitation in her kiss had been withdrawn. She'd be gone in a couple days and that would be the end of it. He put his coffee cup down.

"You're right," he said, suddenly tired to the bone. "I'm gonna try to get some sleep."

* * *

Sarah realized Ben might not like her driving his truck, but she wanted to get into Lowman. She didn't want to wake him, and the keys were in the ignition. It had been years since she'd driven a stick shift, so it took a few bumpy fits and starts before the memory came back and she set off down the gravel road, exhilarated by her freedom.

She stopped by Big Jack's, and he told her he'd gotten the parts and he'd have the Volvo ready in two days.

Lowman was bustling with morning activity. Everyone smiled and waved at the truck as she passed. People wished her "Good mornin'" when she parked and entered the market. It appeared the whole town was so cheered by the safe return of Billy Gorman that even an unwelcome stranger had become a friend, or maybe they were showing their appreciation of her volunteering in the gym.

The man behind the meat counter smiled broadly as he handed her a wrapped chicken. "Wait a minute," he said, reappearing momentarily with a plastic bag filled with large beef bones. "For the, uh, dogs," he whispered with a wink.

She was driving out of Lowman on the highway, mulling over the apparent change in people's attitude toward her, when a green and gold fluttering in the desert off to the right caught her attention. She pulled over and walked back, certain as she walked toward it that it was in fact her scarf. She'd missed it but had no idea where she'd lost it. Maybe it had blown out the window of the car and she hadn't noticed. It looked like someone had found it, tied it around a rock, and placed the rock on a boulder. She walked toward it in the desert, looking down so as not to step on anything awful or poisonous, and was quite close before she looked up again.

Then she gasped in a short scream. The scarf wasn't tied around a rock. It was tied around the decapitated neck of some kind of grinning animal. A fox, she thought, shuddering. Sure enough, the body of the little creature was curled up at the base of the boulder. Who would do such a bizarre and cruel thing? She spun around and ran back to the truck.

* * *

Instead of sleeping, Ben had started working on the marble again. She could hear a steady *chink* coming from the storeroom as she unloaded the groceries. She walked back and told him what she'd seen.

He shrugged. "Prob'ly someone's idea of a joke. People don't like foxes much more an coyotes."

"It made me think about your camp installation. Not that there was any real similarity, just the idea of decapitation. There's something I've wondered about. You padlocked the storeroom the day I came. Why? Just because of me?"

He looked at her with a smile. "Mostly." He shrugged. "I lock it sometimes, when I'm gonna be away for a while."

"Why?"

"Jus feels better."

Seemingly untroubled, he resumed work on the marble. She called the coyotes, and in the hope of scraps, they followed her into the house to keep her company. The scarf had no doubt blown out the window and someone had used it. It was repellant and bizarre, but Billy had been found and there hadn't been any women hurt or missing on the reservation. She felt safe with the coyotes milling around her feet and the sound of Ben's steady mallet coming from the storeroom.

Within a few minutes, she'd put the little fox out of her mind and immersed herself in the labor-intensive process of making kreplach.

She began with a hearty chicken stock: onions, garlic, celery, carrots, cooked slowly with the bird. The fragrance filled the house as she measured and combined flour, salt, and eggs with a little water for a dough.

While the dough rested, she removed the soup, poured it into another pot, and placed it in the refrigerator. Then she sautéed a pound of ground beef with onion and garlic for the stuffing. She floured the top of the table and rolled the dough and cut it into three-inch squares. After filling each with a tablespoon of meat and pinching the edges to form little pockets, she dropped them into boiling water. She tossed a salad and mixed and baked soda rolls while the broth chilled enough to be skimmed and poured through a colander. After discarding the cooked vegetables and reserving the chicken for chicken salad sandwiches, she set the broth back on the burner and spooned in the meat kreplach as it began to simmer.

She cleaned up, set the table, and changed her clothes before walking out into a deepening sky laced with vibrant pink and gold. The storeroom held a scene similar to the one she'd witnessed the first day.

Shirtless, covered with dust, oblivious to everything but the stone, he'd switched from the jackhammer to a mallet and chisel. To her eye the marble was simply an amorphous chunk of mottled white stone, and she wondered if he could already see the sculpture inside, waiting to be revealed. She stood quietly, unobserved, captivated by his inordinate physical beauty, the skill with which he moved.

She suspected he took pleasure from women as he did from food, his entire attention captured for the moment, then on to the next amour as readily as to the next meal. It seemed a shallow choice for a person capable of such depth, but perhaps it served to keep his primary focus on the art. It bruised her pride a bit, but her heart remained intact.

"Ben," she called. "Dinner's ready."

• • •

The soup engendered a lively discussion during which Sarah explained that even he could not overestimate the importance of food in Jewish culture.

"The Jewish year starts the first night of Rosh Hashanah with dinner before temple. From there you have ten days, the

Days of Awe, to set your life in order, apologize for whatever you've done wrong and generally clean up relationships. Then on Yom Kippur we start a fast at sundown and attend temple that night where they play a beautiful piece of music about mortality called the Kol Nidre. My mother says if a Jew goes to temple only one night a year, that will be the night. The fast continues all the next day, until sundown when we break it with a fabulous feast.

"My favorite holiday is Passover. For seven days there can be nothing in the house made of leavened flour, no bread or rolls, only matzo. Everything we eat is special, and there's a ritual feast called a Seder. It's like Thanksgiving, for two nights. My mother starts baking weeks in advance. She uses lots of nuts and dried fruits, and she makes this torte with chocolate and coffee that's everybody's favorite dessert. When I was growing up all my friends begged to come for Seder."

"That's what you want, ain't it?"

"What?"

"Husband, kids, makin' a home."

"Yes."

"Nothin to be ashamed of."

"I'm not. It's just strange to admit it to a man."

"How come?"

"You know very well how come. What did you do the last time a woman started talking about marriage? Tell the truth."

Caught, he grinned. "Ran like hell."

"And why was that?"

He shrugged. "Not interested, I guess."

"Don't you want a home? Children?"

"Seems like I got enough on my hands jus takin care a myself."

She sighed. "I feel like such a cliché."

After dinner they sat on the patio with coffee, surrounded by endless black velvet space, strewn with a billion flickering suns.

"I wonder if you'd consider letting me borrow your truck tomorrow. On the map it looks like Alan Trublo lives about two hours from here, and I thought, if you were going to sculpt all day, maybe I could go to see him. That way I'd have only the Hopi village left before I start back to New York."

"I'll go with you."

"Are you afraid of my driving record? I assure you that up until I met your road it was spotless."

"Like to say hello to Alan. Been a long time. You can drive if you want."

"What about your work?"

"It'll keep. But it's around four hours there. We should get an early start." He stood up. "Unless you want company in that big bed, I'm gonna hit my hard pallet on the floor." He smiled.

"Good night," she said, smiling back.

# CHAPTER 14

**T**hree coyotes jumping on her bed, sniffing and licking any body part they could find, awakened Sarah. Ben stood in the doorway.

"You gonna sleep all day, woman?"

She threw her pillow, easily deflected by his arm, and sat up. The smell of coffee, eggs, and toast wafted into the little room.

"Don't take an hour fixin yourself up. Trublo's too old to care."

He let her drive, enjoying her struggle with the clutch and the gravel immensely. The ride took them through the Four Corners area on the Navajo reservation, where Arizona, Colorado, Utah, and New Mexico met. He told her the number four held special meaning to the Navajo: four seasons, four directions, the four sacred mountains bordering their territory.

"An we're livin in the fourth world. The first one was

black, the second was blue, the third was yellow. This one's called bright. The people kept havin to move on into different worlds cause they couldn't get along with the other animals. Everythin was okay in the yellow world until men an women had a problem with each other. They couldn't work it out, so they decided to divide the world in two, one side for the men and one for the women. Course, after a while, the men got so horny they couldn't talk to each other without a fight. Pretty soon, they stopped speakin altogether. The women got bored cause there was nothin to do, no babies being born, no weddings. They stopped talkin too. World got so quiet you could hear a whisper from one end to the other."

"What happened?"

"They finally got together an admitted they needed each other. They decided to find a new world an start over."

•  •  •

Alan Trublo, an Apache—cousin to the Navajo—had lived in Colorado near the Four Corners area for most of his life. A recognized American sculptor with an international reputation, he had chosen, in spite of his success and monumental commissions throughout the world, to continue his residence on the reservation where he'd been born.

He lived in a large wooden house surrounded by grassy fields. Ben pointed out his studio, a barnlike structure behind the house, where he used to sculpt immense pieces, which would then be loaded into vans and shipped.

They knocked at the front door; an Indian woman of about sixty opened it a crack and stuck her head out.

"If you've come to see Alan," she said in a hushed voice, "I'm sorry to turn you away, but he's no longer receiving visitors."

"Hello, Emma," Ben said.

She peered at him. "Ben?" she said, opening the door. He bent over so she could hug him.

"This is Sarah Friedman," he said. "Think Alan's expectin her."

"He is," Emma said with a bright smile, tears glistened in her eyes. "He talked to Sam for a few minutes last week. Did him a world of good. Sorry for tryin to send you away, but Alan had a stroke a few months back. Strangers always droppin by, wantin to meet him. Used to be okay, but now it takes too much outta him."

Entering the house was like walking into a huge, polished walnut, all rich, dark wood, tempered by time.

Emma Trublo directed Sarah down a hallway. "You better go on alone. He's havin a tough day. Less confusin for him to see one person at a time." She took Ben's arm. "Come into the kitchen for a minute an catch me up on you."

The hallway led to a sunny room, beautifully furnished with antiques, walls lined floor to ceiling with books. Alan Trublo, sitting in a wheelchair at his desk, looked up as Sarah entered and introduced herself.

The old man wheeled out from the desk and indicated a chair for her to sit. His gaze penetrated, although he spoke slowly, with effort.

"Gonna miss seein Sam. Worse part a gettin old's knowin there's folks you won't see again. Him an me go back forty years. Had some good talks. All night sometime. Telephone ain't the same."

"I know he misses visiting you too. I remember when he took me to see your sculpture at the United Nations. I've never known him to be so proud of anything."

Trublo nodded. "It all started cause a him. Contacted me from a picture in a newspaper."

An article in the *New York Times* from 1950, featuring

promising American Indian artists. Sam still kept it in his desk drawer. Alan had moved on to more formidable representation after a couple of years, but Shoen's still carried a small piece from time to time. Something special Sam would bring back from the trip and exhibit with enormous pride, until a collector snapped it up.

"Woulda stayed with him too. His idea for me to go to Levitt."

"It was?" Sarah asked, surprised. Bernard Levitt, one of the most prominent gallery owners in New York, had given Alan Trublo the one-man show that launched his international career.

"Said I needed the best to take me where I was goin. Member the first time he showed up here. I opened the front door an there he was, little Jew in a suit standin on the porch wipin his face with a handkerchief." Trublo laughed. "Sight to see."

Sarah considered it extremely unselfish on her father's part to encourage Trublo's move to Levitt. She wondered if Sam had ever regretted the decision to stand on the sidelines and watch Alan soar. What of his own ambitions? Now that he was on the verge of retirement, it was hard to believe Shoen's Furniture and Gallery had been all he'd ever wanted for himself.

"Got somethin for you to take to him," Alan said. He wheeled back to his desk and picked up a roll of paper, secured by a rubber band. He removed the rubber band and spread a series of drawings on the coffee table in front of Sarah.

They were the detailed plans for the Holocaust monument in Jerusalem, completed more than a decade ago. A mammoth relief Alan had carved on a wall of limestone, along the lines of a sculpted *Guernica*. The drawings contained measurements and notes on various portions of the masterpiece.

"I can't imagine anything that would please my father more."

He rerolled the pages and inserted them into a cardboard tube for safe traveling. "Tell him I send my prayers . . ." Trublo stopped speaking; his eyes rested on Ben, standing in the doorway.

Sarah glanced from one man to the other, baffled by the look that passed between them.

"Lonefeather," Trublo intoned. "Thought you was dead."

Ben walked toward him and knelt at the foot of the chair. Trublo rested his hand on Ben's head, briefly as if in a blessing.

"Had to go low, Alan, real low. You was right. Ain't had a drink in six years. I'm carvin again, an my hands are steady."

Trublo nodded. "You know what I promised you?"

"Yeah. I remember."

"Still got em. Kep em, jus in case. All but give up hope. See it?" His wave indicated an end table next to the sofa upon which rested a simple and lovely marble statue of an Indian woman in a long robe, nursing a child. Only the woman's face, breast, and the child's face were defined. The rest was enveloped by the silken folds of the robe. "I look at it ever day."

Emma Trublo joined them, and Ben wheeled Trublo out to his studio to receive a leather case from the master's trembling hands.

"This here's a good day," Alan said.

Later he and Emma watched from the front porch as Ben and Sarah pulled away. Alan raised his arm from his chair and called out again what a good day it was.

Ben drove quietly.

"He gave you a pretty good day too, I'd say," Sarah said after a few minutes, hoping to be included.

He smiled and told her the story.

Eleven years ago he'd gone to the University of Arizona to study with Trublo, who was by that time already semiretired, more involved in teaching than in his own work. At the end of the first year, Trublo told him he had a great gift but he was pissing it away with liquor. In an effort to curb the waste, he'd offered his tools to Ben, if Ben would quit drinking for the rest of his college time. They were extremely valuable. Handmade, imported from England, the ones he'd used himself for many years. Ben dismissed the offer, denying he had a problem, claiming instead the booze made him freer, more creative. They'd argued about it for almost two years until Trublo refused to waste any more of his time teaching a drunk, and Ben quit school.

"I kept meanin to come by. Not cause a the tools. I didn't think he'd a saved em all this time. I jus needed to see him again, but I put it off, til you came."

They passed Big Jack's station on the way home, locked up for the night. The Volvo was parked near the pumps, sitting straight on its new tires. It seemed Big Jack had been true to his word.

Sarah made an easy dinner of hamburgers and salad, and chattered away as they ate.

"I hate to take up another one of your days tomorrow. Maybe we should load everything into your truck in the morning and then switch it to the Volvo in Lowman. That way you could come home and get right to work."

"What're you scared of?" His low tone cut through the babble, confronting the tension between them.

"I beg your pardon?" she vamped, marshaling forces to avoid him.

"You're bullshittin. Actin like nothin's goin on . . ."

The sound of a truck pulling up in front offered a reprieve. Two doors slammed. Tom and Millie Gorman appeared in the doorway.

"It's okay, Littleman," Ben said, rising. The coyote had jumped up at the sound of the truck.

Tom came in first, his hand extended to Ben. Ben stepped forward and took it. Tom pulled him into an embrace.

"I don't know how to thank you, man," he said.

When he released Ben, Millie stepped between them to hug Ben tightly.

"He's gonna be okay. He has to spend one more night in the hospital so they can make sure he stays still, but he's gonna be fine." She sobbed against his chest. He patted her back. His eyes met Tom's over her head.

"You saved my son," Tom said, clasping Ben's shoulder. "He'd a died up there in that cave before we found him."

"He's a good kid." Ben smiled. "Reminded me a you."

"I bet." Tom laughed. "First thing he tol me was he knew bout my daddy's car." He sobered, with a break in his voice. "Don't think I'll ever forget what I owe you, man. Never."

Millie stepped back, wiping her face with a rumpled hand-kerchief. She glanced at Sarah. "Thank you too. I know you helped."

"It was nothing," Sarah mumbled.

They stood in the room talking about the rescue for a few minutes until Millie took Tom's arm and said it was time to get back to the hospital.

Ben walked them out. He came back to face a confused and unreasonably hurt Sarah standing in the middle of the room.

"Why didn't you tell me you found Billy?"

He shrugged. "Guess cause I couldn't figure a way to work it into the conversation that didn't sound like braggin. Anyway, it was the coyotes found him. I was way off, stumblin around. Kept goin up when I shoulda gone down."

"You saved a little boy's life," she said softly. "No wonder you looked so tired when you got back. You probably didn't sleep, all night, alone in a cave with a sick child."

He moved forward, his eyes like onyx disks. "No, I didn't sleep. But not cause a the kid." He stopped in front of her, his jaw muscles tight. "You think I'm a liar, that's up to you. But I'm telling the truth. I never in my life wanted anything as bad as I want you right now."

City girl, country boy, Jew and Navajo—it was impossible; she knew it even as she put her arms around him.

"It's the same for me," she whispered.

●  ●  ●

They undressed between kisses. Sarah couldn't unbutton his jeans. He helped her, yanking them open, pushing them down, and stepping out. He unfastened her shorts, and they slid away as he pulled her to him. She slipped her thumbs inside the elastic waistband and pulled his jockeys down.

She gasped and stopped cold, too stunned to speak.

"What?" A frown compressed his gorgeous features.

Oh, God, she thought, open the earth and let me fall in.

"Uh, you're not circumcised. But . . . Well, I just . . . Uh, I just need a minute." He must think she was some kind of dithering nutcase. She looked up at him helplessly. "The Nazis made men drop their pants, to check. You see? It meant all the difference."

"I'm not a Nazi, Sarah."

"No, of course not. It's just that I don't think I can sleep with an uncircumcised man. I'm sorry." It was a kind of bottom line.

"Oh." He nodded, slowly. "I see. Well, then"—he shrugged—"guess you won't sleep."

He grasped her under the arms and lifted her over his shoulder, striding to the bedroom and kicking the door shut before the coyotes could follow. He set her on the bed and stretched out beside her, head on his elbow, regarding her with a smile.

"Ben, I—"

"It's okay," he whispered, running his finger slowly along her cheek and across her lips, gently as a breeze.

• • •

When Sarah thought about that night, in the months and years that followed, it was the feeling of his hands on her flesh that she remembered most clearly. Workman's hands, warm and callused, slowly roaming down her neck, circling her breasts, caressing her stomach, hips, buttocks, until she forgot everything except pleasure and arched up to kiss his mouth, reaching for him with greedy fingers.

"You are so beautiful like this," he whispered, rubbing her nipple between his thumb and forefinger, bending to take it in his mouth, biting as his hand drifted down her body again, separating her thighs, stroking her, smiling as her skin caught fire.

He slid down to kiss her, entering first with his tongue until she moaned with need and he pulled himself up to enter her in earnest. She rose to meet him, to fit like puzzle pieces. And in the other's eyes they saw themselves reflected, undamaged, unflawed, in bliss.

• • •

"Oh, my God," she said, sitting up.

"What now?"

"You didn't use anything."

How could she have let this happen? She was always so careful.

"Thought you're on the Pill. I saw the little box in the bathroom."

"That's not what I mean."

"It's okay, Sarah," he said, reaching for her shoulders, easing her down. "I give blood two, three times a year, an the few times I been with anyone the past couple years, I always used a rubber. You don't need to worry."

He held her against his chest.

"You're not gonna go tomorrow, are you? Call your folks, tell em you gotta stay a few more days."

"All right," she said.

• • •

Throughout the night they found each other in different ways, echoing a million years of dark, shared secrets between men and women. Sarah discovered he was not always in command. He excited easily; he groaned and reached for her if she leaned over and let her breasts and hair touch him lightly, if she kissed the inside of his thighs or his belly button, if she ran her tongue down his stomach and took him into her mouth.

Lying next to his regular breathing in the early morning darkness, she told herself that the future was merely a concept. She could steal a few days to take what he wanted to give, give what he wanted to take. If you could believe there was really only the present moment, they had all the time in the world.

# CHAPTER 15

The Hopi reservation encompassed a number of pueblo villages scattered over three mesas, baring the prosaic names First Mesa, Second Mesa and Third Mesa—the entire area contained within a small western area of the Navajo reservation. The two tribes managed to coexist in reasonable accord primarily because their cultures rarely overlapped.

The Hopi kept to themselves, content with their small portion of desolate land.

"Nothin there anyone else wanted," Ben told her as they bumped along potholes in his truck on their way to Camilla Huna's house. "Forty, fifty years ago whites mined the hills for coal, made a real mess, but it's mostly cleaned up now. Other than that, no one's bothered em for a thousand years."

"What are the main differences between the two tribes?"

He laughed. "Just about anything you could name. They're farmers. Each village holds the land in common an all of em work it together. Live next to each other too. Navajos used to be nomads, moved with the herds. Wasn't even a tribe til a couple hundred years ago. Then we settled here an took up ranchin. We got a language an a religion, but it's nothing like them. The Hopi religion's real intense, with the kachinas an the dances an all. It's a mystery that touches every part a their lives. You gotta be Hopi to get let in. They initiate kids when they're around twelve."

"Have you ever been sorry you weren't a part of it?"

"Nope. I'm way too independent for a Hopi. One guy sneezes in Hopiland and ten guys catch cold. No privacy at all. Everybody knows everythin bout everybody."

Just like the Jews of Long Island, Sarah thought. "I'm not so sure the Navajos are all that different," she said. "Considering the way people in Lowman stared at us yesterday."

Empty stomachs and an empty larder had finally propelled them out of bed long enough to drive into town. They'd caused a stir, Sarah suspected, walking down Main Street holding hands. "I've got a feeling half of Lowman knows what you're up to."

"Here," he said, reaching for her hand. "You can feel what I'm up to."

"That is so without finesse." She laughed, denying him the hand, placing it instead across the back of his seat so she could turn and let her knee touch his leg. "I'm not interested in sex now. I'm working. Tell me more about the Hopis."

"You tell me bout the woman we're gonna see. If she's the one I'm thinkin of, my grandma and her mom were friends. I might a met her when I was a kid."

Sarah told him what she knew. Camilla Huna lived in a village on Second Mesa, where she'd been born into a family of master potters. Her great-grandmother had been among the first to revive the ancient potter's craft among the Hopis, and

Camilla continued to form rounded pots from reservation earth she processed herself, achieving perfection in the shapes and thinness of the walls without benefit of a potter's wheel. She used only hand-gathered natural dyes in white, red, and black and painted the intricate, traditional patterns onto un-fired clay with yucca brushes of her own creation. She fired in a hand-built, cinder-block kiln behind her tiny house.

Sam always said that when someone bought one of Camilla's pots, they acquired not only a product of hard work and something of extraordinary beauty but a piece of true American history. Because of the time-consuming delicacy of the process, Camilla completed at most twenty pieces a year, all of which were purchased by Shoen's for between three and four thousand dollars each. They were then sold to collectors or museums within the next few months, with the exception of one pot, which would be kept on display in Shoen's for the year until Sam returned with the new group.

"He likes to have something of hers in the store. He's been her sole representative since he discovered her at the Indian Market in Santa Fe twenty-five years ago."

• • •

After the almost reverential way Sam and even Ben had talked about the Hopis, Sarah thought the Mesas a disappoint-ment, although she kept her opinion to herself. High bluffs surrounded by barren country, bleak villages of dirt roads, where chickens, children, and dogs roamed unfettered. Cinder-block structures with common walls seemed a poor imitation of the lovely ruins of the Anazazi.

They pulled up and parked next to a pickup indistinguish-able from Ben's. An almost toothless old man sitting on a bench in the sun pointed out Camilla's detached wooden house. Their knock was answered by a pretty, light-skinned little girl of about seven, who flung open the front door, revealing a small, cluttered living room dominated by a gold cross on the wall over a flowered sofa.

"It's not my mom," she called over her shoulder.

Camilla Huna appeared from the kitchen, wearing an apron over a pair of black slacks and a knit turquoise top. She was a small, pleasant-looking woman, fiftyish, with a full body and merry black eyes.

"You must be Sarah," she said, opening the screen door and her arms, to grasp Sarah in a warm hug. "I recognize you from your picture."

She backed up so they could pass into the room, expanding her smile to include Ben.

"You look familiar."

He nodded. "Alma James was my grandma."

"You're John's son." She examined his face. "I see him in you, but you're taller and even more handsome. Saddest thing when he died." She indicated they should sit. Sarah took the sofa. Ben sat in a stuffed chair. Camilla joined Sarah on the sofa and continued to Ben. "I forget what they called you, somethin unusual."

"Lonefeather. I'm Ben Lonefeather."

"Your grandma brought you by a few times just before my mother died," she said, nodding. "You musta been about eleven or twelve years old."

"Yes, ma'am."

"Aunt Cammy, can I watch TV in your room?"

Camilla introduced her grand-niece, Casey. "She's Maria's child. I don't know if you remember my brother's daughter, Maria?" Camilla asked Ben. "Lived next door? She's twenty-seven now, but she must a been younger than Casey when you saw her."

"No, ma'am. I don't think I do."

"You really finish all the readin your mother give you?" Camilla asked Casey.

"Cross my heart."

"All right, but I'm gonna pick the program." She said, getting up.

Ben's eyes sought Sarah's with an impish wink.

Camilla brought them glasses of iced tea. They sat in the living room, and she told them about the first time she'd met Sam.

"I spent ever dime I'd saved to get to the Market in Santa Fe. I wasn't even invited officially, but rules was easier then an one a my friends let me share her table. Sam come over, an all I had was three small pots. He bought all of em an give me a commission for more."

"Well, he's never had a problem finding people who want to buy your work."

Camilla smiled. "I been lookin forward to meetin you. Sam's real fond a you. You'll stay for lunch? Maria's comin." She turned to Ben. "She probly won't remember you either. She was such a little thing when your grandma brought you by. But I know she'd like to see you. She's on her way from Many Hills."

Sarah accepted the invitation and Camilla went on talking about her niece, who'd returned to Arizona several months ago with her daughter and without her musician husband. She'd gotten a teaching position on the Navajo reservation in Many Hills for the next school year.

"They hired her after the first interview. She always was a smart girl. Got a scholarship to the University of New Mexico in Albuquerque and made the honor roll every semester, even after she had the baby. We all wanted her to take a job here instead. The tribe offered her a teachin position in the same school where her mother teaches, but she turned it down. Says there's too much community." Camilla sighed. "Just makes it more difficult. She don't know a soul in Many Hills. She's had some kind of trainin the past few days, so she had to drive all the way over here to leave Casey cause she couldn't find a babysitter."

She lowered her voice to be certain Casey wouldn't hear.

"It was a bad marriage. I don't know what happened. None of us ask, but it was bad for a long time. And it changed her. It'd do her good to meet some people her own age." She stopped speaking as the door opened and a young woman walked in.

Maria Huna Farrell was slender and tall, with large, liquid eyes and exquisite, deep brown skin. Sarah didn't think she looked like someone who would have any trouble making friends.

"Nice to meet you," Maria greeted Sarah, with a small smile. "I remember your father from when I was a child. Say hello for me." She turned to Ben, her smile brightening into luminous. "An I remember you too, Ben Lonefeather. You used to chase the chickens."

Sarah instantly regretted not bowing out of lunch.

"Come on, it's gonna get cold," Camilla said, scurrying into the kitchen. She returned to the table with a steaming pot and called Casey.

"You're in luck," Maria told Ben. "My aunt rarely cooks."

Ben sat between Sarah and Maria. Camilla served a hearty chicken stew, flavored with herbs, filled with hominy and corn. The spices were unusual, and when Sarah asked about them Camilla told her she'd used cumin and cinnamon as well as oregano, sage, and thyme. She served it with flat, yeasty bread, warm from the oven.

Ben ate heartily, chatting away with Maria, who recalled a piggyback ride he'd given her around the village when she was five and he was twelve. He was evidently a great one for piggyback rides, Sarah thought as she watched him turn on the charm. An attractive man surrounded by women, like a rooster.

"Been a long time since I had this kinda stew. Reminds me a my grandma," he said, shoveling another helping onto his plate. "You like to cook, Maria?"

"Sometimes."

"She makes cinnamon toast," Casey piped up. "An hot dogs an turkey pot pie from Swansons."

Sarah decided Casey was a delightful girl.

"Do you like cinnamon toast?" she asked.

"Uh-huh." Casey nodded.

"Me too."

"Hear you're livin in my neck a the woods," Ben said to Maria. "Whereabouts?"

She told him she'd rented a little house just outside Many Hills.

"That's a half hour from me," he said.

Maria said she thought she'd like it. She'd been a third grade teacher in Albuquerque, and they'd hired her to teach second.

There was no denying she was a beauty, Sarah thought, although there was something guarded, almost hard, about her. Most noticeable when she mentioned her husband, in response to something Casey said. He was actually somewhat famous, a singer with a band that had a couple of hits a few years ago. Sarah thought she might even own one of their CDs.

As soon as the lunch plates were cleared and they'd had a sip of coffee, Ben put his arm around Sarah's shoulder and pressed his leg against hers under the table.

"We'd better start packin," he said. Sarah had no wish to argue.

Camilla had wrapped and boxed her pots in preparation for Sarah's visit. They loaded them into the back of the truck, and Ben secured them while Sarah went into the house to say good-bye.

Sarah peeked into the bedroom to wave at Casey, who was sitting on the bed watching TV. It was a pleasant, homey room: a queen-size iron bed with a patchwork quilt, Victorian wooden dresser laden with perfume bottles, and a single, silver-framed photograph.

She stepped over for a closer look. The photograph, taken perhaps fifteen years ago, was of her father, relaxing on Camilla's sofa, under the crucifix, smiling happily into the camera.

She'd never seen anything like it; he looked like a stranger.

●  ●  ●

"You don't understand. A photograph on a strange woman's dresser is the happiest image I've ever seen of my father. He's never had that expression on his face. And why did she have it there? She didn't have any pictures of her family, of the niece she's so fond of, or of Casey."

The truck bumped back along the same potholes as Sarah went over and over it.

"If you could hear the dismissive tone he uses with my mother, his loyal, faithful wife for over forty years. He's certainly never smiled at her like that. If you had any idea how hard she works, how hard we all work to get the least little glimmer of happiness from him. And there he is on her dresser, just smiling away."

Her sad, elusive father. She'd always believed he'd kept himself distant because he'd been hurt so terribly by the loss of his childhood family. But perhaps he'd given them only a part of himself because he was saving the rest for Camilla Huna. It made her physically ill to think about it.

She was still edgy later that night after dinner.

"You're buildin a mountain outta a ant hill," Ben said. "They're prob'ly jus friends."

"It's mole hill. And how on earth would you know?"

"You're right." He nodded calmly. "It's none a my business. Maybe it ain't yours either."

"Who are you to tell me that?"

He contemplated her for a moment.

"You got a right to be angry at your dad because a somethin he did to you, but far's I know, until today you thought he was a fine dad. I don't see how it makes any difference if he was happy somewhere else."

"Ah. So in your worldview, it's all right to cheat as long as the people around you are happily ignorant of the fact."

"If your dad broke any promises, it wasn't to you. Your parents got what they are to each other. It belongs to them, not you."

"Obviously you don't know what it means to be part of a close family."

He looked at her thoughtfully. "Nope. I don't guess I do."

She closed her eyes, resting her head in her hands. "I'm sorry. That wasn't a nice thing to say."

"It's the truth. You didn't hurt my feelins."

He drew her up into his arms, running his hands down her back to lift her. She wrapped her legs around him and kissed his neck, biting the thick, pulsing vein as he carried her to the bedroom.

# CHAPTER 16

"What about the sculpture?" she asked the next morning at breakfast. It was Saturday. She'd told her parents that the Volvo dealer in Albuquerque had sent a damaged part and the mechanic had to wait for another one. She'd have to leave Monday midday, at the latest, or come up with another excuse. She swept the thought aside. "Aren't you dying to use the tools Alan gave you?"

He shook his head. "Thought I knew what I was gonna do, but it ain't right. No good forcin it. What I want is to draw you again, without all the bullshit."

"Bullshit? You mean clothes?"

"Yeah, an you pretendin to be shy."

He posed her on the bed sitting on her knees, one arm up, her hand in her hair. He moved around with a large pad, sketching quickly, to catch her from the back and sides, as well as the front.

"Close your eyes." He reached out and wound his finger slowly along her jaw and down her neck to her breast.

He retreated to draw, and she kept her eyes closed, still feeling his touch, listening to the sure, swift passion of his pencil on paper.

He was more comfortable with sex than any man she'd ever been with, and less controllable. For the first time in her life, she let go of the internal critic that told her to hold back, that her desire was too hungry and too huge. The intensity of his ardor matched hers. He wanted to touch, taste, smell, hear, see everything: her toes, her fingers, her ears, her hair, her genitals. He wanted to see her excitement and hear it, and she took pleasure from him fervently and freely. She loved making love with him, loved making him come, loved the dark depths of his smoldering eyes, his voice husky with lust, the deep groans of his orgasm and the lying together after, their bodies entwined, still tingling.

• • •

"If you ever show these to another living soul, I swear I'll never speak to you again," she said later. The initial sketches of her were sensual and lovely; then, as they'd continued into the afternoon, the experience had become more erotic and more graphic. Ben eventually got a mirror and drew them in flagrante delicto until he became so absorbed in what they were doing he dropped the pad and pencil. "I should probably take them back with me."

"Nope. They're mine."

From out front came the sound of a car crunching gravel.

"Oh, God," Sarah squealed, hopping off the bed and grabbing her clothes from the floor. "Who's that?"

Ben went out to see. She could hear Tom Gorman enter the house, setting the coyotes yapping, while she scurried

around frantically dressing, profoundly grateful he hadn't arrived twenty minutes earlier. Ridiculous to think that, living in
a place so remote, there wouldn't be enough privacy.

"Pain in the ass, you not havin a phone," Tom yelled over
the yaps. ". . . drive all the way . . . to tell you . . . come over
for dinner . . . goin line dancing."

Ben got the coyotes outside. He said something Sarah
couldn't hear, but Tom interrupted. "Millie . . . take no for an
answer . . . drag you if I had to. Got somethin cooked up . . .
babysitter an everythin."

Sarah emerged from the bedroom.

Tom turned, surprised. "Hey, Sarah. Didn't know you was
still here." He looked her over with a grin. "Man, must be fun
to have all day with no kids around."

Sarah caught sight of Ben's smirk and looked down at her
T-shirt, which was inside out.

"Excuse me," she said, flushing to the roots. A silence of
about ten seconds followed her departure. She slipped off the
shirt and switched it. ". . . got steaks," Tom continued. ". . . barbeque . . . thick an juicy."

"Steaks, huh?" Ben grinned at Sarah as she reemerged.

"You used to like line dancing," Tom said.

"Yeah, but I never done it sober." Ben laughed.

"You ever been, Sarah?" Tom asked.

"No, I haven't."

"You willin to give it a try?"

She felt on the spot, sensitive to the fact that she hadn't actually been included when the invitation was extended. She
looked at Ben; he seemed eager to go.

"Sure," she said. "Why not?"

"That was embarrassing," she said after Tom left.

"Huh?"

"He just sees me as another notch on your belt."

"Why do you care what Tom Gorman thinks?"

Why indeed? "I always care what everyone thinks," she babbled. "It's a basic flaw in my character. Even someone I won't ever see again. I run around trying to be popular with any group in which I find myself. If I were in jail I'd probably be elected Miss Prisoner Conviviality. Actually though, I'm surprised you accepted the invitation. I thought you didn't enjoy socializing."

"Not usually," he said.

• • •

Millie opened the door with a big smile and hug for Ben. She extended her hand to Sarah. "Nice to see you again. Come on in."

She linked her arm through Ben's. Sarah followed into the rambling, ranch-style house, through a living room with worn, overstuffed chairs and sofa and wrought-iron tables.

"I was all excited because we just hired a new teacher whose grandmother knew yours," Millie confessed to Ben. "Thought I was going to surprise you, but she just told me she already ran into you at her aunt's."

They walked out a sliding door into a large yard where Maria Farrell stood talking to Tom while he barbecued the steaks, thick and juicy as promised.

They ate outside at a picnic table. Billy, with crutches and a large cast, of which he was quite proud, had a TV tray at the end. Chippy sat between Ben and Sarah. Maria sat opposite Ben. She wore jeans, a fitted red checked cowboy shirt, a silver concho belt, and beautiful cowboy boots. Even prettier than yesterday, Sarah thought. She supposed Millie had assumed she'd gone back to New York and was hoping Ben and Maria would hit it off.

She'd dressed as Ben had advised: jeans and a tight short-sleeved summer sweater in sienna that set off her long loose curls, accented her fair skin, and turned her eyes amber. She'd momentarily contemplated her boots, slumping in the corner next to her suitcase, but even the desire for the perfect look and the cognizance that everyone else would be wearing them for line dancing weren't enough to entice her into that torture again. She'd settled on tennis shoes. Millie offered her a cowboy hat.

Alvin materialized just after dinner to babysit. He didn't acknowledge Sarah's greeting and wouldn't meet her eyes, but she noticed he had no trouble extending his hand politely to Maria. Everyone else seemed to like him, but just before they left she caught a hostile glance in her direction and decided there was something dark and secretive about him that gave her the creeps.

• • •

They drove to a large bar an hour away, off the reservation. The crowd was mixed: whites and Indians, twenties and thirties, more men than women, three deep around the bar, thinning a bit at the tables. Tom led Millie and Maria. Sarah followed Ben, aware of the guarded stares, the obvious appraisal. She searched the room for other mixed couples—only a few, all reversed, Indian woman, white guy. In fact, she quickly realized, there were few white women present.

Millie had reserved a table for four. Tom got an extra chair.

"You okay?" Ben asked Sarah.

"Fine," she said quickly.

Tom and Ben decided to go for something to drink.

"Whatcha want?" Ben asked her.

"Would it bother you if I had a beer?"

"Course not."

They returned with a Coors for her and sodas for everyone else. Tom, Millie, and Maria got up to dance. Sarah and Ben watched from the sidelines. He explained that every half hour they'd teach a new dance; otherwise you had to know the steps in order to keep up.

Neither Tom nor Millie was a particularly good dancer, but they laughed a lot and flirted—side by side in line, brushing against each other surreptitiously. Maria danced in her own world—one arm at her side, the thumb of the other in her belt, eyes cast down, cowboy hat hiding her features. She had an economy of movement that reminded Sarah of a line drawing, slim and sensual without sexuality.

A new song started. Ben's eyes lit up. "I know this one."

"Then go," she said.

He took a place in the line and muddled it a bit at the beginning, but he caught on after the first couple of passes through the routine. Smooth, unhurried, sexy as hell, a mixture of almost boyish charm and cockiness. But it was the slight missteps that got to her, the vulnerability he let slip.

Left alone at the table, she kept her eyes on the dance floor, uncomfortably conscious of being a source of attention. People wondering about her, she supposed. They'd probably conclude that Ben and Maria were a couple and she was just a white tourist tagging along.

A new song started, and Ben looked over; apparently it was another one he knew. She gave him an encouraging thumbs-up.

Maria came back and sat down; Sarah made a halfhearted attempt at a smile and returned to watching Ben.

"I don't know if you're feeling like an outsider," Maria said quietly after a few minutes, "but I used to."

Sarah looked at her. Maria met her eyes without the least hint of guile.

"I am," Sarah admitted.

"I was the only Indian wherever we went for most of the time I was with my husband."

She was an innocent, Sarah realized. The guarded quality came out because she'd been terribly hurt.

"I guess what I want to say is that it doesn't matter when you really love someone. After a while, you don't feel it anymore. It only starts to matter again if you stop loving."

In a gesture she would not have imagined five minutes ago, Sarah reached for Maria's hand resting on the table.

"Thank you," she whispered. Maria smiled and squeezed her hand.

Fortified by the beer, Sarah joined Ben on the floor the next time they taught a dance. He took a position in front of her to model the steps. She caught on quickly, concluding country music sounded a lot better when you danced to it. The line turned, Ben went the wrong way and bumped her.

"Hey, thought you never done this before," he said, laughing.

She smiled archly and pulled her cowboy hat down, sliding to the side with two taps and a kick before she turned and took three steps back.

# CHAPTER 17

The coyotes took off ahead as Ben led her up a steep trail, over boulders, along a thin, rocky path. Sarah—heart pounding, lungs gasping, sweat dripping into her eyes—pushed herself as hard as she could, determined not to accept help. Whereas he, completely unaffected by the climb, yawned and sat down to watch her navigate a series of rocks.

"Careful where you put your hand," he said lazily. "Might be a rattler hidin in the crevices."

She yelped, withdrawing her hand from the shadow of a boulder and scrambling up to reach for his outstretched arm.

"Knew that'd hurry you." He laughed.

When they got to the back of the canyon, near the top, Ben whistled and the coyotes bounded out from various places. Sarah sat on a boulder to receive Sage's chin licks, catch her breath, and look around.

No question about its being worth the climb. Immense

boulders, cottonwood trees growing between them, surrounded a deep green pool. A waterfall cascaded from a
precipice at the far end. Ben told her he and Henry had removed rocks from the bottom and deepened the pool with a
dam made of downed trees and boulders.

"This belongs to you?"

He gave her a quick smile before ducking his head to untie
his shoes. "We don't own land like you do. It's all held in trust
by the tribe but I got customary use a the clan lands round my
house. Long as I live on it, it's good as mine. Last one in's a rot-
ten egg," he said as he peeled off his clothes. She walked across
a boulder and touched the water with her finger.

"It's freezing. I'll just relax in the sun."

She watched him step swiftly from rock to rock toward the
back of the pool and then climb up the sheer wall of stone to
the top of the falls. He stood and stepped off, plunging feet-
first into the water, like a twelve-year-old. She watched the
surface until he broke through, her heart beating unreasonably
fast. He pushed the hair back from his face and smiled, and she
felt like she was falling, just falling.

She pulled off her shoes and socks and gingerly stepped
over the rocks to test the water again with her foot.

"Take off your clothes and jump in," he called from the
center of the pool.

"I'm a Jewish girl. I never allow any liquid below eighty
degrees to touch me."

"You got one choice, clothes wet or dry."

"Okay, okay. I don't want to get this shirt wet."

She took her time undressing, delaying the inevitable; he
swam toward her.

"I'm coming. Just let me do it at my own pace."

She moved over the rocks to a place where little pebbles
led into shallow water and experienced almost instant glacial

numbness to her ankles. She set her jaw, stepping up to her knees. And then, before she could think, she closed her eyes and pushed forward, shocked breathless as the tingling water enveloped her, covering the top of her head and spreading her hair like a fan.

Ben swam around as if in a heated swimming pool; he was looking for her when she came up behind him. As he turned, she splashed him full in his face. He sprayed her back with both hands, dousing her without mercy until she had to swim away to get a breath.

"All right, you win," she said, swimming toward him. He'd started a cocky grin, but she pulled her legs forward and, lying on her back, kicked water at him so forcefully it wiped the grin right off his face. He went under, coming up behind to press on the top of her head, effectively dunking her up and down like a jack-in-the-box, until her foot connected with his chest and she pushed away, kicking water in his face again. He swam behind her, catching her, wrapping his arms around her, while she struggled against him.

"Give or you're goin under."

"No."

Under she went. She popped up and grabbed hold of his balls.

"Give or you're going soprano."

He released her, holding his arms in the air, laughing. She let go. He swam to the rocks and climbed out. She walked out the way she got in—goose-bumped and shivery on gritty pebbles. He met her with a towel, wrapped it around her shoulders, and rubbed her until she stopped shivering.

In addition to towels, the daypack was stuffed with a picnic Sarah had packed: chicken sandwiches, chips, oranges, Mountain Dew. Within a few minutes they were warm enough to spread the towels out on a large, flat rock and sit down to eat.

"Adam wasn't circumcised or Moses either," she mused.

"It still bother you?"

She smiled. "I think you're well aware of the answer to that question. My mother, on the other hand, would be horrified."

"Wasn't plannin on showin her." He grinned.

He handed her an unopened can of soda and she turned to lie on her stomach, arrested by the sudden seriousness of his gaze. A clutching in her throat: Oh, God, please don't tell me how impossible it is.

"What?" she asked coolly, with a smile.

"Sarah . . ."

She popped her Mountain Dew and swallowed. "Yes, Benjamin?" she said lightly. "It is Benjamin, isn't it?"

He regarded her thoughtfully, changing gears. "No."

He turned to stare out across the pool; it was a moment before he continued in a dull tone. "It's John. John Kanuho, same as my dad. He was drunk the night he killed my mother an some folks in another car. My grandparents thought maybe if he took his name with him, he'd take his luck too. Prob'ly couldn't face raisin a kid with the same name. Called me Little Son, til I was bout four. One day, me an Henry was out back in the desert an I found a feather. Kinda green an gray, not from any bird Henry knew. Figured it must a come from somethin off a migratory pattern, rare an special. He tol me I found my own name, Lone Feather. It's more like the Cheyenne or the Sioux to name kids like that, but Henry thought borrowin stuff was what kept the Navajo strong."

"Where did Ben come from?"

"When I started school I wanted a name like the other kids. Named myself for the bear, in the movie."

He took a long drink, crumpling the can when he'd finished. "Thing is Henry died thinkin it was all a waste an I'd turned out a drunk anyway. When I get real low, I believe that's what killed him."

She sat up and reached for his hand—massive, nearly twice the size of hers, long brown fingers, short cut nails. Rough, strong, sensitive to nuance, subtle and tough, she turned it over to touch the calluses.

"I think Henry saw how it would be, that your journey might be circuitous and perhaps you'd spend some time traveling down the wrong road, but in the end you'd find your way."

His hand closed on hers. Ask me to stay, she silently pleaded. But he was looking out over the water and didn't say anything.

She shivered. "I'd better put my clothes on."

* * *

She was running through the desert, coyotes nipping at her heels, as if to grab hold and keep her. She stumbled, ripping her dress on a cactus, and they surrounded her, their warm tongues licking her scraped arms and legs. In spite of a comfortable numbness, she dragged herself up and ran on until she came to a steep cliff. The coyotes stopped behind her, whining as she stepped off the edge and fell through the air. From a distance she watched herself splinter and fragment.

* * *

Sarah woke in darkness, her heart pounding, tears fresh on her cheeks. She slipped out of the bed, lit a lantern in the living room, and sat on the sofa. A few moments later Ben came in and leaned against the wall, looking mournfully at her from across the room.

Don't let me go, she silently begged. Tell me we're crazy to let something like this slip through our fingers.

"Couldn't sleep either," he said. "You okay?"

She nodded, but then tears sprang to her eyes, and she shook her head. He walked over and squatted in front of her, taking her hands. It was as if they were already moving away from each other, the lace woven of their separate threads unraveling in front of their eyes.

Quiet tears fell. She extricated her hands to wipe them away, her breath ragged.

"Sarah?"

"Yes?"

She thought he might have something more to say, but apparently he changed his mind or was at a loss for words. He reached out and put his hand on her head, looking into her eyes with an expression both sad and compassionate. And she knew he was going to let her go. He wasn't pretending it didn't hurt or hiding it. She could see the pain in his eyes. But he'd known pain and he'd known loss—and they'd both known this was coming. She let out a tiny sob, more like a hiccup, and managed a smile. He wiped her eyes with his thumb.

"I think I'd like to get an early start," she said.

She did it without much more crying. "Finish the sculpture," she told him. "And think about what you want to do after. I'm sure the jewelry will sell. I'll let you know what kind of response we get. And you have my phone numbers."

She knelt and called the coyotes, hugging and patting each of them. Sage put her paw on Sarah's shoulder, and Sarah couldn't hold back the tears. Ben was outside loading her car so she let herself weep for a moment into the coyote's furry neck.

As she was about to drive off, Ben leaned in the window

and traced her jaw with his finger. She grasped the finger without looking at him and kissed the tip. Finally she looked up. Their eyes met. She started the car. He leaned and brushed her lips with his, then straightened up and backed away.

"Walk in beauty, Sarah."

# PART TWO

# CHAPTER 18

"Hello?" Maria Huna Farrell whispered into the phone. She looked at the clock's face, glowing in the dark. Three a.m., only one person it could be.

"Jimmy?"

"Hey, baby," he answered softly. Not stoned.

Maria found the lamp next to the bed and turned it on. She sat up and collected herself, waiting for her heart to slow down.

"Mary?"

"I'm here."

"You didn't even say good-bye, you know? How could you do that?"

"I didn't want Casey to see you."

She'd come home from work and found him sprawled on the floor of the master bathroom, mumbling incoherently. She'd called 911 and packed a suitcase before pulling Casey away from her homework and loading her into the car. They'd managed to get away before the police and the paramedics arrived.

Maria felt the same empty chill in her heart she'd had that day, cold as the death of love.

"How'd you get my number?"

"My folks hired a detective. I been staying with them to get cleaned up. Don't get mad, baby. They wouldn't give it to me til I'd been sober for a month. I had to hear you, Mary. I been goin crazy."

Maria's hand clutched the phone. He began to cry softly.

"Please come back. I can't do it, Maria. You're my soul, baby, you know that. I can't make it without you and Casey."

"Listen to me, Jimmy." She stopped to get her shaky voice under control. "I'm not coming back. I can't take care of you anymore. You've got to learn to take care of yourself. Try to get it together enough to be a decent father. For Casey, not for me."

"Okay . . . okay, Maria . . . I know it was hard for you here. I know you want to be with your people. That's okay . . . I was thinkin maybe I could come there . . . get away from all the shit and breathe. Get back to writin tunes. We could be happy if we were just left alone for a while."

How many times had he promised things would be different? How many times had she believed him?

"Call me again in a month, if you're still clean. But in the meantime, leave me alone. I mean it, Jimmy. No phone calls and no coming here."

"Yeah, but the thing is my folks want to see Casey. They've got a lawyer an shit. I told them to hold off, that we could work it out. But I don't think they'll wait another month."

Maria knew better than to defy Pam and Steve without support. She'd have to see a lawyer herself in the morning.

"Tell your mom to call me," she said.

She hung up the phone and turned off the light. A pewter moon shone through her curtains. She lay still, in the cold gray, listening to crickets, waiting for dawn.

• • •

Maria Huna had grown up loved and protected in the tiny village of Hewa on the Hopi reservation. She was like all of the children, a child of the village itself. So, when she was twelve and her father died of an aneurysm, every man in the village simply took up a larger part of her upbringing to compensate.

She had been twice blessed at her birth. Once, by being the most beautiful girl anyone remembered being born on Second Mesa. Twice, because she was the great-granddaughter of the other Maria Huna, who'd rediscovered the ancient art of Hopi pottery and restored self-respect to the entire tribe.

By the time she was eighteen, she'd distinguished herself as a student in the tribal school and was recognized as a young woman of the highest virtue, although her complete lack of both talent and interest in the art of her ancestors had caused some consternation.

When she applied and was accepted into a college scholarship program offered by the university in Albuquerque for American Indian students who planned to become teachers, the village accepted the path she'd chosen with an outward display of celebration for her good fortune, although the internal feeling was bittersweet. Many children left; most did not return. No matter the initial intentions, once they departed the protection of their villages, very few found their way home, and those who did had been scarred in the fire of a world that lived by the motto "Every man for himself." Still, the village consoled itself with the belief that Maria Huna was special.

Maria did not think she was special. At least not in the way the village did. For as long as she could remember, she'd felt discordant with the life around her—the sameness of the days, the constricting circle of the reservation. Even the "manifestations" of the kachinas held no power over her imagination. She behaved as was expected and kept her thoughts unspoken. No one knew who she really was, or how she felt about anything important.

They didn't know, for instance, that her favorite color was green because of the ocean, which she'd never seen. Or that she loved Bob Dylan, especially the early songs she'd purchased on tapes and played in secret. Few of them would even know who he was. It was easy to stay away from the Hopi boys who swarmed around her with their earth-brown skin, hair, eyes, when what she longed for was the sky.

The day she boarded the bus that was to take her away from everything she'd ever known was the happiest of her life.

She'd packed all her belongings, everything she cared about stuffed in a suitcase tied with rope or in her backpack. She carried two thick sweaters that wouldn't fit in the suitcase, her winter jacket, a small plastic purse, and a worn copy of *East of Eden*. A dozen people from Hewa had driven over to see her off. They stood around the bus stop on Third Mesa in the hot sun, waiting for the Greyhound.

"There it is," Nelson Winnow called.

Everybody turned to watch it veer off the highway from Flagstaff and wind up the long road to the bluff.

Maria anticipated her future, great expectations rumbling in an empty stomach. She hadn't eaten in two days because the expectations filled her so full there'd been no room for food.

The driver climbed down and shoved her suitcase into the bowels of the luggage compartment.

"Take this," Aunt Camilla said, thrusting a paper bag at Maria's hand, already gripping the pole, chafing to hoist its owner up.

Maria let the pole go in order to grab the bag, her other hand being occupied with the sweaters and jacket.

"I'm not hungry."

"You will be. Put it in your backpack for later."

"My backpack's full," she complained, stuffing the bag into one of the pockets of her jacket and grabbing the pole again.

"Be careful," her mother whispered. "Watch out for cars when you cross the street. They drive crazy in the city."

"You worry too much." She pecked at her mother's cheek and pulled herself up, quickly moving down the aisle to an unoccupied row. She slipped off her backpack and lowered the window.

At the sight of her hopeful face, a general murmur went through the crowd, and they came to stand under her window.

"Watch your stuff."

"Good luck."

"Don't get off til you get to Albuquerque."

Anchored at the window, she leaned out to wave as the bus started, like a movie star to adoring fans. She stayed there until the bus pulled away and she realized that she could sit down. For the first time in her life she could do what she pleased with no one to watch or esteem her. She could finally be herself, she thought, pulling the bag from inside the jacket and unwrapping a peanut butter and jelly sandwich.

The first six weeks were a sad adjustment. She shared a small, cramped dorm room with a girl from the Santa Ana Pueblo named Lorna. A communal bathroom at the end of the hall served all the girls on the floor. In the predominantly Indian student body, everyone she met seemed to know someone else she knew. If anything, there was less privacy than at home and more of the sameness.

Her scholarship required a full load of classes plus twenty hours a week of work in the teachers' cafeteria. Whatever free time she had she reserved, rebuffing friendly advances from other students in favor of going back to her room, on the chance that Lorna would be absent and she could listen to Bob Dylan sing "Mr. Tambourine Man" in peace.

One Friday evening, toward the end of the second month, she returned to the dorm, dismayed to discover Lorna, who was almost always out on Friday night, sitting on floor, sniffling.

"What's the matter?" she asked, wearily sitting on her bed.

"I wanna go home," Lorna whined.

Who doesn't? Maria thought.

"Nobody likes me. I ain't made one friend since I been here. Everybody's got a boyfriend by now, or a least they got a roommate that ain't so stuck up they won't talk to em."

"I'm not stuck up."

"Yeah, you are. You don't like me. I could tell by your face you was sorry to see me here right now. How come? What I ever done but try to be friends?"

"Nothin. I'm sorry. I'm just tired a workin so hard. Besides, it's not true about you not havin friends. You go out every weekend."

"That's cause a my cousin. His mom tol him he hadda take care a me, but now he says he's done with it an I gotta make my own way."

"That was mean."

Lorna looked up, wiping her face. "That's what I said. Least he coulda let me go along with em tonight. I been savin for a month, countin on it. But I don't wanna go all by myself."

"Where are they going?"

"Chancho's. Jimmy Farrell's playin there for a week, startin tonight."

"Oh."

"Don't you know who he is?"

Maria shook her head.

Lorna looked at her like she was from the moon. "Only the best singer you ever heard. I'll pay if you go with me. Come on. You gotta see him at least once in your life."

• • •

They had to stand in the back. All the tables were full. Even the standing room was sold out a few minutes after Lorna paid the cover charge and they slipped in among the crowd. Maria had to crane her neck to see the stage, just a shallow platform up a few steps against the far wall, set with a stool in a puddle of light.

He came in through the audience, head down, carrying his guitar. He took his place on the stool, and began tuning the instrument unhurriedly, as if he were alone. The audience, lively and rowdy moments before, hushed. Then, with no discernible break from the tuning, he began to sing.

Hunched over, in a soft voice you had to strain to hear, he sang about loss and loneliness so desperate it made you reach for anything on hand to numb the pain even if you knew it would kill you in the end. He sang of the destruction of the land and of the hearts and minds of people left without dignity, about greed and spite and the havoc wrecked by men ruled by them, and of despair, the dark empty bottomless ache that robbed you of hope and left you wailing in the wind.

He was telling the truth. It came from the heart. Once in a while he looked up, and Maria could see the pain it cost him, etched across his pale face. He was slight, with fair, uncut hair and light eyes that searched heaven and earth for one thing to believe in, one person who wouldn't let him down.

He played for an hour, then took a break. He left his guitar on the stage and moved back through the crowd, ignoring the applause and words of praise. As he passed within a few feet of Maria, his eyes glanced around to find his way through.

They were green.

Fifteen minutes later he came back and played for another hour. Then it was over. He walked out through the crowd and disappeared, leaving the room feeling empty.

"What'd I tell ya—ain't he great?" Lorna said, heading with the throng toward the door.

Maria followed, unwilling to speak about it. On the bus ride home, she let Lorna babble away and counted money in her head, glad she'd saved practically everything she'd earned. She had enough for three nights.

The next evening Lorna watched her dress, discerning her plans.

"You wouldn't a known about him at all if I hadn't a took you an paid," she whined. "Now I ain't got the money to go again. You got enough. You should take me. That's fair."

Maria couldn't think of a way to say no.

They arrived early enough to get a small table off to the side. Within a half hour the room was jammed to the outer corners.

He sang most of the same songs but changed the order a little. He added one, about a child losing a leg to a land mine.

Sunday night, she ignored Lorna's sulk and went alone.

The crowd had thinned out, and she was able to get a seat at a tiny table on the left side against the wall, where she could listen alone, lost in words and music, already as familiar as her own thoughts.

When it came time for his break, instead of heading outside, he wound his way through the tables. He stopped for a moment to talk to someone at a table near the center of the room and then continued, coming closer, until he was standing next to her.

Maria sipped her Coke through the straw and stared at the tabletop in front of her.

He squatted down so their eyes would be level if she looked up.

"Hey," he said. "What's your name?"

"Maria." She kept her eyes on the table, feeling transparent, like he could see her heart beat.

"I was hopin you'd come back."

She risked a peek. "What?" Crystal eyes looked right through her.

"I saw you Friday and then again last night."

"Oh."

He smiled. Even his smile was sad, as if he could see the end of things at the beginning.

"You're the most beautiful girl in the room."

"Oh," she said again.

"You don't know it, do you?" he said, searching her face.

She felt stupid, as if she'd missed something important.

"What tribe are you from?"

"Hopi."

"Hopi, huh?" He nodded slowly. "Which Mesa?"

"Second," she answered, surprised he knew to ask.

"Cool." He nodded again. "You want to hang when I'm done? Get a drink or something?"

"Yes," she whispered.

A few minutes after he finished, most of the people left. Maria waited at the table, her hands folded in her lap.

"Hey," he said, pulling up a chair. He had two beers and a pack of cigarettes.

"You a student?"

She nodded.

"What're you studying?"

She told him about her classes and the work-study scholarship, wishing she could make it more interesting. Her life was a boring sameness of days stretching back as far as she could remember. That moment, talking to him, was the most exciting thing that had ever happened to her.

"You want this?" he asked, indicating the second beer.

She shook her head, gathering the nerve to ask him a question. "Where are you from?"

"Phoenix."

"Oh."

"Yeah. I was born in LA, but I grew up on my stepdad's ranch. Come on," he said, finishing the beer and picking up his guitar.

She stood to follow him, glancing at the clock on the wall. It was half past eleven.

"Oh, no," she said in a panic. "I gotta catch the bus back to the dorm. It's Sunday. They lock up at twelve on school nights." What was she going to do? She was probably already too late.

"No sweat. I'll give you a ride."

He led her around the back of the building to a huge black motorcycle.

"It's beautiful," she said, thrilled at the thought of riding such a thing.

"Yeah," he said, lighting a small joint and taking several quick, deep drags. "Want a hit?" he asked, holding his breath.

She shook her head, and he put it out on his tongue before swallowing it. He strapped the guitar onto his back, then loosened it and moved it around to the front so she could climb on behind and hold on to him.

The rumbling power scared her. She gripped his leather jacket. Cold wind whipped her hair, stinging her eyes. She hid her face against his back, shielded from the wind.

At five minutes to twelve, they roared to a stop in front of the dorm.

"Thank you," she said, reluctantly releasing him and climbing off.

"Maria?"

"Yes?"

He kicked the stand down and pulled the guitar out of the strap, resting it on the ground against the bike. "Come here for a minute."

She took the few steps back. He put his arm around her and pulled her onto his knee to kiss her. He tasted of beer and cigarettes and marijuana, sweet and strong. His hand moved up under her sweater, over her bra, and then inside it to her breast. She gasped and held still.

"You're a virgin, aren't you?" he whispered.

"Yes."

He removed his hand and let her slip off his knee, holding her steady so she wouldn't fall.

"You better get in. The guy's standing at the door."

She looked behind her, through the glass doors, where the first-floor R.A. stared out.

"You coming back tomorrow?" Jimmy called as she ran for the door.

"I can't."

"Okay. See ya," he said. She watched him rumble off, feeling as if everything important in her life went with him.

Friday night, a week after the first night she'd seen him, she was already in bed when someone knocked on her door.

"There's a guy downstairs named Jimmy, wants you."

She bolted up, pulling on jeans and a sweater.

"Where're you going?" Lorna mumbled, half awake.

"Shhh. Nowhere—go back to sleep," she whispered, hustling out of the room, rushing down two flights of stairs. The lobby held a few kids watching TV and a couple kissing on a couch in the corner. No sign of Jimmy. What if she'd taken too long and he was gone?

She stared through the glass doors and saw him sitting out front on the motorcycle.

They went to McDonald's and then into an empty warehouse in the industrial part of the city. He took her up some rickety stairs to a room furnished with a ratty couch and some orange crates with lamps on them. He had a hot plate, a refrigerator, and a microwave set up in one corner and a couple of old chairs and a table. On the other side of the room, next to the wall, was a rumpled mattress on the floor with a lamp next to it. The bathroom was downstairs, in the warehouse.

"I write at night and sleep during the day so I need to be somewhere quiet. I'm putting a band together. We're gonna use the downstairs space for rehearsal."

They took off their shoes and sat on the bed. Maria leaned against the wall, trembling. He smiled at her, lit a joint, and held it out to her. "Here, help you relax."

She shook her head.

He smoked it and played for a while, singing softly, stopping to go back over places he wanted to change, rewriting some of the lyrics as she listened. It was almost like he forgot her. Like it was normal for her to be there.

"You okay?" he asked, putting the guitar down on the floor and stretching out.

"Yes," she said. He turned out the lamp and pulled her down next to him, kissing her gently before pulling off her sweater.

"I don't want to hurt you. If you want to stop, just tell me."

She wasn't scared anymore. She wanted to.

It hurt, but she didn't care. It was wonderful to give him something that made him happy. When it was over, she got under the covers before he turned on the light.

"That was nice," he said, smiling into her eyes. "You okay?"
She nodded.

"You want to go home or stay?"

"Stay," she said.

He nodded. "I'm gonna work for a while." He picked up a
bottle of pills from the floor, took the guitar, and walked over
to sit in a chair at the table.

Maria turned off the lamp next to the bed and dressed
quickly, her back toward him, although he was already playing.
She used the bathroom downstairs, staring in wonder at the
stranger in the cracked mirror.

She struggled to stay awake, to make it last, watching his
delicate silhouette outlined against the lamp shade behind him,
listening to the sweet, sad throb in his voice, until she couldn't
fight sleep any longer.

When she woke, it was day. He was still awake in the chair,
hunched over the guitar. Cigarette and marijuana smoke hung
in the air like a fog.

"Morning, sleepyhead." He smiled, his voice hoarse and
raspy. Sea-green eyes, swimming in red, pale cheeks, stubbled
with fair hair. "Got somethin for you."

He took a sip of beer and tuned the guitar a little.

It was a song about a soft-eyed girl named Maria whose
hair smelled like rain. He was weary and heartsick, at the end
of the line. Believing in nothing no more. She'd opened her
heart, she'd opened her arms, and when he came knockin she'd
opened her door. "Lost inside Maria," he sang. "Rocking to
sleep like a baby. It just might be, at the end of the line, I found
the one who can save me."

# CHAPTER 19

The answering machine had recorded sixty-three messages. Sarah stared at the red blinking numbers with the weary impulse to simply press the erase button, take the phone off the hook, and fall, face-first, on the bed.

She'd sobbed for the length of the gravel road and beyond, the wrenching away as bad as anything she'd dreamed. By the time she'd stopped for the night in Albuquerque she'd been through every day, almost every moment, they'd had together and convinced herself she understood how he might care deeply for her and still let go.

He knew her—the kind of life she wanted, a happy, messy home with children, the pride and respect of her family and friends. He respected her deep connection to her people and religion. And he knew his own needs—quiet, solitude, peace, work, coyotes, the land. He'd looked rationally at the two of them and recognized the impossibility she'd lost sight of.

In Albuquerque she'd gone into a bookstore and selected a beautiful coffee-table book on the Louvre. *To Ben, with all my love, Sarah,* she'd written on the frontispiece.

Then she'd purchased a blank card.

Dear Ben,

Thank you for the most wonderful ten days of my life. A rare gift I will always treasure. I see now what I think you knew all along. The lasting aspect of what we are to each other is friendship and our relationship as artist and dealer. I count you as my dear, true friend, and look forward to doing my part to ensure your great success in the years to come.

Love,
Sarah

She'd awakened from a restless sleep in the motel before dawn, wired and drained, the magnet pull toward home compelling—as if she might outdistance her thoughts and escape the pain. She'd driven almost nonstop after that.

Buster jumped up on the bed with a demanding meow, his unblinking golden eyes fixed on hers. She ran her hand down the length of his body, and he writhed beneath it, purring.

"If I didn't know better, I'd say you missed me," she whispered, scratching under his ears as he moved his head around her fingers. "See? I had to come back for you, didn't I?" Her very bones ached.

The apartment—dark, dusty, a mountain of newspapers, fliers, solicitations, unpaid bills covering the dining table—felt cold and unkempt, smelly from cat boxes let go too long by neighbors who hadn't bargained on a month's responsibility. She'd have to get them something special.

Buster abruptly jumped off the bed, his need for affection sated, and she knelt to unzip her suitcase. She got it open and stared at the contents, wishing they belonged to someone else.

Unable to face unpacking, she turned on the light in the bathroom, rinsed out the tub and ran hot water, pouring the remains of some bath salts she'd saved under the steaming flow. Ben would want to know she'd gotten home safely; he might call tonight. No, not tonight. Maybe tomorrow or the next day. He'd expect the drive to take that long. She could safely take the phone off the hook when she got out of the bath. And then she'd sleep.

• • •

She woke twelve hours later in semidarkness: five thirty a.m. Still tired but no longer in need of sleep, she lay in bed, gathering fortitude to face the tasks in front of her—unpacking and sorting clothes into laundry and dry cleaning, perusing the mail and paying bills. The apartment needed vacuuming, the kitchen scrubbing, the refrigerator stocking. She'd have to shop for groceries, return phone calls, make plans with friends. The only call she'd felt remotely able to make when she got back yesterday afternoon had been to her mother.

Evelyn's voice had been warm and mothering, and for the first time since she was a child, Sarah had longed to lay her head in her mother's lap and sob.

"Oh, for God's sake," she said out loud. "Enough!" She propelled herself up and out of bed, rummaged in her dresser for a pair of old jeans, selected a bulky sweater from her closet, pulled on socks and tennis shoes, grabbed her umbrella, and ran down eight flights of stairs.

It was sunrise on a drizzly Saturday morning in mid-September; the streets were quiet for New York. Light traffic, a few dog walkers and joggers. The Korean grocer at the end of the block had his lights on and stood outside under his awning arranging freshly delivered flowers.

The leaves in Riverside Park glistened in the rain. The earth smelled richly of itself. She breathed it in, remembering how much she loved green and moisture and the glory of the fall that was on its way.

Walking back from the park, she bought a coffee and stopped at the grocery for a tomato, an apple, two pears, a plum, fresh mozzarella, basil, lettuce, carrots, onions, a free-range chicken, and a bouquet of lilies. Her pulse leapt as she approached her door and heard the phone ringing. She practically dropped the shopping bags in order to get into her pocket for her keys and then left them in the door as she ran to answer. It was a woman from a long-distance phone company inquiring if she'd like to try their service.

Really, she thought, late that evening as she climbed onto a chair to put her empty suitcase on the top shelf of the closet, it was good he hadn't called. He was wise to give it time.

• • •

On Sunday afternoon she met Sam and a man hired for the occasion at Shoen's to unload the Volvo.

"So? Tell me?" her father said, ushering her into the office while the man worked. Sam looked smaller and older, although he seemed in better than usual spirits.

"I don't know where to start. I had a wonderful time. You'll see what I did. Some pots I think you'll like from the Market. Jon Wilbur sent beautiful things."

"Did you see Alan?"

She remembered the astonishment on the old man's face when Ben had stepped out from the shadows, the way Ben had knelt, his hands on the arms of Alan's chair, the blessing. That was before they'd become lovers. But she'd already been in love with him.

"Oh," she said, turning her face away, "of course. You'll be thrilled." She jumped up to run out into the storeroom, furtively wiping tears as she searched for the cardboard tube.

• • •

Sam pored over the plans, extremely moved. So much of his life counted for so little, but this, his friendship with Alan, the part he'd played in helping Alan gain the recognition he deserved, was the best of it. And Jon and Camilla, of course. Without him they'd have found dealers, their pottery would have sold, but not for the kind of money he'd gotten. He'd done well by them all. It was a small thing to be proud of. Not enough to tip the balance of his life's worth, but something.

Later, as he and Sarah stood in the showroom unwrapping the pieces from the Volvo, he was surprised to discover how interested he was in her descriptions of her experiences and the pleasure he took in the purchases she'd made.

"You have a good eye," he said more than once.

It had been difficult to stay home and watch her go, but he found it easy to welcome her back, open surprises, and listen to her depiction of the Indian Market and the Taos Pueblo. Bitter, he supposed, to admit Evelyn had been right and he wasn't up to it anymore, but sweet to see that his daughter was. Perhaps Sarah could continue bringing the work of these artists back to the city, and he'd be here to unwrap them. He felt elated and somewhat relieved at the thought.

• • •

Sam was unusually effusive and surprisingly uncritical, Sarah thought. They spent several pleasant hours together unpacking the boxes while she gave the particulars about where and why an individual item had caught her attention.

"Jewelry?" he asked, surprised, glancing at Ben's wonderful pieces with only mild interest.

"It's beautiful, and I think it will sell."

"I thought you wanted to move into fine art."

"This man is a fine artist. He's only making jewelry to support himself for now. But that's not the point. I think this will bring people in."

"Fine." Sam held up his hand. "If it makes you happy."

She leaned over and kissed his cheek. It seemed all right.

Until they got to Camilla's pottery.

The flushed smile as he unwrapped the first bowl and ran his fingers over the rim brought bile to her throat.

"I had lunch there," she said. "With her niece and her niece's daughter."

"Yes, I know." He nodded, his attention on the next pot, which he unwrapped with the tenderness and anticipation of a lover undressing his beloved. "You brought a friend with you, someone Camilla knew from years ago. I forgot who it was."

He stopped speaking and looked up. "I spoke to her when your mother told me you were delayed."

Two things her father never did—explain and apologize. In all her life she couldn't recall him offering an explanation for anything. And she hadn't even asked how he knew about the lunch.

"She had a picture of you on the dresser in her bedroom. I believe it was the only photograph she had in her house. I wondered when it was taken." It would be hard to miss the undercurrent of accusation in her voice.

Sam's expression didn't change. In a moment he turned back to unwrapping. "I don't remember a picture," he said in his usual flat tone. "Did you save the receipts? Gas? Food? Hotels?"

"Yes."

"How much was the repair on the Volvo?"

She told him.

He sighed. "I suppose I should think about getting rid of it."

"Yes, I think you should."

After they'd completed the unwrapping with a minimum of further conversation, Sam went home, leaving her to clean up and begin the process of rearranging the gallery space to accommodate the new pieces. The next morning he called and said he was taking the day off. Tuesday he was already ensconced in the office poring over the books, when she arrived. He greeted her absently and left at lunch.

On the surface there was nothing particularly unusual in his removal and apathy. The difference lay in the quality of the silence between them, the coldness and distance. As if they'd had a terrible argument, when in fact little had been said. Her implication, however, had been monumental.

Sam disappeared into himself, and Sarah had no will to pursue. She considered Ben's caution: that it was none of her business, that her parents' relationship was theirs and her relationship with her father had not been compromised. She didn't know if she agreed with him, but when he called she'd talk to him about it again, as a friend. Maybe he'd help her find the largesse she needed to move beyond her sense of betrayal.

● ● ●

During the time she'd been gone David had completed his move from Bloomfield and Sheeve. His secretary left a message on her answering machine at home, informing her of the new number. She called it Thursday afternoon, during the post-lunch lull.

"David Klein and Associates."

Sarah gave her name, and David came on the line sounding rushed.

She congratulated him on his new business venture.

"Thanks. It's going great. Look, I want to hear all about what you've been up to and we need to talk, but I've got a meeting in three minutes. How about dinner? Des Artistes, eight o'clock? I'll have my secretary make a reservation."

"No," she said quickly. "I can't."

"Oh. Well, I can't make it tomorrow, but let me look at my calendar. Maybe Saturday . . ."

She had zero interest in rehashing their relationship and even less in telling him what she'd been up to.

"I can't, David. I'm sorry. I was gone longer than I planned and there's so much to do. Why don't I call you again in a week or two?"

"I thought you said you weren't angry."

"I'm not," she said. "I was, but it doesn't matter anymore."

"What do you mean?"

"I mean it doesn't matter. You have a meeting. Go on. We can talk another time."

"I'll call you later."

He tried to reach her that night at home, but she let the machine pick up.

# CHAPTER 20

Friday afternoon, after Sam left, Evelyn came into Shoen's. Sarah had spoken to her several times since she'd been back. Without revealing particulars, she'd been able to describe the desert and the reservation. She'd turned Millie and Tom into the family with whom she'd stayed and admitted it had been lonely coming home. She found it surprisingly easy to deflect her mother's more personal questions and to see that Evelyn's interest in her experiences stemmed from love.

"What's wrong?" Sarah said, responding to Evelyn's worried face.

"I just came from Saul's." Saul Plotkin was Evelyn's gynecologist. "I didn't want to say anything. I thought it was probably nothing, why get everyone upset? But he says it's not nothing."

"What are you talking about?" Sarah sat down, suddenly unsteady. "Ma?"

Evelyn sighed. "I had a lump, Sarah. The mammography looked suspicious. He did a biopsy. I've got cancer."

• • •

The tumult of tests, doctor visits, second opinions, and surgery options preempted the following week. The next was lost to the mastectomy itself. Sarah waited for word with Sam, Eli, and Lisa in the surgical waiting room of a Long Island hospital near her parents' home. Interminable hours, her tiny family drawing close against a common enemy, one they knew could sever them in a moment, as mercilessly as Evelyn's breast was being severed from her body.

Sam seemed shell-shocked, staring at the wall vacantly, a gray pallor to his skin.

"I thought it would be me," he whispered.

"Hush, Pop," Eli soothed.

None of them wanted to hear it, Sarah thought. They'd all expected it to be him. They'd spent years thinking he was the one who needed to be watched.

"She'll be fine after the surgery," Lisa said.

She should know. Her mother died from cancer when she was fourteen years old. She'd seen it all unfold. Now she looked tormented, as if she'd brought a curse with her when she married. Eli put his arm around her and kissed the top of her head. Sarah's heart lurched in remembrance. The edge of Canyon de Chelly. She ached with wanting him.

He wouldn't be here, she told herself. She'd have come back to deal with her mother's cancer alone, alienated from him because he couldn't understand the importance of her family, alienated from her family because they'd never understand her choice of him. Again and again, as she forced herself to be realistic, his wisdom spoke the words he'd never said. But why hadn't he called? If he truly cared for her, wouldn't he want to know she'd gotten home all right?

The surgeon came in—Dr. Goldman, stodgy and serious, his bald head reflecting the fluorescent lights from the ceiling. "She came through like a champ. It could be a difficult recovery. The important thing is to maintain a positive attitude. We want her to regain her strength so she can fight this thing."

Eli put his arm around Sarah and gave her a squeeze. Love for her brother surprisingly overwhelmed her. When had he become such a man?

The lab results showed cancer in three of the lymph nodes under Evelyn's arm. The doctors recommended aggressive chemotherapy, which could make her feel quite ill. She'd need a lot of support. On the day she was to be released from the hospital, Sarah, Lisa, and Eli met in the hospital cafeteria to divide the chores.

"You've got to deal with Dad," Eli said. "He'll listen to you, if he'll listen to anyone."

That afternoon, when they brought Evelyn home, Sarah told Sam she was prepared to take over the financial reins at Shoen's.

"Ma needs you here. She shouldn't be alone. Rosalie can come two mornings a week to do the laundry and heavy cleaning, and Lisa will make dinner, but you've got to handle the rest. Lisa will give you marketing lists, but there's all the other things, the cleaners, the pharmacy, and everything else Ma does that we don't even know about. We have to put her first for once."

She read guilt in the quizzical look she received, in the very slump of her father's shoulders, in the fact that he didn't argue or even question the sharpness of her tone.

Guilty or not, she told herself, he's hurting. She softened her voice and touched his hand.

"You can come into the city tomorrow morning and go over the books with me. Lisa will stay with Ma until you get back."

He nodded and walked upstairs.

Sarah unpacked groceries and set out cereal choices for the morning on the counter. She cut several of her mother's beautiful roses and carried a vase upstairs to set on the nightstand.

She kissed Evelyn's cheek and whispered she loved her. Sam was sitting on his side of the bed reading *Newsweek*. She kissed his cheek. He nodded. She tiptoed out and drove home.

●  ●  ●

Evelyn rested on her side, her features drawn in repose. Sam sat next to her on the bed, a magazine on his lap, lost in memories.

March 1939, barely fourteen, standing on the platform of the Cologne train station. Always the spoiled, pampered baby, he'd accepted his trip to America unquestioningly, as an exciting adventure. He'd never considered the feelings of his sisters. Gerta had tickled his ribs until he couldn't catch his breath and he'd slapped her arms away; Elizabeth had pretended to be a Frenchman and kissed each cheek. If they'd resented him getting the chance to leave, they hadn't showed it.

He could still smell the blend of mink and leather and Joy perfume that had enveloped him with his mother's sobbing embrace. As he'd boarded the train, he'd looked back at her, his cool, perfectly groomed mother with her lipstick smeared and tears streaming down her face.

"*Vergiss mich nicht,*" she'd called. Don't forget me.

Sam sighed and glanced at Evelyn to ask if she needed anything, but she'd fallen asleep. He quietly put the magazine on the nightstand and settled his back against the headboard, remembering.

No place at that time could have been further from frigid, restricted, dying Cologne than New York City. The city was filled with pulsing energy; music and colors poured into its streets from the rich array of cultures jammed together. He'd spent his days wandering in dizzy joy. He'd filled his first letters to his family with exhilaration at his newfound independence, the opulence surrounding him in the Park Avenue apartment, and funny observations about Milton and Erica Reese, the elderly cousins who'd taken him in. The letters he received in return stunned him. The envelopes had been opened, and the contents bore the black marks of censorship. In guarded language, they described empty days spent at home.

By the end of 1940 their responses had diminished to one letter a month. In 1941 he received only seven letters, referring to the meager Easter dinner, meaning Passover, or that Christmas, meaning Hanukkah, had been quite cold. They'd moved to smaller quarters, as they "couldn't possibly use all that room anymore."

It seemed unreal. They wrote to him as if to a child, but he'd changed from the boy they'd known. He couldn't have erased the distance increasing between them, but he'd felt even then that he should be sorrier about it. However, he was enjoying himself too much to be sorry about anything, looking forward, not back, captured by each fresh experience waiting for him.

By the time he was seventeen he'd discovered girls liked him, especially the Jewish girls of Polish and Russian ancestry he met in school, who called him a "yakki" behind his back but were very willing to neck with him at the movies on Sunday afternoon. Then he met Rosa Santiago. She was sixteen the day he picked her up in a coffee shop in Spanish Harlem. He could still remember the throaty laughter, the scent of her skin, the touch of her long, brown fingers.

He enlisted the day he graduated from high school, on fire to kill the bastard Nazis, but instead spent three years in a basement office in Baltimore translating documents and listening to rumors about what was happening to the Jews in Europe, whispers about death camps. By then he had no means of contacting his family. He broke it off with Rosa during a weekend leave. She ran after the bus crying and calling his name. He'd watched through the window, crying himself, but he couldn't continue to love her, tormented by thoughts of his family's condition and what they would think of his behavior.

It wasn't until he returned to Germany and found their names listed among the dead at Auschwitz that he'd realized the magnitude of his betrayal. While he'd been enjoying himself as an American high school student, his family had been murdered. At some exact moment, perhaps when he was telling a joke at a party, or feeling Judy Rossman up in the movies, or spewing himself into Rosa's mouth, each of them had died.

The shame was more than he could bear.

He remembered 1959. He was thirty-four years old, living in an East Village walk-up and running a small gallery a few doors down from his apartment on the same street. Milton Reese had died six months earlier, and Erica had moved to Florida to be near her sister and her sister's children. He'd had dinner at their home two or three times a week. Suddenly he didn't know what to do with the time.

Shoenberg's Furniture, high-priced home furnishings on the Upper West Side of Manhattan, was just one of many stores he'd passed for years on his way here or there. One day he carried in four framed paintings by Village artists.

"Can I help you?"

The daughter. He'd seen her before, at temple. Thirtyish,

dark dress, no makeup, indistinguishable from other female casualties of the war. A nice Jewish girl settling into spinsterhood.

"I think we can help each other," he'd answered. "Whenever I walk by here I notice the bare walls."

She'd convinced Old Man Shoenberg to let him hang the paintings. When they sold, he brought in more.

"Your shoes could use a shine," she'd said the third or fourth time he came to replenish the art. She looked like a different girl, wearing a pink summer dress, matching lipstick and nail polish, her hair done up in curls. "Sit down. Have a cup of tea. Give them to me." She sat him at the desk in the office, poured him some tea, and took his shoes into the bathroom. When she came out her manicure was ruined, but he could see his face in the shine.

He was tired of living alone, tired of the Village walk-up. Shoenberg offered him a partnership—as a son-in-law. Love had nothing to do with it.

It hadn't been because of the money. Her father was not a rich man. Milton Reese had proposed much more financial security when Sam graduated from City College, but the thought of banking had been unbearable. He'd taken Shoenberg's offer because he could endure running a furniture store cum gallery. He could bear marriage to Evelyn Shoenberg.

He'd regarded it in the light of a business arrangement. His obligation: to make a reasonable living and maintain an honorable place for them in society; hers: to raise children and create a home. Of course, it had never been discussed in such terms, and he'd known that Evelyn would be hurt by his point of view.

Throughout their life together he'd held himself aloof. It had been his will to remain uninvolved. As a punishment for surviving, he supposed. A protest against a God he didn't believe in.

Evelyn, on the other hand, squeezed life for every drop of juice. She too had settled for what was offered, but she took it fully. She seemed to have an inexhaustible capacity to care about people: her parents, the children, her friends. She enjoyed books and movies and plays. She loved socializing and holidays and children's soccer games.

He remembered once, when she was angry over his refusal to attend a baseball game of Eli's, she'd said, "You know what it is with you, Sam? You don't appreciate what you've got. You're miserable because you can't care for anything until it's gone." The reproach had infuriated him. But now, when he saw the pleasure Eli took in the sports activities of his boys, when he watched his son become the father he'd never been, he realized that she was right.

Evelyn woke and looked over.

"What is it? Why are you crying?"

In all the years, he'd never once thanked her for what she gave to him and the children. He'd never thanked her for saving his life.

"I'm not dying, Sam. Listen to me. I don't think I can stand it if you start feeling guilty because of the cancer."

He swallowed, staring at her.

# CHAPTER 21

**S**arah assumed complete operation of the business, grateful to have her time filled and her mind occupied. She got up early most mornings to run in the park, worked late most evenings, and at the end of the majority of her days fell into an exhausted sleep. Fridays she closed shortly after lunchtime to drive to Long Island, cook Shabbat dinner for her parents, and visit with Evelyn while Sam went to temple. She spent the night in Woodbridge.

Now that Lauren had moved to Miramar, all three of her closest friends lived in Long Island. Becky and Miriam had children. On Saturday Sarah often met one or the other for a walk or brunch. Each on separate occasions broached the subject of a husband's good buddy who'd recently divorced or seemed ready for a relationship, but Sarah so adamantly refused that no one mentioned it more than once.

She hired Joshua Greenblatt, a gay artist friend, to help in the store. He'd come out to his Orthodox family during the time she'd been in the Southwest, and it had been less a surprise, or trauma, than he'd feared.

"I can finally be who I am," he told her. "I'm ready for a real job."

He relegated his mixed-media collages to a weekend hobby and committed to being an excellent employee: showing up for work on time, willing to do without lunch if necessary and to stay late on Friday so she could keep the store open and still get out to Long Island.

David had called her the week of her mother's surgery to offer his support. He'd heard about it from his mother who'd heard about it, Sarah supposed, from Molly at the bridge game. He suggested they meet for lunch, "to talk."

She'd told him she appreciated his call but she couldn't get away. He had not insisted, and when she didn't hear from him again, she'd assumed it had been an obligatory attempt. Perhaps, if she let it alone, he'd feel he'd done his duty and would move on without the "talk."

Wednesday, five weeks after the surgery, business was slow. Sarah prevailed on Joshua to help her move two vintage craftsman chairs, the last vestige of Shoenberg's Furniture, into the office and rearrange the showroom space.

"I think we should drop the furniture and just call it Shoen's or Shoen's Gallery."

Joshua nodded absently, no doubt thinking about plans to meet his partner for apartment hunting during lunch.

"Hey." She smiled. "Let me run around the corner for a sandwich and you can take the rest of the day."

She ordered a turkey on rye with an iced tea to go and moved off to the side to wait, just as David came into the deli, his arm encircled by an attractive young woman at least ten years his junior. They took seats at a table near the front of the restaurant.

Sarah had to admit it bruised her ego a bit. He sat with his back to her, but she could see the young woman's smile and the intimate way she reached across the table to touch his hand before picking up her menu.

Unfortunately, passing near them on the way out was unavoidable. She kept her eyes averted as if lost in thought and walked quickly.

"Sarah?"

"Oh, hello," she said, turning with a bright surprised smile plastered on her face.

"How are you?" He asked. "How's your mom?"

"She's hanging in."

"This is my sister, Hannah. Hannah, Sarah Friedman."

She'd forgotten he had a sister. At Wellesley. Hannah gave her a wide grin and they chatted for a few minutes. Seemed like a nice girl. Sarah would have enjoyed staying longer, but Joshua was waiting. She said it was a pleasure and excused herself to get back.

Joshua—literally standing next to the door—left as soon as she came in, and she could swear he moved without touching the ground.

The world was in love. She sighed, sinking into one of the craftsmen chairs in the office to unwrap her sandwich. Before she could take a bite the buzzer went off, signaling a customer. She dropped the sandwich on the desk and went out to the floor.

An attractive young woman in an expensive suit looked around, frowning.

"I'm afraid I'm in the wrong store. I saw a stunning necklace last night at a dinner party and was told it was purchased here. I canceled lunch with an important client to get here."

Sarah assured her she was in the right place. "The necklaces are by an artist named Lonefeather. Unfortunately, I only had five, and the last one sold a week ago. He's supposed to send more, but I have no idea when it will be."

"Will you let me know? I mean immediately?" the woman said, handing Sarah a card.

• • •

Sarah sat down at Sam's desk, debating. She picked up the phone and punched in Dawsen's number.

Anna answered. She said it was good to hear from Sarah. Both she and Frank were fine.

"Ben told me I could leave a message with you if I wanted to contact him. It's good news, not an emergency. Just tell him that his necklaces have all sold. I'm ready for more."

"I'll send Frank out to his place. Give us an excuse to check up on him. I haven't seen him in more an a month. Frank went over couple weeks ago with a casserole. Says he's workin day an night on a sculpture an don't wanna be disturbed."

Sarah hung up and took a bite of sandwich. Her throat closed like a fist, and for a moment she was unable to breathe.

The buzzer went off again. She looked up through the glass partition. A gorgeous basket of Iceland poppies floated into the gallery.

"Sarah Friedman?" the delivery boy asked, peeking out from behind.

The card said:

I miss you.
David

She called him. "They're beautiful. And they came at the perfect time. I was wallowing in self-pity."

"Have dinner with me tonight."

"I can't possibly. I've got to get home. I have a million things I've been putting off."

"You have to eat. I'm not taking no for an answer, Sarah. I'll pick up Chinese and be at your place at seven."

• • •

At six fifteen she unlocked the door, dumped her purse on the entry table, and absently riffled through the bundle of mail from her box, considering trying to reach David at the office to cancel. Her home was dusty and cluttered, cat hair everywhere. She had loads of laundry. Nothing sounded more like heaven than a hot bath and a few hours' zoning in front of the TV.

The phone rang.

"Sarah." Ben's voice.

She dropped the mail and collapsed onto a chair. Everything she'd been keeping under control burst out in a torrent of words, intermingled with sobs. She told him about the cancer, the surgery, taking over at Shoen's, how worried she was about her mother.

"I'm real sorry," he murmured. "That's rough."

She sat clenching the phone like a lifeline, but its hard plastic and the disconnected voice imparted nothing of the Ben she remembered. She felt a little foolish. She wiped her face and pulled herself together. "No, I'm sorry for unloading. It was just so good to hear from you. How are you?"

"Okay. Dawsen came by my place. Tol me you called."

"Where are you now?"

"Gas station."

She reiterated what she'd said to Anna about the jewelry. "I was hoping you could get me some more pieces by early November—that would give us the holiday market."

"Okay," he said.

She asked about the sculpture.

"It's comin along."

He didn't elaborate, and Sarah was at a momentary loss what to say next.

"I guess now's not a good time to talk about it," he said quietly.

"What?"

"The letter I wrote."

"What letter?"

A mechanical voice interrupted, demanding a deposit.

"Shit, I'm gonna run outta change." There was a click. Sarah could hear the coins going in and another click.

"Ben?"

"Yeah."

"I haven't gotten a letter. Sometimes the mail's terrible here. Things show up weeks late. What did you write?"

"Nothin. It ain't important. Thinkin a makin some pins along with the necklaces."

"Oh. Well, sure, that sounds fine. You got the book, didn't you?"

"Yeah. Look at it every night."

"Anna said she hasn't seen you."

"Been workin ten, twelve hours a day."

"But you have to get out. Be with people."

He gave a short laugh. "You wanna run my life, you can't do it from New York."

"I'm sorry. It's just that I need to know you're all right."

"I'm okay," he said. "Sarah?"

"Yes?"

"I think about you . . ."

Another mechanical click cut him off. Sarah sat numbly holding the phone for a moment, listening to the dial tone. She hung up, but he didn't call back.

• • •

David came. He talked. He ate. She tried to concentrate on what he was saying. Something about loyal clients and decorating his new office. He thought she looked pale and tired.

"This move was extremely stressful. The timing couldn't have been worse. You're going through hell with your mom, and I haven't been there for you."

"Would it be all right if we made this an early evening?" she asked. "I'm dead tired."

He reached across the table and took her hand. She looked at him, surprised by the concern in his face.

"I behaved like a jerk. I saw someone else a few times—"

"It's all right, David," she interjected.

"I have to say this, Sarah," he continued. "I don't know when or even if I'll ever be ready. I can't face another divorce."

"I know." She nodded, wishing he would go.

"But I'd like to pick up where we left off and see where it leads."

"Give me some time to think. I'll call you," she managed, closing the door after him.

She ran water for a hot bath, scalding hot. Ben said he thought about her. When? Every day? Once in a while? It had been seven weeks, and he'd called only to return her call.

Heartbreak seared through her center, a visceral, physical pain.

Stop it, she told herself. He'd never lied or promised anything. She could choose to rejoice in having been lucky enough to have had what they'd had, or dissect it and destroy the memory for no purpose.

She stayed in the bath until the water turned cold, wrapped up in a robe, climbed into bed, and cried herself to sleep.

•  •  •

Ben kept the generator on all night, seeking refuge in the sculpture. In a fever of humiliation, he damned himself for the years lost. If he'd listened to Trublo, things would be different now. He damned Alexander Graham Bell for inventing the telephone in the first place. Didn't he know what he was doing to other men? Men who didn't have easy words, who got tongue-tied if they couldn't see who they were talking to?

When Dawsen told him she'd called, he'd raced into town without a thought on his mind. Just her face in front of him and a knot in his guts. Then he'd stood there like a fool, holding the phone, listening to her cry, people pulling in and out waving at him, Big Jack and Horace Pruitt leaning on the pumps watching, like he was on TV.

He'd sounded like an asshole, but he couldn't get past his own bullshit; all he could think was she deserved a man who could get on a plane and hold her when she needed him, not some clown who had to call her from a pay phone, like a kid, running out of money.

He watched himself struggle against the current for a long time before he let loose his grip and slipped into the marble. Nothing he could do but let it carry him and have faith that the process itself would take him where he needed to be.

# CHAPTER 22

**R**osh Hashanah arrived in October. The leaves had changed, and a cold rain littered the ground with fallen splendor. The family sat together in temple.

"This is a time to ask forgiveness," the rabbi said. "To reach out to our loved ones, to our community, and to the world beyond. It is a time to forgive freely those who have wronged us, those who ask our pardon, and those who cannot ask. It is a time to forgive our own mistakes. It is a time to forgive God."

Sarah, her parents on one side, Eli and Lisa on the other, recited the traditional responses with the cantor and the rabbi, struggling for perspective.

She peeked at her mother, so frail, next to her. But Evelyn amazed them all. She'd completed six weeks of chemotherapy without complaint, her sense of humor intact. Sarah glanced at Eli and Lisa, their hands clasped in his lap. She'd spent time with them lately, enough to garner how their marriage worked. It wasn't some transcendent gift of love that kept the wheels greased. Perhaps it was, underneath, but on a daily basis it was dedication to each other and their boys, compromise, shared priorities, honesty. More than once she'd seen Lisa bite back a sharp response and answer mildly when Eli was grouchy. And often she'd seen Eli lift a task from Lisa's shoulders, such as picking up the boys from school or taking them away on a Saturday afternoon, without being asked, because he judged she needed time to herself.

Like a dance in which they took turns leading. It wasn't perfect. They disagreed. They lost patience and snapped. But they were committed to making it work.

"We're in it for the duration," Lisa told her wryly.

Sarah had always considered her parents' marriage off balance: her mother scurrying after her father, attempting to please a man who could not be pleased; her father bored and annoyed by his wife's nagging and solicitation. But the weight had shifted. Evelyn's illness terrified Sam. He'd become reluctant to leave her side, and it was he who was solicitous, worried that she'd tire herself, wondering if she was cold or hot, asking numerous times if she'd taken her medication.

Who was she to judge if guilt motivated him? What she knew was that her father had been happy in the Southwest but he'd chosen to honor his commitments. He'd remained with his wife and family and done his best.

"For the next ten days we take the opportunity to look back on the person we were a year ago to see how far we've come. We imagine the person we want to be next year. What changes can we make to create deeper, richer, more fulfilling lives?"

The Days of Awe offered a chance to reframe her life. She vowed to put her faith in the ritual and perform the tenets prescribed by the rabbi.

The next morning, before work, she examined her checkbook and made a list of her priorities, reshuffling them from an overload in the physical appearance category. She sent checks to several charities and volunteered to collect canned goods and work at a shelter on Christmas Day.

She took a walk with Lisa on the Saturday that fell in the middle of the holiday. They bundled up and tramped through her parents' neighborhood on a cold, clear morning discussing Evelyn's health, the boys, and Eli, until Sarah took a breath and blurted, "I had an affair when I was in the Southwest. He's an Indian."

She stopped short with a small laugh. "It's sad, isn't it? How we pigenhole people?"

Lisa didn't say anything; being a therapist made her easy with silence.

"I was there for ten days. It's been over two months, and I think about him constantly. I still dream about coyotes." Sarah sighed. "Obviously, I'm having trouble letting go."

Lisa nodded once and waited.

"With him, maybe for the first time in my life, I stopped trying to figure out what parts of myself to hold back. He seemed to want it all, even the smothering and neurosis. He'd just laugh and I'd relax."

"You've changed," Lisa said. "Eli and I were talking about it the other night. You seem more at ease and softer. We thought it was your mom's illness, but it's also this." Lisa linked her arm through Sarah's and gave a squeeze. "It'll get easier. You've taken a big step by talking about it."

•  •  •

The next evening, Sarah met David for dinner at an intimate Italian restaurant in the theater district. They were seated at a candlelit table in the rear, as David liked, behind the antipasti and a distance from the bar. He ordered a bottle of Chianti and then turned his attention to her.

"How are you, Sarah?"

His serious demeanor oddly gave her the desire to be flip, possibly from a residue of anger at the way he'd treated her. She took a sip of wine.

"I'm fine. Tell me how it feels to be self-employed?" Questions about business generally switched him into autopilot.

"Good," he said. "It's good."

"Did you get as many clients as you'd hoped?"

He smiled. "More."

"Really?"

He sat back, smiling. "It's been amazing."

"Tell me."

"Well, when I decided to do it, as you know, I went to Bloomfield because he's always been decent to me and I felt I owed it to him . . ."

They finished the bottle of wine with dinner, and whenever he started flagging, a question or two would set him off again.

The plates were cleared, the coffee served, and he came to the end of a story about how one of Bloomfield's wealthiest clients had called several days ago and asked to meet with him next week.

"That's wonderful," she said, putting her coffee down.

He looked at his watch with a laugh. "I did go on, didn't I?" His smiling eyes held hers. "What are you doing Saturday?"

She shook her head. "I don't see any point, David. I propose we congratulate each other on a game well played and call it a draw."

He lost his smile and stared at her. "I think I deserve more."

"All right. I had an affair in the Southwest. And I've decided it was my last affair."

"Meaning?"

"I don't want to pick up where we left off."

He asked for the check and insisted on riding home with her in the taxi. She assumed he'd simply drop her at her apartment, but he came up.

"What do you want, Sarah?"

"Honestly? I don't know. Right now I don't want anything. But someday I'm sure I'll feel unfulfilled without a family of my own. Actually, if my mother offered me the option of an arranged marriage, I might let her have a go." She opened the door for him. "I truly wish you the best, David."

He shook his head and sighed. "Call me if you change your mind."

• • •

"Why chicken and dumplings?" Sarah asked in the kitchen of her parents' house on the eve of Yom Kippur. Evelyn sat at the table reciting the recipe from memory. "You never make it any other time and it's not very good."

"Bobbi always made it." Evelyn's maternal grandmother had lived with the Shoenbergs when Evelyn was growing up. "She used to say dumplings made an easy fast."

"But she was a terrible cook."

"My brother Aaron always said the reason her dumplings made fasting easier was because they were still in his stomach during Kaddish."

"The half cup of goose fat might be a clue why. How about we substitute olive oil?"

"Olive oil, shmolive oil. We're Jewish, not Italian. I don't understand why you put olive oil in everything."

"Because it tastes better, why else? Borrowing good things from other cultures makes your own culture richer. Look at the Japanese."

"I don't know any Japanese. I only know Jewish. And olive

oil doesn't go with kreplah. But we have to substitute something. Your father forgot the goose fat when he went to the kosher butcher. I thought we could use chicken fat."

"Yuck, no way. As a matter of fact, I made kreplach with olive oil a couple of months ago, and it was terrific. I'm trying it with dumplings."

Evelyn acquiesced with a shrug, and Sarah involved herself in the process of dumpling making. A few minutes later she looked up and caught her mother gazing at her.

"What?"

"You are so pretty, Sarah. Such a good girl. A good daughter, a good cook. A lovely person."

"But?"

"But nothing."

Sarah smiled. "Thanks, Ma."

"For what?"

"For not saying, 'So how come you're not married?' "

Evelyn smiled back. "You're welcome."

• • •

After an early dinner to begin the fast, Eli took the boys home and the adults met at temple for Kol Nidre service. Played that night by a cellist from the New York Philharmonic, the deep, aching melody lingered in the soul.

At the end of the service it was traditional to embrace and wish one another a good holiday. Sarah hugged Evelyn and Lisa and then Eli.

He squeezed back just a little too hard, the way he had when they were young. "I'm sorry I spied on you in the shower that time with Robbie Blau, and I'm sorry I used to call you Melons."

"Don't start or we'll be here all night." She laughed.

She turned to Sam. She could never tell him in words, but

she believed she understood now how much he'd given up for all of them. "I'm so sorry, Daddy," she whispered.

"For what?" he whispered back. "You're a wonderful daughter."

They moved slowly through the crowded aisle, jammed with people greeting and hugging one another on the way out. Sarah felt a tap on her shoulder.

"Good Yontif," David said, enfolding her in a hug.

"What are you doing here?"

"I decided temple might be good for me," he answered.

"David Klein?" Evelyn said, her dark eyes registering a twinkle when Sarah made the introductions. "I don't recall Sarah ever mentioning you. Do you, Sam?"

"No," he said honestly.

"Did you two meet recently?"

"We've been friends for, how long has it been, Sarah, about nine months?"

"Nine months," Evelyn repeated, a slight surprise in her tone, glancing at Sarah in wonder at her never so much as mentioning him. Sarah turned away to hide her smile. "Well, it's a pleasure to meet you."

"I think you and my mother have a friend in common," David said, positioning himself next to Evelyn as they inched up the aisle. "Molly Lieberman?"

"No. Really? Molly is one of my dearest friends. How does your mother know her?"

"They play bridge every couple of weeks."

"Why, your mother must be Paula Klein!" Big surprise. "Well, isn't it a small world? I suppose you're breaking the fast with your family tomorrow night? Give your mother my regards."

"I will the next time I see her. They don't fast. I'm on my own tomorrow."

"Well, you're more than welcome to join us," Evelyn said.

"Thank you. I'd enjoy that."

Outside, David asked Sarah if he could speak to her for a moment.

"I've thought about what you said the other night," he said, extending his hand as if to shake. "How do you do? My name is David Klein."

•  •  •

Sarah spent Yom Kippur in the synagogue.

She pictured the day at the waterfall, her love for Ben overreaching anything she'd ever felt, the deep solace he'd seemed to take from her. In her mind she thanked him for all the precious things she'd carried away and tried to imagine touching his face. "Good-bye," she whispered.

That night David came to her familial home and fielded her mother's questions, her father's judgment, her brother's commiseration, and her sister-in-law's assessment, all with singular equanimity.

He and Eli knew each other from school and had mutual business interests. Eli had a client who was in need of a new business manager. David was always looking for a reliable attorney to refer to. Lisa gave her a thumbs-up behind his back. Evelyn's eyes sparkled and she didn't appear the least bit tired as he thanked her and bid her good night. Sarah walked him out to his car.

"I think that went reasonably well," he said, leaning over to give her a peck on the lips before opening his door. "What about you?"

"I had a nice time."

"Good. I'll call you in a couple of days."

Two weeks later he took her to dinner with his parents.

•  •  •

In November, shortly before Sarah's thirty-fourth birthday, a package from Ben arrived at Shoen's. It contained nine pieces: six necklaces, two pins, and a bracelet. At the bottom of the box was a present wrapped in white tissue and tied with a curly red ribbon. The card read:

> Happy Birthday. I made this thinking about you in lantern light. Wish you were here.
>
> Ben

It was a beautiful necklace, interwoven strands of water pearls and red and pink coral beads, scattered with touches of lapis, a gold clasp inlaid with lapis. Suddenly she was in his living room, in the glow of the lanterns, with the scent of oil and the texture of the Navajo blanket he kept on the sofa. He was thinking of her. He wished she were there. What would happen if she hopped on a plane? She could rent a car in Flagstaff and be at his house by late tonight.

And then? They'd make mad, passionate love for a few days and she'd come limping back to start forgetting all over again? Or worse, she'd drive out to his house and discover he wasn't alone.

She put the necklace in the case along with the others and wrote him a quick letter on Shoen's stationery, to enclose with his check.

> Dear Ben,
>
> I just received the jewelry. As expected, it's beautiful. Enclosed please find a check. You will notice it's for quite a bit more than you expect. I've increased pricing. I've also included payment for the necklace you sent for

my birthday. I can't possibly accept such an extravagant gift until you're a famous artist and can afford it. The thought was lovely. Thank you for the good wishes.

Sarah

. . .

"I'm not ready," Sarah told Lisa. They were sitting in the Friedmans' living room a month after Yom Kipper. Eli had persuaded Sam to go to soccer practice to watch Aaron. Joseph and Jeremy had a play date. "He says he's willing to wait."

Evelyn came into the room with tea service on a tray. "What are you two talking about?"

Sarah bounded up to take the tray.

"Don't start," Evelyn said, holding on. She carried it over and set it on the coffee table. "Sam's bad enough. He's driving me crazy. You've got to convince him to go back to work. This is the first time I've had the kitchen to myself since I came home from the hospital." She looked between them. "So?"

Sarah grinned at her mother. "Sex."

Evelyn nodded and poured the tea. "Sarah, let me tell you something. When a peach is ripe it's time to pick it. Don't stand there wishing it was an apple."

"What are you talking about?" Sarah laughed.

"The other one," Evelyn said, handing her a warm cup.

Sarah looked at Lisa, who raised her hands in innocence.

"Lisa didn't say anything to me," Evelyn said, handing Lisa a cup. "She didn't have to. Anyway, we don't need to talk about it. I can see you're feeling better. David is a nice boy. I think you'll be happy. Don't you, Lisa?"

"I do. Yes."

"We're not to that point yet," Sarah protested.

Evelyn sipped her tea. "Well, if you don't pick this peach, someone else will," she mused. "That's what my mother said to me. I was thirty years old, working in my parents' store. She sat me down and told me Sam Friedman was the last peach on the tree."

"Who was the apple?" Sarah asked.

"Danny Geller."

"The boy killed in the war? I thought he was just a friend."

"No. We were going to be married."

"You were engaged, and this is the first time you've ever mentioned it?"

"We had enough dead people to live with when you were growing up. I married your father and left Danny in the cemetery. That was one of Sam's wedding gifts to me. Finally I could stop feeling sorry for myself. I found someone who had more reason for sadness than I did. There's always a gift, my darling."

"I know, you say that whenever anything bad happens. I suppose you're going to tell me the cancer has given us a gift?"

"Many gifts." Evelyn smiled. "You'd be surprised."

# CHAPTER 23

At times Ben thought of the figure emerging from stone as something that had always existed inside the marble. At others, he knew it to be entirely his vision, substantiated by his skill alone. Always the marble participated: sometimes giving itself, releasing under his pressure; sometimes he was its minion, his will suppliant to its power. Mostly there were no thoughts, just a rhythm conjoining them and a process shared. It was his passion, his obsession, the nucleus of his life.

His days took on a regularity that allowed for maximum focus. He woke before dawn, ate, and cleaned up. At sunrise he took the coyotes for a swift hour's hike up the canyon in back of the house. When he returned he went to work, often unaware of the passage of time until his arms shook from exhaustion and it was dark outside. He showered, opened a few cans, usually pork and beans or chili and some kind of vegetable. The coyotes kept him company while he ate.

He worked every day, except the Sunday afternoon once a month when Alvin came over. In late October, he took two tedious weeks to fabricate jewelry because he needed money and he'd promised Sarah he'd send some things for Christmas sales.

He wondered if she was happy on her birthday. He pictured her talking to someone, laughing, moving her hands in the air the way she did, and then it was like he was staring into a dry well, dark and bottomless.

A week before Christmas, Anna Dawsen came out to invite him to their Christmas open house and read him the riot act about isolation and responsibility to his friends. He'd been managing to keep house by going into Lowman for a few hours every other week, but she caught him with a pile of dirty laundry and a bare cupboard.

"I'm not gonna let you live this way, Ben," she said. "You need to be with people, an we need to know you're okay. I'm not leavin til you promise to come to the party. Bring a carton a sodas."

"Okay," he said.

"But that's not enough. You gotta take one day a week off. Make it Sunday. You can come over for dinner, an I'll do your laundry."

"I'll think about it," he said.

The next day he bought a used combination washing machine and a dryer. Time he grew up.

● ● ●

On Christmas morning, Maria drove Casey to the airstrip near Willard so that Steve and Pam McDonnell, Jimmy's mother and stepfather, could pick her up in their Cessna Skyhawk and fly her back to spend a week with them and Jimmy in Phoenix.

Casey bounced up and down watching the plane land.

"Daddy came," she shouted, bounding out of the car as the plane touched ground. She raced over and flung herself into Jimmy's arms as soon as he jumped down from the last step. Maria stayed in the car until he started toward her carrying Casey, legs and arms wrapped around his middle, planting kisses on his forehead and cheeks.

"Hey," he said, waiting while Maria got out.

Steve waved to her from the cockpit. She returned the wave. "I guess your mom didn't come."

He shrugged. "She's still upset about you taking Casey and not letting us know where you were. And the stuff your lawyer brought up about me in court didn't help."

During the divorce, Maria's lawyer had used Jimmy's drug problems in an attempt to fight a joint custody arrangement. "You didn't need to do it. We coulda worked it out."

In truth it hadn't helped much. The judge had ruled that for one year they would share legal custody of Casey, but she would live with Maria and attend school in Many Hills. Jimmy and his folks got her every other weekend, a week at Christmas, and two months during the summer, as long as Jimmy submitted monthly documentation of consistent attendance and compliance with a drug rehabilitation program.

But once the year was up, her attorney told her, she'd have a fight on her hands. They'd take her back to court and try to get the arrangement switched on the grounds of Casey's education.

Pam McDonnell had cornered Maria in the hallway outside the courtroom.

"Why are you putting Casey through this?" she'd demanded. "Is it to get back at Jimmy? You can't possibly think it's in Casey's best interest to grow up on an Indian reservation with strangers, rather than with her family."

"What is it that bothers you?" Maria had answered. "That we don't know many people yet or that it's a reservation?"

"Both," she'd answered.

"I had to do what I think is right," Maria said tersely to Jimmy as she pulled Casey's suitcase out of the backseat.

"I know, but there's no reason for us to fight. Everybody wants the same thing. What's best for Casey. Ain't that right, baby?" he asked Casey.

"I wanna live with you. Mommy's mean. She won't let me watch TV an I can't drink sodas or stay up past ten, even when there's no school."

"Well, I wanna live with you too. You and your mom. But she doesn't want to right now."

"Why not?"

"Jimmy," Maria hissed through a clenched jaw.

"Because Daddy's been a bad boy, baby," he said, his sad eyes on Maria. "It's gonna take some time for Mommy to forgive him. But hey, we're gonna have a great time. Let me put you down so I can get your suitcase."

He covered Maria's hand on the handle before she could let go. "You gotta trust a little, Mary," he said softly. "Nobody wants to take anything away from you. What happened to that sweet girl I used to know? When'd you get to be so angry?"

She stared at him. You happened to me, she thought, tears starting. Twisting her hand away, she bent down, hiding her face from Casey, hugging the reluctant little body.

"Be a good girl," she said, standing stiffly. "I'll see you in a week."

•  •  •

The Dawsens had a full house for Christmas dinner. It looked like half the reservation was jammed into their home and spilling outside. Maria parked in the back pasture behind the barn and walked up past a group of jubilant children playing tag. She carried a large covered casserole, her contribution to the potluck, which she deposited on one of the tables set up in the living room. She stepped over more children to make her way to the kitchen, searching for a familiar face.

Millie Gorman, head of the PTA and her only friend, had invited her to the annual open house. She'd accepted because it was time she met people socially and began to make a life for herself apart from work and Casey. While this was awkward and uncomfortable, the thought of going back alone to her place was worse.

"Hi, Alvin," she said to the slumping figure passing through the doorway between the living room and kitchen. "I'm glad you're here."

She'd met him at Millie and Tom's and they went to the same church. She found his scar unnerving and never knew what to say to him, but today she actually had something to talk about.

"Maria," he said, looking about as uncomfortable as she felt. "Y-you look nice."

"Thank you," she said.

"I like blue."

"What?"

"Blue?" He pointed to her dress.

"Oh." She nodded. "Alvin? I heard you're a good gardener."

"I g-guess."

"I need my lawn mowed once a week, and my house is kind of dull outside. I was thinking the right flowers would make it nicer, but I don't know what to plant. Would you be interested in a job?"

"S-sure."

"Can you work Saturdays?"

"I g-got two jobs in the mornin an I b-babysit S-Saturday night. Maybe I could d-do it about f-five o'clock?"

"That's good."

"Okay. I'll come by."

"But you don't know where I live."

"Yeah. I d-do." His head bobbed. "Maria?"

"Yes?"

"You wanna g-go t-to th-the movies in Willard s-some-time?"

"I don't think so, Alvin. I don't have much free time."

"Casey can come too."

"I'll think about it."

"Okay," he said.

"Have you seen Millie? She invited me and I wanted to find her to say hello."

"In th-there," he said, pointing to the kitchen.

Millie was standing next to the refrigerator talking to an older white man. She introduced him to Maria as the host, Frank Dawsen.

"Pleasure," he said. "I bet you ain't got any trouble gettin the boys to come to school."

She didn't know what to say.

His eyes softened. "You're Hopi, aren't you?"

"Yes."

"I'm going to take her in hand, see she meets everybody," Millie said.

"An enviable task." Dawsen smiled. Millie kissed him on the cheek. Maria followed her out of the kitchen. The living room had become even more crowded than moments before.

"Do you know anybody?" Millie asked.

"Not really. I'm scared I'm going to run into some parents I should know but whose names I forget."

"They can't expect you to remember every parent's name. How many times have you met them? Once? Twice? I don't know how teachers even remember all the names of the kids in their classes. I'm always mixin mine up, and I've only got two—well three, if you count Tom." She laughed, sobering at the sight of Maria's face. "Don't worry, just stay with me. I'll make sure you know who's who."

They mingled for a while. People were discussing the arrest of a trucker in Gallup the previous week, accused of the murder of the little girl from Many Hills.

"He's been linked to five dead girls, about the same age, all on his regular route," Millie told Anna Dawsen.

"Good they found him," Anna said. "We can all sleep better. Still looks like we still got some nutcase cuttin heads off animals though."

It was weird. For at least two years someone had been shooting coyotes and foxes, cutting the heads off and leaving them set up on rocks. Then last year there'd been three sheep tied to a fence, so it looked like they were sitting up with their legs crossed, like humans. But the really crazy thing had turned up two days earlier, only a few feet off the highway outside town. Three cats, stiff and shellacked, sitting at a broken child's table with a tea set, dressed up in doll dresses, their heads on top of the table. A lot of it had been pilfered from the trash and repaired. Must have taken weeks of work. It was gruesome, but also kind of funny, except that the cats had been pets. People were riled.

Maria and Millie filled plates at the buffet and went outside in back to eat at one of the card tables the Dawsens had set up on the dirt driveway.

"Well, Merry Christmas, stranger. It's about time," Millie called, waving as Ben Lonefeather headed toward them, carrying a case of Mountain Dew. "The food's almost gone."

"Hey, Millie, Maria," he said.

"Why don't you put those in the kitchen, get a plate, and come out here and join us?" Millie said. "There's some things I wanna discuss with you."

"I know. The council's offer to offset the price of pavin the road and puttin in a phone line. You put in a lot a work an I appreciate it, Millie. I'm sorry I ain't responded. It's just I been real busy."

"Go get dinner." Millie laughed. "Stead of standin like a kid caught with his hand in a cookie jar. We'll be here."

Since the night they'd gone line dancing, Maria hadn't seen Ben. But she'd wondered if he was going to be at the party and had been disappointed when it appeared he wasn't.

It took him a long while to make it back to their table. By the time he did, they'd finished eating and had almost exhausted the main topic of conversation between them, Chippy's gifted intelligence and the limited options available to enrich his education. Millie thanked Maria for taking extra time with him. She said he'd been especially excited by a Hopi story Maria had found about the chipmunk chewing a hole up from the underworld so the people could come out.

They looked up as Ben sat down with a plate full of food and a heavy sigh. "You look like you're carryin the weight of the world," Millie said. "What's the matter?"

"Oh, I jus had a fight with one of them answerin machines."

"I guess it won."

"Millie?" Tom called from the back door. "Chippy's got a bloody nose."

"Damn," she said. "Excuse me."

Maria looked at Ben as he watched Millie go, aware that he probably would not have come back if Millie hadn't been there.

"Aw, I don't even know what I'm doin here," he said, ill at ease, turning to his plate. "I ain't fit company. Ain't even hungry. Think I'm gonna take this back into the kitchen an head home."

"Will you come to my house?"

He looked up quizzically. Before she had the chance to stop and think, she ran on. "My ex-husband just picked up my daughter to spend a week with his parents. I feel like somebody died—I'm so lonely. I can't face going back to an empty house."

"I know what you mean," he said slowly. "I don't much wanna go home either."

•  •  •

Ben got the picture as Maria talked: drug addiction, broken promises, in and out of rehab. Not as if he didn't have his own life to draw from, he supposed. Even so, he couldn't find much sympathy for her husband, dragging a wife and kid through hell. Looking for someone to save him from himself. It troubled him that Maria seemed to think she'd deserted the guy. More like she'd stayed longer than she should have.

She asked him about Sarah, and he told her she'd left a few days after the line dancing and they hadn't had much communication since. She asked if that made him sad. He said he didn't know, more like frustrated, and he guessed a big part of the problem was he wasn't much good on the phone. He explained about Sarah's insisting they be friends.

"Wouldn't even take a present I made her. Paid me for it. It's getting so I hate the idea a takin money from her for my work, you know? Makes me feel like a employee."

"But you're not working for her. She's just buying what you sell."

He sighed. "She was only in my house for ten days. It's been four months an I still miss her. Prob'ly sounds stupid, but I never missed anyone who wasn't dead before. Tried to call her from Dawsen's today. Got her answerin machine an hung up before I made a fool a myself."

"It sounds like you're lonely."

"Whew." He laughed. "You must be tired a listenin to my troubles." It was around midnight.

"I like listening to you."

"Yeah, that's somethin I'm just learnin—women are good for talking." He paused. "To," he added with a grin.

She looked confused.

"Sorry. Bad joke. Better be goin." He got up from her couch. "I mean it, Maria. It was good talkin to you. Made me feel a lot better."

She stood and moved into him, placing her hands on his shoulders. He was in the middle of a kiss before he'd given it a thought.

"Hold on," he said, pulling back. "What are we doin here?" His demurral was somewhat muted by the eagerness of his dick, which he figured she must have detected. Though, if she saw the humor, she gave no indication of it.

"It's okay," Maria said. "I'm not looking for anything permanent. I just need to be with somebody."

"You're a beautiful woman, Maria. There's lots a men like nothin better an to be with you."

She met his eyes. "Jimmy didn't . . . He couldn't do anything. The heroin took that away, along with everything else. I got to feeling like . . . I don't know. Like I wasn't real. I need to feel real."

Her hair smelled like vanilla. When she raised her face, he kissed her again. It had been too long for him too. Before Sarah, when he'd been half asleep, he'd had no problem doing without. Now he was wide-awake. He stood with his arms around Maria wondering if two people could ever get together without anybody getting hurt. Then he kissed the top of her head and told her he had to get home.

"Don't go."

"Got to. There's three hungry coyotes waitin. But, if you want, you can follow me."

•  •  •

He lit the lanterns and fed the coyotes. When he came into the bedroom, her clothes were folded neatly on the trunk and she was in bed, the covers pulled up to her chin.

"Let's see what you got under there?" He laughed, playing at trying to pull the blanket off.

"Don't," she yelped, grabbing it, her eyes huge. Scared.

"You sure you wanna do this?" He was beginning to think it wasn't such a good idea. "You don't have to."

"I want to."

She averted her eyes while he got out of his clothes and slipped under the covers. He felt for her and found her shaking like a rabbit.

"What's the matter?"

"I've never even kissed anyone but Jimmy."

He groaned internally. "It's okay," he said soothingly.

"Do you think you could just hold me for a while, first?"

"Sure," he said. He eased his arm under her so she could rest against his chest. "No problem," he said, stroking her hair. "You don't need to do nothin to get held."

She relaxed, and he drifted off to sleep. Sometime in the middle of the night she woke him, her hand on his face, her breast brushing his chest. "Do you still want to?"

He considered taking a pass, but his dick wasn't going for it. He got up and searched the bathroom until he found a single rubber wedged behind the medicine cabinet.

She waited quietly in the bed. He slipped in and moved to kiss her, slowly running his hand down her long, lean body.

She didn't respond much, so he slowed down, concentrating on the kissing. Still, she seemed cool. He pulled back and kissed her hairline, her cheek.

"What do you like?" he whispered.

"I don't know," she said.

It was okay for him, but he wasn't sure if she really enjoyed it. When he woke the next morning she'd taken her clothes into the bathroom with her. He pulled on his jeans and went out to make some coffee and start the generator. A few minutes later, she came up behind him at the stove.

"Thank you," she said softly.

"For what?"

"For understanding, I guess. An making me feel safe."

She was a pretty woman, but for some reason that didn't cheer him. He felt tired and a little sad.

"You hungry?"

She nodded, so he fried up some eggs and they sat out on the patio with coffee. He kept up his end of the conversation for a while, then he let it go, hankering to get back to the marble. She took the hint and told him she was going home.

"Can I come back sometime?"

"Sure," he said, walking her to her car. "You know the way."

# CHAPTER 24

For Hanukkah Sarah gave Lisa and Eli a promise to babysit on New Year's Eve. When David found out, he offered to pay someone to take her place.

She laughed. "Do you know how hard it is to find a babysitter for that night?"

"My secretary will do it," he told her the next day. "I have to give her two days off with pay."

"It's a gift, David. I can't take it back. Besides, I'm looking forward to it."

He grumbled and cajoled. There were several important parties given by clients he should attend.

Sarah had no intention of disappointing her nephews. David finally gave up and volunteered to assist her.

"You don't know what you're saying," she said.

"I have two brothers and a sister. I know what kids are like."

"Don't say I didn't warn you."

• • •

Sarah dressed for laser tag and packed a shopping bag of supplies: a large plastic container of her nephews' favorite stuffed cabbage, two bags of microwave popcorn, and four movies on DVD. David picked her up in a sparkling new silver Mercedes with a charcoal leather interior.

"They delivered it last night. I told them the deal hinged on getting it to me for today," he said, smiling at the success of his surprise.

She adjusted her comfy seat and relaxed. "Who cares about traffic?" she said languidly. "This is heaven."

They drove across town through slushy, sleeted rain and inched along with other cars jammed on the Queesboro Bridge, listening to mellow new age piano.

"I paid an extra twenty-five hundred for the sound system. Was it worth it?"

"Absolutely. Is it fun to drive?"

"It's different. I'm used to a sense of the road and the tight steering of the BMW. This is very smooth, almost loose. We'll see. I only took a two-year lease."

After the redbrick, working-class sprawl of Queens, the Long Island Expressway picked up a little speed.

"I think you're actually happier on your way to babysit tonight than you'd be all dressed up for party-hopping on Fifth Avenue," he said.

"I think you're right."

They left the Expressway and stopped at a supermarket for ice cream and sparkling apple cider.

She left David talking business in the living room with Eli, greeted the boys, and found Lisa in a killer black dress, applying eye shadow.

"I can't believe you talked David into this."

"I can't believe you're the mother of three."

Lisa raised her eyebrows. "Well?"

"What?"

"Have you?"

"Not yet."

"Don't you think it's about time?"

If David had envisioned a romantic evening, or even a re-laxing one, he'd been grossly mistaken. It started with a rous-ing game of laser tag outside, then a race around the house and up and down the stairs with plastic swords like the Three Mus-keteers, then skipping and pausing through the Star Wars tril-ogy, enacting battles and jumping on the couch. Jeremy slipped on the kitchen floor and bumped his head hard, biting his tongue so that it bled. Aaron swallowed a molar. They ate the cabbage, popped the corn, and polished off two cartons of ice cream.

At the stroke of twelve they opened the bottles of sparkling cider and toasted the New Year. Sarah gave each of them, in-cluding David, a peck on the lips and bustled the boys upstairs to bed. She read them the story of Medusa from a book of Greek myths, which frightened Joseph, so she stayed with him until he fell asleep and dozed off herself.

When she got back downstairs it was after one. David, stretched out on the couch, reached for her hand. "Lie down here and tell me—were you always so good with boys?"

She let herself be drawn down and kissed, pleasantly. His hand massaged the small of her back under her shirt, then moved up and unhooked her bra. The kiss intensified; Sarah rubbed her leg against him, wishing she felt more excited. He groaned and cupped her breast.

"Wait," she said. "I'm not about to risk my brother walk-ing in on anything too compromising. I'd never hear the end of it."

"Come home with me tonight," he said.

"It's not night anymore."

"Sarah?"

It had been two months. He'd made his intentions clear and hadn't wavered. She believed he'd accept it if she put him off a little longer, but would a few weeks really make a difference?

"All right," she said.

They got to his apartment by two thirty. As the front door closed, David gripped her arm and pulled her into a hungry kiss, quickly moving his hands under the sweater to her breasts. Sarah tried to go with it, but she wasn't aroused.

"Slow down, tiger," she whispered, backing up. He came forward, and she unbuttoned his shirt, one button at a time, looking him in the eye.

She moved into the bedroom and knelt on the bed, pulling him to her.

"Oh, God, Sarah," he whispered, cupping her head. "I've missed you."

"Your turn," he said a few minutes later, pressing her backward on the velvet bedspread. She looked up at the crystal ceiling fixture, imagining someone drawing her, just the sound of the pencil, until she was ready to slide down and slip him inside.

• • •

Sarah and Evelyn sipped tea in the coffee shop at Bloomingdale's late one afternoon near the end of January. They'd picked up Evelyn's prosthesis that morning and the majority of the day had been spent buying her a new wardrobe.

"Tired?" Sarah asked her mother.

"I feel good."

"Well, you look great."

Her hair was cut very short, and she'd let it go gray. Sarah thought it suited her. Still thin, she'd put on a little weight and no longer seemed frail. Her face had color. The doctors were giving her a six-week break from the chemo.

"Do you know how many years it's been since I wore a size eight? I just hope I can keep it long enough for the wedding." Her eyes twinkled.

"Ma, don't start." Sarah laughed.

"I didn't say whose wedding. There's always some wedding."

"I'm sure that's true. And, if you sat here long enough, someone you know would walk by and invite you to theirs."

"And I would have the perfect thing to wear." Evelyn indicated the Bloomingdale's bags. "All right. I correct myself. I hope I can stay a size eight long enough to show off everything we bought at least once. I spent a fortune."

"You deserve it, and Daddy can afford it."

"Sarah? Tell me something. Why were you angry with him when you came back from the Southwest?"

"I don't think I was angry," Sarah flubbed. "I just remember being a little tired. And worried."

"It was because of a woman named Camilla Huna, wasn't it?"

She stared at her mother.

"Sarah?"

"Yes."

Evelyn put down her teacup and closed her eyes. Sarah reached for her hand.

Evelyn opened her eyes. "It's all right, sweetheart. I think I've suspected for years. He looked forward to that trip months in advance, and he was always more affectionate when he came back. I just didn't want to rock the boat. Maybe I was afraid it would tip over." She sniffed and wiped her eyes with a napkin. "So what's she like?"

"Middle-aged. Mid-fifties, I guess. Heavy. I feel awful talking to you about it. Men are such bastards."

"He's not a bastard—he's your father. Is she married?"

"No. I don't think she ever has been."

"She's an artist?"

"Yes."

"American Indian?"

"Yes."

Evelyn smiled. "Everything he loves."

"I can't believe you're taking it like this."

"What should I do? Confront him? Throw a fit? Leave?"

Sarah didn't have an answer.

"Why should I make myself and everyone else miserable over something that's finished? He's not going on any more buying trips. And he's been wonderful since the cancer. It's good between us. He's even started taking medication for depression. He's doing everything I ask. I know he's trying to make it up to me." Evelyn sipped her tea. "The best thing I can do is let him."

• • •

"When are you coming back to the city?" David asked, reaching Sarah on her cell phone one freezing Saturday morning in February. She was at Lauren's, where she'd been trapped in the still unfurnished living room of the new Miramar house, listening to complaints for the past two hours. She was fed up with Lauren's whining about morning sickness and her annoyance at Louis's lack of interest in her pregnancy.

"Soon, why?"

"There's something I want to ask you."

"So ask."

"Not on the phone. I'll meet you at your place."

"I thought you wanted to work."

"I've decided to be a generous boss and give myself the afternoon off."

She drove home nervously. What did he want to ask that was so important? Obviously they were headed in the direction of marriage, but she wasn't ready. She had a question of her own. In the past she'd given a lot of herself in relationships, which seemed to make most of the men with whom she'd been involved, David among them, feel overwhelmed and smothered. Now the world had flipped, and she worried that David might eventually feel cheated because she gave so little.

"What's up?" she asked, opening the door of her apartment to David's smiling face. He strode in with confident excitement.

"Well"—he beamed—"I talked to your father this morning. He said it was fine with him."

"My father? What's fine?"

He reached into his coat pocket to retrieve a thick envelope. "Five days in the Bahamas, the first week in March. I haven't taken a day off in two years, and it's the last possible time I can take before tax season. I booked a flight and hotel."

"Oh," she said, giddy with relief. "That's a fabulous idea. I'd love it."

•  •  •

Sam awoke in semidarkness. The iridescent lights on the clock radio said 5:47 A.M. He turned very gently toward Evelyn. She was on her stomach, her head on a pillow, facing him. He liked watching her sleep. He remembered when they were first married, how she used to awaken smiling at him, and they'd make love.

He found her face fascinating, the arch of her brow, the depth of her cheek. It had been years since he'd contemplated the softness of her mouth. Most women her age had thin, shriveled lips, but Evelyn's were full.

He got up quietly and left the house. The bakery was closed but the twenty-four-hour grocery had croissants, fresh orange juice, fruit, and cold cuts. On his way out he stopped at the flower section; Evelyn liked lilies and tulips.

He felt like a boy filled with spring.

He put the flowers in a vase, set them on her nightstand, and sat on the bed. She opened her eyes and smiled, and it was as if a stone shattered in his heart.

"I'm sorry I haven't been the husband you deserve. I . . ."

"Sam," she said, cutting him off, touching his cheek, "you're a good husband. You've made me very happy. But there's one important thing you can do for me."

"What?"

"Let the guilt go. Just let it go."

•  •  •

David had given the travel agent carte blanche for the trip to Andros Island in the Bahamas, from the waterfront suite in a five-star hotel and massages in the afternoon to dinner at a different restaurant each night. Sarah was to be wined, dined, and pampered.

David spent the better part of the first morning on the phone with a client concerning the purchase of a new house. She explored the hotel and returned with espresso and croissants. They ate at a table on the balcony. He got another call, and several faxes were delivered to the room. She took a long walk down the glorious beach. When she came back to find him still on the phone, she stripped seductively in front him. He hung up before she put on her swimsuit.

"I thought you wanted to work," she said, running her finger along the zipper of his shorts.

"I'd rather be with you."

"Uh-huh." She pulled him toward the bed by the zipper.

She turned and sat in front of him on the bed, her legs crossed, unzipping, slowly. "Um," she said, smiling up at him and slipping her fingernail through the gaping opening in his boxers, "I want to negotiate."

"I'm listening."

"You can have one hour for business in the morning when I'm taking a walk and another in the afternoon when I'm getting ready for dinner. And that's all."

"Don't you think your tactics are a little unfair?"

She ran her nail along his erection and looked up at him.

"Agreed," he said.

• • •

"You're spending a fortune," she said the third night. They were lying in bed after a morning sail, lunch, snorkeling in the afternoon, massages, dinner, and the casino. The only thing they'd done for free was have sex.

He folded his arms under his head. "It's not a problem, Sarah. You know I own my apartment, but what you don't know is that I own two others in the building. My grandfather left sizable investments for each of us in trust. I haven't touched mine. And business is good; I'm hiring an associate and more secretarial staff. I intend to make a lot of money."

He rolled over toward her, resting his head on a bent arm. "I took a class, my first year as an undergraduate at Yale, Intro to Business 101 or something. I don't even remember the professor's name. What I remember is that he had us do an exercise that he promised would be the most important thing we'd ever learn in college. I forgot it as soon as the class was over and I had my A, but I started doing it again about a year ago. Make a list of the five most important things you intend to accomplish within the next five years. Then make one of the five things you intend to accomplish within the next year, then within the next month, then the next week, and finally the next day. Every day cross off what's been achieved and revamp your lists. Takes ten minutes or so. He guaranteed we'd achieve our five-year goals, whatever they were. It works like a charm. I've got two of mine already. Why are you smiling?"

"No reason," she said. In truth she'd had a thought she didn't feel compelled to share.

"Do you know how exciting you are?"

"Why?"

"Because I don't know what you're thinking. Sometimes you're so aloof, it drives me crazy, but I think that's why I couldn't let you go. I used to be sure of you, then suddenly I had no idea how you felt."

"And you like that?"

"I probably shouldn't tell you, but it turns me on, big time."

The last night David surprised her with a catered dinner in the room served on the terrace by candle and moonlight, a waiter in attendence.

As they raised their glasses for a champagne toast, Sarah found herself eyeballing a mammoth diamond ring, bubbling at the bottom of her glass.

"You're not drinking." He smiled.

"I'm afraid I'll choke," she said. My God, what was it? Three carats? She fished it out of the glass and dried it with her napkin. It sparkled brilliantly, a beautifully beveled circle set in platinum.

"Sarah?" David asked.

His tone let her know that he wasn't entirely certain of the answer, which she thought very sweet. She stared at the ring in her hand, feeling quite calm.

"I have a question for you," she said, impishly. "Is this on one of your lists? I mean, does it say, 'Ask Sarah to marry me,' or something equivalent, on any of them?"

He hesitated for the briefest moment. "Don't be ridiculous, Sarah. Of course not."

She smiled, slipping the ring on the finger for which it was intended, and which, she was pleased to discover, it fit perfectly.

On the return flight she sank into the cushy seat, ruminating.

He was overly ambitious and self-centered, but his family mattered to him. He was a good brother and son, capable of love and loyalty. He was used to being in control. She would have to pick her battles to get her way with the things that mattered most to her: where they'd live, which temple they'd attend, where their children would go to school.

He loved his work and could fairly be called a workaholic, but he was willing to have children, and he'd support them beautifully. He'd work long hours to support them. No doubt he'd eventually complain about it.

If she was savvy, if she kept herself attractive, played it smart and didn't nag too much, if she created a lovely home with happy children and a pleasant social life, he would be content. If she made the effort to meet him in the city for lunch, if they occasionally spent the night together in a hotel after they had children, she believed he would be faithful.

She imagined she could see the future. They'd argue about him spending more time with their children. She'd badger him to take a vacation. She didn't love him in the wild way she'd always thought she wanted, but she cared for him, very much. She could make him happy. They could be happy together. And they would make the people around them happy.

"What are you thinking about?" he asked.

"Did you have a big wedding, when you married Sharon?"

"Do we have to talk about that?"

"Yes. I want to know. Where was it?"

"The Beverly Hills Hotel, two hundred and fifty people, most of them doctors or hospital board members, whom I'd never met before and never saw again. In a word, awful."

"Well, you'll be relieved to hear my idea. What would you say to a small ceremony at my parents' house, just family and close friends? We could spend the night somewhere on the beach."

"Hmm. It sounds sweet. Unspoiled, like you." He smiled. "But it's your first, I mean, it's your only, wedding. You've waited a long time for Mr. Right. I think we should do it properly. Invite everyone."

"Is this about business?"

He laughed. "Not entirely. But the truth is some of my clients are friends. They'd be insulted if I didn't invite them to my wedding. And they know each other. I can't invite a few and not others. I'd like to do it someplace beautiful and ask them all."

"What do you mean by beautiful?"

"My mother has a contact at the Four Seasons. How does that sound?"

"Extremely expensive. My parents can't afford it. And I certainly can't."

"We're not teenagers. I'm perfectly capable of paying for my own wedding. I thought we could have it in the summer."

"Don't be silly. It will take months to plan, and the Four Seasons is probably booked for a year."

"I have no intention of waiting a year. Let me talk to my mother and see what she can do."

Sarah called Evelyn as soon as she got home. Then Lisa. Then Lauren, Miriam, and Becky.

"It's never too soon to start discussing the wedding," Lauren gushed. "I've kept all the information. The most important thing is to decide on a list of venues ASAP. *When* you do it is going to depend on *where* you can get a reservation."

But David had that handled by the next afternoon when he called her at Shoen's.

"We can have the ballroom of the Four Seasons and a suite for the weekend, if you're willing to be married the first Saturday in July. I checked with a rabbi. That night the Sabbath officially ends at eight twenty-five p.m. We can have the ceremony in candlelight."

"I don't believe it."

He laughed. "It's not that big a deal. They had a cancellation. My mother did it in ten minutes."

"My God, she's a powerhouse."

"She is. She's probably calling your mother to arrange a strategy session right now. But if she gets to be too much, just tell her to back off. I think she'll listen. Her other two daughters-in-law have paved the way."

Only Sam seemed less than ecstatic about the news.

"I suppose this means you'll be taking more time off."

"I'm sorry, Daddy. I've got less than four months to plan a wedding. Joshua's capable of picking up the slack for now, but you might want to think about hiring additional help. I don't know how long I'm going to keep working after we're married."

She hoped to move to Long Island and start trying for a baby right away. David wanted to stay in the city and wait a year or so. They were discussing it.

Sam sighed. "I suppose it's time for me to think about retirement."

"What's wrong? You don't seem very happy for me. You like David, don't you?"

"I like him all right. I suppose I wouldn't think anyone is good enough for you."

"Oh, Daddy," she said, kissing him on the cheek. "That's so sweet."

# CHAPTER 25

Ben completed the sculpture at the end of March. It seemed one day he was engrossed in it and the next he stood looking from the outside in the grip of profound loneliness.

Strange, because his life had never had so many people in it.

Every week since Christmas, on Sunday morning when he collected the week's mail, there'd been a note in the mailbox telling him where he was expected for dinner. Anna was determined. How else had she stayed married to Dawsen for so long?

He liked the evenings at Millie and Tom's the best: kids running in and out, doors slamming, Millie on the phone with one hand and cooking with the other. He and Tom would be outside throwing a ball with the boys, and Tom would be yelling back into the house, telling her about something that happened that day. Sometimes he'd get home grateful for the quiet, but even so, he looked forward to going back.

Maria came over every other Saturday night, when Casey was with her dad.

She'd started a few weeks after the first time, surprising him late in the afternoon while he was sculpting in the storeroom. It had almost been a replay of the day Sarah came. Littleman yapped, a woman's voice said his name. He'd spun around, so sure. But it was Maria who stood there, holding a bucket of chicken, her smile fading into an apology. He recovered quick as he could and told her he was glad to see her. A little while later he realized it was true.

Since then it had become a regular thing. Twice a month, she'd drive out in the evening after he was finished for the day. They'd eat dinner together, usually something she'd picked up at Stuckey's, and she'd spend the night.

They kept what was between them private. She was headed for another custody battle and didn't want to have to defend her reputation in court. Which was fine as far as he was concerned. He didn't want people treating them like a couple.

He told her she should go out and give some of the other guys around a chance. But she said she didn't want to. He kept expecting her to yell at him, tell him he better start appreciating her more or she'd stop coming by. He had to admit he'd miss her. She was a beautiful woman. Plenty of guys would love to be in his shoes.

Alvin, for one.

Shortly after Christmas, when he came for his monthly lesson, Alvin told him the real name of the beautiful woman who went to his church and he called the Madonna. Ben couldn't very well say she'd spent the night with him the week before. He felt like a dick, but he let it slide.

Alvin had gotten to be a real pain. He'd taken to stopping by again, and he always wanted to go with Ben to dinner on the nights he came for his lesson. He'd get moody if Ben re-

fused and whine that nobody liked him. Since he babysat on
Saturday night and left early for church on Sunday, he hadn't
seen Maria drive past his house. But it was only a matter of
time. Maybe the best thing to do would be to tell him the
truth and let the chips fall.

But none of these people, not Maria or Alvin or Tom or
Millie, or even Dawsen or Anna, came to mind as he stood in
front of the completed sculpture. It had taken everything he
had—physically, mentally, and spiritually—for seven months,
and he was more proud of it than anything he'd ever done. He
doubted any of them would understand.

He drove over to the Trublo house and ended up sitting in
the kitchen with Emma, the only room that hadn't already
been packed up. She was moving to Dallas in a few days to live
with her daughter.

"He died ten weeks ago," she told him. "I was gonna write
you, soon's I got settled. It's been crazy round here. What with
sellin the house an packin up thirty years' worth. People from
the gallery in New York came out for a few days, went through
everythin, shipped off his papers an odds an ends, for a retrospective. Thought I was gonna kill em before they finally got
outta my hair an let me pack in peace."

"I'm real sorry, Emma," Ben said.

"It was good he got the chance to see you last summer. It
troubled him, not knowin what happened to you." She
reached over and patted his hand. "I'm grateful you made it
over in time"

"So am I."

"Sorry you had to make the trip today for nothin but sad
news."

"Yeah. I was hopin to get some business advice. I'm ready
to look for a dealer, but I don't know the best way to go
about it."

"I'm afraid I'm not gonna be much help," she sighed. "Alan handled all that. The best one I can think for you to talk to is Sam Friedman. He could give you advice. Wait a minute. Don't you know his daughter?"

"Thing is I don't want to ask her."

"Well, the only other person I know is Bernard Levitt. A cold fish if you ask me. Alan's dealer for thirty years. Sent a card from France when he heard the news an didn't even come himself to collect Alan's papers an things. I got his number, if you want it."

Ben called the Levitt Gallery the next day from Dawsen's. The receptionist informed him that Bernard Levitt was in Europe. When he said he'd been a student of Alan Trublo, she connected him to Arnold Stern, an associate.

"It's great you called," he said. "I'm putting together a Trublo retrospective, for the Desert Museum, in California. But I'm a bit slight on the teaching years. Would you mind answering a few questions?"

They spoke for a half hour about Alan's time at the university.

"You've been extremely helpful," Stern said. "If you like, I'll arrange for you to receive tickets to the opening gala."

"Uh, thanks, but the reason I called is that I'm lookin for representation myself."

"Really? What kind of work do you do?"

Ben said he had some paintings but he was primarily a sculptor.

"Well, send me some pictures. I'll take a look."

The operator called back and told him the charge for the phone call was fifteen dollars.

"Shit," he complained, forking over the money to Dawsen. "I gotta call before eight in the morning from now on. An keep the calls short."

"Yeah, life's expensive. Hate to add more to the mix, but there's a couple things I been meanin to talk to you about. You gotta get your own telephone. Not that I mind you usin ours, but I'm sick a havin to drive out every time I wanna talk to you an so's everybody else. An you need a fence. You keep lettin them coyotes run wild, someone's gonna shoot em."

Driving home, he turned his attention to money. He hadn't earned any since November, when he'd sent the jewelry to Sarah. He'd lived frugally off what she'd paid, in order to finish the sculpture. He had three thousand dollars set aside, enough to pay for new materials and get by until he completed the work. She'd pay him right away, and he could keep on the way he was going. But he wasn't willing to work for her anymore. He was a sculptor not a jewelry maker.

The next day he drove into Gallup to speak with Horace Dodge. The banker was a friend of Henry's who'd loaned Ben the money to pay the Indian Market for damage he'd done the last time he was in Santa Fe, when he'd demolished four stalls worth of pottery. At that time Dodge sent an appraiser out to assess all the antique weavings and furnishings in Ben's house and had taken about a third of it for collateral.

Ben brought in the entire contents of his grandmother's trunk plus all the Hopi baskets and pottery he owned. He handed Dodge the appraiser's list and the receipts for all of his equipment. He signed an affidavit declaring he still owned the furniture the appraiser had valued so highly. Dodge set up a seventy-five-thousand-dollar credit line, and handed him a checkbook.

"Hope you know what you're doin," he said. "Hate to see you get into debt again." It had taken Ben seven years to pay off the last loan, for less money.

"Yeah, me, too," Ben said, standing up to shake hands.

• • •

Millie Gorman's responsibilities as head of tribal public relations included photographing people and events in case something happened the outside world might find interesting. Ben asked her to go with him to Flagstaff to advise on the purchase of photographic equipment.

"I'm glad to do this, but I'm not what you'd call a professional," she told him, climbing into the truck. "I jus took one class in photography six years ago."

"That's one more an I took," he answered.

He bought an expensive camera, a tripod, and four adjustable lights. That night he studied the manuals that came with the camera and lights trying to understand how to use them and compose shots. He examined the photographs in the book Sarah had sent, noting the difference between the full-page colored pictures and the high-contrast black-and-white coverage of some of the details in close-ups.

The next morning he set the storeroom up like a gallery—paintings spread along the walls, front and side, woodblocks at the back behind the camp installation, stone sculptures in the center on the table. Millie showed up in the afternoon to help get him started.

"Gosh," she said after she'd walked around the room. "I don't know a lot about art, but it seems really good. What's under the sheet in the corner?"

"My latest piece. I'm not photographing it."

She circled the camp scene again. "You show this to anyone?"

"Couple people. Why?"

"It just made me think of those animals last year."

"Well, I sure ain't been runnin around cuttin the heads off animals."

She smiled. "I know that. You were too busy lookin for lost kids."

She gave him a quick photography lesson, imparting what she knew about the difference between natural light from the windows and the artificial lights he'd bought.

He listened, looking through the viewfinder, snapping test shots, impatient with the learning curve. He'd have to wait for them to be developed before he'd understand the impact of light on film. Millie left with the exposed rolls of color film, and that night he shot close details in black-and-white. He moved the lights around and changed the speed of the film, anything he could think that would make a difference. He wouldn't be able to correct the black-and-white pictures because they'd take longer to develop, but he wanted to experiment in case he got lucky.

The next afternoon he dropped off six rolls of black-and-white film and picked up the developed color pictures. They looked washed out from too much undifferentiated light, so he taped sheets over the storehouse windows and tried covering the artificial lights with some drawing paper he colored in pastels. The developed pictures he picked up the following afternoon were much improved.

The next few days he shot dozens of rolls of color film, working slowly and methodically, piece by piece. By the time they were developed, the black-and-white pictures were ready. He examined all the photographs, selecting one in color of each of his paintings and several of each of the wood blocks, using the black-and-white close-ups for details as was done in the book Sarah gave him. He chose a dozen color pictures and four black-and-whites of the camp installation and three each in color of *Deer Hunters, The Supplicant,* and *The Wild Horse.* He printed notes on materials, dimensions, and titles for each piece.

When he was satisfied he'd done the best he could, he drove into Willard and mailed the package to the Levitt Gallery, Federal Express.

During the time he'd been working on the photographs, the tribe had started to erect telephone poles alongside the road, continuing the line from where they stopped in front of Alvin's house. Ben hated the way they looked, and he had to split the cost, but if things went well, he'd need a phone for business.

Tom's crew had been out for three days digging a trench around five acres of land in back of the house so they could set the chain link a foot into the ground to keep the coyotes from digging under it. The fence would be in by the middle of next week.

In two weeks, they were going to start paving the road.

Fences, telephones, paved roads, and debt: things Ben had sworn he never wanted in his life. Yet here he was, inviting them in. He shook his head at the wonder of it.

• • •

Maria stood in front of her little house, holding a twenty-dollar bill, waiting for Alvin to finish watering the marigolds he'd just planted so she could pay him.

In an hour, after a shower, she'd put on the white cotton dress she'd bought in Willard yesterday when she took Casey to the airstrip, pick up something for dinner, and drive out to Ben's. He liked her in white and she was already anticipating his smile.

Alvin whistled while he watered and glanced sideways at her. Over the past months he'd weeded the front yard and planted yellow daisies around the walkway and along the front of the house. They brightened things up so you almost forgot about the drab brown stucco. A few times during the week he stopped by to water, which was a good thing, because between PTA and Brownies, as well as teaching, cooking, cleaning, and helping Casey with homework, she would forget.

He asked her to the movies almost every time he saw her. At first she'd been concerned about his feelings and had invented excuses. When he didn't get the message, her reasons got more and more flimsy until a child could see through them. Still, he continued to ask, taking her rejection with a quick nod as if it was expected. She no longer bothered with excuses at all and occasionally wondered what he'd do if she actually said yes. It seemed like he didn't really expect her to go but just enjoyed asking for some reason of his own.

A rumble at the end of the block turned her head. Her heart lurched as she watched Jimmy thunder up the quiet street on his Harley. He stopped abruptly in front of her, pulled the bike back to rest on the kickstand, and slipped off his helmet.

"Hey," he said, regarding her wistfully.

"What are you doing here? Where's Casey?"

"With my folks."

"You're supposed to be with her. That's the point of visitation."

"I needed to see you. She's okay with them."

"I asked you not to come here unless it's for Casey."

Tired lines etched the sides of his mouth. His ocean eyes were rimmed in red, from lack of sleep or the long ride, she couldn't tell.

"I know, baby, but you got to talk to me sometime. You can't just close the door without a word." He swung his leg over the bike and pulled off his saddle pack.

"Maria?" Alvin said, shutting off the hose. "I g-got to be g-goin. Millie's waitin f-for me to babysit."

"Oh, sure," she said, handing him the twenty. "Thanks."

"Y-you're welcome." He remained standing next to her, uneasily.

Jimmy extended his hand. "Jimmy Farrell. Maria's husband. How's it going?"

Alvin took the hand, confused. "F-fine th-thanks." He glanced at Maria before pocketing the money and walking to his truck.

Jimmy shouldered the saddle pack. "You got something going on there, Mary?" he asked as they walked inside the little dark house.

"That's none of your business. You're not my husband anymore."

"Seems a likely lad," he said sarcastically, dropping the saddle pack on the couch.

"I don't have to listen to your opinions about people I know."

"Probably not much choice around here."

"Jimmy, you've got to let go. I'm making a new life."

"Yeah." He looked around the room. "I can see."

She'd gone to a discount furniture store in Gallup with her first paycheck and furnished the whole house in one day. She kept it neat and clean, but it didn't feel like a home. Nothing did.

"What I don't understand is why here? You're not even Navajo."

"I got a job here."

"My mother thinks you're doing it to get back at me."

"When did you start listening to your mother? Anyway, she's wrong. I'm doing this to get away from you."

"Damn, that's cold. You sound just like a white chick. How come you're being such a bitch?" He walked around the corner to the kitchen and got two Cokes out of the refrigerator. "You were so gentle, Maria," he said, handing her one. "Brown skin an big eyes. Didn't know how pretty you were. Didn't know nothin bout sex, drugs, an rock an roll." He gave a short, ironic laugh and reached into his pocket for a cigarette.

"I'd rather you didn't smoke in here."

He lit a match. "Sorry." His hand shook lighting the cigarette. He dropped the match in the sink. "You know me, baby. Gotta break the rules."

She knew only too well. Why else had he married her a month after they met? She'd slept with him whenever he wanted. She would have moved in, if he asked, without any demands. But he wanted to get married. She'd been so happy. He'd told her it was to surprise his folks, so they did it on her eighteenth birthday, in Nevada, on the way to meet them. It had been a surprise. She'd sat on the sofa in the living room, holding her backpack, trying not to hear the yelling—a horrible, ugly argument about her. Jimmy had come into the room and grabbed her arm and the backpack, practically yanking her out the door.

"Fuck em," he'd yelled into the wind as they raced away on the Harley. "Fuck em both."

"Why do you want to get away from me?" he asked softly. "I love you so much." He reached out, pulling her in, resting his forehead against hers. "Oh, God, Mary, I'm sorry."

He'd brought a pint of J&B that he poured into the Coke can as he drank. When he'd finished the cigarette, he fumbled in his saddle pack for a joint.

"What are you doing? You're supposed to stay clean."

"Yeah," he said with a rueful smile. He took a few quick drags and held the smoke in his lungs. "It's a joke, Maria. Steve's got a friend owns a bunch of rehabs. The forms are filled out and sent. They've never even seen me." He shrugged and took another hit. "They got the bases covered, baby. You know how it is. They even hired a guy to drive by and check up on you. They know you're spending the night with someone near Lowman when Casey's with me. I said they got it wrong—you were probably going to your mom's. If you got a lover, baby, you might want to cover your tracks."

"Why are you telling me this?"

He didn't answer.

"What's going on, Jimmy?"

"Nothing. I'm just sick of them. Unless you've seen them operate firsthand, it's tough to appreciate their venality. They make me feel like a saint. Nothing gets in the way of whatever they want. Casey's better off here with you."

"Then why are you living with them?"

He sighed, leaning his head back against the couch and putting his feet up on the coffee table. Mellowing out with the buzz he got from the grass and liquor. " 'Cause I ain't got nowhere else to go,' " he sang his own lyric, smiling. "I sold the warehouse, Mary. Everything's gone. The guys won't take me back. I don't blame them. Can't find words anymore. Steal from myself an don't even know it half the time. Stay up writing all night and end up with crap. I'm tired, Maria. I've said it all. Don't have any more to say." He opened his eyes. "It's over between us? You're sure?"

She'd sworn she'd never leave him. She'd stay as long as he wanted her. But in the end, she couldn't keep her word. She'd deserted him to save herself.

"I'm sorry, Jimmy," she whispered.

"It's okay, baby." He smiled, closing his eyes again. "You did your best. If anyone could have made it work, it would have been you. None of it's your fault. You don't have anything to be sorry for."

She went to him on the couch and sat close, raising her hand to soothe his rubbled cheek. He took it, kissing the palm.

"I stopped by the Hopi reservation on my way here."

"You did? Why?"

"It's something I always wanted to see, and you never would take me. Use to bother me. It's your home, baby. You should be living there. The most peaceful place I've ever seen. I stood up on the bluff there with your mom and we talked for a while."

"You met my mother?"

"Yeah. I told her how sorry I was about the way things turned out. Told her it wasn't your fault. She's a nice lady. I left something for you at her house."

"What?"

"You can find out the next time you visit."

He finished the pint and dozed off. Maria took a shower and slipped into the white dress. Ben was probably hungry and wondering where she was. She decided to pick up some chicken and take it out to him, just to explain what was going on. She'd have to hurry to be back when Jimmy woke up. He never slept for long, and she needed to make sure he ate and sobered up before he got back on the Harley.

But when she got out to the living room, he was sitting at the dining table hunched over a candle, the wretched sweet scent of melting heroin in the air.

"Oh, Jimmy, please don't."

"Got to, Mary." His attention captured by the sticky brown junk melting in the spoon. A little saliva escaped from the corner of his mouth as he took a cotton ball and soaked up the liquid, drawing it carefully into a new syringe. He cleaned up the discarded wrapping and washed the spoon, then carried the candle over to the coffee table.

Maria stood in the center of the room, torn as she had been throughout her marriage. Wanting to leave but unable to go, wondering if she should make him go instead. Where? Some alley like before when she'd kicked him out?

He sat on the couch looking at her, pale with solemn long-ing, reading her mind.

"Just this once, Mary," he begged softly. "Stay til I nod off. Never asked you before. Never will again. Please, baby? I don't wanna be alone. Just one time. Hold me while I shoot."

She couldn't fight it anymore.

He wrapped the rubber tube around his arm, flicked the skin, and injected the needle. "You look like an angel," he whispered, pulling her arms around him. He moaned as the drug came on, sinking into her, mumbling his thanks. "Like heaven," he sighed. She stroked the hair back from his forehead, remembering the way it used to be when she first heard him sing, before the band and the recording contracts and tours, before the heroin. How he could hold a room of people spellbound for hours with nothing but his guitar and his whisper-soft voice telling the truth. She kissed his cheek.

Something was wrong. He was too still. She slapped his face, but he didn't respond. She climbed out from under him, pushed him onto the floor, and pumped his chest, breathing into his mouth. Yelling at him, she slapped him again. Noth-ing. She crawled, dragging him with her, to grab the phone and call for help.

● ● ●

Ben waited at his place for Maria until concern got the best of him. He locked the coyotes up in the house and drove to her place. He arrived as the ambulance pulled away and stayed with her through the police questioning and the phone call to Jimmy's parents.

Looking through the dead man's saddle pack, he came across a folded piece of paper. He read it, then handed it to her.

Maria,

I wanted to die in your arms. If I've done that, I'm at peace. I'm sorry for putting you through it all. Forgive me.

Ben carried her to bed, crawled in next to her, and held her until she finally stopped crying and fell asleep. He was half asleep himself when something disturbed him. For a moment he still wasn't sure if he was awake. Alvin's face peered in the window, pale as the moon. By the time Ben got out of the bed and made it to the front door, Alvin's truck was turning the corner at the end of the block.

# CHAPTER 26

**B**en boarded the coyotes at Dawsen's and drove Maria to Phoenix, where they picked up Casey at Jimmy's parents'. Maria gripped his arm while they waited on the front porch. The child ran to her mother and held on tight. The door closed behind her.

In the truck she told her mom that her dad had come into her room the previous morning. He'd said he was going away and might not see her again. If he didn't come back, he wanted her to know her mom was the one who loved her best of anyone in the world and she'd better appreciate it.

"How could he die, Mommy?" she asked. "He wasn't old. Grandma said he had an accident on his motorcycle, but I don't believe her."

"Sometimes people die even when they're not old, Casey. They get sick, like my daddy, or they lose heart. I think that's what happened to Daddy. He lost heart."

They rented two rooms next to each other in a motel until the funeral could be arranged. Maria crept into Ben's bed for comfort late at night, when Casey was sleeping.

• • •

More than two thousand people showed up for the funeral, too many to fit inside the church. It was covered by the local news. The service went on for hours as friends and fans took turns speaking about Jimmy Farrell and what his music had meant to them. Boom boxes played his recordings outside the church, and people sat on the steps crying.

Two days later, Maria met with Jimmy's parents at a lawyer's office for the reading of a brief will. Jimmy was to be cremated, his ashes scattered over the Grand Canyon. He'd created a trust for Casey—all royalties and the proceeds from the sale of everything he owned—to be administered by the Hopi tribal council until Casey was twenty-one. He'd written a letter to be read aloud to the family.

It was his hope that Casey would be raised on the Hopi reservation among her mother's people, but he realized it was up to Maria to determine where she and Casey would live. His parents were to abide by any decision Maria made. They were not to sue for grandparents' rights. They were advised to treat Maria with the respect she deserved: "If you meet her halfway, she'll share Casey with you. If you don't, you shouldn't be entitled to see her daughter."

On the way back to Many Hills Ben and Maria stopped by the Hopi reservation, where Jimmy had left his guitar for Maria.

• • •

Ben dropped Maria and Casey off in Many Hills and swung by Dawsen's to pick up the coyotes. They jumped on him, yapping like he'd been gone for a year instead of five days. Maybe it seemed a year to them.

"You look like hell," Dawsen said.

"Yeah, well, I feel like hell," he said, fishing in his pocket for the boarding payment. Money seemed to be flowing through his fingers like spilled beer. The trip to Phoenix had cost over a thousand dollars, and that was a drop in the bucket when he considered his other expenses.

He drove home, the weight of obligation settling on his shoulders. Maria was making no demands. A woman of grace and beauty, she'd let him know she cared for him but was content with whatever he was willing to give. Which wasn't much. But he couldn't keep pretending it was just sex twice a month.

He stopped at his mailbox for the week's mail and tore open the letter from the Levitt Gallery.

Dear Mr. Lonefeather,

Thank you for giving us the opportunity to view your work by photograph. I can't remember ever receiving so many and such well-done pictures from an artist. Unfortunately, although your work shows talent and skill, it isn't cutting-edge.

If you wish the photographs returned, please contact Alice and she will send them. Bernard Levitt joins me in wishing you the best of luck.

Arnold Stern

Ben unlocked the storeroom and stood in front of the sculpture, running his hand lightly over the smooth, polished curves. He'd done it as much for the look on her face as for any single reason. The look she'd had the first time she'd seen his work.

Disappointment rocked him.

He couldn't go to New York without the guarantee of a dealer. He was in major debt. In less than two weeks he'd have to write a check from the credit line to make the first payment on the loan. He'd better order jewelry supplies tomorrow. At some point he guessed he'd humble himself and ask her help finding a dealer for the art.

Suddenly Littleman—yapping furiously, hair raised all up his back—raced in from the desert past the storeroom door toward the house.

Why the hell was it he couldn't seem to get a minute's peace? He walked across the patio, intercepting the two females and commanding them to stay outside. The frantic yaps continued, then a loud explosive crack, like a rifle shot. What the fuck? He dodged to the side of the doorway and peered in. Alvin was standing in the center of the room, a rifle aimed down at Littleman on the floor, bloody, whimpering.

"Alvin!"

Alvin's eyes burned black. His face pale as a specter, he raised the rifle. Ben ducked back. The blast nicked his upper arm and sailed out the open doorway behind him. Alvin unlocked the chamber to reload from bullets ready in his hand. Ben sprang forward, scrambling to reach him in time. He tackled Alvin's legs, knocking him over as the chamber locked and the rifle discharged straight up, bringing down clumps of plaster and shattered tile pieces from the ceiling. Bullets from Alvin's hand and pocket clattered in the debris on the floor as Ben crawled over him, reaching for the weapon, and Alvin scooted backward to attempt another shot. Ben spied Eagle coming up along the side. He yelled for her to go back and gripped the barrel with his hand, shoving Alvin's arm down. The round discharged along the floor, missing her by an inch or less, blowing a hole through his front wall.

Alvin screamed as Sage clamped his ankle. Ben pulled the

rifle out of his grasp. Eagle moved in, snarling. "Hold," Ben commanded, tossing the rifle out of the way. The coyote took position above Alvin's neck. "Don't move or she'll rip your throat out."

"D–don't hurt me," Alvin moaned, lying still.

Ben ignored him, ripping at his bloody shirt, tying it tight around his bleeding arm as he crawled over to Littleman. "Okay, boy?" he queried.

The coyote whined. His eyes moved, trying to find Ben, but the rest of his body remained still. The wound, in the chest and shoulder area, gaped open. Blood seeped out, covering his coat, dripping onto the rug.

"I'm s–s–sorry," Alvin blubbered. "Ben? I'm s–s–sorry. I d–didn't mean to s–shoot. It s–scared me."

"Back," Ben commanded. The two coyotes backed off warily. "Gimme your shirt," he yelled, cutting through Alvin's incoherent whimpering. While Alvin sat up and unbuttoned his shirt, Ben found the pressure point on Littleman and pressed it with the remains of his T-shirt. Alvin got his shirt off; the red scar ran over his shoulder and down his arm.

"It's okay, boy," Ben crooned to Littleman. Alvin stared at him, his eyes scared. Ben locked on them.

"You still wanna kill me?"

Alvin shook his head.

"Then you got a choice. Get the fuck outta here or help me."

Alvin swallowed. "Help."

"You got a knife?"

Alvin nodded.

"Get a sheet. From the bed, in there." He indicated the direction with his head. He bent to Littleman. "You with me, boy? Stay with me," he whispered. "Make a cut an then rip it into strips," he shouted at Alvin.

Alvin did as he was told. Ben kept the pressure on with one

hand and wrapped a strip of sheet around Littleman's upper
body with the other. He removed the soaked piece of T-shirt
and lifted the torso. Alvin pulled the strip around underneath,
and Ben tied it tightly in place. They repeated the process three
times before the wound was covered, but Ben still had to keep
the pressure on with his hand, otherwise blood streamed out.

"Get the blanket from the couch."

Alvin slipped it under the coyote as Ben held him up. Ben
gently wrapped the blanket around Littleman and lifted the
bundle into his arms.

"You drive. My truck. The shocks are better." He whistled
to the females and walked as smoothly as possible outside the
open front door. The coyotes jumped into the truck bed.

"Make sure the back is locked." He didn't want to lose another one because of Alvin's driving. Alvin opened the passenger door and Ben slid in, gently as he could. "Littleman?" he
whispered. The coyote looked at him, still conscious.
"Smooth," he told Alvin. "Fast as you can, but smooth."

Alvin started the truck and pulled away.

Ben's hand was inside the blanket so he could feel the
heartbeat and keep pressure on the wound. He murmured
comfort to the frightened animal as they drove, monitoring the
heart and breathing rate, which by the time they got to the intersection with the highway were increasingly rapid.

"D-D-Dawsen's?" Alvin asked, finding his voice. Eyes staring straight ahead, hands clenched on the wheel, his jaw tight,
fighting tears.

"Yeah," Ben said. "You think you can get us there sometime today?"

•  •  •

Alvin opened the door to Ben's side and ran inside.
Dawsen came to the back door, holding the screen.

"What happened?"

"Alvin shot him."

"Shit," Dawsen said, moving ahead to the clinic. He was scrubbing up as Ben carried the coyote in.

"I can't feel a heartbeat. I had one up to a minute ago, but I lost it."

"Lay him on the table with the injury up," Dawsen said. "Just let the blanket drop." He bent over Littleman, shining a light into his eye. He listened with the stethoscope. "His heart's stopped. He's in shock, lost too much blood."

He reached into Littleman's mouth and throat with his fingers, coming up with a wad of bloody mucous. "You're gonna give him artificial respiration," he said, opening a cupboard and drawer, grabbing a vial of Adrenalin, throwing instructions to Ben as he worked.

"Hold his snout closed. Get down and cover it completely with your mouth. Take a breath an try to blow it slow and steady into his nose."

Ben squatted and did it while Dawsen loaded a syringe. "Slow down. Only wanna do about six a minute." He gave the shot and then began pressing and releasing the side of Littleman's chest, counting.

"Stop," he said, pausing to listen with a stethoscope. "Keep goin." They worked for another minute.

"Okay." He cut the bandages Ben had made from the sheet and told Ben to take them out to the barn where Kyle, his assistant, could run a blood check and draw blood from the other coyotes. "Tell him to come in an help soon's he can. You wait in the living room."

Alvin was sitting on the couch, crying, when Ben came in and sat down facing him. "I started seein her at Christmas. I shoulda told you."

Alvin didn't look up. "Why d-did you need to ball her?"

"I don't know. Cause I liked her. We liked each other."

"D–dirty liar."

Ben sighed. He guessed he was.

"D–don't think I don't know what you do. I know. I r–read what you wrote. You make me s–sick."

"What are you talkin about?"

"You know."

"What'd you read that I wrote?"

"Huh?" Alvin looked up, ashen.

"I swear I could break your neck as easy as look at you, if you bullshit me."

Alvin didn't answer.

Ben reached out with one hand and gripped him by the neck. "You take my letter?"

Alvin stared like a caught mouse. "I g–got it at my house. Y–you c–can have it back."

Ben let go and got up abruptly to move across the room, a fire working his guts. If he wasn't careful, he could kill Alvin. He leaned against the wall and folded his arms so he could hold on to them.

"This ain't jus about Maria. You been fuckin with me."

"Don't s–shut me out," Alvin whimpered.

"Shut you outta where? Whadda you talkin about?"

Alvin's eyes narrowed and turned dark. His voice deepened. "You don't see anythin. It's in front a you but you don't see. I'm sick an tired a doin your dirty work. I don't wanna be like you anymore."

"What dirty work?"

"You know." His eyes darted around the room. Red blotches appeared on his pale cheeks.

"What dirty work, Alvin?"

Then the bluster slipped away, and he put his head back in his hands and started crying again.

"You kill them animals?"

Alvin didn't answer. Ben's rage slipped away, replaced by cold loathing. Too bad, he thought, walking outside—anger felt better.

Dawsen came out after three hours.

"The bone was shattered. Had to take the leg off at the shoulder and repair it best I could. If he makes it, I can't say for sure he'll be able to walk. May have to put him down anyway." He put his hand on Ben's shoulder. "It was smart, you bringin in the other coyotes. Without their blood he wouldn't have a chance. Animals usually do okay pretty quick or they die. If he's still around tomorrow, I'd say it's a good sign."

"Thanks, man. You need to keep a tally, let me know what I owe."

"I ain't worried. Come on. I better take a look at your arm."

Dawsen cleaned the wound, took ten stitches, and gave Ben a tetanus shot. While he worked, Ben told him what happened with Alvin.

"I'll call the tribal police," Dawsen said. "They're gonna wanna take him in, least for a couple days."

"He's got somethin a mine I want back, an his truck's at my place. I gotta go home, take a look at the damage an pack some stuff so I can stay here with Littleman. Tell em they can pick him up in a hour at his place."

● ● ●

Ben got a pang of the sorrow of missed opportunity when he drove Alvin home and entered the house for the first time since Fanny died. If he'd ever stopped by for any reason, he'd have seen that Alvin had crossed the invisible but very real line, from ordinary crazy into madness. Maybe he would have cared enough then to try to help him.

The place was close and dim, rank with mildew and rotting garbage, like a cave in hell. Dozens of drawings—stuck through nails on the walls, ripped apart and strewn over the filthy carpet—with only one subject. Alvin wasn't much of an artist, but Ben could recognize himself.

"Get the letter," he said tersely.

Alvin slumped into the bedroom and returned with a smudged envelope. He handed it over, avoiding Ben's glare. Ben slipped the folded paper out, so faded and worn from handling it had turned gray.

Alvin still needed a ride back to Ben's to pick up his truck. They rode in silence.

"Go home an wait for the police," Ben told him. Alvin couldn't look him in the eye, which was just as well. "Stay outta my way. I show up somewhere, you leave. Jus keep the fuck outta my way."

He stood in front, watching until Alvin's truck disappeared.

His house was a wreck. A hole the size of a cannonball in the roof and one with cracks all the way to both corners in the front wall. The floor was littered with debris, the rug and tiles soaked with blood. He left it as it was and, for the first time in memory, locked all the doors and windows.

He sat out in Dawsen's barn with the coyotes, next to the cage where Littleman lay. He was there when the coyote groggily opened his eyes—about three a.m. After that, he slept.

●  ●  ●

Ben's downward trend turned into a spiral that seemed bottomless. Almost funny, he thought. Too bad he'd lost his sense of humor. Must have come off with Littleman's shoulder.

Three weeks after the shooting the coyote couldn't walk, couldn't even get himself up. Dawsen figured it was because he'd had to take so much tissue and bone that the body balance had been thrown off, and Littleman couldn't figure a way to compensate. Ben had brought him home after a week but had to keep him in the storeroom because he pissed over himself. He'd only eat if Ben fed him by hand, and he was so light that lifting him was like picking up a cat.

His spirit seemed broken. The other coyotes knew something was wrong and stayed near him, at least one of them, all the time, even though he curled his lip at them or snapped for no reason Ben could fathom. He wagged his tail weakly when Ben came in the room or spoke to him. Sometimes he whined and tried to struggle to his feet to follow when Ben left. But mostly he lay still, staring at nothing.

"Time to put him down," Dawsen said, cutting the stitches from the wound that had healed in an angry circle of rough skin, indented into the chest. "Shame we put him through it all. Continuing on is cruelty," he said.

Ben felt the ground slipping away from under him. "I'll bring him back tomorrow." His throat was parched. He wanted a drink.

"Now's as good a time as any."

"For you maybe. I need the night."

He was uncomfortable with Dawsen. Like Littleman's lost leg, the balance was off. He'd always taken more from both the Dawsens than he could ever give back. That was their way. They liked to give: time, advice, food, a place to stay. It had never made him feel beholden. He'd looked on them as family. Things were different now. Maybe because he was past the age to be dependent on anyone, maybe because he resented not having a family of his own.

He carried Littleman out through the kitchen where Anna had a pot of soup going.

"Get a bowl and sit down," she said.

"Naw. Thanks, Anna. Not hungry. I gotta get back." He avoided the concerned look on her face and continued outside.

In turmoil—sick at the thought of tomorrow, his guts knotted in impotent rage—he couldn't find a place to stand and see clearly. He was twenty-five thousand dollars in debt to the bank, and he just kept sinking deeper. Even though Dawsen had cut payment for his own services down to a fraction, Littleman's vet bills were over five hundred dollars because of antibiotics, lab tests, X-rays. The repairs on his house, materials alone, had cost another two thousand. He'd stopped them paving the road; it ended a mile past Alvin's, but he had to pay for half of what they'd done.

All thoughts of sculpture had been put aside. For the next year at least, he'd be making jewelry. He'd ordered supplies. It would take another week for the package to arrive.

The coyote nestled close on the truck seat, resting his head on Ben's lap.

"Had two good years, didn't we, boy?" he said, clearing his throat and stroking the soft head as he drove. "That's more an a lot a the wild ones get."

He stopped at the market and bought a steak. Heaviness in his legs like a muscle ache made it hard to keep putting one foot in front of the other. Like trudging uphill with a back full of stones.

He had a bottle at home, under the sink.

"Buddy, you gonna get the best meal you ever ate," he said as he got back in the truck.

Maria's car was parked in front when he got home. He'd only seen her once since the trip to Phoenix. She'd come by while he was at Dawsen's to tell him she was sorry about Littleman. Casey was having a tough time, and it was hard for her to get away. He'd told her he was fine and not to worry. He'd been relieved. Like she'd let him off the hook.

• • •

She faced him, her eyes filled with hurt trust, the way he pictured Littleman's would be tomorrow. A trial run.

"I can't, Maria. I wish I could."

"You said it was over with her. Don't you want to move on?"

"I gotta do it alone."

"But, why? It's not like I'm asking you to marry me or anything. I'm not even tryin to change what we have. If you just wanna keep it the way it's been, it's okay."

"You may be willin to settle for that, but you deserve better. It ain't okay with me for you to go on treatin the little I give you like it's somethin special. Makes me feel like a liar."

After she left he picked up his new phone and dialed Sarah's number at home.

"So, you finally got a phone," she said, surprised to hear from him. "Congratulations. But where have you been for four months?"

"I was finishin the sculpture an then some stuff happened. It's complicated. Things got outta hand."

"What things? You sound terrible. What's the matter?"

"I'm kinda in financial straits. I ordered a lot of jewelry supplies, but before I start, I need to know you're gonna buy it all."

"Well, I'm not spending much time at Shoen's right now and I'm not sure my father will want to take it on. We may have to find another venue. How many pieces did you have in mind?"

"I gotta sell whatever I can make, maybe seventy-five, a hundred pieces in the next year."

"What about your art?"

"On hold."

"And you won't tell me why?"

"It's a long story. Can you handle the jewelry?"

"Send it as you make it, a few pieces at a time. We'll start with them at Shoen's. If I have to, I'll find another dealer. Don't worry. It'll be okay."

"Thanks."

"You're welcome."

"Sarah?"

"Yes?"

"I never stopped thinkin about you."

She was quiet. He waited.

"I'm sorry. I don't know how to . . ."

"Jus say it."

"I'm getting married."

•  •  •

He sat on the floor to feed the steak to Littleman. Afterward, he carried the coyote outside to the table so he could see the moon and stars. The night sky spread like a pinpricked canopy, warm and fragrant with the spring.

He kept replaying her piteous tone telling him how sorry she was. The thought of her writing him a check humiliated him. He couldn't abide the idea of her running around New York trying to find someone to take on his jewelry.

He was losing hold of his life, like sliding down a crevice with nothing to grab on to but twigs that kept breaking. He'd known Sarah was in love with him, yet somehow he'd let her go. He'd sunk himself in major debt, based on the notion that when Levitt saw his pictures he'd cream in his pants. He'd seen Alvin was troubled, but hadn't considered he might be a threat. How much more wrong could he be?

He couldn't face tomorrow.

Reaching far into the back of the cupboard under the sink, he remembered something Henry had said one night when he came home drunk and found the old man sitting outside alone.

"The strength of a man is found in the dark times. How much he can take an still go on appreciatin the small things, like a pretty night, or the taste of a good cup of coffee."

Well, he couldn't find the strength, he thought, grasping the bottle, Tom n' Jerry's, half full. He unscrewed the cap. The sharp honeyed scent hit him between the eyes; his mouth went dry and his hand shook as he carried it outside and sat down on the bench next to Littleman. The coyote wagged his tail. Ben stroked his head and with effort replaced the cap, setting the bottle on the table. Not tonight. Tomorrow, after he left Dawsen's.

He whistled for the females and carried Littleman into the bedroom of the studio. He'd been sleeping in the main house in Sarah's bed, but tonight he wanted his old pallet, so the three of them could be next to him.

They snuggled close. For a long time he lay awake, listening to their breathing, the soft yaps and whimpers of coyote dreams. Then he must have drifted off, because he woke to darkness and the silence of an empty room.

He got up and walked outside. The moon had set; the only light came from stars. He could just make out the shadowy figures on the patio. Littleman was lodged between the two females, their bodies close enough to keep him from falling over. He hopped a few steps and leaned, first to one side and then to the other, using them for balance. It was slow going, but the distance gradually increased, and after a while he was moving haltingly on his own. He stopped next to the wall of the storeroom. Sage positioned herself so one of her front legs was almost under him. He shifted his weight against her and slowly lifted a back leg an inch or two off the ground to take a piss.

Ben could hear it splatter against the patio as he stood in the doorway of the studio, crying like a kid.


The next morning he was on the phone giving Alice at the Levitt Gallery his address so she could send the pictures back when Littleman made his way from the patio into the house, sniffing around the kitchen floor for crumbs before dropping down with a thump and a groan at Ben's feet. Like it was the most normal thing in the world.

"It's probably none of my business," Alice said, "but I hope you're going to try some other galleries."

Ben bent over to give the coyote a scratch behind the ears. "Tell you what," he said. "Hold on to em for a day or two. I may have somewhere else you can send em."

He punched in the number.

"Shoen's." It was an old man's voice.

"Can I speak to Sam Friedman?"

# PART THREE

# CHAPTER 27

Evelyn's call woke Sarah up.

"What are you doing today?"

Sarah opened her daily calendar.

"Um, this morning I'm giving the guest list a final check and faxing it to the secretarial service. The invitations should go out this week. Then I'm shopping for shoes with Lauren and Becky. In the afternoon I have appointments with the music coordinator and a photographer, and I'm meeting David at Layers to taste cakes."

"Don't move. I'm coming in."

She arrived with bagels and the Long Island real estate section from the paper, an hour and a half later.

"Your father's closing Shoen's."

"When?"

"Next week. He's going to empty the entire store and turn it into a gallery for a one-man show."

"I don't believe it." How incredibly aggravating, she thought. It was exactly what she'd always wanted to do.

"He's planning to open the last Friday in June. He says he's a reform Jew and God would understand Friday is the best night for an opening."

"A week before my wedding? What's the rush?"

"The artist insisted. And you know how your father is. 'What's the big deal? A wedding is one night.' But I sat him down and told him if he wanted us to support this, he had to promise it wouldn't interfere. He's to be on time for the rehearsal, he's hosting the rehearsal dinner, and he's going to the bachelor party. Did I leave out anything?"

"Who's the artist?"

"Someone who studied with Alan Trublo. Something feather. I've never seen Sam like this. Jumping out of his skin, he's so excited. He says it's like another chance with Trublo. I brought pictures. You have to tell me if he's crazy or if this man is really as good as he thinks."

Sarah didn't need to look at pictures but she did, to gather her wits. "They're wonderful," she said. Who took them? she wondered. Did Ben even own a camera? She'd talked to him a week ago for the first time in months. He wasn't sculpting. He needed money. He was supposedly deep into jewelry. Now suddenly he's connected with her father and is coming to New York?

"Sarah, listen to me. Your father has a dream. In all the years we're married it's the first dream he's had. You have to help him."

Sarah sank into a chair, or her legs gave way, she wasn't sure which. Evelyn rattled on. "After this, he's promised to retire and take me on a cruise. If we have any money left. I'm kidding. He's explained it all to me. It's a risk, but even if he loses his shirt we'll still be all right."

"Ma, I," Sarah began.

Evelyn waved her arm, interrupting. "You spent four years in a gallery." She paused meaningfully. "Now it will be worth it."

•  •  •

Sarah couldn't get to Shoen's until just after closing time that evening. A large sign—FINAL SALE 50% OFF ENTIRE STOCK—hung in the window. The showroom looked like a garage sale, everything out and labeled, a third of the inventory already gone. She found Sam in the office going over the day's receipts and told him she thought the show was a bad idea.

"Make up your mind," he said. "You've been after me for years to find young artists and move into fine art. Now you don't think I know what I'm doing?"

"I meant for us to start slowly and build a reputation with artists who couldn't get other representation," Sarah said. "I've seen this man's work. He deserves a first-class show, with serious collectors, first-string press, museum attention."

"And I'll do my best to give him one. He's not a simpleton. He understands the situation. How well do you know him? You met him once to buy jewelry. We've talked about the risk. I suggested he take some time to look for another dealer. He doesn't want to. He knows he can trust me, because of our connection through Alan, and it's important to him to do it soon."

"Why?"

Sam shrugged. "Why else with an artist? Money. He's taken a loan and he needs to sell some pieces before it comes due. I told him I'd do the show and handle immediate sales, and I'll help him find another dealer."

Why, after years of biding his time, was Ben rushing into this? And why hadn't he come to her for help? She found it extremely frustrating.

She looked over the notes on her father's desk: plans for re-furbishing the gallery space, lists of personal contacts all over the country—collectors, museum directors, art historians, re-viewers, dozens upon dozens of names—every professional with whom he had any association. At least he had a place to start. The draft of a letter underneath, however, was garbled. She picked up a preliminary press release laced with typos and odd syntax.

"I'll handle the press and correspondence from my com-puter at home starting with this list. I'll type up a general let-ter and we can add personal remarks as we go."

Sam shrugged. "It's up to you. Don't do me any favors."

"And, um, do you have a phone number for Mr. Lone-feather? In case I need to ask him a question?"


She called that night.

"Oh, hey, Sarah. How you doin?" His voice sounded per-fectly cheerful and relaxed.

"I'm fine. My father just told me he's . . . you're doing a show. At Shoen's."

"Yeah, took your advice."

"Yes. Well, I was wondering why you're . . . I mean, what's the hurry? I thought you said you wouldn't be ready so soon."

"Work went faster than I thought. Somethin wrong?"

"Well, I'm confused actually. I thought I made it clear I'd help you when you were ready."

"Yeah, I know. But then you said you weren't workin much an I figured you were busy with the weddin an all. Emma spoke highly a your dad, so I called him."

# CHAPTER 28

For the next six weeks Ben worked methodically, sparing no expense. In addition to preparations for the trip, he finished paving the road and completed the fencing. Before it was over he figured to go through a lot of the credit line.

He spoke to Sam several times a week as things moved along in New York. They cleared the space, repaired the floors and walls, sanded, painted. A few collectors who'd seen the pictures had expressed interest. Sam had submitted his name to a new museum in Chicago for a possible sculpture commission. Of course it was all just potential, but Sam's enthusiasm was real.

Whenever he considered what he stood to lose, he'd just turn his attention to Littleman. The coyote got stronger every day, hobbling into the house to yap if strangers showed up, hopping through the desert in back trying to catch jackrabbits. He'd never catch a jackrabbit again, but he was alive and trying.

Even if the worst happened and the show was a total bust, Ben knew he'd make it through. He'd start back on jewelry or cutting stones, and work his way out of debt again. Long as he could feed the coyotes, long as they had a roof over their heads, even if it turned out to be on an empty house, he'd survive.

He planned to make the trip short but he was still concerned about leaving them penned up at Dawsen's.

"They'll be okay," Dawsen said. "Two or three weeks, they won't know the difference."

"I'll be back in two."

He had no intention of staying for the wedding. He'd pushed Sam to do the show the last week in June because he wanted to see her before she got married. Look at her face-to-face, make sure she knew what she was doing and it was done between them. He'd hoped he could get her to let him stay at her place—after all, she'd stayed at his. But once she called about the show he knew that wasn't going to happen. She'd been guarded and confused, trying to figure out what he wanted. He'd take a bet her family didn't know about the two of them, and she didn't want them to.

He thought maybe he could sleep at the gallery for the first week and move to a motel for a couple nights after the show opened. But when he brought up the idea Sam wouldn't hear of it and insisted he stay with them on Long Island. He had to admit he was curious to see what her family was like, put the faces to the stories.

He hired a moving company out of Los Angeles that specialized in transporting art and antiques. Cost a fortune, but he judged it worth every penny when he saw their equipment and the way they handled his stuff. He just stood back and let them do their job, prepared to head off as soon as they were loaded. He was driving his truck to New York and planned to

get there a day before they did, to be at the gallery for unloading.

He tried to keep his thoughts off her. That wasn't all this
was about. It was also about him, standing up and taking his
shot—the chance to show his work in the arena where the big
boys played.

# CHAPTER 29

**M**iriam and Daniel Lowenstein, partners in a landscape architectural firm, had been married ten years. They had two children, a thriving business, and a lovely Long Island house surrounded by a gorgeous garden. The perfect setting for a baby shower.

Thirty-five women laughed and chattered at brightly covered tables under a long arbor. Caterers bustled about with elegant dishes, offering mimosas to the women who weren't pregnant, iced tea or Perrier to those who were. Dozens of children squealed and laughed, swinging on the swing set, climbing the jungle gym, chasing the ducks on the lawn, all under the attention of a variety of caregivers.

The gifts were extravagant, or clever, or extremely functional; the weather was warm and clear. Lauren, nearing the end of a difficult pregnancy, rallied and kept her complaints to a minimum, issuing only one comment about being stuck like a beached whale in suburbia all week while Louis enjoyed long days of freedom in the city.

All in all, the elements combined to make it a smashing party.

Sarah basked in the afterglow with Miriam and Becky and a pitcher of iced tea in Miriam's living room.

"Worth every penny," she said, handing a check to Miriam. "I'm sorry I wasn't more help." Technically, she'd been one of the hostesses.

"Don't be silly. Your plate's full."

In addition to preparations for the wedding in thirteen days, she'd also been working long hours on the show at the gallery.

"I have to say, I'm enjoying it," she said. "I wish my father wasn't closing. I'd stay on."

"Why is he?" Becky asked.

"Because he and my mother agreed it would just be for the one show. They want to spend more time together. Apparently they've fallen in love. She had no problem with him using a chunk of their retirement to realize his dream."

"My mother would have a cow." Becky grimaced.

"Unfortunately, it may prove to be too much to start a gallery and an artist's career at the same time. I'm having difficulty getting press coverage. We may have a wonderful show that no one will see."

"We'll see." Miriam smiled. Becky nodded.

"Thanks." Sarah laughed. "But I mean press and serious collectors."

Ben was due to arrive at her parents' house that afternoon. What would they think of him? What would he make of them? On second thought, she could live the rest of her life without knowing. She'd like the whole thing to disappear, except that Sam walked around smiling like the picture she'd seen at Camilla Huna's, which thrilled Evelyn no end.

"You seem stressed. Are you all right?" Becky asked.

"Just overloaded."

She dreaded seeing Ben again. Lisa, the only person with whom she could talk about it, wondered why, if Sarah was content with her decision to marry David, seeing an old lover should disturb her so much. Maybe the best thing would be to confront the situation quickly and move past it. She had a good reason to stop by her parents' house that afternoon. There was to be a dinner party at David's club that night, and she needed somewhere to change. But how could she see Ben for the first time in front of her parents and pretend he was merely an acquaintance?

"So what are you going to do after the wedding?" Miriam asked.

"I'd like to start trying for a baby. I'm in the process of convincing David we should look for a house out here. But he's encouraging me to find a job in Manhattan, at another gallery or even a museum. I was up half the night worrying about my future—husband, house, children, work."

"You can't have it all," Miriam said seriously.

"*You* do," Sarah replied.

"Sarah, I work five miles from where I live. I don't ride the train an hour each way to get to the city every day. Once you have a baby, believe me, the commute will be impossible. It's two hours of wasted time."

"And if you aren't working and David's in the city all day, you'll be bored to death out here," Becky said. "Look at Lauren."

They all groaned.

"What about you?" Sarah asked Becky.

"Truth? I feel isolated sometimes, even with Gymboree and Mommy and Me, and Matt only goes in three days a week. The way David works, you'd never see him."

"I thought we'd keep an apartment and I could go in a couple of nights a week."

"That's a terrible idea," Becky yelped. "You don't want to be out here being a mommy and leave your husband in the city with an apartment at his disposal. Forget it."

"So you think we'll have to live in Manhattan?"

"If you're both going to work there? Absolutely."

"It's possible to raise children in the city," Miriam said. "People do it all the time."

She'd already agreed to move into David's apartment after the wedding. She'd assumed it would be temporary, but now she wasn't sure. It would be foolish to try to push him into a lifestyle they both might regret.

• • •

Sarah had changed clothes at Lauren's house that afternoon for the formal dinner, hosted by David's older brother, Michael, and his wife, Judy, in the library of the Oakview Country Club. The guests included David's three best friends with their wives, along with Lauren and Louis, the only couple among her friends David enjoyed. Which meant the only man among her closest friends' husbands who golfed and liked to talk investments. Sarah shifted in her seat, fatigued from a long day of socializing.

The Oakview had been founded in the 40s by several Jewish families in response to their restriction from the surrounding country clubs. It remained predominantly Jewish as well as expensive and exclusive. David's family had been members since he was a child; he'd spent the best times of his youth swimming in the pool, playing games in the rec room, meeting girls at the dances.

It was still his favorite place to socialize. He played golf on Sundays with friends throughout the summer, as he had that afternoon, and usually had dinner before driving back to the city. He liked Sarah to join him, along with his friends' wives who played golf in their own foursome. He'd suggested she take lessons.

Her thoughts drifted to Ben, at that moment sitting at the dinner table in her parents' home, surrounded by her family.

"It depends whether you want to see your husband on Sunday or have the day to yourself," Lauren said, in reference to the golf lesson issue. She and Louis were applying for membership in Oakview. At Sarah's request, David had written a recommendation.

"Must be your first child." Shelly, the wife of Stuart, an investment banker, indicated Lauren's pregnancy with a superior smile. "You'll soon find out you never have Sunday to yourself. Walking around the course gossiping with my friends sure beats staying home finger painting."

"It's also the best way to keep an eye on things," Leah chimed in, smiling at her husband, Carl, a stockbroker. She was a real estate agent. "You'd be shocked how many single women spend Sunday afternoon in the bar, waiting for the foursomes to come in."

It was almost ten. Sarah stifled a yawn. By the time she got home, it would be too late to call Lisa.

"Have you met Mickey, the pro?" Julie, the wife of David's third friend, Max, a tax attorney, asked.

"Not yet."

"Oh, God, you've got to see Mickey . . ." Leah interjected.

"Mickey's the best . . ." Shelly asserted.

"He's adorable. You'll love him," Julie assured her.

Michael stood up and offered an after-dinner toast. "To my brother David. It took some time, but you finally got it right." He raised his glass to Sarah.

• • •

It was after one a.m. by the time Sarah slipped on her robe and walked David, redressed in his suit, to the door of her apartment. He liked to go to work from his own place.

"It's going to be a long week," he said.

She rarely knew in advance when she'd see him on week-nights. Things often got hectic for him late in the day; nine evenings out of ten he worked late. They spent weekends to-gether and had lunch two or three times during the week, which fueled David's arguments against moving away from the city. He often used lunch for social business meetings and wanted her to join him when his clients brought their wives. If he didn't have a meeting, instead of eating in a restaurant, they would grab a sandwich and convene at one of their apartments for time alone.

"Don't forget tomorrow," he said.

"I remember, the Guttermans."

"Guttman," he corrected with a chuckle. "Phil was a sig-nificant factor in my ability to leave Bloomfield. They've just made an unexpected profit on some real estate. We're going to discuss shelters. I'm counting on you to keep Liz entertained. You'll like her—she's on the board of one of the museums. The Frick? The Guggenheim? I've forgotten. Wear that green suit you bought last week. She'll be dressed."

• • •

Early the next morning Sarah called Lisa.

"How was it?"

"Dinner? The brisket was a little salty."

"Lisa."

Lisa laughed. "It was fine. The boys were thrilled because they got to actually meet a real American Indian. They pep-pered him with questions, but he seemed okay with it. He told them about the Navajo rite of passage, and he must know something about Judaism, because he compared it to a Bar

Mitzvah, which they thought very cool. After dinner, he told them stories in the living room and we all came in and listened. He's so easygoing. He relaxed us all, even Eli. And of course your father was in heaven."

"Do you think Ma guessed?"

"I don't think so. She didn't say anything." Lisa sighed. "I can see why you were attracted to him. He's very handsome."

• • •

Even with the time change, Ben was up before seven. He wandered downstairs and found Sarah's mother alone in the kitchen.

She offered him a cup of coffee.

He took it, thanking her.

"I hope you slept well?"

"Yes, ma'am."

"You're in my daughter Sarah's old room."

"Yes, ma'am," he said.

"She couldn't join us last night. She was having dinner with her fiancé. But then you've already met her. She came back from the Southwest with some of your jewelry."

"Yes, ma'am."

"Sit," Evelyn said, indicating a seat for him at the table.

Ben sat down.

"You know she's getting married very soon?"

Ben nodded.

Evelyn sipped her coffee. "Preparing a wedding is a stressful time in a woman's life. Especially the kind of wedding Sarah and David are planning. Right now Sarah's very emotional."

She paused, glancing at him. "Have you ever been married?"

"No, ma'am."

"Well, it's normal to get cold feet before a wedding. Everybody wonders. It would be a shame for someone who knew her in the past to take advantage of her natural nervousness and create doubts that might spoil this special time for her."

"Mrs. Friedman, I didn't come here to try an convince her she's makin a mistake."

Evelyn looked him dead in the eye. "Sarah came home from the Southwest terribly hurt. But she's very happy now. If you care for her at all, you'll wish her well and let it go at that."

Blindsided, Ben remembered her pale face as she drove away. He'd been pissed off by that bullshit note she'd sent, and he'd figured to hear from her when she got his letter, so he'd focused on the sculpture and waited. He'd never thought she might be suffering like he was. When he finally talked to her on the phone and she was crying about her mom and the cancer, all he'd thought was how helpless he felt. He hadn't considered that she might also have been crying over him.

Evelyn regarded him thoughtfully. "Will you make me a promise?"

He waited.

"Promise that you will take no for an answer."

He nodded slowly.

# CHAPTER 30

**S**arah got to Shoen's Monday morning just after ten.

She saw Ben before he saw her. Tall, broad shoulders, wearing jeans and a T-shirt. He was hard to miss, standing behind the moving van parked in the loading dock. She spun around and took refuge behind the corner to breathe.

A few minutes later she came up beside him. "Hello."

He turned and said her name.

She'd misjudged the distance. She stepped back, flushing, not quite meeting his eyes. "Sorry. I'm a little nervous. About the situation . . . Uh, my father doesn't know. I've never told my family."

He shrugged. "Nobody's business."

She nodded and turned to watch the compression elevator lower to street level. "I'm glad you're doing this."

He didn't say anything. In a moment, his attention shifted back to the truck. He seemed easy and unruffled.

She walked into the gallery, her shaky legs contributing to the foolish feeling that maybe she was overreacting just a tad.

A number of screens stood in the corner, ready to be put to use as a backdrop for some of the paintings. Dozens of new lights ran along tracks across the ceiling. Sam had left the interior design to her. She'd chosen an eggshell white, matte finish, for the walls and had arranged for the floors to be repaired and refinished a light wheat color.

Sam bustled out from the office, his face radiant. "You have to see," he said, beckoning her over to the *Wild Horse* already displayed on a pedestal.

She ran her hand along the curling wind-whipped mane, grounded by the interplay of mortality and eternal stone Ben's marble evoked. The rest is gone in a heartbeat, she thought. This lasts forever.

"It's something, isn't it?" Sam beamed proudly around the new gallery.

"It's going to be spectacular."

She stayed through the morning to work on the program in the office and answer the phone. The unloading process absorbed Ben's attention, so she could observe him through the window without being noticed. After a while, as she watched the art begin to claim the space and complete the transformation of Shoenberg's Furniture into Shoen's Gallery, her heart found its accustomed rhythm. She could do this.

The movers took their lunch break, and Sam suggested the three of them go around the corner to the deli.

"I can't," she said, checking her watch for the first time. "I'm meeting David for lunch at one. I have to leave in ten minutes."

"You mind goin alone, Sam?" Ben said. "I wanna finish markin this wall."

"I'll bring you a sandwich," Sam answered, opening the door. "What would you like?"

"Anything'll be fine."

"Daddy? Give me a second to get my things, and I'll walk with you."

"Uh, Sarah?" Ben said quickly. "I was hopin you'd hold the other end a the tape. Be a help if you could."

Sam smiled and walked out the door.

Sarah watched him pass the front of the gallery. Her heart took a leap as she moved toward Ben, reaching for the tape measure. Their fingers touched. He didn't release it. She raised her eyes.

"Thought we was friends."

"We are," she said.

"Then how come this is the first time you looked at me? How you doin, Sarah?" he asked gently.

"I'm all right."

"You look different, all done up. Never seen you wearin high heels. You happy?"

"Yes," she answered quickly, then asked softly, "Are you?"

"I'm okay."

A moment passed between them. Bittersweet, Sarah thought, to face him again, but not awful.

"Want you to know I appreciate what you're doin for me. All the work you put in."

She nodded, surprised to find herself smiling.

He let go of the tape measure and told her where to stand so he could get the measurement. He did the math in his head. "Got room for all the woodblocks along this wall, with bout thirteen inches between em. What do you think?"

"Thirteen inches is too close. I think they should go against the back wall, behind the screens, otherwise they're going to dwarf the other pieces."

He nodded. "You figure puttin the camp installation in the center's a good idea?"

"Yes. You want people to be able to walk around it without bumping into each other. Daddy's right—it's the crowd pleaser."

It was almost one. She went into the office to call the restaurant and leave a message for David that she would be late. Ben was sitting in the center of the room, measuring the floor space and marking it with pieces of paper and tape, when she walked out.

"The prototype for the program is on the desk. You and my father should both take a look at it, to make sure I've got it right. Change anything you want. I'll stop by around four and we can go over it together. I'd like to get it to the printer tomorrow."

• • •

David stood and gave her a hug.

"Where've you been?" he grumbled in her ear. "We were about to order."

"Sorry," she said, kissing his cheek.

He took her hand and turned to the couple sitting at the table. "Here she is, the woman I've been waiting for all of my life."

The Guttmans, in their sixties, had three children and scores of grandchildren, a house on Nantucket, and an apartment overlooking Central Park. He'd made a lot of money in California real estate and was now semiretired. David paid their bills and taxes, managed their various trust funds, and advised them on tax shelters and investments, for which he was paid a hefty retainer.

They'd just sold the last of their property in Los Angeles for an unexpected million-dollar profit.

"Fun money," Liz said. David had been right. She was dressed: an original black and white Chanel suit from the 60s, Sarah guessed.

David had some ideas about what to do with the "fun money." He elaborated a few to Phil, primarily reinvestment in real estate. Liz glanced at the menu and asked Sarah questions about the wedding.

"I'm so sorry we can't be there. We're leaving in a few days for three weeks on Nantucket with the kids," Liz said. Then she launched into a description of their youngest daughter's recent nuptials. Sarah listened with one ear and the other tuned into David's conversation.

"Art is a terrible investment," he said. "Buy it because you like it. Hang it on your walls for a few years, then, when you get tired of it, donate it and take the write-off. But don't expect to make money on it."

Phil laughed. "Talk to Liz—she's the one. She's already spent half of her half."

"Did I hear my name?" Liz said, interrupting her own conversation.

"I just broke the news to David that you've already spent half of your half."

"I did, this very morning." She smiled, raising her eyebrows and glancing around in humorous stealth. "It's under the table," she whispered.

Something worth a quarter of a million dollars, under the table?

"What is it?" Sarah couldn't help asking, especially as Liz clearly wanted to be asked.

"It's wonderful," she said. "Would you like to see?"

"Of course."

It took a little maneuvering of chairs but Phil and David

were able to reach under and retrieve a sealed box about two feet square.

Liz cut the tape with a knife and pulled out a wad of excelsior along with a marble sculpture. She brushed off the strips of paper and set it in the center of the table. Sarah was stunned to be confronted by Ben's *Mother and Child*.

"Isn't it extraordinary? It's by Alan Trublo. He died recently, and this was discovered among his personal things. I fell in love with it the moment I saw it."

"It is"—Sarah swallowed—"absolutely beautiful. But it's not by Alan Trublo."

"Of course it is," Liz said. "We just bought it from Bernard Levitt. He handles all of Trublo's work."

"I'm sorry. I don't know what Mr. Levitt told you, or why, but it's the work of an artist named Ben Lonefeather."

"Don't be ridiculous," Phil said. "Bernard is a personal friend. He isn't about to lie to us."

"Then he made a mistake."

Phil glanced at David before giving Sarah a strained smile. "Bernard didn't make a mistake. He's been handling Alan Trublo's work for thirty years."

Sarah felt herself flush.

Liz touched her husband's hand and leaned forward in a conciliatory effort. "It was found among his things after he died. Very few people have seen it. If you're familiar with his body of work, you're probably having difficulty recognizing it because it's never been photographed."

"I'm familiar with this work," Sarah responded. "I saw it in Alan's study last summer with the artist who carved it. He was a student of Alan's." She ignored the pressure of David's shoe on hers. "Either Mr. Levitt truly doesn't know that, or he lied to you." Her tone, louder than she'd intended, echoed. Several people from other tables glanced over. "This is silly," she said. "Ben Lonefeather signs his work with a single feather. Would you mind if I have a look?"

"Please," Phil Guttman said.

She drew the piece toward her and turned it slowly, searching for Ben's trademark. She stood and gently laid it on its side. No feather. *Alan Trublo* was written in felt marker across the bottom. "I guess he didn't sign it. I have no idea who wrote Alan's name, but I'm certain it wasn't Alan," she concluded lamely.

Phil began to say something. Liz touched his hand and shook her head. She stood to repack the sculpture. "Art is so emotional. People make mistakes all the time. You can be convinced about something and it turns out there's a perfectly reasonable explanation, that it isn't at all what you thought."

"What do you do, Sarah?" Phil asked.

"I work with my father. He owns Shoen's Furniture and Gallery and has been dealing American Indian art for forty years. He was Alan's first dealer. Actually, he introduced him to Bernard Levitt."

"That's interesting. I wonder why Trublo chose to go with Bernard?"

"Because my father thought Alan would be better served by a name gallery."

"I see," Phil said without conviction.

"Shoen's Furniture and Gallery?" Liz said. "I know that shop. It's very sweet. Lots of pottery and crafts."

"Isn't Lonefeather the artist your father is representing?" David asked her.

"Yes. Why?"

"No reason. It's just that you've been spending a lot of time there and I recognized the name."

"What are you saying? That I'm so involved with the show I'm seeing Lonefeathers everywhere?"

He smiled coolly. "Let's order, shall we?"

She picked up her menu and selected the first thing under entrees.

"I apologize if I've spoiled lunch," she said after the orders were taken. "Regardless who the artist is, you've purchased a beautiful sculpture."

Phil Guttman nodded coolly. Liz smiled insincerely.

"So tell me about your son's company. Do they design games?" David asked.

"Educational games," Phil answered. "It's highly competitive, but it looks like he might be onto something with corporate training."

Sarah excused herself to go to the ladies' room. She called the gallery. Ben answered the phone.

She told him what had happened.

"Prob'ly didn't sign it," he said nonchalantly. "Two hundred and fifty thousand? I'll be damned."

"Yes. But they only paid that because they thought it was by Alan."

"Still. They musta thought it was worth somethin."

What should her father do? Confront Bernard? If he chose to stick to his story, how could they prove anything?

"Sam went around the corner for a cup of coffee. Somethin's botherin him too. The newspapers ain't comin or they're sendin someone he don't think is any good. I'm stayin out of it. Figure you two can handle that part. The unloadin's goin good. We got most a the paintins in."

•  •  •

"It was a pleasure meeting you," Sarah told the Guttmans after lunch.

Phil answered with a cool nod.

"Good-bye, Sarah," Liz said. She kissed David's cheek. "Have a nice wedding."

Sarah turned to David. "I need to go to the ladies' room. You'd better get back to work."

She had an appointment with the photographer she'd hired for the wedding, and she'd planned to stop at Bloomingdale's to return a nightie from her lingerie shower. She sat on the lounge chair and canceled the photographer. She used the toilet and freshened her makeup, emerging disappointed to see that David was waiting to share a taxi and some of his thoughts with her.

He'd never seen her behave like that.

"They're nice, pleasant people," he said, maintaining a reasonable tone with some effort. "They bought a piece of art from a reputable dealer who happens to be their friend. They were pleased with it. Why couldn't you leave it alone?"

"It wasn't the truth."

"How can you be certain there aren't two very similar sculptures? Didn't you feel my foot? I know you did—you just chose to ignore it."

"Can you hear the way you're talking to me? As if I were a child. I can distinguish one sculpture from another."

"They're my *clients,* Sarah. My business runs on people placing absolute trust in my judgment. Without it they'll go to someone else."

"What if it turns out I'm right? Won't everyone feel better?"

"And if it turns out you're wrong? Or even worse, it's unresolved and becomes your word against Bernard Levitt? What happens then?"

"I don't know."

"I do. You've put the Guttmans in the position of having to

choose whose judgment to trust, Levitt's or mine." He paused
to make certain she understood his point. "I want you to drop
it. Write them a note and say you were mistaken. Offer some
excuse. Confusion with another work, PMS, nerves because of
the wedding. Whatever. His business is important to me."

Sarah didn't say anything. The taxi stopped in front of
David's office building. He opened the door. "I should be finished tonight around nine. I'll call you."

When she got to the gallery, most of the paintings had been
unloaded and stacked against the walls.

Ben was moving them from one spot to another in order
to determine where to hang them. "Whadda you think?"

She'd forgotten the vibrancy and action of the earliest
pieces. Her nephews would like them. Even Eli, who had no
interest in art, might relate.

"Right out front—the first things they see."

He remained unconcerned about the whole Bernard Levitt
thing. "Think we got a solution," he told her.

Her father was in the office, more troubled at the moment
by the lack of coverage they were getting in the newspapers.
They hadn't even been guaranteed a gallery openings listing in
the *Times,* and none of the top newspapers or magazines had
mentioned them.

"I'll call Bernard," he said, picking up the phone. "I'm certain he had no intention of deceiving anyone."

Phil Guttman had already spoken to Bernard. Sarah sat
down and listened to Sam's half of the conversation.

"I know you believe it's Alan's. He kept it in his study because his most promising student carved it. I spoke with him
about it several times. No one's questioning your integrity,
Bernard. I'm sure it was simply an honest mistake. Look," Sam
said sharply, "we won't get anywhere arguing about it. Ben
Lonefeather had a suggestion. Why don't we call Emma

Trublo and ask her? I'm aware of that, but I think she knows her husband's work, don't you? Fine, unless she's certain whose it is, we will agree to its being by Alan. Fine. I'll wait to hear from you."

Sam hung up and looked at Sarah. "He'll call tomorrow."

Sarah turned to regard Ben through the glass. The movers were bringing in the two additional sculptures to set on the low pedestals he'd placed at intervals around the room, about three feet from the wall. She thought about his response when she'd called from the restaurant. That the Guttmans' willingness to pay so much meant the sculpture must be worth something. It struck her as absurd that the name of the artist so completely determined the value of a piece of art. Because Ben made it instead of Alan, would it instantly become worthless? No, but worth less. How much less, and why, exactly?

A little before six they carried in the first of the wood-blocks and secured the dark monolith against the back wall. Alone the piece was imposing—all six together would be magnificent. Unfortunately it seemed the critics would not be availing themselves of the opportunity to see it.

Before the movers left for the night they brought in another low wooden platform that Ben had them set a few feet from the right wall in relation to the three sculptures.

"What's still in the truck?" Sarah asked. It was on its way to a storage facility for the night and would return early in the morning.

"The rest of the woodblocks, the camp installation, which I gotta assemble. An another sculpture."

"The marble you were starting when I was there?"

"Yeah. I wrote down the dimensions so you could add it to the program." He handed her a piece of notebook paper.

He'd titled the piece *Yin*.

"I'm going home," Sam said, coming out of the office

with his jacket. He extended his hand to shake Ben's. "I couldn't be more pleased with the way it's coming together. I hope you are?"

"Yeah, Sam, I am."

"You've got your key? And the directions? Don't be afraid of disturbing us if it's late and we're not up. I'll see you in the morning."

"Where are you going?" Sarah asked Ben.

"Figured I'd walk around, get somethin to eat. Wouldn't mind company."

What would be the harm? she thought. Besides, it was a practical way to dodge David's call.

"All right. I'll show you a little of my city."

They walked over to Central Park West and down toward Midtown, across the street from the park, past the beautiful Beaux Arts buildings with elegant doormen standing outside. She asked about Anna and Dawsen, Millie and Tom, Billy and Chippy.

When they got to Fifty-ninth they turned toward Columbus Circle and continued on Broadway to the neon garishness of Times Square, mobbed by tourists, hustlers, police, peppered with actual New Yorkers all day and most of the night. Even on a Monday when the majority of Broadway theaters were closed, the noise and jostling of the crowd interrupted conversation until they turned on Forty-third. As they walked west to Ninth Avenue, Ben told her about Alvin and Littleman. She'd sensed Alvin was a loose cannon but had never anticipated he might be danger to Ben.

"You're the most important person in the world to him. Why would he do something so certain to drive you away?"

They entered a little trattoria she loved and were seated at a table for two along the wall. He related the story about Maria's husband killing himself and seeing Alvin at the window.

"So, you've been seeing Maria Farrell?" It just popped out. Not the point of his story and really none of her business. Worse, in the face of everything, it stung.

He gazed at her keenly.

She flushed. "I mean, that's nice. She's a nice person," she said, picking up her menu.

He quickly perused his menu and set it down, grinning. "You order."

She selected scampi with penne for him and sole for herself, a radicchio and parmesan salad, a carpaccio appetizer, focaccia with sun-dried tomatoes, and a bottle of sparkling water.

"Where is Alvin now?"

"Hospital in Flagstaff. Millie says he's psychotic. Hears voices. Can't tell the difference between his thoughts an the truth."

"Have you seen him?"

"No."

"I feel sorry for him."

"You wouldn't if you saw Littleman," he said harshly.

She didn't say anything. He looked at her. "I can't, Sarah," he sighed. "I'm too angry."

The food came. He ate his scampi with all the exuberance she remembered.

"Has your life changed now that you have a telephone?"

"Get more dinner invitations. Guess cause people can jus call up stead a drivin out."

She wondered where Maria fit in.

"There are two questions I have to ask," she said. "Why didn't you come to me when you decided you wanted a show? And why did you press to open it so soon?"

He sat back in his chair and looked at her. "Didn't want your help."

"Why not?"

"Don't matter," he said with a wry smile. "Ended up gettin it anyway."

"It's absurd not to ask for help if you need it."

He didn't respond. Apparently he'd said all he was going to.

"But why the rush?"

He shrugged. "Already had the loan. Knew if I didn't do it fast, the money'd be gone and so would the opportunity."

Was it possible her wedding had nothing to do with it?

"I'm concerned it's not going to be what you expect or deserve. Shoen's doesn't have a reputation as a gallery, and it's been tougher than we thought to generate interest in the show."

"Won't be your fault, or your dad's. He's doin everything he can to make sure I get my shot."

"Thank you for saying that."

As they walked toward her apartment after dinner, she told him her thoughts from that morning, watching his art infuse Shoen's.

"My mother's father started the store when he was twenty-two. My mother worked there all through her twenties and into her thirties, until Eli was born. My father has been there since his thirties, and I started there when I was twenty-eight. I'll be sad to see it close. But I'm very proud of the way it's going out."

"You make me believe in myself," he said.

She almost took his arm to give it a squeeze.

"You gonna be there tomorrow?"

She had a full day scheduled in addition to what she'd put off today. "I'll try."

"Appreciate it. Wanna get your opinion on somethin."

"I thought you didn't want my help," she said archly.

"Changed my mind. I need all the help I can get."

It was after eleven. She stopped in front of her building.

"You gonna invite me up?" He was standing close, looking down at her.

"It's late."

"You tired?"

"Yes," she lied.

"Naw. You're jus scared I might try an kiss you." He touched her lower lip with his thumb. "No need to worry, thought ain't even crossed my mind." He grinned, stepping back and walking away before she could collect herself for a response.

• • •

David had left a message on her machine to call no matter what time she got in. She picked up the phone, hoping that a talk with him, even an unpleasant one, would rid her mind of Ben.

She told him about her father's conversation with Bernard.

"That's good. I was most concerned it would be left up in the air. As soon as it's decided, let me know so I can call Phil and smooth everything out. You'll write a note?"

She assured him she would, if she was wrong.

He dropped out of business mode.

"I've been lying here thinking about you. Where were you tonight?"

"I had dinner with Ben Lonefeather, and he walked me home."

"Just the two of you?"

"Yes."

"Hmm, I don't know if I like that. What did you talk about?"

"Art, life, the show."

"Did you have a nice time?"

"Yes, I did."

"He's an Indian, isn't he? Or should I say Native American?"

"What else would he be?"

"Sometimes artists take on strange names, you know, as an attention grabber."

"Oh. No, he's a real Indian."

"Good."

"Why is it good?"

"I might be jealous otherwise. Anyway, I'll be interested to meet him. I don't think I've ever met one before."

# CHAPTER 31

**S**arah got up early to complete the program so she could drop it off at the printer's. There was a biography of Ben with a picture that Ben had sent. Who had taken it? she wondered. He was standing in front of the wall at his home, staring into the camera, his arms crossed. He looked very much the way he had the first day she'd seen him: a forbidding surface with no clue to the man underneath. There were descriptions and dimensions of each piece, prices on request. They were yet to be determined.

Sam finally called at ten thirty. Emma Trublo had confirmed the sculpture was Ben's work. Apparently the associate Bernard sent to collect Alan's things had mistakenly taken it.

Nothing like a little vindication to make one's day, she thought.

"So what's going to happen to the sculpture?"

"The Guttmans are returning it. Emma wants Ben to keep it as the first piece in his personal collection."

"That's great, but it doesn't help us, does it? We don't have any idea what it's worth."

"Bernard offered Emma four thousand on behalf of the Guttmans."

She hung up, sickened. Well, now they knew the value of the artist's name in this case. At least according to Bernard Levitt.

A few minutes later David called to say he'd just talked to Phil. He apologized for doubting her. "I was an ass, and you have my permission to throw it in my face if I ever argue with you about art again," he said.

But in reality what had she accomplished? Nothing except the profound devaluation of a beautiful piece of work. On the basis of one man's opinion. Why? Because no one else with credibility would look at it. The whole thing infuriated her. In addition to the usual press releases, pictures, biography of the artist, she'd sent heartfelt personal letters to art critics at the most influential newspapers in the city and received form letters in response. The exact language differed, but they'd all said the same thing: not enough time and staff to cover everything in the city.

Surely she must know someone who knew someone, but who? Then it hit her. Her future mother-in-law was a honorary board member of the AIDS Project, and for the last three years, Gunter Morton, first-string art critic for the *Times*, had chaired the art auction, one of the AIDS Project's fund-raisers.

Unfortunately, Paula Klein wasn't the warm and fuzzy favor-doing type; she was more the Queen of Hearts in *Alice in Wonderland* type, chilly and formidable. Sarah suspected that she believed David was marrying beneath him. She'd be unlikely to offer help. Gunter Morton wasn't on the guest list for the wedding, so they must not be close friends.

Still, he'd be certain to know who she was.

Sarah picked up the phone and dialed the *Times* before she had the chance to lose her nerve. She requested Arts, identified herself as Paula Klein's assistant, and asked to speak with Gunter Morton.

"I'll see if he's in," the woman said. She returned a moment later.

"He's on another line. Can you hold? Or should he call you back?"

Sarah swallowed. "I'll hold."

When he came on the line all she could think was *hang up*.

"Mr. Morton? I'm Amy Jones calling on behalf of Paula Klein. She was hoping you might possibly do her a small, personal favor?"

"Of course," he said, sounding mildly surprised. "If I can."

"She's considering the purchase of a sculpture. The artist is unknown, and the gallery is new, on the Upper West Side. She wondered if you might have time today or tomorrow to just drop by and have a look. I can call you late tomorrow to see what you think."

A moment's pause. She held her breath. Was this just too ridiculous?

"Please tell Mrs. Klein that it would be my pleasure."

She hung up, had a moment of relief, and then took a long anxious shower. Her plan had only limited potential for success and a definite downside. The good news was that Gunter Morton had agreed to go by Shoen's, and there hadn't been any other way she could think to accomplish that. The bad news was that generally people hate to be manipulated. She just hoped he'd recognize Ben's brilliance and forgive or forget the manipulation. In the meantime, she'd try to figure out a way to prevent him ever mentioning it to Paula Klein.

Maybe it would be best for her to come clean when she

met Paula and her mother that afternoon and just deal with it. She emerged from her bedroom running late, grabbed a yogurt and a banana, and rushed to the Four Seasons' ballroom to negotiate a seating chart for the reception.

Planning any aspect of the wedding with the two mothers taxed Sarah's diplomatic skills; they were both extremely opinionated, and every detail took on defining importance. In usual circumstances, Evelyn, being the bride's mother, would have more clout, but since David was paying for the reception Paula felt justified in asserting herself to "look after his interests." Sarah didn't much care where people sat. She spent three hours refereeing. In the end, she'd achieved her goal of parity in that both Evelyn and Paula seemed in equal measure satisfied with the decisions reached. Within the first five minutes she'd discarded any notion of discussing the Gunter Morton conversation.

She walked out with her mother into a warm summer afternoon.

"Our house guest stayed out late last night. I hear you showed him the city," Evelyn said.

"It was fun."

"What about David?"

"David's seen the city."

"You know what I mean. Does he know?"

"It's okay, Ma. Relax. Ben and I are friends. He has a girlfriend in Arizona."

"Does David *know*, Sarah?"

Sarah sighed. "What do you have, second sight? No, he doesn't."

Evelyn shook her head. "You're playing with fire."

• • •

Sarah got to the gallery at four thirty. The moving van had gone. Through the front window she saw Ben standing rigidly next to the *Wild Horse*. She opened the door as a flash went off.

"Okay. Thanks," the photographer said. Ben relaxed and grinned at her. On his way out, the photographer waved at a man Sarah recognized standing in the office with Sam. She walked through the not yet assembled pieces of the camp installation as Sam came out of the office with Gunter Morton and introduced her.

"Ah, Miss Friedman," he said. "Maybe you can clear this up. Someone named Amy, claiming to be Paula Klein's assistant, asked me to look at a piece Mrs. Klein is considering. Your father was unaware of any interest in a purchase, and when I attempted to contact Ms. Jones for more information, Brad, Mrs. Klein's assistant, had no idea who she was."

"That would be my doing, I'm afraid," she said humbly, but also, she hoped, with charm. "I'd tried every legitimate thing I could to pique your interest. Finally, in desperation I picked Mrs. Klein's name from the list of board members on an AIDS Project mailer and pretended to be her assistant. I'm a minor contributor, by the way. I think you're doing wonderful work."

He didn't smile.

"I was out of line. I apologize."

"It's an interesting story about the confusion with the Trublo."

"Yes."

"I'm doing it as a feature for Friday's paper."

•  •  •

As soon as Gunter Morton had safely walked past the front window, Sam took her by the shoulders and kissed both cheeks. "Do you know what you've done? How did you get so smart?"

He told her Morton had rushed in impatiently around

eleven thirty and stayed for two hours. A half hour ago he'd returned with the photographer.

"Yes!" Sarah whooped. "You do understand?" She turned to Ben. "This is very good."

He nodded, a slow smile warming his eyes.

"What's that?" she asked, breaking the look between them, indicating a large bubble-wrapped mound on the low platform.

"A mystery," Sam answered. "He wouldn't unwrap it, not even for the *Times*."

Ben walked over to cut the tape with his pocketknife. He pulled the wrapping away and stepped back.

A female nude rose out of rough marble. She knelt, as Sarah had that day on his bed, knees slightly parted. One hand rested on her thigh. The other arm was raised and bent. The head turned into the elbow, hiding the facial features. The fingers cupped the nape of the neck laced through a knot of curls. One ringlet escaped down the delicate back. The heels of her feet arched as if pulling away from the stone; only her toes remained captured and undifferentiated.

Sam ecstatically commented on its vitality. It was a work of maturity, classical and erotic. Should they keep it in its current position or move it closer to the front? Placed as it was, near the camp installation, it served as a counterpoint—two extreme aspects of Ben's vision, which was very interesting. Didn't Sarah think so?

Sarah couldn't think. In spite of herself she started to cry.

Ben leaned against the wall, watching her.

She wiped her face with her palms and tried to smile at him. "It's beautiful."

He stared back, his jaw clenched.

The buzzer went off.

"Sarah?" Liz Guttman called, walking in with a potted orchid. Phil followed, carrying the box with the *Mother and Child*.

"You have to accept our apology," Liz said, handing the plant to Sarah.

In a semifog Sarah made the introductions. Phil gave the box to Ben and asked if he would reconsider its sale.

"Talk to Sam," Ben replied, setting the box on the floor. "I'm goin out for some air." He walked past Sarah without a glance.

Sam stepped in. "Please don't take it personally. I think there's just been too much sudden attention. The *Times* was here all afternoon interviewing him."

Sarah excused herself. Sam chatted on as she made her way into the office.

"The *Mother and Child* was his first marble, and we've decided it should be kept."

"My goodness, this is exciting," Liz said. "Can we look around?"

"Of course, I'll be happy to answer any questions . . ."

Sarah dropped the orchid on the desk, continued into the restroom, and shut the door.

He'd chiseled her image in stone. He'd told her it was difficult to get someone to pose, and God knew artists often slept with their models, but he'd waited to show her particularly. And she'd burst into tears at its beauty, which apparently made him angry. What did he expect? She had no idea what to think. Her father hadn't guessed, but someone more astute might. Did it matter? She didn't know how she felt about any of it.

Sam had shown the Guttmans the collection by the time she returned, pulled together, freshened up.

"I'm dazzled," Phil Guttman said. "I expected to see derivative Alan Trublo but that's not the case."

"I'm crazy about the woodblocks," Liz said. "Especially the *Shut Up and Open Your Mouth*. Is it for sale?"

"Everything's for sale," Sam said. "Except the *Mother and Child*."

Sam took them into the office. They sat in the craftsman chairs. Sam sat at the desk. Sarah stood next to the office door, her eyes on Sam.

"Because Ben has never offered his work before, there's no precedent for a price. I'm reluctant to set one before I know what the marketplace will bear. Gunter Morton is doing a feature in the *Times*, Friday before the opening, and of course he's reviewing. I think we'll get quite a bit of attention."

"Just for the sake of argument, what would you take today?" Phil Guttman asked.

"Seventy-five thousand dollars."

Sarah almost fell over.

"It may be too much," Sam continued evenly. "But the first piece sold will set the standard, and I intend to be certain the artist gets what he deserves."

"It seems a little steep. Would you consider fifty?"

Fifty? Sarah swallowed. Fifty would do.

"Not until I have a clearer idea of how it's going."

"I think we should give it more thought," Phil Guttman said to Liz. "Perhaps speak to Bernard."

She answered with a slight negative shake of her head.

"Why don't I hold it for you until the show opens," Sam said. "When we determine where we are with the woodblocks, I'll give you the opportunity to buy at the market price."

"Which could be lower or higher?" Liz asked.

"Exactly."

"And would mean we wouldn't be the first people to purchase a Lonefeather?"

"Yes, that's correct."

The Guttmans looked at each other. Phil Guttman pulled out his checkbook. "All right, seventy-five thousand."

Sarah released her breath. Sam had handled the situation beautifully, she thought. She would have settled for less and been wrong. She gazed through the window into the gallery. From the first day in the storeroom, she'd believed Ben's work would be recognized, but she hadn't realized until that moment how responsible she felt for it.

The Guttmans agreed to allow the woodblock to remain for the duration of the show, and Sarah stuck a little red dot next to the piece indicating it had been sold. The minute the front door closed behind them, Sam clasped his hands together, and whispered, "Oh boy. Oh boy, oh boy, oh boy."

"Daddy." She laughed. "You were incredible."

"Hallelujah," he sang from Handel's *Messiah*, dancing toward the office to look at the check again and call Evelyn.

• • •

Ben came into the office where Sarah sat in one of the craftsman chairs. Sam, still on the telephone, handed the check to him. "I want to take these kids to dinner," Sam said into the phone.

Ben sank into the other craftsman chair, staring at the check.

"It's for one of the woodblocks," Sarah told him.

"Holy shit," he said quietly.

"All right, we'll order hors d'oeuvres and champagne." Sam hung up. "She's coming in to join us."

# CHAPTER 32

Le Jardin de Fromage: very beautiful, very expensive. Sam, Sarah, and Ben were seated at a round table set for four. Sam ordered the champagne and a large bottle of Perrier for Ben, who still seemed stunned. They toasted to the show's success. Sarah gulped her drink, mulling over some way to excuse herself from dinner. Attempting lucid conversation with both Evelyn and Ben at the table was beyond her current mental state. She needed to clear her mind and get some perspective.

The waiter came with appetizers, filling the table with a multitude of tiny, skillfully presented bits to capture their attention. The food looked fabulous, and all she'd eaten that day was yogurt and a banana. She decided she could have another drink, munch a little, and then remember she had to meet David somewhere.

Sam poured them each another glass and smiled at Sarah.

"This afternoon before Morton came back with the photographer, Ben and I had a talk about his next dealer. I had several people in mind, but he wondered if you might be interested."

"Me?"

"Haven't you always wanted to run a gallery?"

"But I have so little experience."

"Your dad could teach you," Ben said.

Sam nodded cheerily. "I'd stay on part-time, but it would be your business."

Out of the corner of her eye she saw the maitre d' moving toward their table with Evelyn. And behind her, David.

Sam jumped up and Ben stood, towering over David when they shook hands. The busboy added another chair and table setting next to Sarah for David, and they crowded together in a circle.

"Bring us something special," Sam told the waiter. "I'll leave it to you, but no pork or seafood."

David put his arm over the back of Sarah's chair, kissed her cheek, and whispered, "I'm so proud of you. I spoke to Phil just before your mother called and invited me to join the celebration." He turned to Sam. "I hear some friends of mine bought a sculpture from you this afternoon. They were very impressed with the way you do business. Congratulations." He raised his glass to Sam and included Ben.

Ben looked at him and nodded.

"We were just talking about Sarah continuing on with Shoen's Gallery as Ben's dealer," Sam said.

"That's a great idea," David said.

"What?" Evelyn said.

"Ben"—Sarah leaned forward seriously—"you need someone with credibility and connections."

"Don't be silly," Evelyn said. "She'll have her hands full with a house and children. She can't run a gallery in Manhattan."

"I don't know the first thing about securing commissions," Sarah continued. "And I'm not a very good negotiator."

"You'll learn," Sam told her.

Her eyes met Ben's.

"It would be a wonderful thing, wouldn't it?" Sam turned to Evelyn. "The next generation of Shoen's?"

Evelyn gave him a small smile and drank her champagne.

David squeezed Sarah's shoulder, pleased because it would effectively put an end to a source of friction between them and they'd stay in the city.

It was what she'd always wanted, presented on a platter. So why was she anxious and nauseated instead of jumping out of her skin with joy? Ben's gaze rested on her, with slow warmth and a message.

Like debris in a glass of murky water, her swirling thoughts finally settled to the bottom, affording some clarity. They'd speak every day or two by phone, and before long she'd visit him to view a work in progress or discuss a potential commission. He'd come to New York to check on sales and meet with collectors and commission prospects. *Sooner or later* was the message, or so she imagined. Perhaps it was simply her own desire she was reading.

If she was smart and careful, David need never know.

She couldn't eat anything after the soup. Evelyn didn't eat much either, although she drank four glasses of champagne. David ate sparingly and passed on dessert. Sam drank five glasses of champagne. Ben ate all six courses, including two desserts.

They walked out into muggy air, hanging over the city like a dirty gray sheet, trapping the day's heat.

Ben bent to her, speaking quietly. "Your parents okay to get home alone? Thought maybe you and me could talk."

"No," she whispered. "Um, would you mind going with them? They've had a lot to drink."

He glanced at David and got into the taxi to Penn Station.
David put his arms around her.

"Come home with me?"

"Um, sounds tempting, but I've got a huge day tomorrow
and I need to get on my computer early in the morning."

He kissed her forehead and hailed a taxi.

*   *   *

Sarah took a bath and tried to force herself to think clearly.
Her own capacity for duplicity shocked her. She was heading
for disaster.

A few minutes before one a.m. her phone rang.

"I'm at Penn Station. Took your folks home, but there was
no point in me stayin out there tryin to sleep. Can I come to
your place?"

She dressed in a T-shirt and sweats with no makeup and
met him in front of her building.

"I feel like a walk," she said.

He stepped close. "It's gonna be okay, Sarah," he whispered,
brushing a hair from her forehead with his finger, his eyes luminous. She felt like a mouse hypnotized by a snake. He bent
and grazed her lips with his, slipping his arm around her and
drawing her in, bending for another kiss.

No, it wasn't okay. She twisted out of his grasp and walked
down the street quickly. He came up alongside.

"Why did you ask me to be your dealer?"

"Because I trust you more an anyone."

They walked a block in silence.

"Best thing to do is spit it out," he said.

"If I told you there was no way we'd ever be alone together,
no weekends in Arizona, no meeting in various cities to install
your work. If you knew there was not a chance of anything
physical between us, would you still want me to represent you?"

"You sayin I'm tryin to buy you?" He chuckled. "I ain't that horny or stupid. But you might wanna ask yourself why you're so afraid a bein alone with me."

She stopped and faced him. "What does Maria think of your latest sculpture?"

"Never showed her."

"Why not?"

"Ain't seen her in two months." He took a step toward her. "Sarah, it's jus somethin that happened between Maria and me. Truth is she got a lot less than she deserved."

"I understand. No promises broken . . ."

"You got no reason to be jealous."

"I beg your pardon? I'm not jealous."

"Yeah, you are."

"You're so wrong. I wouldn't trade places for anything in the world."

His jaw clenched, but he kept his voice low. "You think I like the idea a you with him? You think I wanna spend my time waitin for you to get angry or bored an come lookin to do a little business in Arizona?"

She didn't answer.

"You'll come, Sarah. You know it," he said softly. "An if that's the best I can do, I'll take it."

"And so you're willing to give me the job representing you? I thought you were a better negotiator."

"Stop it now." He grabbed her shoulders, searching her eyes. "Don't marry that guy. Come home with me."

"Let me go," she hissed.

He removed his hands.

"The hardest thing I've ever done in my life was drive down that road away from you. And you didn't even try to stop me." She swallowed. Tears started in her eyes, but she kept her voice steady. "If you wanted me to wait, all you had to do was say it."

He reached for her. She stopped him with her hand.

"It took all I had to hold on to the good. But I did. I'm grateful for everything I got from that experience. It was a magic time. But I will rot in hell before I repeat it."

His confidence drained away. He looked at her helplessly, his arms at his sides.

"I've been giving you mixed signals, I know," she continued evenly. "I'm sorry. Right now, I'm not sure we can ever get to a place where it's just business between us. But you need to understand that would be the only way I'm prepared to go on. I suggest we both take some time to think about it."

He stepped back, his eyes shrouded like ice-covered stone, and walked away.

●  ●  ●

Sarah spent a fitful night. The next morning she met the DJ for the wedding reception at nine a.m. to go over his mix, picked up the printed programs, and walked into the gallery a little after eleven, astonished to see the camp installation completely assembled, the screen dividers up, the paintings in place.

She found Sam in the office.

"Where's Ben?"

"He worked all night. When I got here this morning, he was hanging the last painting. He thanked me for my hospitality and said he was going out to Woodbridge to get his things. He's moving to a hotel. Said he'll see us at the opening."

"Oh," Sarah said, sinking into a craftsman chair, relieved and deflated.

"What's going on between you?"

She sighed. "We had an affair last summer. That was the reason I was gone so long."

He showed no surprise. "Would you mind some advice?"

"Be my guest."

He regarded her sadly, not as a father but as a fellow traveler familiar with the road. "Let him find another dealer."


The *Times* ran two pictures, one of *Mother and Child* and one of Ben standing next to *The Wild Horse*. The accompanying article touched briefly on the slippery price of art but focused mainly on a uniquely talented American Indian artist whose entire body of work would be on display for a short time at a new, innovative gallery on the Upper West Side. For anyone with an interest in making up his or her own mind about the value of art, a view of the show was highly recommended.

# CHAPTER 33

People swarmed to the opening, arriving in a continuous stream: family, friends, collectors, reviewers, art aficionados, curious tourists. Sarah, doing her best to appear poised, greeted, made introductions, answered questions, all the while feeling like she was racing to catch a bus but never quite getting on and finding a seat.

She'd set the bartender up in the tiny storeroom. It had seemed the best place to put him, but it created a flow problem and at times the wait to get a drink looked like the line at the concession stand of a ball game, people fanning themselves with the program, trying to remain polite.

She and Sam had decided they should split the time, taking turns handling the floor and the office. He started in the office.

Gunter Morton was just leaving when Ben turned up, forty-five minutes late, carrying a six-pack of Mountain Dew and wearing a T-shirt with a big red apple on the front and NEW YORK emblazoned in purple on the back.

"I've enjoyed the show," Morton said.

"Uh, thanks," Ben said, glancing at Sarah uncomfortably. "I gotta get these in the cooler. Scuse me."

She nodded with a strained smile, equally uncomfortable.

"He's a little nervous," she explained.

"It's refreshing," Gunter Morton said. "Unfortunately, it will pass. A year from now, he'll be a different man."

When it was time to exchange places with her father, Sarah adjourned to the office, where a steady flow of inquiries kept her seated at the desk, her mind occupied. Occasionally she looked out on the floor to watch Sam in his element, standing next to Ben, making introductions, happily chatting away.

David, with a dozen yellow roses, found her in the office. "Phil Guttman called again. He wants to know what the woodblocks are selling for."

She took the flowers and kissed him. "Tell him he did very well."

"How long will you be?" he asked, glancing at the young couple currently sitting in the craftsman chairs.

"I'll try to come out in a little while. Have a look around. Get a drink, if you can bear the line."

"Excuse me while I find somewhere to put these," she said to Mr. and Mrs. Martinez. He was an actor she recognized from several independent films. His wife, a beautiful blonde, was about six months pregnant. They were in the process of purchasing a painting—young men drinking beer in the back of a pickup, entitled *Deer Hunters*.

The only thing large enough for the bouquet was an old plastic jar Sam kept under his desk that was half filled with jellybeans. She dumped the candy in the bathroom wastebasket, filled the jar with water, dropped the long stems in, and placed the bouquet on top of the filing cabinet next to the orchid.

"Now," she said, smiling at the Martinezes, "where were we?"

While Mrs. Martinez wrote a check, Sarah caught sight of David shaking hands with her father and Ben. She couldn't see David's face, but Ben's eyes locked on hers over the back of his head.

A few moments later, he leaned his head into the office. She introduced him to the newest owners of one of his pieces.

"How ya doin?" he said, eyeing the Martinezes. His glance switched to Sarah. "I gotta get outta here."

• • •

The Bruers replaced the Martinezes. As she discussed the *Times* article with them, she watched David wander indifferently through the art with a drink. Although they'd met at a gallery opening, he'd confessed soon after that he'd only gone because he'd read somewhere that galleries were a good place to meet intelligent women. He really had little interest in art. He walked around the camp installation fairly quickly and stopped in front of *Yin.*

Mr. Bruer asked for a total including tax and handed her a credit card.

When she finished the transaction, David was still standing in front of the sculpture. She moved to him and touched his arm.

"Why didn't you tell me who he was?" he whispered harshly, staring straight ahead.

"I'm sorry."

"My God, Sarah. Did you think I wouldn't get it when I saw this?"

"I haven't been thinking. That's the problem."

He turned to look at her, his voice low. "Just tell me, is it still going on?"

"No."

He searched her eyes, then nodded. "I'll call you later."

• • •

Late that evening an exhausted Sarah straightened and readied the gallery for the morning. Joshua had agreed to come back for a few weeks to help as she had a full calendar of wedding activities, but clearly he couldn't handle it alone. Either she or Sam would have to be here most of the time. She'd have to make a schedule. Tomorrow. Tonight nothing sounded more like heaven than home and falling into bed, but she should probably go to David's.

She paid the bartender and walked back through the gallery to get the lights in the office, catching a glimpse of herself in the mirror of the bathroom as the iridescent glow dimmed—large weary eyes, a pale, green-tinged face.

When she turned around, Ben was standing in shadow by the office door.

"Oh . . . you startled me."

"Wanted to make sure you got a taxi."

"That's thoughtful," she said carefully. "Well, I can safely say you won't be making jewelry anytime soon. In fact you probably never have to work again, if you don't want to. I had to insist people leave the pieces until the show closes, otherwise you'd have walked through a half-empty gallery just now."

"I'm goin home, Sarah. I need to clear my head. Give me a month an we can talk business."

It was for the best, she thought with sad relief.

He reached into his pocket and pulled out a torn envelope. "Wrote this the day you left. Was glad you never got it. Felt like a fool for sendin it, specially after I got your card." He held it out to her. "Want you to read it now, so everythin's said and done between us."

She sat down at the desk and turned on the lamp. He went out to the gallery and stood in dim light, his back to her.

She removed the letter. The writing was faded but legible.

Dear Sarah,

You been gone twenty minutes and I miss you so much I do not know how I am going to make it through the next five. I wanted to speak before you left but held back. You were in no frame of mind to think clear about what I am asking. You need to be home with your folks to take stock. And I am in no frame of mind to listen if you said no for all the good reasons there are. If you were here I would not let you alone with it. I would use my sweet tongue as you call it to try to convince you. I got to say the sweetest thing my tongue ever tasted was your body and your name. I am asking you to marry me. I know I do not have near enough to offer but if you feel like I hope you do you might be willing to take a chance on me. I figure we could get along on jewelry for a while and when the sculpture is done we could put on a show in New York. I know what I am asking. If you cannot do it I understand. I love you. Never said it to anyone before. No matter what happens I want to thank you for giving me that. I am going back to work now and will be okay. I had to try.

Ben

She turned off the light and rested her head in her hands. She hadn't misjudged what was between them. He *had* cared for her. As profoundly as she'd cared for him.

Like a benediction, like heaven's kiss, the letter breached the schism of her soul. For as long as she could remember she'd felt the tug-of-war between her need to be deeply and passionately cherished and her understanding that in the real world she asked too much, between her longing to give all of herself and the discernment that all of her was more than any man would want.

Her terror of smothering, the holding back, trying to get it right, keep it light, accept the limitations of the love offered— all slipped silently away.

She raised her head to look through the office window. He was moving through the shadowy showroom toward her, his body delineated in the glow of streetlights. Slowly, on legs gone numb, she pulled herself up to meet him.

# CHAPTER 34

**S**arah woke to pounding. It took her a moment to realize she was in her own bed. Six fifteen a.m.

"What's that?" Ben said, sitting up.

"Stay here." She slipped into her robe.

She opened the door to David. Ashen, his clothes wrinkled and his eyes red, he looked as if he hadn't slept at all.

"Why didn't you answer your phone? I've been calling all night."

With Ben behind her, kissing her neck, she'd ignored the blinking answering machine and turned the phone off.

"I'm sorry," she said quietly. "I'm so sorry." She slipped the ring off and held it out to him. "You've done nothing to deserve this."

His face flushed as if he'd been slapped.

"I wish there was something I could say to make it easier."

"For whom?"

"For you. For both of us."

He slumped against the wall. "I can't believe this."

She didn't know what to say. Her heart dissolved in pity for his rigid chin, the fearful and pleading look in his eyes. "Oh, God, David. I'm so sorry." Useless words. She wanted to hold him, cry with him, convince him everything would be all right.

"Don't," he said, reading her mind, straightening up. He moved away to look down the hall toward the bedroom.

"Is he here?"

"Yes."

His expression solidified into a mask.

"Have you told your parents?"

"No."

"You're going to kill them. You know that, don't you?"

It was the worst thing he could have said.

"I must have called ten times." He looked at her with pain-filled accusation.

She looked away, ashamed. "I'm sorry."

Ben appeared at the corner of the hallway dressed in jeans and T-shirt. The men faced each other. Neither of them spoke.

David turned. "I'll call my mother. She'll deal with my half of the guest list." As he passed her, she touched his hand. He glanced at her with tears in his eyes and then continued walking out of her life.

• • •

Ben stayed in the city to wait for Sam at the gallery. Sarah went out to Woodbridge to talk to Evelyn alone, hoping to defuse her mother's ire by a calm outline of how she intended to go about canceling the festivities. She'd already contacted the secretarial service. They were in the process of sending cards to everyone on the list.

"Of course I'll cover all of the expense—"

"How can you do this to him?" Evelyn interrupted. "A week before the wedding? Do you think you can make this up with money? You have an obligation to people. Sarah, what have you done?"

"What I had to do."

"You're spitting on all the values we taught you: responsibility, honor, commitment. For what? Sex? Let me tell you something. No matter how exciting you think it is, it will fade. You'll be left with nothing. A mess for a life."

"I don't love David. I can't marry him to make you happy . . ."

"Me? Me happy? Are you blaming me for this?"

"No, of course not."

"You're turning your back on everything that makes you what you are. What kind of man would ask such a thing?"

"A man who loves me."

"How do you know? Because he says so? What do you know about him? His family? His friends? He's a stranger . . ."

"Ma, think, just for a moment. What would you have done if Danny Geller reappeared?"

"Don't be ridiculous. The one has nothing to do with the other. Danny was dead. *You* think, Sarah. What about your grandmother Sarah, and Elizabeth and Gerta—"

"What are you saying? They're as dead as Danny Geller. I can't live for them—"

"You have a duty to generations of your family, on both sides. You have a commitment of honor as a Jewish woman . . ."

"I have a commitment to myself first . . ."

"Sarah, listen to me. A woman's reputation is the most precious thing she has. You're throwing yours away."

"You've always said children are the most precious things a woman has."

"Yes." Evelyn nodded. "Children come first. They give you the greatest joy and they break your heart. It's a terrible feeling to stand by and watch your daughter ruin her life. I wanted so much for you, a lovely home, children . . ."

"I know, Ma."

"You're tossing it all out the window. Don't you want children?"

"Of course I do. We do."

Evelyn shook her head. "Think about what you're saying, Sarah. They won't fit anywhere. What kind of lives will they have, caught between two worlds?"

"The kind they choose to make. As I do. Ma? Try to understand . . . please."

Evelyn, very pale, rested her head on the back of the sofa, closing her eyes. "I'm tired. I need to go upstairs to lie down. Do me a favor. Call your father. Ask him to come home."

Sarah sat alone in the living room for an hour, waiting. Finally she heard the front door open. "Daddy?" she called softly.

He came to the doorway and looked in at her without a smile.

"I can't believe that you, of all people, don't understand," she said.

"I understand. Where's your mother?"

"Upstairs."

He turned away and started toward the stairs.

"But you know him, you know how wonderful he is. And you don't even like David."

"Right now I'm not thinking about you."

• • •

It was afternoon by the time Sarah got to the gallery and found Joshua and Ben out of their depth, hungry from missed lunch, and overwhelmed by customers and calls. She sent

Joshua around the corner to the deli for takeout and sat down at the desk to return the calls: inquiries about specific pieces; two newspapers requesting interviews; the Desert Museum wanted the camp installation held until they could send someone on Monday or Tuesday to take a look at it. Ben sat down in one of the craftsman chairs and grinned at her.

"What?"

"Sure was nice in here last night." He kept his eyes on her. "Your face is gettin red. You shy? Or rememberin?"

She flashed on yanking his shirt up, needing the touch of his skin as she needed air to breathe, his hands inside her pantyhose, ripping, shredding. Him kicking the door closed, backing her against it.

"Stop," she said, smiling. "Did my father say anything to you?"

"Not much except he's retirin as of today. If you want anythin, you can get him at home. He don't want to hear about us gettin married. Tol me I'd better get back to Arizona to concentrate on my work an you'd have your hands full here. I think, more an anythin, he's worried about your mom. Guess she was real upset?"

"Yes, she was."

Sarah managed to sandwich in four phone calls. To Miriam, Becky, and Lauren she repeated a brief variation of the same thing—the wedding was off, she was in love with Ben Lonefeather, she couldn't explain it all now but she'd call when she could. Then she called Lisa, who'd already spoken to Evelyn.

"What do you think?" Sarah asked.

"If I told you I thought you were crazy, would you do anything different?"

"No."

"So why ask? It's going to be tough, at least for a while. But if you really love each other, I've got to believe it'll be okay."

• • •

The juicy story circulated like a virus through the electronic bloodstream of insular, provincial Woodbridge, gathering strength as it traveled. David called his mother. An outraged Paula Klein called everyone she knew. Within a few days, practically everyone who'd ever met Sarah Friedman had heard she'd behaved like a slut.

Poor David had gone to an art show a week before their intended marriage and been confronted by an obscene carving of his wife-to-be. When he went to her apartment to discuss it, he found her in bed with the artist, an Indian—not the kind from India, the other kind. The nicest thing to be said about Sarah Friedman was that she must be emotionally unbalanced.

Her friends were concerned. She came in late in the evening to numerous messages on her machine. Some from people she hadn't heard from in years. She returned the ones she cared about but cut the conversations short. She had little interest in rehashing her broken engagement on the phone when she could be with Ben. What could she say except the story was essentially true? Ben had carved her naked image in marble, and she intended to marry him. She made no excuses or apologies and found it strange how little what anyone thought mattered to her. She, who'd always been obsessed with other people's opinions, suddenly couldn't care less. His slow smile was what she cared about, his warmth. The way they were together. The dawning realization that the whole world could disappear in a twinkling and he wouldn't give a damn as long as she was next to him.

She would have been blissfully happy during the week they had together, except for the unhappiness of her family.

Evelyn kept her phone unplugged or turned off for hours at a time, tired of the continuous calls from people who wanted firsthand gossip. When Sarah managed to get through, her mother barely said hello before she handed the phone to Sam.

Sam's interest consisted solely in business at Shoen's. Talk of Sarah and Ben's future or any hint of his intervening with Evelyn ended the conversation.

Eli called her with his opinion. There was no excuse for the way she'd treated a "great guy" like David. She'd shown terrible judgment and would come to regret her behavior. He had no idea who she was anymore.

Sarah reminded him of several nice girls he'd dumped, rather cruelly, on his way to Lisa, but that only made him angrier. "A week before a wedding is on another level," he responded.

• • •

Friday morning before work she tried her parents. The line was busy, so she called Lisa.

"I want to come out for Shabbat tonight, but I can't get through to my mother."

"I'm taking the boys to school in a few minutes. I'll stop by and talk to her."

An hour and a half later Sarah answered the phone at Shoen's.

"It's not good," Lisa said.

"She won't let me come to Shabbat?" Sarah sat down feeling like she was on the receiving end of a mallet, hammering her into the ground.

"She says she's not up to it."

"She couldn't even call me herself?"

"She doesn't want to talk about it," Lisa said. "I tried to get your father to speak to her, but he won't, and neither will Eli."

"What's going on?" Sarah sensed a gaping chasm opening under her feet, her family on one side and Ben on the other, as if she had to pick a side and jump.

"My guess is it's equal parts worry and humiliation," Lisa answered calmly. "She believes her beloved daughter is making the biggest mistake of her life, and she's getting no consolation from her friends, in fact the opposite. Her social world is crumbling."

"Do you think this could set her recovery back?"

"That's what's got your father concerned. I don't think so, but who knows? I do know if you start allowing guilt to run your life, you're very foolish. Eventually, she'll work through it."

But, Sarah thought, eventually might be too late. When anxiety hit late that night she lay in bed wondering if she was insane to risk everything that mattered on her belief in this man. Was she counting on him to be her lifeboat, and would her faith be shattered against the boulders surrounding his house?

"You okay?" he whispered, wrapping his arms around her.

He was no more her lifeboat than she was his; they were partners, rowing their boat together. If it smashed on the rocks, they'd both drown.

She pulled him close.

"I'm sad," she whispered. "It feels like I've crossed some kind of boundary and left them all on the other side."

• • •

On Sunday morning Ben packed up, said a long good-bye to Sarah, and took the train out to Long Island to pick up his truck and head back to Arizona.

She planned to stay on in the city to finish the show and clear out her apartment. She'd put it up for sale, although he suggested they keep it for a while, in case she got stir-crazy on the rez. She said she'd rather buy a little vacation house in Santa Fe and had already subscribed to the opera season there next summer.

He'd called Tom a couple of days ago and told him to start on plans for a remodel, joining the two small houses together, enlarging the kitchen, adding another bedroom and bath. He was going home with a fax machine so he could plug it in and fax the plans to Sarah. He also had his first commission, a triptych in wood for the entrance to the new Museum of Indigenous Culture in Chicago.

In two months he'd fly back to oversee the loading of the pieces they'd decided to keep: *Yin, The Supplicant, Mother and Child*, and two paintings. At the same time, the movers would pick up Sarah's things at her place and she'd fly home with him.

•  •  •

He rang the Friedmans' front doorbell. Evelyn answered the door.

"Mrs. Friedman? I wonder if I could come in an speak to you an Sam."

She wasn't pleased to see him, but she let him in. Sam shook hands. They took him into the kitchen for a cup of tea. A small, old couple confused and hurt by a world turning too fast. It was the day after the wedding was supposed to be. He noticed the phone was unplugged.

He told them he was sorry for all the pain he'd caused them by loving their daughter. "I tried to stop, but I couldn't."

In spite of himself, Sam smiled. Evelyn turned to the stove.

"Smells like shortbread," Ben said, taking a seat and eyeing a plate of homemade cookies on the table.

"Please, help yourself," Sam said. "I hear the camp installation went to the Desert Museum. Congratulations."

"Thanks."

They watched Evelyn measure loose tea into a flowered teapot and pour milk into a little pitcher. Sarah was a combination of the two of them, but she'd look like her mother when she got old. Probably be just as fierce, he thought.

Evelyn brought teacups and saucers to the table.

"Mmm, this is good," he said, crunching the cookie. "What's in em?"

"Butter, flour, sugar, a little salt, and vanilla."

She carried the teapot to the table and sat down across from him next to Sam.

"I never had tea like this. Real pretty."

She placed a tiny metal grate over the cup to catch the tea leaves as she poured. Sam took the saucer from her when the cup was full and poured in milk from a little pitcher. She poured for Ben and then for herself.

"Mrs. Friedman, when we talked before, you asked me to take no for an answer, an I agreed. Now I'm here to find out what it's gonna take for you to accept yes."

"We think you're making a mistake," Evelyn said. "Like a bird and a fish, you're too different."

Ben smiled. "We ain't different species."

"How do I know you'll take care of her? I have no idea what kind of man you are."

Sam took her hand. "We believe you're a decent person, Ben. But the truth is we don't know you. Marriage means different things to different people. Cultures are different."

Ben nodded. "You got a point. You got no reason to trust me. I can say I intend to be a good husband, but words are cheap." He took a sip of tea; the tiny cup almost disappeared in his grasp. He set it on the saucer. "Truth is everybody takes a chance when they get married. Mrs. Friedman, seems to me you'd be in better shape to keep an eye on things in Arizona if you an Sarah was talkin on the phone every day, an you an Sam come out to visit us. Not gonna do you any good sittin here angry, wonderin what's goin on."

"I'm not angry."

"Sure you are. Angry an hurt. So's Sarah. An the longer it goes on, the worse it'll get. I know the way somethin like this can rip up a family. I don't wanna be the cause of tearin this one up."

"What are you proposing?" Sam asked.

"Sarah wants to get married here, with her family around her. We want your blessin. I'm plannin to sit here until we come to some agreement about what it's gonna take to make that happen."

"You barely know each other. It's ridiculous to talk about a wedding," Evelyn snapped.

"What's the rush?" Sam asked. "Take a year or two. Give yourselves a chance to be certain this is really the best thing for both of you."

"We already been apart almost a year. We wanna start tryin for a family. But I gotta get home, an Sarah's got a lot to do here to get ready, so we're prepared to wait two months."

"Sarah's Jewish," Evelyn said. "Her children will be Jewish. How do you feel about that?"

"Fine with me."

"What religion are you?"

"Navajo."

"That's your religion?"

"It's what I am, kinda like bein a Jew. I thought maybe you'd feel better about me if I converted, so I had a talk with a rabbi. Seems like if you're born Jewish you don't have to believe in anything to stay Jewish. You can be a Buddhist or a atheist and still be a Jew. But if you're convertin you gotta believe in Judiasm an let go a bein what you were before. I can't do that."

"I see," Evelyn said grimly. "It doesn't seem to me you're willing to do very much to alleviate our concerns." She looked at Sam.

"The other thing about convertin is that you gotta get circumcised," Ben said softly.

Evelyn's head snapped to face him, her eyes wide. He met her look.

A half hour later Sam walked with him to the front door. "You're a good man," he said, extending his hand. "Have a safe trip."

Ben shook the hand and thanked him for everything. Then he got in his truck and headed home, successful but not victorious.

# CHAPTER 35

"**A**re you nuts? I can't do that," Dawsen screeched.

"Can't or won't?"

"Both. Why you wanna do somethin like that anyway?"

"I tol you."

"You tol me you was gettin married. Lots a men get married an I never heard a one of em havin to get his dick cut up to do it. Heard a some of em getting their balls cut off but never their dicks."

"It's a Jewish custom."

"You ain't Jewish."

"Her ma wants it, an I want her blessin. I made a deal."

"What's Sarah say?"

"She don't know. It's somethin between her parents an me."

"Shit." Dawsen laughed. "Mother-in-laws are tough, but you might a got the worst a the bunch."

"You gonna help me or not?"

Dawsen sighed. "I guess. I sure can't do it, but I'll find out who's the best guy. Maybe there's someone in Flagstaff. Prob'ly best to go into Albuquerque, though. If it was my dick, I would. I'll have to drive you."

• .• •

Dawsen made the arrangements. Two weeks later, Ben left the coyotes with Anna, and the two men drove to Albuquerque and checked into a Days Inn near the hospital where the surgery was set for early the next morning. If everything went okay, Ben would spend only one night in the hospital and then a couple more at Dawsen's just to be safe. He didn't want to think about things not going okay.

Since he talked to Sarah every night on the phone, he'd had to come up with something to tell her about why he'd be unavailable for a while. He figured talking to her right after would kill him, so he came up with the story he was going to look at quarries in the backcountry for a week.

He was lying on his twin bed in the motel room listening to Dawsen sing old Pete Seeger songs in the shower when the phone rang. He thought it must be Anna. She was the only one who knew where they were.

"Ben?"

"Uh, hey, Sarah."

"My father came into the gallery this afternoon to tell me about a conversation he and my mother had with you before you left New York. He's been concerned about it and finally decided I had at least the right to know. By the way, when did we start lying to each other?"

"I didn't tell you cause I knew you'd jus get upset."

"Isn't that usually why people lie? Because they don't want to go through the process of dealing with what other people feel?"

"Sarah . . ."

"Well, never mind. It's no big thing. So tomorrow morning they're going to mutilate your penis?"

"Jesus, don't say it like that."

"No? Why not?" she continued in the bright, brittle tone she was using. "Because, I mean, it's really nothing." Her voice broke.

He held the phone listening to her cry.

"What is this, the dark ages? My mother gets her pound of flesh?"

"Shhh, Sarah, don't," he soothed. "I want to." Almost the truth—it had been his ace in the hole, and he'd played it. "Don't cry," he said.

"You are not to do this."

"You're a Jewish woman, Sarah. You can't marry a man who's not circumcised."

"Are you out of your mind?" she yelped. "I'm marrying a Navajo and moving to a reservation. It's a little late to start worrying about living a proper Jewish life." She hiccuped and sniffed. "Ben?"

"Yeah?"

"I love you for being willing to do it."

"Okay, then."

"But I want you to listen to me. It doesn't work for me to have my mother in my bedroom. I'm absolutely firm on this. I want you the way you are or not at all."

●  ●  ●

Sarah understood Evelyn's motive in driving such a bargain. It was a test of Ben's devotion, like God testing Abraham with Isaac. What mattered was Ben's willingness to go through with it; there was no need for him to actually do it. Nor could she see any reason for her mother to know he hadn't.

• • •

Ben wore a navy blue, double-breasted suit with a white dress shirt and a burgundy silk tie. Sarah had taken him shopping.

He was nervous, waiting for the ceremony to begin.

"Still time to run," Dawsen whispered. They were standing in Sarah's parents' backyard, under a tree.

It was a Sunday, the third week of September. The guests were seated in white chairs on the lawn, listening to the birds compete with a string quartet playing music by Bach. Tom and Millie sat next to Anna in the front row with the two boys. It was their first visit to New York, and they were having a high time.

The music changed, and Ben looked up as Sarah walked toward him, escorted by her parents. She was wearing a pale green dress, carrying tulips. He stepped forward and took her hand from Sam.

They stood together under a canopy. They took turns drinking grape juice from the same cup. They exchanged rings, repeating what the rabbi said: "By this ring you are consecrated to me, in accordance with the laws of Moses and Israel."

The rabbi spoke for a few minutes about the melding of separate entities into one, stronger and richer than either alone, yet containing all of the elements of both. Then he held up a glass wrapped in a napkin.

"The glass is broken under the groom's foot at all Jewish weddings," he said, "to remind Jews about the destruction of the Temple of David in Jerusalem. The implication is that even in times of great happiness, Jews must never forget what our people have suffered. When I explained this to Ben, he asked if it would be proper for him to remember the Long Walk of the Navajo, an event of great sorrow for his people."

The rabbi bent down and placed the glass on the ground. "Let us all join him in remembering."

It didn't break at first because the grass was soft under it. Ben had to stomp a couple of times. Then everybody shouted, "Mazel tov."

He liked that.

•  •  •

In the oddly consistent movement of life from harmony to chaos, the telephone rang at eleven p.m. a month after the wedding, just as Sarah and Ben were drifting off to sleep.

Ben answered, and from the gravity in his voice and the few words he spoke, Sarah understood that it was Eli. Sam had had a heart attack and was in an ambulance on his way to the hospital.

She raced around, throwing things haphazardly into a suit-case, while Ben called and arranged a flight out of Flagstaff. It had been too much, she thought. First the show, then the re-lationship between her and Ben, then the wedding. Every-thing. Was it punishment for her happiness? Her selfishness? She was so far away. Oh, God, was he going to die before she got there?

Ben wrapped his arms around her as she stared into the suitcase.

"It jus happened, Sarah."

The force of his love infused her. The world stopped tum-bling. She was not to blame. She was not in charge.

He handled it all with quiet efficiency: the long drive to the airport, the flight, the luggage, the taxi to the hospital. Holding her hand throughout. If she'd had any lingering doubt about the husband she'd chosen, she would have lost it then. But there was no doubt.

•  •  •

Sammy! Look where you're running!

Sunlight streamed through French windows. White damask curtains billowed. The room he raced through smelled of furniture polish and freshly waxed floors. A vase crashed to the floor. His mother knelt to pick up the pieces. She looked up, her lipstick smeared, tears running down her face.

Don't forget me!

Rosa's strong brown fingers gripped the metal bar. The Ferris wheel began to climb. *Dios mio!* Sam, we're gonna die! Half giggle, half scream. Her black hair whipped in the wind. He buried his face in it as they rose to the top, leaving the crowds and noise of Coney Island far below. She laughed, flinging her arms wide. It's like flying!

"Sam? Can you hear me?"

Bright lights. The man's head and mouth covered by a green mask.

"Sam? Are you in pain?"

You're a brave boy, Sammy, to scrape your knee and not cry.

"Sam?"

A cold gray room. Water dripping from the sink in the lavatory, the stench of mildew, a bare lightbulb. He traced the lines across the pages. The glare from the light made it hard to read. He picked up the ledger, so many names.

The gallery tilted, paintings hung suspended in midair. People walked along the walls smiling and nodding. The rabbi from his old yeshiva, the baker from the corner, the woman who made lace like snowflakes. So many names he'd forgotten. Alan waved and motioned him over.

Sammy, come! We'll be late, his mother called. The train hissed behind her. His father hurried ahead with the suitcases. Elizabeth and Gerta opened their windows and leaned out. Come on, Sammy! Hurry up! His mother smiled and held out her hand. Come, darling.

He caught sight of Evelyn as he stepped on. She was running up and down the platform searching for him. He called to her, but the train was already moving.

• • •

Sam was buried less than forty-eight hours after death in accordance with Jewish custom. His body returned to the earth in a plain pine box, under red and golden maple trees, to the tune of chirping sparrows, on a crisp fall day redolent of newly turned moist ground.

"May he come to his place in peace," the rabbi intoned. Then the dull, final sound of dirt against the coffin as the mourners took turns shoveling from the mound next to the grave.

Sarah bid good-bye to her father, standing between her mother and her husband, her arms around them both. There is no answer to death, she thought. No response but to reinvest oneself in one's own journey. To live as fully and well as possible, to love completely, and to be grateful for the short time we have together.

# CHAPTER 36

"**G**ood-bye," Evelyn said, taking her hand luggage from him and kissing his cheek. "Ben? You do know how dear you are, don't you?"

He mumbled he guessed he did, and she laughed before turning to walk through the doorway to the plane.

He was sorry to see her go. Sarah enjoyed her company, and he'd miss her cooking. Between Amelia, new duties for the school board, and time spent on the computer and telephone handling his business, Sarah didn't often cook the way she used to. Anyway, she was partial to healthy, low-fat food. He doubted he'd get kreplach before Evelyn came back.

She'd been out the first time two years ago, just before Amelia was born, and had been back four times since. Said the dryness got rid of her arthritis. But Sarah said she'd visit them in Timbuktu to see her granddaughter.

Sarah would want him to make sure her mom was safely

on her way, so he stayed at the airport until the plane took off. Then he got back into the truck, turned up his music, and headed out.

It was late afternoon, and he was familiar with the traffic pattern between his house and the airport. Even if he didn't hit a jam on the interstate, he wouldn't make it back before Amelia went to sleep. He was eager to get home, but there was no point in rushing.

He wondered what had gone on that afternoon between Evelyn and Camilla Huna.

They'd stopped off at the Hopi reservation on the way to the airport so Evelyn could give Camilla a gold necklace Sam wore with a Hebrew letter on it.

"Why on earth would you want to do that?" Sarah had asked.

"He called her every week from Shoen's. I'm sure she still misses him," Evelyn had answered. "And I want to meet her."

When they got to Camilla's, Evelyn told him to run along for an hour. She wanted to speak to Camilla alone. He'd gone over to Maria's with a package.

Maria lived on First Mesa, married to a Kachina carver named Nelson Winnow. She met Ben at the door with a big smile. He gave her the present, a pajama set from Bloomingdale's Sarah had ordered for the baby.

"Honey?" she called into the bedroom. "Ben's here." She turned back to him. "I got the grant."

She'd been studying film at Arizona State for two years and during the last couple of months had been trying to get the tribe to approve funding for her first documentary. The Hopi were opposed on principle to having themselves filmed, but Maria had persisted until she came up with an idea they were willing to live with.

Winnow walked out of the nursery, a tiny baby in his arms

and Casey riding on his back, smiling at Maria like she invented light. "Ain't she somethin?"

Ben liked Winnow, and Sarah liked Maria. Every couple of weeks they got together, sometimes with Millie and Tom, to line dance at a place in between the two reservations.

Ben pulled up to the wall and parked in the dusk. He walked quietly into the dim house, switched on the light in the kitchen, drank a glass of milk, and scarfed a couple cookies from the counter before tiptoeing to the bedroom where Sarah and Amelia had both fallen asleep in the rocking chair. The coyotes stood up, shaking sleep off. Sarah opened her eyes and held a finger to her lips, convinced—no matter how fast asleep—if Amelia heard him she'd wake up.

Amelia of the dancing eyes, Sarah called her.

She was twenty-one months old and everything about her danced. She followed Ben around on her tiptoes all day, chattering away, the coyotes trailing behind, reluctant to let her out of sight. Sometimes he felt like the pied piper. She was already interested in art, had her own set of paints and brushes. He'd set up the new studio, what used to be the storeroom, so she could be in with him while he worked. Long as he wasn't carving marble. He didn't want her breathing the dust. She'd stand at her little easel, sometimes for a couple of hours, painting. Evelyn was sure she was a genius.

He lit a lantern in the living room, and Sarah came out a few minutes later. He watched her walk into the kitchen to turn off the light. She was pregnant again, a little more than four months and visibly swelling. The doctor had shown them two small masses on the ultrasound. Sam and Henry, Sarah called them. Said she could already feel them wrestling.

"Millie and I came up with some fabulous ideas for the English curriculum today. Do you want to hear them?"

"Sure."

She came back with a cookie and took a bite, looking him in the eye. She licked her lips.

"Later," he said, reaching for her.

She eluded him with a laugh. "I smell like applesauce, and I feel like a tired mommy. I'm going to take a nice long shower. Give me a half hour."

He walked outside to cool his ardor and contemplate the moon.

The two female coyotes dashed past him in pursuit of a jackrabbit. Racing about two feet behind it, they split up, edging it to the center of blacktop road to prevent it going off the sides into the desert. Still, it looked like the rabbit was gaining a lead when Littleman appeared from the shadow of a boulder, perfectly timed and directly in its path. He leapt with his powerful rear legs, knocked it over and pinned it under his front paw, quickly breaking its neck with his jaws.

Harsh on the rabbit; Sarah wouldn't like it, if he told her. She held the perspective that one animal killing another was a sad thing. She also had an odd fondness for what she called bunnies.

But it made him smile.

If a three-legged coyote could still catch a jackrabbit, anything seemed possible.

# COYOTE DREAM

## JESSICA DAVIS STEIN

This Conversation Guide is intended to enrich the
individual reading experience, as well as encourage us
to explore these topics together—because books,
and life, are meant for sharing.

# A CONVERSATION WITH JESSICA DAVIS STEIN

Q. Coyote Dream *is a very romantic story told realistically. What inspired you to write about these characters?*

A. I really like love stories. I suppose I'm a romantic because I believe that a passionate lifelong commitment is still possible in this sexually disposable world. I think most people crave deep, meaningful connections and even sophisticated, cynical, disaffected souls long for true love.

About eight years ago, when I was in private practice as a psychotherapist, I had a group of fabulous single career women in their early thirties who were all looking for love. It was during the course of that group that I must have started unconsciously working on this novel. Although none of the characters in the book bears any resemblance to any member of the group, their discussions informed Sarah's dilemma at the beginning and some of her thoughts throughout.

Another, and equal, inspiration came from my son, Kee, who's adopted from Korea. First, because I'm compelled to explore interracial relationships, given it's our family situation and, second, because when he was a child we traveled several times to the Southwest and I was struck by his resemblance to the American Indian kids we met. I have a picture of him sitting with a group of children at Taos and he looks just like he's from the Pueblo. He's always been his own person, with a different dynamic and rhythm from the rest of our family, and I think imagining him as an adult having grown up in a different place and time started me on the road to Ben.

Q. *Why write about coyotes?*

A. They live in the desert where I grew up, and in the hills of Los Angeles where I live now, so they've always been around. About ten years ago, a couple of them killed two cats I loved. Since it's absurd to hate an animal for behaving instinctually, I was compelled to learn about them. I got hooked. They are urban wolves.

The Southwest American Indians often used Coyote in their tales as a stand-in for Man, in order to represent the morally ambiguous behavior of the human being. I've learned to appreciate their cunning intelligence as well as their bravery and beauty. They're amazingly adaptable and can live almost anywhere. They're almost universally despised and are continually hunted, poisoned, trapped, shot, and driven out of their home territories. But they survive . . . like the Jews and the American Indians.

Every so often I come across a coyote on my hikes and sometimes, if I don't happen to have a dog with me and I stop, they do too. They'll stand and stare for a long time, until they get bored or distracted. It's very special to look into the eyes of an animal in the wild.

*Coyote Dream* places people very much in the hierarchy of the natural world. An underlying premise is that contact with nature keeps us sane and an understanding of our place in the order of things can give us the ability to participate without destroying the delicate balance of life on earth. Like Ben's grandfather, Henry, I'd hate to see a world without coyotes.

*Q. The haunting effect of the Holocaust on Sam and his family is a theme of the book. Did you write from personal experience? You also use the word* holocaust *to describe the American Indian experience. Can you elaborate on that?*

A. My husband's Jewish parents came to the U.S. from Germany in 1939. They left everything, including most of their family members, and barely managed to get out in time. When they were alive, I was extremely aware of the many ways the experience impacted them and every aspect of their lives. It continues to echo with their children. I don't take the Holocaust perpetrated on the Jews lightly. On the other hand, at some point it's imperative for the children of victims to come to terms with what happened and to stop living in response to it.

When I visited Germany for the first time and saw the inscription *Never Again* at Dachu, it happened to be at the same time Pol Pot was creating his own holocaust in Cambodia. And it occurred to me that Germany didn't hold the patent on mass human extermination nor were Jews the only objects of that kind of hatred. Kurds, Armenians, Russians, Cambodians, American Indians (of whom approximately twenty million were killed during two hundred years of white settlement) have all been victims of holocausts. I've seen a picture of the last Tasmanian Man taken for posterity by the Australians who'd wiped out his entire race.

The strangest part, and in a way the most calming for me, is that "ethnic cleansing" is not a human anomaly. Chimps commit their own brand of it in the wild. They live in extended family groups (tribes?) and sometimes a strong group will begin to systematically destroy another neighboring group. It's not a war because it only goes one way. Over the course of weeks, possibly months, every male and female member, including infants, of the other group is murdered. It's probably some kind of territorial drive. Which is also an element of what human holocausts are about.

It may seem odd but the reason I find that thought calming is because I believe if we humans really understand where our behavior comes from, given our wonderful huge brains and our ability to transcend instinct for reason, we can make different choices.

*Q. What advice would you give to someone just beginning to write fiction?*

A. Good writing lives in rewriting. The best advice I got at the beginning was from a friend who has made his living as a writer for over thirty years. He read my first draft and told me to begin rewriting the way people did before the word processor: i.e., start with a fresh piece of paper and tell the story again from the beginning. I rewrote and revised and polished the book that became *Coyote Dream* for over six years and, sometime during the process, I became a writer. I've started work on my next novel and I'm happy to say I don't think it will take nearly as long to complete.

I would also say find readers you trust, who are willing to be honest with you, treasure them as if they were gold and listen to what they tell you. And overwrite; *really say it all,* and then edit it; *really* edit. I read somewhere—I'm sorry to say I don't remember who said it—that the only way to create a beautiful garden is to be a merciless killer. The same is true for writing.

*Q. What books most influenced you in the writing of* Coyote Dream?

A. This book sprang from my interest in the roots of human behavior and might even have been nonfiction if I'd had the scientific expertise to write something unique about male/female bonding. I wanted to create a timeless courtship. The kind of attraction/pair-bonding between a man and a woman that could have existed thousands of years ago, if one of them, from one hunter-gatherer culture perhaps, ventured into neighboring territory. In other words, essential Man and Woman dressed up in Millennium clothes. Which is what I think we modern-type humans are. The books that influenced me:

*In the Shadow of Man* by Jane Goodall.

*The Third Chimpanzee* by Jared Diamond.

*The Beak of the Finch* by Jonathan Weiner.

*The Moral Animal* by Robert Wright.

*Bully for Brontosaurus* by Steven Jay Gould.

*The Human Animal* by Desmond Morris.

Q. *What kind of fiction do you enjoy?*

A. I enjoy all kinds of fiction with the exception of formulaic genre. A quick list of books I love: *Pride and Prejudice, House of Mirth, House of Spirits, The Mill on the Floss, David Copperfield, Anna Karenina, Mrs. Dalloway, East of Eden, Lonesome Dove, The World According to Garp, Love in the Time of Cholera, Turtle Moon, Atonement.* I also like light, funny books like *Compromising Positions* and *Bridget Jones: The Edge of Reason.*

# QUESTIONS FOR DISCUSSION

1. Why does the book begin with the coyote? What part do the three coyotes play throughout? Ben seems to care more about them than for most people. Do you think it possible to have a truly significant relationship with an animal?

2. How is the Holocaust theme used in the story? Do you believe *holocaust* is the proper word to use in reference to what was done to the American Indian? In what way has Sarah's life been impacted by what happened to her father? Has your life been influenced by experiences your parents had when they were young?

3. Do you think Evelyn is overly involved in her children's lives? Is she smothering or supportive? Does she change during the course of the book, or is it Sarah's perception and feelings about her that change?

4. At what point does Sarah begin to view Ben as a potential partner? When does Ben's point of view about her change? Do you think their differing perspectives throughout the book are more personal, cultural, or sexual?

5. How does Maria change during the course of the story? Does she bear any responsibility in the breakup of her marriage? Do you think she could be right for Ben? Why or why not?

6. Did Alvin's attack surprise you or did you see it coming? Does Ben bear any responsibility for Alvin's violence?

7. What do you think happened between Sam and Camilla Huna? How do you feel about Sam's behavior throughout the story? Would you say he is a good man?

8. Why do you think David decides to pursue Sarah? If Ben had not reentered Sarah's life, do you think she and David would have been happy? How do David and Ben view marriage/Sarah differently? What are the differences for Sarah between being David's wife and Ben's?

9. Do you believe it's a good idea for people of different races/religions to marry? How would you feel if your child married someone from another race or culture? Did Sarah make the choice you would have made?